CAMP
SO-AND-SO

MARY McCOY

carolrhoda LAB
MINNEAPOLIS

Carolrhoda Lab™
An imprint of Carolrhoda Books
A division of Lerner Publishing Group, Inc.
241 First Avenue North
Minneapolis, MN 55401 USA

For reading levels and more information, look up this title at
www.lernerbooks.com.

Cover and interior images: © iStockphoto.com/Skyhobo (crow); © Elena
Schweitzer/Shutterstock.com (wooden sign, path in trees); © iStockphoto.
com/NI QIN (necklace); © Robsonphoto/Shutterstock.com (green forest);
© iStockphoto.com/lukaves (thorny bush); © iStockphoto.com/billnoll (purple
polka dots); © iStockphoto.com/titoOnz (golden sparkles); © iStockphoto.
com/Hulya Erdem (blue sparkles); © Your Design/Shutterstock.com (wood
background); © FINDEEP/Shutterstock.com (brown texture); © iStockphoto.
com/DesignGeek-1 (green bottle); © iStockphoto.com/VeenaMari (swirls);
© iStockphoto.com/kite-kit (leaf border); Laura Westlund/Independent Picture
Service (chapter icons, map).

Main body text set in Janson Text LT Std 10.5/15.
Typeface provided by Linotype AG.

Library of Congress Cataloging-in-Publication Data

Names: McCoy, Mary, 1976– author.
Title: Camp So-and-So / Mary McCoy.
Description: Minneapolis : Carolrhoda Lab, [2017] | Summary: "Twenty five girls
  are invited to attend the mysterious Camp So-and-So over the summer where
  they work with their cabinmates to compete in the All-Camp Sports & Follies"
  —Provided by publisher.
Identifiers: LCCN 2016006371 (print) | LCCN 2016024758 (ebook) |
  ISBN 9781512415971 (th : alk. paper) | ISBN 9781512426939 (eb pdf)
Subjects: | CYAC: Camps—Fiction. | Summer—Fiction. | Friendship—Fiction. |
  Sports—Fiction.
Classification: LCC PZ7.1.M43 Cam 2017 (print) | LCC PZ7.1.M43 (ebook) |
  DDC [Fic]—dc23

LC record available at https://lccn.loc.gov/2016006371

Manufactured in the United States of America
1-39945-21395-8/22/2016

To Patricia:

friend, champion,
and
Head Counselor
of
Camp So-and-So

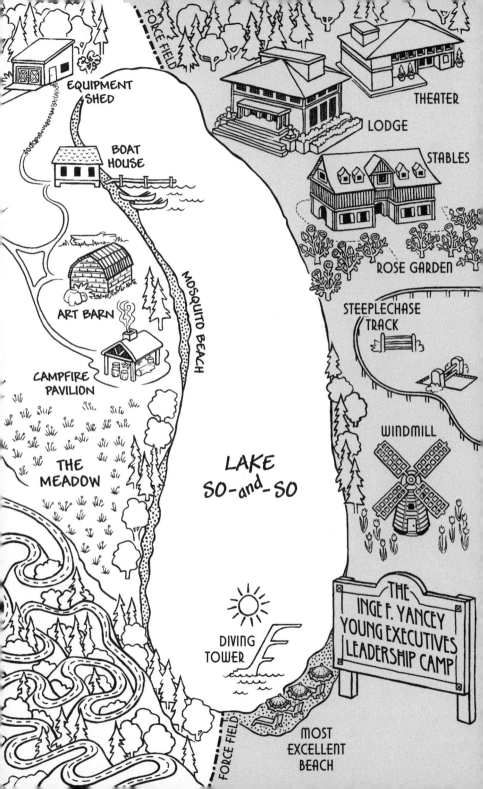

PROLOGUE

The letters went out in mid-February, when the weather had been so cold and so gray, and everything had been so buried in snow for so long, and the idea of riding a horse or rowing across a lake seemed so impossible, the brochures might as well have been promising magic.

There were twenty-five letters in all. They went to girls who lived in apartment buildings in cities and farmhouses in the country and condos in the suburbs. Each letter invited its recipient to spend a week at Camp So-and-So, a lakeside retreat for girls nestled high in the Starveling Mountains, on a merit scholarship. Each letter came with a registration form, a packing list, and a glossy brochure with photographs of young women climbing rocks, performing Shakespearean theater under the stars, and spiking volleyballs. Each letter was signed in ink by the famed and reclusive businessman and philanthropist Inge F. Yancey IV.

By the end of the month, twenty-five applications had been completed, signed, and mailed to a post office box in an obscure Appalachian town.

Had any of these girls tried to follow the directions in the brochure and visit the camp for themselves on that day in February, they would have discovered that there was no such town and no such mountain and that no one within a fifty-mile radius had ever heard of Camp So-and-So.

ACT 1

DRAMATIS PERSONAE:

KADIE

CRESSIDA

DORA

VIVIAN and KIMBER

SHARON, *their counselor*

ROBIN, *a counselor-in-training*

TANIA

RON

Their MINIONS

CABIN 1

THE ALL-CAMP SPORT & FOLLIES

[SCENE: As they arrive at Camp So-and-So,
campers are assigned to their cabins.]

Up the long, unnecessarily winding road to Camp So-and-So, the narrator (who, I should mention, is me) watched them come. I watched as they traveled around the hairpin turns, and past the spots where the guardrails had fallen into disrepair and next to nothing prevented the cars from dropping fifty feet into the carpet of treetops that stretched as far as the eye could see.

It was nearly suppertime when Kadie Aguilar arrived. She was the first camper to check in with Camp So-and-So's counselor-in-training, Robin, and though the sun hung low in the sky, the air was still hot and sticky.

A Note from the Narrator: As counselor-in-training, Robin was assigned all the jobs no one else wanted to do and, as a result, more or less ran the place.

Robin had stationed herself in front of the mess hall, a ramshackle building with high ceilings and hewn lumber beams that also housed the camp director's office and the nurse's station.

"Aguilar, Aguilar . . ." she said, tapping her clipboard with the tip of her pencil.

"It's probably at the top," Kadie offered. "With the A's."

Robin looked up from the clipboard, annoyed. Kadie eyed her cargo shorts and athletic sandals, which looked like she might have been wearing them for at least five summers, and wondered if she was a former camper. She didn't seem that much older than Kadie, but Kadie didn't remember her from last year.

"Here you are. Kadie Aguilar. Cabin 1."

Kadie's eyes brightened. She'd been in Cabin 1 the summer before, and hearing Robin say she would be there again opened up a floodgate of memories: the musty bunks, the sound of raindrops on the cabin roof, the secrets she and her cabinmates had whispered to one another after lights out.

Robin opened Kadie's backpack for inspection. "It says here you're a return camper, so I take it you know the rules?"

Kadie nodded as Robin put on a pair of latex gloves and swept her hands through the contents of the bag, looking for contraband. Once she was satisfied, she waved Kadie to the side and called for the next person in line.

There was no one more excited to be at camp than Kadie was. She had hardly slept the night before, but she wasn't tired. She was in her favorite place on earth. Mrs. Aguilar looked considerably less enthusiastic. She chewed a handful of antacids as she opened the station wagon hatchback and helped

Kadie unload her other bags She didn't remember the drive being this harrowing last year.

As Kadie looked in vain for Cabin 1's counselor, more cars pulled up. Two friends wearing thick liquid eyeliner drawn out past the corners of their eyelids and tight black jeans hitched low on their hips slouched out of the backseat of an SUV. As their respective parents hefted their many pieces of luggage from the back of the car, piling them in the gravel in front of the mess hall, the two huddled together, sharing a pair of earbuds. When Robin asked for their names, which were Vivian and Kimber, they pretended not to hear her, leaving their parents to sign them in.

When Kadie heard Robin assign them to Cabin 1, she bounced up and cheerfully introduced herself, ignoring all the warning signs. At home, Kadie was involved in team sports and extracurricular activities, and was forever being thrown in with groups of relative strangers to write a mock resolution curbing nuclear proliferation for the Model UN or to put on a production of *Into the Woods*. More often than not, Kadie found, people wanted the same things in these situations. They wanted to like each other because they were all there for the same reason, and if they got along, it was likelier that they'd do well.

"Can either of you ride a horse?" Kadie asked.

Vivian and Kimber regarded her with stony silence.

"Sorry, that was weird," Kadie said with a self-deprecating smile. "Horsemanship is an event in the All-Camp Sport & Follies, and I'm not any good at it. Archery, either. I hope someone in our cabin is halfway decent with a bow and arrow."

The girls' lips curled in identical contempt, and Vivian

turned up the volume on the song she and Kimber were listening to.

"Excuse me," Robin called out to them, an irritated look on her face, a curling iron cord dangling from her fingertips. "Didn't you read the brochure? You're not allowed to have this."

Grumbling, Vivian and Kimber turned their backs on Kadie and shuffled over to the registration table, where Robin continued to confiscate items from their bags. The list of items forbidden at Camp So-and-So included phones, curling irons, hair dryers, razors, and nail clippers, all of which Vivian and Kimber had tried to smuggle in.

Ostensibly, the policy existed so the time that campers would otherwise have spent grooming themselves or staring at screens could be devoted to having enriching experiences and creating memories. Kadie supposed this made sense, although the list itself was strangely arbitrary. Manicure tools of all kinds were forbidden, but nail polish was not. Campers weren't allowed to wear jewelry but could use any eyeliner, perfume, or lotion they wanted. Maybe girls hadn't worn eyeliner or used lotion a hundred years ago, or whenever the camp had instituted the policy, Kadie reasoned.

More cars drove into the roundabout now. More girls unloaded their bags, met their cheerful counselors, and were spirited up the steps to the mess hall, their bags now stacked in piles outside by cabin number. Kadie's stomach growled, and she wondered again where Cabin 1's counselor was.

The next Cabin 1 camper to arrive was Dora, though Kadie almost didn't notice. Dora was the kind of girl whose hair, skin, eyes, and clothes were a forgettable sort of tan, like the wallpaper in a dentist's office. When Kadie introduced herself, Dora mumbled a hello that was directed more at the tops of her shoes than at Kadie.

Each cabin held five girls, which meant Kadie only had one more chance of landing a decent bunkmate.

Please, she thought, *let it be someone nice.*

Instead, it turned out to be Cressida.

If Dora blended into the scenery, Cressida stood out. Even from my vantage point, I noted the translucent, faintly bluish cast to her skin, her watery eyes, the baby-fine wisps of blonde hair, scarcely enough to cover her head.

"I hope you brought a hat," Vivian said, while Kimber chuckled unkindly.

"I hope you brought a shit for me to give," Cressida shot back.

Kadie recoiled at Cressida's voice, which was not unlike the sound of a circular saw on sheet metal—insistent, raspy, and shrill all at once.

"I'm Kadie," Kadie said, giving Cressida a smile that she hoped would defuse the hostility already brewing between her cabinmates.

"Good for you," Cressida said, pretending to study the map of Camp So-and-So that had been carved into a giant disc of tree trunk and was mounted in front of the mess hall.

Kadie watched as two girls from Cabin 3—a tall, stick-like goth girl and a girl in an orange hoodie—went into the mess hall together, conspiring like old friends, and let out a sigh.

"I don't recognize anybody from last year," Kadie said. "I think I'm the only one who came back."

A Note from the Narrator: This was partly true, but also not true at all.

"Should we go in for dinner with the others?" Dora asked.

Kadie was startled. She had forgotten Dora was there.

"Maybe that's where our counselor is," Kadie said hopefully.

The five of them left their bags in a pile, climbed the mess hall stairs together, and peered in through one of the screen windows. Some of the other counselors had decorated their cabins' tables with streamers or balloons or little signs that said things like "CABIN 2! 4-EVER!" but Cabin 1's table was bare and empty.

"Hot dogs," Kadie muttered under her breath. "Lame."

"It's camp," Cressida said. "That's what you're supposed to eat at camp."

Kadie glared at her. Camp was *her* thing, and she was not about to let some Camp So-and-So virgin tell her how things were and were not supposed to be. Besides, none of the other campers seemed terribly enthusiastic about the grayish hot dogs either, and the peppy centerpieces their counselors had made did little to distract from the grim lighting and dusty tabletops.

"The Welcome Campers dinner was better last year," she said. "They had a carving station with prime rib and hot rolls and a salad bar and everything."

"Probably not the only thing that was better last year," Cressida said, glaring at Vivian and Kimber, who were pacing the mess hall porch as though looking for an escape hatch that would take them away from this place.

Dora shrugged and said, "I'm not hungry anyway. Should we take our stuff to the cabin?"

"We might as well," Kadie said. "Maybe our counselor's there."

She remembered where their cabin was and led them from the mess hall. They stopped to pick up their bags on the way. Kadie, Cressida, and Dora slung camping packs over their shoulders while Vivian and Kimber half-wheeled, half-dragged their roller bags about a quarter of a mile down a wooded path into a clearing where they saw five cabins situated in a semicircle around a fire pit. When the girls saw the cabins, all of them but Kadie wailed in dismay. They were squat wooden platforms built up on stilts. Four posts supported the roof, but the cabins had no walls—only vinyl tarps that could be rolled down and secured in a rainstorm.

Inside was no better. Here they found low wooden bunks with mattresses so lumpy their backs ached just looking at them—and Sharon.

Sharon was their counselor, and she made it plain that they were beneath her contempt. She did not remove her headphones or look up from her handheld game console when they went inside the cabin. She grumbled her name from beneath a nest of hair so dirty it was impossible to tell its original color, then said, "Leave me alone, entertain yourselves, and don't start any trouble, or I will *end* you."

It was the only thing she would say to them during their entire time at camp.

They dropped their bags by the bunks, then stepped out into the semi-circle of girls' cabins and shuffled their feet in indecision.

"Should we go back to the mess hall?" Dora asked.

"Gah!" Cressida exclaimed. "If you want to go back, go back. Nobody's stopping you. We don't have to do everything together just because we're in the same cabin."

Vivian and Kimber nodded in agreement and started to wander toward the fire pit. Dora turned away to hide her disappointment and headed back inside the cabin.

"I forgot," she called over her shoulder. "There's something I need to get out of my suitcase."

Kadie's heart sank. This was not how things had been last year. By the end of the first day, her cabinmates had already seemed as close as sisters. Their counselor had been trained in the theater and taught them show tunes and how to modulate their vibrato. They'd lost the All-Camp Sport & Follies, but it had been close, and besides, they'd had fun doing it.

Even if she hadn't done a very good job of keeping in touch with them, she still thought about her friends from last summer all the time, and she'd been thinking about coming back to Camp So-and-So all year. Of course you didn't have to do every single thing with the people in your cabin, but if you didn't do most of the things together, what was the point? Cressida hated everyone, Vivian and Kimber didn't think the others were cool enough, and now Dora said she was "getting something out of her suitcase," but Kadie knew she was probably hiding in the cabin to avoid Cabin 1's toxic stew of meanness.

A Note from the Narrator: Dora's feelings were a little hurt, but she really was getting something out of her suitcase—her grandfather's steel pocket watch, which she carried in her pocket and squeezed with her fingers whenever she needed a little boost of confidence or bravery. Timepieces such as this one had been listed as contraband on the Camp So-and-So packing list, but Dora couldn't see the harm in it and, in an uncharacteristic act of rule-breaking, had smuggled it into camp inside a pair of socks.

"Wait," Kadie said, hoping to intervene before the bond between her cabinmates was irreparably damaged. "I know where we can get better food. And where there are boys."

Vivian and Kimber stopped and turned around. Dora, who had come out of the cabin, looked willing, and at least Cressida didn't say no. Kadie breathed a sigh of relief. It was desperate, but she knew that if she didn't keep her cabinmates together now, they'd never achieve the bond, the trust, the communication you had to have to compete in the All-Camp Sport & Follies. Once they got to know the camp for themselves, they'd understand. They'd love it like she did. She would have her team.

They went back the way they'd come, back toward the mess hall. The girls from Cabin 5 waved to them when they met on the path, but only Kadie and Dora waved back to them. They headed east until they reached the banks of Lake So-and-So, the kidney-bean-shaped lake that stretched from the camp's northernmost point to its southernmost tip two miles away, with me, your humble narrator, following from a discreet distance. They headed north along the shore with Kadie pointing out landmarks along the way—Campfire Pavilion, the art barn, the boat house, the equipment shed.

"This is where we'll be spending most of our time for tomorrow," she said, grinning like the dismal cinder block structures were Malibu real estate.

"Why?" Cressida asked, wrinkling her nose.

"Because this is where they hold most of the events in the All-Camp Sport & Follies."

"All-Camp Sport & Follies?" Dora asked.

A Note from the Narrator: Dora was an easygoing girl who did her chores and homework without being asked, accepted every baby-sitting job she was offered, and would rather have thrust a sharpened stick through her own foot than tell anyone "no." She had neither wanted nor not wanted to come to camp, but when told she had been registered, she cheerfully packed her bags.

In truth, Dora's mother had begun to worry that Dora was a bit too pliant and accommodating. Dora's friends borrowed her sweaters and hair products and never returned them. The people she babysat for always came home late and underpaid her. Her class-mates were always leaving messages, asking, "Dora, do you have a partner for the Spanish project yet?" "Dora, have you written your civics paper yet?"

No good would come of it. And so, Dora's mother researched places where she could send the girl for the summer in the hopes that she might develop a less selfless and eager-to-please spirit. Unfor-tunately, most summer activities for people Dora's age existed for the sole purpose of cultivating these characteristics. There were many summer opportunities for Dora to help and serve others. She could build schools or volunteer at a medical clinic or teach Shakespeare to underprivileged youth or dig wells in malarial villages, but Dora's mother wanted her daughter to do something for herself for a change.

The colorful camp brochure caught her eye immediately, but it was the tanned, youthful face of Inge F. Yancey IV smiling from the sidebar, and his inspiring words, that drew her in:

Welcome to Camp So-and-So! For over 75 years, the Yancey family has been proud to provide young people with opportunities for physical, mental, and social growth through independently directed study, wilderness activities, and cultural enrichment. My great-grandfather believed in giving campers the freedom to discover themselves—and our amazing grounds—at their own pace, and that's a promise we continue to this day. Whether your passion is horsemanship, archery, rowing, fine art, or outdoor adventures on our high ropes course, there's something for everyone to explore at Camp So-and-So!

It sounded like the very thing for Dora, a place where nothing was demanded of her, where all she had to do was open herself up to the possibilities of her own likes and preferences and interests. Dora's mother signed her daughter up immediately.

"What," Cressida asked, "is the All-Camp Sport & Follies, and why on earth would anyone want to do it?"

Vivian and Kimber shuddered at the earnestness of the name, while Cressida broke out in tiny red spider veins across her cheeks just from speaking the word *sport* aloud.

A Note from the Narrator: Or at least that's what everybody thought. The other girls in Cabin 1 assumed that Cressida, frail and pasty as she was, had a horror of sports, and Cressida was more than happy to give them this impression. In fact, she was trained in tai chi, karate, and ballet, and had been a backstroke champion at one time before her other pursuits put such a strain on her time that she had no choice but to drop it. It was one of those other pursuits that brought Cressida to Camp So-and-So. She didn't know what the All-Camp Sport & Follies were, but she had an idea that they were incompatible with her current mission. *She had to shut down Kadie's idea before it gathered any momentum with the others.*

"It's really fun!" Kadie said.

"It doesn't sound fun," Vivian said.

"What is it?" Dora asked, which was all the encouragement Kadie required to elaborate.

"One day, five events, dawn 'til dusk," she said, the excitement building in her voice as she listed them off one by one. "Archery. Camp craft. Rowing. Horsemanship. Song and dance number. We compete against the other campers, and whoever wins the most events is crowned champion! There's a trophy and everything."

Kimber brushed her long bangs off her eyes. "Do we have to do it?"

"They've done it for seventy-five years," Kadie insisted. "It's a camp tradition."

"But do we *have* to do it?"

Kadie sighed. "No."

"I guess not then," Kimber said with a shrug.

At the boat house, Kadie showed them the tiny crawl space with the broken lock along the building's north wall where the counselors stashed their junk food and the occasional wine cooler. However, her heart wasn't in it. Besides, the counselors had spent last night consuming their stores. The girls found a few empty bottles and cellophane wrappers, but nothing more interesting than a few granola bars, which they took partly out of spite and partly because they'd missed dinner.

"I hope the boys are better than this," Vivian said.

Kadie said nothing, but doubled back and led them down the beach along the tree-lined shores of Lake So-and-So. They were the kind of boggy, algae- and rock-covered beaches that attracted leeches, snapping turtles, and, of course, swarms of mosquitos. Not a place one wanted to linger in a bikini for any length of time.

As they walked further down the beach, though, things improved somewhat. The clouds had turned cotton-candy pink as the sun began to set over the hilltops. The insect-clogged thickets and slimy rock shores gave way to sand, even if it was only a thin strip, hardly wide enough to lay down a towel.

"Isn't there a better beach than this?" Vivian asked.

Kadie, who had hardly spoken a word since the boat house, said, "Yes, but we're not allowed to use it."

The girls made a grumbling show of outrage that surprised and touched Kadie deeply. Even Cressida, who looked as though she'd burst into flame in direct sunlight, seemed deeply concerned about beach access once she learned that it was denied to her.

"Why not?" Dora asked.

Kadie's eyes flashed with pure hatred, and she pointed across the lake. "Because of that."

The girls squinted, then wondered how they hadn't seen it right away. A hill rose up on the far shore of Lake So-and-So, and built into it was terrace upon canopied terrace, edifice after shimmering glass edifice. It was crisp and modern-looking, yet festooned with rustic touches—wooden latticework, heavy oak beams—as though Frank Lloyd Wright and J.R.R. Tolkien had teamed up for one grand, strange experiment.

"What is that place?" Kimber asked, her mouth agape.

"That is our competition in the All-Camp Sport & Follies," Kadie said, then spat in the dirt. "The Inge F. Yancey Young Executives Leadership Camp."

When Vivian stifled a giggle with the back of her hand, Kadie spun around and her voice got scarily quiet and intense.

"It's a rich kid camp," she said. "Any one of their parents is worth more than all of ours put together. Just wait. I'm sure when we meet them, they'll tell you all about it."

"So, they're rich. So what?" said Vivian, taking a step back from Kadie.

"Every year for seventy-five years, they've competed against Camp So-and-So in the All-Camp Sport & Follies. And every year for seventy-five years, the Inge F. Yancey Young Executives Leadership Camp has beaten us."

Cressida rolled her eyes. "Didn't anybody ever tell you winning isn't everything? Besides, I thought you loved it here. I thought this camp was your awesome, super-special place."

Kadie wasn't about to spend the week letting these girls talk to her like she was some kind of loser just because she'd had the audacity to be friendly to them. She wasn't a loser, and besides, she wasn't finished talking yet.

"You've seen our camp," she said.

Cressida nodded.

"You've seen theirs."

Cressida nodded again.

"The winner of the All-Camp Sport & Follies gets to pick which camp they want."

All five campers gazed across the lake at the luxurious terraces, the tangle of rose gardens, the princess gazebos, then thought about their cinder block art barn and the boat dock, slick with algae and slime.

"When does it start?" Kimber asked.

Kadie smiled. "Archery is tomorrow morning in the meadow, just after sunrise. Then camp craft at the art barn, and then rowing. Starting line is our boat dock, finish line at Most Excellent Beach."

"The beach we're not allowed to go to?" Cressida said.

"The very same."

"Can we at least go look at it?" Kimber asked.

They continued south, the shores of Lake So-and-So to their left, and to their right a sprawling green meadow. In the distance, they recognized the girls from Cabin 2 talking to a spindly-jointed man in coveralls who sat on a riding mower in the middle of the meadow. They seemed to be hanging on his every word, but whatever they were discussing was of no interest to the girls from Cabin 1, who kept their sights fixed on the southernmost tip of the lake, where Camp So-and-So ended and the Inge F. Yancey Young Executives Leadership Camp began.

"There it is," Kadie said, pointing toward a vast expanse of sugary, white sand scattered with towels and beach chairs, upon which rested the most relaxed, contented-looking souls any of them had ever laid eyes on. A giant tower spoked with diving boards rose up near the shore, and happy swimmers leapt off of it at regular intervals. Two girls in bikinis sat on boys' shoulders and tried to shove one another into the water. Their laughter pealed all the way across the meadow.

More of them clustered around a picnic table laden with the kind of dinner the campers at Camp So-and-So could only dream about: deviled eggs, fried chicken, corn on the cob. There were bowls of watermelon and cantaloupe slices, and crystal pitchers of lemonade, and trays piled high with brownies and macaroons.

The whole scene was so inviting that Dora strayed from her cabinmates, wandering toward this idyllic beach scene. The remaining daylight shone brighter over there. The water seemed bluer. There did not appear to be a single mosquito.

"Dora!" Kadie called after her, but it was too late. Only a handful of yards remained between her and Most Excellent Beach, and she was practically running toward it.

Just when her toes were about to sink into the soft, white sand, there was a bright flash, and Dora was blown off her feet and thrown backwards. When she opened her eyes, the girls of Cabin 1 were all standing over her, anxious looks on their faces.

"Didn't you hear me yelling at you?" Kadie asked. "It's electrified."

"Oh no," said Vivian. "They're coming over here."

The bug-zapper sound Dora had made when she hit the force field had drawn a few Inge F. Yancey campers from their beach blankets. They sauntered up to the invisible electric fence, a chorus line of expensive haircuts and swimwear, and smiled as if on cue.

"Oh, hi!" One of the girls stepped forward and waved. She wore a gleaming white bathing suit that exactly matched her teeth and the tips of her French manicure. "I hope you didn't hurt yourself there."

Dora pulled herself up on her elbows and shook her head. One of the other Inge F. Yancey campers whispered something to her friend, and they both giggled. Kimber shook her hair so it fell over her eyes and hid her face, while Vivian looked away, pretending she had never seen any of the girls from Cabin 1 before in her life.

A sandy-haired boy, tan of chest and aquiline of nose, stepped forward, too, taking his place beside the girl in the white bathing suit.

"My name's Ron. You'll forgive me if I don't shake hands," he said with a sterile chuckle. "I hope you're all enjoying yourselves so far."

Kadie stood there quaking with rage, her arms pulled tight across her chest.

"Everything's fine," she said.

"Good, good, glad to hear it," he said. "Kadie, I hope you're showing your friends the ropes around here. We don't want any accidents this year."

Had there been accidents last year? Kadie couldn't remember any, and even though this boy knew Kadie's name and talked to her like there was some history between them, Kadie didn't remember him either.

"A little after-the-fact to be worrying about accidents," Cressida said, looking at Dora, who was still sitting somewhat dazed on the ground.

The girl in the white bathing suit turned her attention to Cressida, her head tilting in a mechanical facsimile of friendliness. "Do I know you from somewhere? What's your name?"

"What's yours?" Cressida asked, her chainsaw voice even less endearing than usual.

The girl looked down her nose at Cressida. "It's Tania. What's wrong with your skin? Is it always like that?"

Ron gave her a pat on the shoulder that seemed like a warning, and she turned to Kadie instead.

"I hope we'll be seeing all of you in the All-Camp Sport & Follies, Kadie. I know how much you enjoyed them last year."

Cressida turned to Kadie, her pale eyebrows furrowed. "Why are they talking to you like that? Like we're their guests or something?"

Tania looked as though she'd swallowed an egg, but Ron laughed his politician laugh again and said, "We were looking forward to a little bit of healthy competition this summer. Maybe this is your year, Kadie."

"Although judging by the looks of it . . ." Tania trailed off as though the rest was so self-evident it did not bear mentioning aloud.

"Who says we're even going to do the All-Camp Sport & Follies?" Cressida said.

Tania took one step forward, then another, drawing closer and closer to the force field. First, the hairs on the back of her arms began to stand on end, then her figure was silhouetted in a halo of light. She looked down at Dora, who still sat on the ground in a half-stupor.

"Get up," she said, her voice crackling with electrical current. She took another step, and the force field hummed around her, radiating heat. Then she stepped through it, as though it were no stronger than a stiff breeze.

As she crooked her finger, Dora's body rose from the ground, her legs suspended out in front of her like a magician's assistant. When she was floating three feet in the air, Tania snapped her fingers, and suddenly, Dora tilted forward, her heels scuffing in the dirt as she rotated into a standing position, feet firmly planted.

"Hope to see you at archery tomorrow," Tania said with a smirk. "Arrows at dawn."

She stepped back through the force field, and the humming stopped.

"Come on," she said, and her clique turned around in almost perfect unison while the girls from Cabin 1 stared after them.

Halfway back to their towels, Tania looked over her shoulder and blew them a kiss. "Can't wait, ladies."

As soon as her back was turned again, Kadie ran over to check on Dora, who was shaky, crackling with static electricity, and missing all the hair on her arms, but ultimately unharmed.

It was odd, Kadie thought, that she hadn't remembered this part of camp. When she combed her memories, she couldn't dredge up Tania or Ron. She couldn't dredge up a single supernatural thing. Last year, they rode horses and made crafts and choreographed dance numbers. Nobody had walked through a force field or levitated anybody.

"Should we tell somebody what happened?" Dora asked, reaching into her pocket and giving her grandfather's watch a squeeze. The heft of it, the coolness of the metal against her fingers, felt reassuring.

Kadie tried to imagine their counselor, Sharon, believing them, or—an even greater stretch—caring.

"Who would we tell?" she asked.

Cressida put a hand on her bony hip as she walked over to join them. "You saw what just happened, right?"

"I don't know," Kadie mumbled, staring after the Inge F. Yancey campers as they settled back down to their picnic.

"You don't know what you saw?"

"No. I mean, yes," Kadie said, fumbling for words. "I mean, I saw the same thing we all did."

"We should call our parents and ask them to come back here and pick us up," Dora said with more conviction than usual.

"There's definitely something wrong with this place," Cressida added.

"Maybe Tania was just playing a trick on us," Kadie said, scanning the ground for fishline or hidden wires or anything the other campers might have used to create the illusion.

"Like, maybe it didn't happen the way we think it did?" Dora asked.

"Doesn't that seem more likely?" Kadie asked.

Dora, who had been growing more and more concerned, seemed somewhat placated by this. It made more sense to decide they were being messed with than to leap to the conclusion that the other campers could levitate them at will.

Cressida, however, was harder to convince. "Even if you're right, why on earth would you want to compete against them in the All-Camp Sport & Follies? Doesn't it seem to you like they might have an unfair advantage?"

At Cressida's words, Kadie suddenly felt less sure of herself and her reasons for wanting to do the All-Camp Sport & Follies so badly. It wasn't that she fed off competition for its own sake. She knew people back home who didn't know what they thought of themselves unless they could hold themselves up to someone else, and some of them were so desperate to call themselves winners that they never tried doing anything they might lose. They took easy classes so they could be the smartest, surrounded themselves with boring people so they could feel interesting.

What Kadie loved was a challenge. She'd faced off against the Inge F. Yancey campers before, and lost, and knew there was almost no hope of winning, and yet she still came back ready to try again. Even when she knew the game was fixed, she still wanted to play it.

"It's what I came here to do," Kadie said. "I've been planning it all year."

"But you're just doing what they want you to do," Cressida said. "Even if you beat them, how is that winning? You don't have to play their games. Our counselor doesn't care what we do. Nobody's making us do the All-Camp Sport & Follies."

Cressida was right, Kadie realized, and she hadn't even been mean about it. Nobody *was* making them do this, and what's more, nobody except her even wanted to. Her cabinmates weren't like the competitive overachievers she usually hung out with, and it wasn't fair to drag them into the All-Camp Sport & Follies. If the rest of them wanted nothing to do with Tania and the Inge F. Yancey Young Executives Leadership Camp, Kadie decided, she would do something else. She would lie out on Mosquito Beach and work on her tan, or explore a cave, or go rock climbing. Maybe she'd finally learn how to ride a horse.

It was then that Vivian and Kimber strolled up to them. While the others had been talking, they'd wandered down the beach, peering longingly beyond the invisible, electrified perimeter.

"We want to do the All-Camp Sport & Follies," Kimber said.

"We want to go to their beach," said Vivian.

"Really?" Kadie asked, hopeful and wary all at once. "What about you, Dora?"

Dora gazed at the white sugar sands and the diving tower. "I bet their cabins have walls," she said.

"So that just leaves you, Cressida," Vivian said. She and Kimber shot pointed, vaguely threatening looks in Cressida's direction.

Kadie felt suddenly protective of Cressida with her bluish skin and her frail, spindly legs.

"She doesn't have to do it," Kadie said, stepping up so she was standing shoulder to shoulder with Cressida, a united front if she wanted it.

As Kadie glanced over to see if she appreciated this unexpected allegiance, a strange, scheming look spread across Cressida's face. It was hard to tell what it meant, though.

A Note from the Narrator: It could have meant anything, and to be honest, on a face like Cressida's, even ordinary thinking looked rather a lot like scheming.

"I'm in," Cressida said at last. "Let's see how smug they are when we take their camp."

TO: Sebastian Langley, Executive Assistant to Inge F. Yancey IV,
   Yancey Corp. CEO

FROM: Octavia Henry, Director, Camp So-and-So

Dear Sebastian,

Only three months until the first day of summer session!!! Everyone here is excited already—we can't wait to kick off another GREAT year!

With enrollment set—and of course, with your permission—I'd like to move forward with hiring for seasonal staff. Below I've included a list of positions that need to be filled:

Counselors (5)
Kitchen Staff (3)
Lifeguard (2)
Archery Instructor (1)
Creative Arts Instructor (1)
Horseback Riding Instructor (1)
Music and Theater Instructor (1)
Registered Nurse (1)

In response to the directive from corporate, staffing requests have been reduced by 20%; however, I'm confident that we can work more efficiently and run a GREAT camp even with this bare-bones crew.

> Eagerly awaiting your reply,
> Octavia

DRAMATIS PERSONAE:

WALLIS

CORINNE

SHEA

HENNIE

BECCA

MEGAN, *their counselor*

OSCAR, *a groundskeeper*

CABIN 2

KILLER IN THE WOODS

[SCENE: A meadow on the banks of Lake So-and-So]

Within two hours of arriving at summer camp, Wallis was standing in a meadow talking to a man on a riding lawn mower about murder. It did not bode well for the rest of the week.

Nothing about Camp So-and-So was like the brochures had promised, starting with their cabins. They were nothing but wooden slabs, support beams, and a sloping roof. There were no walls to speak of, just some vinyl-lined tarps that could be rolled down in the event of bad weather. Wallis had spent some of her allowance money on a brand new sleeping bag to bring with her. Now she wished she hadn't bothered. It was sure to be mildewed and filthy by the time she went home.

She hadn't even really had a chance to meet the other girls properly. Robin, the counselor-in-training, had checked her off on her clipboard and shunted her off to Megan, their freckled, ponytailed, infectiously chipper counselor. Megan had marched them all to the cabin to drop off their things, then turned them around and marched them straight back to the mess hall to sit at a table covered with balloons and a sign that said "CABIN 2! 4-EVER!" Theirs was the most festive table, Wallis could not deny that, but there was not a single working lightbulb in the room and dinner was a plateful of grayish hot dogs. And while the girls from the other cabins chatted together happily, dinner revealed the girls of Cabin 2 for the drawerful of mismatched socks they were.

Nobody went together. At first, Wallis wondered if Shea and Corinne might be friends. They were both pretty in the same kind of carefully groomed way, right down to their shell-pink manicures and tasteful gold hoop earrings. But the moment they opened their mouths, Wallis could tell that was where the similarities ended.

"I like your shoes," Corinne said to Shea, tentatively testing the friendship waters.

"FOUR DOLLARS! I GOT THEM ON CLEARANCE!"

A Note from the Narrator: It wasn't that Shea yelled exactly. It was just that she came from a large family where one frequently had to talk over others to be heard, and as a result, she had no indoor voice.

At the sound of Shea's booming voice and twangy accent, Wallis saw Corinne wrinkle her nose in distaste. If that was what she made of Shea, Wallis did not hold out much hope for Corinne's estimation of the rest of them. Becca flinched if you so much as looked at her. Hennie wouldn't stop smiling at everyone with a toothy, creepy smile that lasted too long.

And then there's me, thought Wallis. Wallis knew she looked young for her age, that she really ought to let down her pigtail braids, trade in her plastic-rimmed glasses and overall shorts for something more sophisticated, but whenever she seriously considered the idea of sticking a contact lens in her eye or stuffing herself into a camisole top and cut-offs, she could feel her lip curl.

Still, she was not entirely opposed to change. Wallis had meant to use camp as a kind of social experiment to try out different forms of self-expression that she might take back to school with her in the fall. Her plan had been to start with her name. She was tired of the strange faces and questions and giggles she got whenever she told people her name was Wallis.

No, not like the boy's name Wallace. W-A-L-L-I-S. Like the Duchess of Windsor. The English one. Well, actually she was American. King Edward VIII abdicated his throne to marry her, and she became the Duchess of Windsor.

By that point no one was ever listening to her. Her middle name was Dorothea, and she planned to introduce herself that way. Not that it was a marked improvement over Wallis, but at least it was recognizable as a girl's name. But the habit was too ingrained. She opened her mouth, and out came all the usual things about the Duchess of Windsor, which resulted in yawns and glazed eyes and people looking over her shoulder for someone else to talk to. So much for that part of the social experiment.

After dinner, Megan sent them off to explore while she prepared what she called a "Big Surprise!!!" for them back at the cabin. You could actually hear the extra exclamation points in her voice, but Wallis heard disappointment there, too, disappointment that the girls had failed to become Best Friends!!! So now, they were supposed to explore Camp So-and-So, in the hopes that this would bond them in a way that a lukewarm hot dog supper could not, and that they could share living quarters for the next week in something other than awkward silence. While Megan was back at the cabin preparing the Big Surprise!!!, the girls from Cabin 2 were walking down the main road from the mess hall.

It was the road their families had taken into Camp So-and-So, and Wallis noticed now, though she hadn't then, how long, how winding, and how unnecessarily far away from civilization it was. The west side of the road was heavily wooded, and according to the map of Camp So-and-So that someone had carved into a slab of wood outside the mess hall, it was where the pony trails and caves were. To the east lay the meadow, which was just what it sounded like. From where they stood, they could see all the way to the unappealing, stony shores of Lake So-and-So.

Fascinating as it was to go on a forced march down a dirt road, eventually the girls of Cabin 2 bored of their route. Corinne was the first to venture off, and one by one the others followed her into the meadow, which was lush, green, and by far the most pleasant part of the camp they had yet seen.

Hennie began plucking clover blossoms, which she arranged into a miniature bouquet and inserted in a buttonhole on her shirt. Corinne lifted her hair off of her neck and arched her back in the sun, while Becca and Shea lay on their backs in the peaceful green field. The only sound was the pastoral sputtering of a riding lawn mower in the distance.

While the others communed with nature, Wallis went off by herself, wandering across the meadow until the other girls were no bigger than her fingertip when she looked over her shoulder. She let out a sigh of relief.

It was not that she had expected camp to be any easier than school. She just hadn't expected girls from other places to reject her in all the same ways.

When she saw Corinne for the first time, she thought, *At least I'm not the only black girl in the cabin.* Maybe they'd be friends, never mind that Corinne was tall and glamorous-looking with her sleek, flat-ironed hair and petal-pink nails, and Wallis was . . . Wallis. Maybe it wasn't too much to hope for. Maybe they'd bond. Maybe Corinne would take Wallis under her wing and let her borrow her clothes and show her how to act like a halfway normal person.

But the moment she saw Corinne and Shea sizing one another up, her hopes were dashed. Even though Shea was white with curly red hair, she and Corinne looked like they belonged together in a way that Wallis knew *she* didn't. And if she didn't fit with Corinne, Wallis wasn't sure who in this cabin she *did* fit with. Shea had a brash confidence that made Wallis feel like even more of a baby than she usually did. Becca didn't seem actively mean, but she wasn't friendly either. She wasn't the kind of person you felt like you could just walk right up to and start a conversation with. Not that Wallis felt that way about anybody.

And then there was Henrietta, or Hennie. Wallis was at least pleased to see that there was one person in the cabin who appeared to be as weird and hopeless as she was. Hennie was perilously tall with beaky features, thick eyebrows, and that goony smile that came on and off as though it were on a timer. It was as if someone had once told her that people would like her more if she smiled, and didn't bother to explain that there was a little more to it than that.

Before going off to camp, Wallis had made a promise to her parents that she would at least try not to be a recluse, that she would not spend the whole time holed up in the cabin rereading her Isis Archimedes books or hiding underneath the headphones that swallowed up her whole head and tuned out the rest of the world. She'd kept her promise so far, more or less. Maybe it was antisocial to wander off, but she'd really needed a break from being around these girls. It had only been three hours since she'd hugged her parents good-bye, and she had no idea how she was supposed to last a week in this place, but she was determined to try. It was time to approach the social experiment from a different angle. If she couldn't be Dorothea for a week, she could at least turn around, walk up to someone, and try to start a conversation.

Hennie seemed like a good person to try something like this out on. At worst, a very weird person would think she was weird. At best, she'd discover that Hennie was fantastically interesting and they'd be camp best friends, after which they'd return home to their respective cities, exchange a few letters, each one shorter and more distant-sounding than the last, until finally they forgot all about one another. The stakes were so low, there was really nothing to lose.

Wallis told herself to approach Hennie, but her feet were having none of it. If this went badly, she'd still have to live alongside her. Hennie might manage to befriend Becca—if Becca stopped flinching long enough. And if Shea and Corinne decided to stick together after all, that would leave Wallis as the odd girl out. Or Hennie might turn on Wallis in an effort to prevent herself from becoming the cabin's obvious outcast, and Wallis would spend the week being tormented and ignored. It was more pressure than she could bear.

Just as she was about to abandon the idea altogether, she noticed that the rumble of the riding lawn mower had grown unignorably loud, and she turned to discover that it was coming right for her. Its rider braked and turned off the engine. His face was leathery and sun-spotted, and he wore a pair of faded blue coveralls that made him look as though he had just escaped from a chain gang.

"Young lady, could you take a step or two to the left so I can keep mowing straight?"

Wallis stood there stupidly for a moment, still so deep in thought that she didn't quite register what he'd said.

"Young lady, are you all right?"

That shook her to her senses. She hopped out of the way and said, "Yes, I'm fine."

"I thought you might have gone a bit sun-struck," he said, sticking a finger in his ear and digging with great enthusiasm.

"Sorry, I was just thinking," Wallis said, then extended her hand to the man, encouraged at the idea of talking to someone new, someone she had not yet alienated with her weirdness. "My name's Dorothea. What's yours?"

Thankfully, he shook with the hand that had not been in his ear.

"Oscar," he said. "I'm the groundskeeper."

"Nice to meet you," Wallis said.

"Likewise."

See? Wallis told herself. *Meeting people is easy. This is going perfectly well.*

"So do you like working here?" she asked. "How long have you worked here?"

A conversation! She was having an actual conversation!

"Twenty years now." He shrugged. "It's a living, I suppose."

Having spotted Wallis talking to the man on the riding lawn mower, the other girls in Cabin 2 made their way toward her. They had all watched enough television shows about murderers and girls in peril to know that these kinds of conversations could end badly.

"HI, WALLIS. WHAT ARE YOU DOING OVER HERE BY YOURSELF?" Shea asked.

"This is Oscar," Wallis said, oblivious to their concern. "He's the groundskeeper."

"But why are you talking to him?" Corinne asked, looking Oscar up and down like she was memorizing a description to pass along to the authorities.

Wallis cringed, but Oscar seemed to take Corinne's suspicion in stride.

"It's good that you're sticking together like you are," he said. "It's good that you're looking out for each other."

If only he knew, Wallis thought, that as soon as this walk was over, the five of them would probably never by choice be within such close proximity again, at least during waking hours.

"Lot of things out there," Oscar continued. "Lot of real bad things."

The girls, even Wallis, now exchanged surreptitious glances and began to inch away from the spot where Oscar sat on his riding mower.

"Not so fast, girlies," he said. "You might want to listen to old Oscar. You might be glad you did."

He wasn't that old, Wallis thought. He couldn't have been much older than her parents, and yet, when he said it, a cloud passed overhead and threw shadows on his face and made it look drawn and withered.

"It all started a few summers ago," Oscar said. "A terrible thing."

Corinne shivered and hugged herself even though the evening chill had yet to fall over the camp.

"A group of kids decided to go exploring in the cave near the pony trails. Not a nice place, never has been. Some people even say it's cursed.

"But the girls from Cabin 2 decided they wanted to have themselves an adventure, so they went to the cave and explored and saw what there was to see, and then they climbed back out again following a rope they'd tied to a rock. But when they stepped out of the cave, they realized they were a body short. One of the girls had gotten separated from the rest, and no one had noticed until it was too late. They went back inside and searched for her, but it was no good. They couldn't find her. By that time, it was beginning to get dark, and the girls had to get back to their cabin. They left the cord tied to the rock for her, and went to get help. But it was the night of the song-and-dance competition in the All-Camp Sport & Follies, and in all the excitement, they forgot to tell their counselor that the girl was still inside the cave. To be fair, the counselor didn't notice she was missing either. She was a quiet girl, timid, easy to overlook.

"The next morning, the girls woke up and suddenly remembered what had happened, and they went back for their friend, but when they got to the cave, they came upon a chilling sight. The rope was gone, and there was no sign of the girl inside the cave. All that was left was the journal she kept, detailing the sad, lonely story of her time at Camp So-and-So. And when they shone their flashlights on the walls, they saw that they were splattered with blood.

"They didn't stop running or screaming until they reached the cabin, where they finally told their counselor what had happened. The authorities were called in, the cave was thoroughly searched, and the blood on the walls was found to be that of a squirrel, but other than the journal, they recovered nothing else of the girl."

"What was her name?" Wallis asked. The part of the story about the girl being quiet and easy to overlook made her more uncomfortable than she liked to admit. She wondered if the others would notice if she were lost in a cave and separated from the group. Had she been psychic, she might have been comforted to know that Hennie and Becca were feeling exactly the same thing at that moment.

A Note from the Narrator: Wallis was not psychic. There were no psychic girls at Camp So-and-So, at least not this summer.

"The girl's name was Abigail, and the worst was yet to come," he said. "Even though none of the other cabins knew what had happened—the camp director decided it would be unnecessarily upsetting and kept the thing hushed up—strange things began to happen to the rest of Cabin 2. They heard noises outside late at night, felt like they were being watched even when there was no one else around. They'd wake up in the morning and find dead snakes and spiders on their pillows.

"More strange things happened. One day they came back from horseback riding and found four dolls made out of burlap sacks, nestled in their sleeping bags, each one with X's where the eyes should have been. After that, none of them left the cabin, none of them slept.

"And then, one of them was killed.

"Her name was Lori, and they found her body pinned to the archery target, an arrow straight through her heart. After that, the remaining three girls in Cabin 2 all went stark raving mad. They had to be carted out on stretchers, and last I heard, all but one remains in institutional care. Camp ended early that year."

"THAT'S TRUE," Shea said. "A GIRL DID GET KILLED AROUND HERE A FEW YEARS AGO. I SAW IT ON THE NEWS."

Corinne gave her a baffled stare. "You *knew* this happened, and you decided to come here anyway?"

Shea shrugged. "I DIDN'T KNOW IT HAPPENED *HERE*. THE REPORTER NEVER SAID THE NAME OF THE CAMP OR ANYTHING. BESIDES, I HEARD IT WAS AN ARCHERY ACCIDENT. THEY NEVER SAID ANYTHING ABOUT AN INSANE MURDERER RUNNING AROUND."

"Did Abigail do it?" asked Becca.

"It's hard to say," Oscar said, shrugging. "There's always more going on around here than I can keep track of. Maybe Abigail killed her, or maybe Lori was just a girl who made some mighty vengeful enemies. I can't say as I know which is the more reasonable explanation. What I do know is that Abigail is still out there."

Becca twisted the ends of her hair nervously. "So you've seen her?"

"Of course not. Abigail's a shy girl. Keeps mainly to herself. But I've heard her rustling around in the bushes from time to time. In fact, sometimes when I'm out here in the meadow, I'll sit real still and quiet until the only thing I can hear is the wind blowing through the grass, and over by the road, I'll hear the crack of a twig or the sound of a girl crying, and I'll know it's Abigail."

He finished talking. The sun peeked from behind the clouds and the shadows lifted off of his face, and he smiled at them and sat up straight on his mower.

"Well, I should probably get back to work, but it was sure nice talking to you girls!"

He revved up the engine on the riding lawn mower, tipped the brim of his baseball cap to them, and rode off across the meadow. The girls from Cabin 2 stared after him, their mouths hanging open.

Shea broke the silence. "WHAT WAS THAT ABOUT?"

Annoyance flashed across Corinne's face. "Just a creepy old man trying to scare us. I'm going to report him when we get back."

"WE PROBABLY SHOULD GO BACK. IT'S STARTING TO GET DARK."

"I don't want to go back," Becca said. "I want to go home."

"DON'T BE SUCH A BABY," Shea said, though not unkindly. She grinned at Becca as she spoke.

"I don't want to go back, either," said Hennie.

"How can we sleep in that cabin, knowing that the girls who had our cots all went insane?" Becca said.

"WE CAN SEE IF CABIN 5 WANTS TO TRADE CABINS WITH US. THEY'RE CLOSEST TO THE LATRINE, SO THEY MIGHT GO FOR IT."

Corinne sneered. "I'm not sleeping downwind from the toilets just because a couple of you are too naive to know when you're being messed with."

"But some of the things Oscar said were true," Hennie said.

"Which things? A girl got killed in an archery accident. We know that. But did the news say that she was murdered? Did it say that a girl disappeared in a cave? Did it say that a bunch of campers went insane and they had to close down the camp?" Corinne counted off each point on her fingers like she was amassing a pile of evidence.

"Don't you think the news would have mentioned something like that if it had actually happened?" she finished.

"I guess so," Hennie admitted.

"Then there's nothing to be afraid of," Corinne said.

"But Oscar said the camp director tried to hush everything up so no one would panic," Becca said, refusing to give up.

"Well, that probably went right out the window once somebody got murdered on an archery target," Wallis muttered. Nevertheless, what Corinne said made sense.

"I still want to go home," Becca said.

Shea put an arm around her shoulder and gave it a squeeze.

"Come on, let's go back," Corinne said.

As they walked back to the road, Wallis thought about asking Shea whether she lived nearby. She must if the camper's death had been covered in the local news. That would be a good icebreaker for a conversation. But Wallis's tongue sat like a lump of clay in her mouth. She put her head down and trailed behind the rest of the girls.

Only Becca still seemed upset by what Oscar had said. Corinne's logic had calmed the rest of them down, and no one said anything about Abigail or Lori or even Oscar. Still, when they passed a trailhead that led into the woods and Hennie whispered, "That's the path to the cave," a chill ran through every one of them.

When they got back, two rows of tea candles illuminated the path to Cabin 2. This must have been what Megan was doing while they were gone. She'd also left a trail of Hershey's kisses between the flickering candles and hung a small disco ball from the door frame.

A Note from the Narrator: Megan had planned to do more to the cabin. She'd brought a roll of streamers and a pack of glow-in-the-dark stars and planets and meant to hang those as well, but the girls didn't know this, and they never would.

Shea giggled. "THAT LOOKS SO CUTE!"

As the rest of her cabinmates went up the steps, Wallis bent down and put three of the kisses in the front pocket of her overall shorts. She was about to reach for a fourth when she heard the screams.

Wallis ran up the steps and into the cabin. Inside, their flashlights had been duct-taped to the four corner posts, all trained on a spot in the middle of the cabin where their counselor's body hung upside down from a beam. Megan's ankles had been tied with a cord and X's drawn over her eyes in black marker. The end of her ponytail grazed the floorboards as the body swung back and forth like a pendulum.

Shea and Hennie screamed. Corinne shook. Becca collapsed into a ball and began to weep. Wallis pointed up at the unfinished wood panels that slanted up to form the roof of the cabin.

"Look," she said, her voice trembling.

Scrawled in blood were the words:

ABIGAIL LIVES.

DRAMATIS PERSONAE:

THE GIRL WITH
BEADS IN HER HAIR

THE GIRL IN
THE ORANGE HOODIE

THE STICKLIKE GOTH GIRL

THE GIRL WITH
THE UPTURNED NOSE

THE GIRL WITH
THOUSANDS OF FRECKLES

CABIN 3

THE HERO'S QUEST

[SCENE: Interior, Cabin 3]

Cabin 2 was still out in the meadow talking to Oscar when the girls from Cabin 3 discovered that something had also been written in their rafters. The five of them circled up beneath it and took turns reading the verse aloud:

In evil times when darkness threatens day,
One soul among you must hold it at bay.
First you must slay the beast outside its lair
And then set free the one imprisoned there;
But know the path you walk is thick with traps
All custom-made to hasten your collapse.
Beware! The Knave who only speaks in lies!
Beware! The Knight who plots out your demise!
Beware! For you will lose before it's done!
First five, then four, then three, then two, then one.

This quest is not a summer's game,
It is not safe, it is not tame.
Consider this before you pack—
Some of you may not come back.

It was never a question of whether they would go.

They were, all of them, readers of Arthurian legends and Greek myths and every volume in the Isis Archimedes series that had been published so far. They were Girl Scouts who blew on dandelions and looked for suspicious cracks in walls that looked like they might lead to magical worlds, and between the five of them had spent exactly 1,362 hours, 42 minutes, and 13 seconds daydreaming about receiving a call to action just like this one.

Of course they would answer it. The question was where they would start.

"There was a cave on the map," said the girl with beads in her hair.

"I saw it, too," said the girl in the orange hoodie.

"It's near the pony trail," said the sticklike goth girl.

"What about our counselor?" asked the girl with the upturned nose. "It'll be dark soon."

"We'll leave her a note so she won't worry," said the girl with thousands of freckles. While she found a pencil and jotted a few lines, the rest of them packed. They filled their water bottles, hooked axes and Swiss army knives to their belt loops, and stuffed flashlights, headlamps, and first aid kits into their backpacks.

"Shouldn't we think about this? Shouldn't we have a plan?" asked the girl in the orange hoodie.

"I've been planning for this my whole life," said the girl with beads in her hair.

To Our Counselor,

By the time you read this, we'll be gone.

Unfortunately, we can't tell you why, only that Camp So-and-So is in terrible peril and we have been called upon to save it.

The road ahead is liable to be long and dangerous. We cannot say when, or if, we will return.

We are sorry that we did not get to know you better, and are sure that you are a very good counselor.

Respectfully,
Cabin 3

DRAMATIS PERSONAE:

VERITY

AMBER, ALIX, ANNIKA, and ADDISON

PAM, *their counselor*

CABIN 4

SOUL MATES

*[SCENE: Behind Cabin 4 on a trail that,
until a few moments ago, did not exist]*

Amber and Alix and Annika and Addison had been best friends
since the fourth grade, and now they had all come to summer
camp together.

But each cabin held five girls, and so the last bunk went to
Verity.

They were nice enough people, Verity supposed. They
were very silly and giggled at everything, but there was nothing mean about them, and Verity reminded herself as she
unpacked that if they were excluding her, at least it probably
wasn't on purpose.

Still, she couldn't settle down. She'd spent the past four
months in a state of anxiety, ever since she'd sent in the applica-
tion for her one-week session at Camp So-and-So. Her parents
had looked so hopeful when they showed Verity the brochure,

so happy when Verity didn't immediately push it away.

It was summer camp. It was a rite of passage, a formative experience. You could come back from something like that a whole different person. The idea appealed so much to Verity that she found herself nodding her head and buying flip-flops to wear in the shower.

Now, she realized it had been a mistake. She had no idea how she would make it through an entire week if she kept worrying like this.

It wasn't like it showed. It wasn't like these girls were paying attention to anything she did anyway. And even if they noticed, they probably wouldn't care. In her head, Verity knew that you could say you were gay and most people would be okay with it. But knowing something like that wasn't the same as announcing it to the world.

It wasn't like you had to tell people when you decided you were straight. People should have to do that, Verity decided. It should be required. It would be less lonely that way.

It seemed like Verity's friends back home never stopped talking about the boys they liked, the boys who looked at them, the boys who didn't look at them, and when they weren't talking about boys, they were asking each other for advice about how to act around boys and what to say to boys and how to feel about boys. Meanwhile, Verity couldn't even give herself permission to look at a girl long enough to know whether she was looking back or not, and she didn't know of anyone she could ask for advice about that.

A Note from the Narrator: You might wonder, how could I possibly know all of these things about people I've never met? Before the campers arrive, I do my homework. I study all their files. I am a keen observer of human behavior. I make good guesses. But I strive for accuracy in my storytelling, so when I find a camper who keeps a journal, I feel that I really owe it to the story to get my hands on that journal.

At some point, she'd tell people, and then they'd all alter their opinions of her accordingly. They'd think about all the years that they had known her, and they would make certain moments stand out in relief, and they would say, "Oh, of course you like girls. How could we not have known all along?"

Verity didn't want other people trying to make sense of her. Not when she hadn't quite made sense of it all herself.

A Note from the Narrator: You might also be thinking that it was wrong of me to read Verity's journal and trample around through her innermost, secret thoughts just so I can tell you this story. I would respond to that by saying that I have not stolen Verity's journal. I am only borrowing it, and there's plenty in here I'm not telling you, no matter how juicy it is.

After dinner, their counselor, Pam, laid out their plans for the rest of the evening. First they would unpack, then they would make up their bunks, then they would go introduce themselves to the girls in the other cabins and invite them to an evening of icebreakers and games. Pam barked out these instructions in a way that made them suspect that in another life, she had been either a drill sergeant or a guard in a women's prison.

"You will split up into two groups. First group takes Cabins 1 and 2; second group takes Cabins 3 and 5. The evening's entertainment will begin at 1900 hours sharp. Trail mix and s'mores will be served, and it will be a nice time. Are there any questions, Cabin 4?"

"No," they said in unison.

"Very good," she said, checking her watch. "Reconvene here in thirty minutes. That is all."

Pam set off in the direction of the mess hall, presumably to collect supplies for her icebreakers and s'mores, and leaving the girls to carry out her instructions. This proved a nearly impossible task for Amber, Alix, Annika, and Addison, who were loath to be parted. After some deliberation, it was decided that Alix and Annika would go with Verity, and they left one another with tearful embraces.

Verity knocked on the doorpost of Cabin 1, but the only person inside was Sharon, the counselor. She had headphones on, her face buried in a gaming console. She didn't even look up at the girls from Cabin 4, and Verity correctly supposed she would not want to join them for icebreaker games.

Megan, the counselor of Cabin 2, was hanging a glittery disco ball from the cabin doorway when they approached.

"Fun!" she squealed when they told her Pam's plans. "I'll tell the girls as soon as they get back."

She hadn't actually said they would attend, but that was the closest thing to a yes that Verity, Annika, and Alix would get.

Cabin 3 wasn't technically their responsibility, but when they walked past, Verity couldn't help but notice that something seemed to be amiss. There was no sign of campers or a counselor, or anyone except for Robin, the counselor-in-training who'd checked them in and assigned them to their cabin earlier that afternoon. She was standing in the center of the cabin and reading a letter, which struck Verity as odd, and possibly a little shady. Did she have any business being there? Was that letter even addressed to her?

"Hey," Verity waved and smiled, and tried to keep these suspicions hidden from her face. "Have you seen the others?"

Robin shook her head. "They seem to have lit out for the territories," she said.

"Is that allowed?" Alix asked.

"Sure," Robin said. "You can pretty much do what you want to at Camp So-and-So. Set your agenda. Follow your bliss."

"Really?" Verity asked, thinking about the series of orders Pam had barked at them. "I had not gotten that impression."

Robin folded the letter she'd been reading into thirds and laid it on the cot closest to the door.

"Oh, wait," she said. "You're in Pam's cabin, aren't you?"

Verity, Annika, and Alix nodded ruefully.

Robin rolled down the vinyl flap over the door and stepped out onto the cinder block steps.

"Well, then I guess you'll have to be a little sneakier about it," she said, winking at them before she jumped down the steps, landing with a puff of dust and pine needles.

When they returned to their bunks, there was no sign of Addison or Amber. Thinking they were still chatting with the campers next door, the three of them went over to Cabin 5, introduced themselves, and learned that Addison and Amber had never so much as waved hello to these girls, much less invited them over for s'mores.

"I wonder where they went," Annika said with a note of annoyance.

Alix shrugged and turned back toward the girls from Cabin 5.

"Anyhow, you'll come over at 1900 hours, whenever that is?" she asked.

"Seven," Verity muttered. "1900 hours means seven o'clock."

"Then why didn't Pam just say 'seven o'clock'?" Alix asked.

"Sure," said one of the girls from Cabin 5. "We'll probably come over after we finish unpacking."

"Cool," said Verity, Annika, and Alix.

"We'll see," said the girl from Cabin 5.

They were halfway back to their own cabin when Amber and Addison came running toward them. Their eyes were bright and fevered, and their voices even more frantic and giddy than usual.

"Youguysyouguysyouguys!" Amber shrieked.

"You'll never guess what we found in the woods!" Addison said with a reckless grin. She pointed back in the direction they'd come from, a dim and uninviting patch of forest carpeted with enough wild undergrowth to discourage casual exploration.

"Why were you back there?" Verity asked. "Pam told you to invite Cabins 3 and 5 to our mixer thing."

"Which you did not do," Annika pointed out.

"I know!" Amber said, giggling. "But when we went behind our cabin, there was this, like . . ."

"It was like a magnet," Addison added. "We couldn't NOT follow it."

"And so, we're in the woods, and all of a sudden, there were BOYS!"

"That's not possible," Verity said.

Boys were strictly forbidden at Camp So-and-So, Pam had said. There was a coed camp across the lake, and more than one camper in the past had tried to steal a canoe and cross the lake under cover of night, or to smuggle a boy from the Inge F. Yancey Young Executives Leadership Camp back into their cabins. They were always caught, Pam had warned them, and punishments were harsh.

Addison tugged Alix by the arm. "Come on. We'll show you."

With Addison leading the way, the girls circled around the back of their cabin and toward the woods in a single file. Verity hung back, partly because she didn't want to get in trouble if they were wandering into some forbidden encampment of boys, and partly because she wasn't sure that Addison's invitation extended to her. But in case it did, she followed along at a safe distance.

She was glad she had, because it gave her an extra moment to make sense of what she saw next. Just before Addison crossed into the forest, her body jerked to the left and she began side-walking into the underbrush as though she were drunk.

"This is just how it happened before!" Addison said as she lurched sideways. "Like a magnet!"

As she spoke, Amber also stumbled, then fell in line behind Addison. Alix was knocked off her feet, but she got right back up and was soon chasing after the other girls, letting the magnetic force pull her along through the woods.

Annika looked over her shoulder at Verity before she too was carried into the forest. "You're coming, right?" she asked.

Well, *now* she was.

If I am killed by a pack of hillbilly aliens or escaped convicts who are hiding in the woods of Camp So-and-So, at least I will die having been invited to something, she thought.

It felt like stepping into a strong river current, and Verity had trouble keeping her balance as it pulled her into the trees. She eventually settled on a half-walking, half-running stutter step. If there really was a cabin of boys waiting up ahead in the clearing, this was unlikely to make a good first impression on them.

Up ahead, Addison and Amber attempted not very successfully to muffle their squeals of delight. They sought cover behind a fallen tree, blackened and split halfway down from where it had been struck by lightning long ago. Addison settled in, lying flat on her stomach behind the log, and Amber motioned for the other girls to join them. Soon, all five of them were laid out in a row, feet sticking out behind them, elbows propped up on the trunk.

"Look," Addison whispered, pointing toward a grove of poplars not ten yards away. In the center of it stood a cabin identical to their own, and sure enough, all around the cabin, there were boys. There was a boy sitting on the cabin steps playing a guitar. A boy with a rockabilly pompadour doing pull-ups on a poplar limb. A boy standing on the peak of the cabin roof, perfectly balanced on a skateboard. A boy building the beginnings of a campfire with kindling and pine needles.

Addison locked her eyes on him and whispered, "Isn't he gorgeous?"

Alix was too busy staring at the skateboarder to reply. To be fair, he was creating a pretty interesting spectacle at the moment. Verity watched, too, as he tipped back on his board, then launched himself down the cabin roof, realizing only once he was airborne the folly of his plan. He flailed only for a moment as the skateboard shot out from under his feet, then tucked his chin and somersaulted in midair before making a perfect landing. Alix gasped, her eyes phosphorescent with love.

Amber missed the whole thing, humming along with the song the boy played on his guitar. "That's my favorite song," she whispered. "How could he know?"

"He couldn't," Verity started to explain, but Annika poked her in the ribs.

"Shhhhh," she said, never once taking her eyes off the shirtless boy doing pull-ups. His muscles looked like they'd been oiled, and they flexed dramatically each time he lifted himself on the branch.

"I wonder how he gets his hair to do that," Annika murmured.

Verity opened her mouth to make a crack about how he probably styled it with pec sweat, but before she could speak, the girl walked out the cabin door.

She was the prettiest girl Verity had ever seen, with cheekbones that looked like they'd been sculpted out of marble, and skin that glowed. Her smile was wide and joyful, and the very sight of it filled Verity with so profound a sense of well-being that she felt she might never feel the need to be sarcastic about anything ever again.

Or was that sarcasm, too? Verity smiled, knowing for no particular reason yet knowing all the same that the girl would smile at that, too. And then, just when she thought she couldn't crush any harder, Verity saw that the girl was holding a copy of the first book in the Isis Archimedes series.

Written by Eurydice Horne, the Isis Archimedes books told the story of a young foundling who swears revenge against the tyrant S'ulla after his armies destroy her village and his soldiers murder the only family she has ever known. In the second book, Isis Archimedes devises a plan to train as a soldier and spy and to infiltrate S'ulla's army, but when that fails, when she's captured and thrown into prison, Isis finally learns the truth about who she really is. That was where the story really got going for Verity. She liked battle scenes and sabotage and political intrigue as much as the next person, but she was in it for the magic.

They were the books Verity read whenever she felt lousy about the world, like there was nothing worth doing or seeing, and they always made her feel better. She didn't know anyone else who read them. The series was supposed to be seven books, but it had been over a decade since the fifth one came out, and Verity had almost given up hope that she'd ever find out how it ended. Even Eurydice Horne herself had gone into hiding, shuttered her website, given no interviews, and made no statements since the publication of the fifth book.

Watching the girl settle into her hammock with the first Isis Archimedes like it was an old friend shook Verity out of her thoughts about the fifth book and its deeply troubling ending. And after another minute, she found she wasn't thinking about the books at all but, rather, what it would be like to be curled up in the hammock next to the beautiful girl.

"Should we go talk to them?" Annika asked, her eyes still locked on the boy doing pull-ups.

Amber let out a little shriek. "No, I could never."

Alix nodded in agreement. "Not yet. Let's just keep watching them."

Annika shushed them again. "If you all keep talking, they're going to hear us."

For a moment, it seemed like Addison's boy, the one building the campfire, had actually heard them. He got up from his crouch by the fire pit and began walking toward their hiding place. If he'd taken two steps into the woods, he would have spotted them stretched out behind the mossy log. But instead, he stopped at the edge of the clearing and began to fill his arms with firewood.

The moment his back was turned, Addison pulled herself up and, keeping her head and shoulders hunched down, crawled over the log. For a moment, Annika, Alix, Amber, and Verity thought she was about to go running after him, but instead, she stole over to the woodpile where he'd been standing, plucked something up off the ground, and stole back unseen.

"Are you insane?" Annika asked, pulling her down behind the log.

Addison grinned and held her palm open to them.

"He lost a button," she said.

Annika whispered, "Are you going to give it back to him?"

"I'm keeping it," Addison said, shoving the button into the pocket of her shorts. "It's my soul mate souvenir."

The five of them froze at Addison's words, and their eyes met, none of them daring to speak aloud what they thought. Because the idea that Addison could know that the boy gathering firewood was her soul mate after watching him for five minutes was ridiculous, and Verity knew it. They all must have known it. But she felt the same way about the girl reading Isis

Archimedes. She knew that in those moments when she felt alone and lost and altogether unknowable, this girl would see her as she really was, would love her—nicks, bumps, broken pieces, and all. And if she could know something like that, why couldn't Addison know that the firewood boy was her soul mate too?

Suddenly, Addison began to crawl away from the fallen log. She shuffled backwards through the leaves until she butted into a yew tree and slumped back against its trunk, clutching her head in her hands.

"We should go back," she whispered, pain etched on her face.

Before the other girls could even protest, she got up and began to run back toward their camp. Amber and Annika and Alix looked at each other. The conflict was plain on their faces, but loyalty won out, and they got up to follow her.

"Come on," Annika said to Verity, extending a hand to help her to her feet.

Verity took one last look back at the cabin and saw that the girl had slung herself out of the hammock and lay under the poplars reading Isis Archimedes. She felt a pang of longing in her chest and, for a moment, considered turning back. But then Annika gave her a pull, and she snapped back to herself and followed after the others.

She had no idea where they were, no idea how they'd gotten there, so it was almost a relief when she felt the same current that had pulled them to this place tugging at her feet.

Once they were almost back to their cabin, Alix said, "When can we go back?"

"Yeah," Amber agreed, turning to Addison. "What's wrong? Why'd you make us leave?"

"I don't know," Addison said. Her face was no longer contorted in pain, but looked troubled instead.

"Maybe it was the woods," Alix said. "Maybe you're allergic."

"You should take some Claritin or something, and then we should go back," Amber said.

"It's really weird, though, right?" Addison asked. "Them being out there. Five of them, five of us."

At this, Verity began to panic. *Five of them, five of us*, Addison had said. That meant that she'd seen the girl, too, that all of them had. Verity felt suddenly exposed.

"If that's true, we should go back to them," said Alix.

"Maybe," said Annika. "But we can't just go back there and stare at them. We have to do something next time."

To her surprise, Verity found herself chiming in, "Otherwise what's the point?"

Annika nodded to her in encouragement. "Yeah, otherwise what's the point? If they're really our soul mates, we have to meet them eventually. We have to be ready."

"We should go back to their cabin and talk to them," said Addison. "We should invite them to do something."

"But what are we going to invite the boys to do?" asked Amber.

Boys? Verity thought.

And then slowly it dawned on her that no camp would allow four teenage boys to share a cabin with a girl. That if anyone from Cabin 5 had noticed the girl with the beautiful smile and the glowing cheekbones, they certainly would have said something.

"Five boys, five of us," said Verity, carefully testing her theory. "We could see if they want to play basketball."

Amber wrinkled her nose. "I don't want to play basketball. Besides, where would we play? It's not like we can invite them back to Camp So-and-So."

"What about paintball?" asked Annika. "Or hiking."

While the four other girls considered the merits of these suggestions, Verity mulled over her own thoughts. There was no doubt in her mind that she'd seen the girl, that she'd really been there. But if Addison and Amber and Alix and Annika hadn't seen her, what had they seen instead? And what if Verity had seen things that they hadn't? For all she knew, the guitar-playing boy could have been strumming a harp and the rockabilly pompadour might have looked like a mohawk or a buzzcut to Annika.

And if they couldn't trust their eyes, what they saw in the woods could have been anything at all.

TO: Sebastian Langley, Executive Assistant to Inge F. Yancey IV,
    Yancey Corp. CEO

FROM: Octavia Henry, Director, Camp So-and-So

Dear Sebastian,

Maybe my last note slipped through the cracks! Just touching base about the staffing situation at Camp So-and-So. It's less than two months until camp starts, and I'm starting to get a little nervous about getting those positions filled in time. Here's hoping I don't have to go over your head and start pestering Mr. Yancey about this. Haha, kidding!

If you have any questions, please feel free to get in touch, day or night. That art barn isn't going to run itself!

    Look forward to hearing from you!
    Octavia

DRAMATIS PERSONAE:

FIVE CAMPERS, *names unknown*

CABIN 5

SURVIVAL

[SCENE: A cabin encircled by thorns]

The ground erupted in a perfect circle around Cabin 5, causing a blast that shook the earth and rattled the cabin eaves, and out of the dirt rose a wall of thick, writhing brambles.

One girl screamed as they were sealed off from the rest of the camp. Another fainted. One attempted a running leap, but the wall rose up too quickly, and she failed to clear it. The last two girls tried to climb up the brambles instead, but the brambles did not want to be climbed and raked their flesh. A vine snaked around one girl's ankle and yanked her off the wall. The other managed to climb a bit higher, until a thorny branch pitched her off into the fire pit, where she landed, limp as a sock puppet and covered in scrapes.

A Note from the Narrator: Cabin 1 was at Most Excellent Beach when it happened, and Cabin 2 was talking to Oscar in the meadow.

Cabin 3 had set forth on their quest for the beast, and Cabin 4 had just clapped eyes on their soul mates for the first time.

No one saw it happen except me. Because I see almost everything.

I saw the screaming girl collect herself. I saw her help the girl who'd tried to hurdle over the wall up off the ground, and I saw them both slap the cheeks of the girl who'd fainted until she revived. I saw the girls who'd been flung from the walls cover their mouths in horror and awe as the vines rose forty feet in the air.

I saw it dawn on all five of them that they were cut off from the latrine, the mess hall, the other cabins, their counselor.

I saw it dawn on one of them that this all might have been avoided if they'd gone over to Cabin 4 for s'mores and icebreakers five minutes earlier.

I saw them gather around the cinder block steps and look to one another in the hopes that someone, anyone, had the slightest idea what they were supposed to do next.

∽⊙PLAYBILL⊙∽
CAMP SO-AND-SO

Cabin 1: The All-Camp Sport & Follies

DRAMATIS PERSONAE:

KADIE

CRESSIDA

DORA

VIVIAN and KIMBER

ROBIN, *a counselor-in-training*

TANIA

RON

Their MINIONS

Cabin 2: Killer in the Woods

DRAMATIS PERSONAE:

WALLIS

CORINNE

SHEA

HENNIE

BECCA

~~MEGAN, *their counselor*~~

OSCAR, *a groundskeeper*

Cabin 3: The Hero's Quest

DRAMATIS PERSONAE:

THE GIRL WITH BEADS IN HER HAIR
THE GIRL IN THE ORANGE HOODIE
THE STICKLIKE GOTH GIRL
THE GIRL WITH THE UPTURNED NOSE
THE GIRL WITH THOUSANDS OF FRECKLES

Cabin 4: Soul Mates

DRAMATIS PERSONAE:

VERITY
AMBER, ALIX, ANNIKA, and ADDISON
PAM, *their counselor*

Cabin 5: Survival

DRAMATIS PERSONAE:

FIVE CAMPERS, *names unknown*

[SCENE: Camp So-and-So, and the woods near it]

NOTE: Intermission will take place at the discretion
of management, and without warning.

CABIN 1

THE ALL-CAMP SPORT & FOLLIES

[SCENE: Inside Cabin 1, KADIE wakes her fellow campers, CRESSIDA, DORA, VIVIAN, and KIMBER, in preparation for the first event of the All-Camp Sport & Follies—archery]

It was still dark when Kadie showered, dressed, and went to the mess hall, where she liberated enough apples, granola bars, and peanut butter crackers to feed three cabins. They had a long day ahead of them: five tests of strength, skill, wit, and endurance. There would be no time for proper meals.

Next, she went to the equipment shed, which, remote as it was from the rest of the camp, was a desolate place before dawn. Kadie had no desire to stay there longer than necessary, so she did not question why the door was unlocked or why the air was thick with the smell of burnt oil and tires. She took the bows and arrows and targets and left.

Back at the cabin, she woke the others, starting with Dora,

who grabbed her towel and shuffled off to the latrine without protest. Kadie wasn't surprised. The girl had all the backbone of a potato. She had not expected that it would be so easy to get Vivian and Kimber moving, but since laying eyes on the Inge F. Yancey Young Executives Leadership Camp, they had visions of feather beds and sugar-sand beaches dancing in their heads and got up right away.

When Kadie went over to Cressida's bunk, she found her lying in the dark, her eyes open, watching and waiting. When Kadie nudged her shoulder, she rolled out of her sleeping bag already dressed, right down to her hiking boots.

A Note from the Narrator: Of course, this is because Cressida had been up even earlier than Kadie, working on schemes of her own.

They crept out of the cabin and left Sharon snoring in the dark. Eventually, the others emerged from the latrine, and they gathered around the fire pit, where Kadie distributed the granola bars and apples and crackers.

"Was that hedge there last night?" Dora whispered. It was still too dark to make out the contours and scale of the thorny wall that now rose up around Cabin 5.

Kadie squinted. There'd been five cabins, hadn't there? Or maybe there'd only been four. Maybe that had changed since last summer, too. Kadie had been so fixated on trying to convince her cabinmates to do the All-Camp Sport & Follies last night that she wasn't able to say for sure how many cabins there were.

"Come on," Kadie whispered, shoving aside her own

nagging suspicions in favor of the matter at hand. "We've got work to do."

By the time the fog had burned off and the Inge F. Yancey campers had arrived at the meadow (they could have rowed across the lake, but preferred to be driven in town cars), the girls of Cabin 1 had what passed for a game plan.

Things had not gotten off to a promising start that morning as Kadie set up the archery targets and ran drills to assess their talent. Dora had been eliminated immediately, being too nervous to grip the bow with any conviction, and Cressida's spindly arms lacked the strength (or appeared to) to pull back the string. To the surprise of everyone, most of all themselves, Vivian and Kimber took the field first, representing Cabin 1 in archery.

Kimber hadn't missed the target after her first try, and Vivian actually managed a bullseye. They'd even figured out how to put the arm guards on by themselves.

"Do you think we can do this?" Vivian asked, as the Inge campers poured out of the town cars, immaculate in their matching vests, visors, and sunglasses.

"You'll be great," Kadie said.

"Besides," Kimber said, tossing her hair as she drew back the bowstring, "just look at us."

They did cut a striking figure with their bows and tight jeans and chunky black boots. The Inge F. Yancey campers noticed it. There was no question that Tania noticed it, and despite looking *Vogue*-ready in her mod white sunglasses and vest, she was not about to tolerate any sort of challenge to her fairest-of-them-all title.

She whispered something to her minions that made them laugh hysterically. Then she shouldered her bow and drew back the string while aiming in the direction of Vivian's head. Kimber had already tackled her friend and pulled her to the ground before she realized there was no arrow loaded in Tania's bow.

Tania let out a peal of laughter and let go of the string.

Kadie shook her head in disgust and helped Vivian and Kimber to their feet. Why had she loved this place so much last summer? She wasn't sure she liked it now, and it wasn't the girls in her cabin who were the problem.

Something was different. And wrong. And possibly unsafe. It dawned on Kadie that if something bad happened, she had absolutely no idea who to ask for help. Certainly not their counselor, but who else was there? If Tania's bow had been loaded when she aimed at Vivian's head, was there anything they could have done about it?

As Kadie thought about this and Vivian and Kimber wiped the dewy grass clippings off their jeans, the last town car pulled onto the shoulder of the road. A peculiar-looking trio lurched from the backseat.

"Don't just stand there," Ron said, snaking a possessive arm around Tania's waist and glaring at a small group of her minions. "See to our judges."

Three boys scurried for the car and offered their elbows, then walked the judges across the meadow and presented them to Tania.

Standing there together, they resembled candles in a candelabra, waxy-skinned and melted down to different sizes and shapes over the years. In the center stood a tall, gray-haired woman who wore a prim, black suit and gloves and a veiled hat, looking as though she'd been transported from another time.

A Note from the Narrator: Which, as a matter of fact, she had been, fifty years earlier when she'd been sent by the bank where she worked to investigate an accounting matter at the camp, accepted a cup of tea from her hosts, and never thought to leave.

To her right was a woman in a sleeveless, floral-print dress with a flouncy skirt and pumps. Her hair was honey-colored and hung halfway down her back, and it was only after you looked at her for a few minutes that you realized you couldn't tell whether she was twenty years old or forty or sixty or a hundred and two.

On the other side of the woman with the veiled hat stood the third judge. If it was difficult to place the age of the second judge or the time of the first one, it was unclear whether the third judge was, in fact, human. He (or she) was small and lumpen and eccentrically dressed in a purple suitcoat with green piping at the lapels. It was difficult to make out the face beneath the thicket of black hair that swept over the judge's eyes, but what bits did show through seemed too pale to belong to a person.

"Welcome," Tania said.

The judge in the black, veiled hat looked up and down the line of girls from Cabin 1 and sniffed.

"It's their camp," she said. "Shouldn't they be doing the welcoming?"

However, all the girls from Cabin 1 found themselves quite incapable of speech, except for Cressida who had fixated on a finer point.

"You brought your own judges?" she asked Tania, her cheeks turning pink with agitation.

Tania strode up to Cressida, her paces graceful and measured as a dancer's. Cressida only came up to her collarbone.

"In what universe is that fair?" Cressida said, taking a step back. Her voice quivered, though Kadie couldn't tell if it was because she was angry or because Tania intimidated her.

"I'm sorry," Tania purred. "Is that a problem? Did *you* have someone else lined up?"

Now Cressida was at a loss for words, as they had not encountered a single adult on the premises of Camp So-and-So except for their counselor, Sharon, who would probably take a baseball bat to their kneecaps if they asked her to serve as a judge at the All-Camp Sport & Follies.

She was about to shake her head in frustration when she heard footsteps approaching and turned around to see Robin, the counselor-in-training, cutting across the meadow.

"What about her?" Cressida asked.

"What about me?" Robin asked, planting her hands on her hips as she joined their little party.

"They want you to judge the All-Camp Sport & Follies," Tania told her.

All the girls from Cabin 1 looked at Robin to see what she would say.

A Note from the Narrator: Except for Dora, who kept her eye on Tania and, in doing so, realized two things: a) Robin may have worked for Camp So-and-So, but she answered to Tania, and b) under no circumstance did Tania want Robin judging the All-Camp Sport & Follies. Dora thought this strange, but kept her observations to herself.

"Inge F. Yancey and Camp So-and-So are owned by the same person," Robin explained, never taking her eyes off of Tania. "This is the board of directors, and I assure you, they are entirely impartial."

"If they're so impartial, where's my town car?" Cressida complained.

The judge in the floral-print dress wrinkled her nose. "I suppose it's a good thing you're not being judged on your manners," she said.

A crackle of static erupted from the walkie-talkie hooked to the waistband of Robin's cargo shorts.

"Can I get an assist with a carcass in the woods near the pony trails? It's a big one."

The voice was monotone, as though this sort of thing happened every day at Camp So-and-So.

"You were supposed to clean that up hours ago," Robin barked into the walkie-talkie before reholstering it at her waist and turning back to the girls from Cabin 1 with a shrug. "You can work this out amongst yourselves, can't you?"

Kadie nodded. What choice did she have? As Robin headed west across the meadow toward the woods and whatever kind of carcass was rotting there, Kadie yanked Cressida back into the line of Cabin 1 campers and whispered at her to keep her mouth shut. Then, tucking her hair behind her ears and straightening her shoulders, she stepped forward and nodded to each of the judges and Tania. If Camp So-and-So was to host the All-Camp Sport & Follies, then they would manage it with at least some measure of dignity and class.

"Welcome, campers, judges, competitors, and guests, to the first day of the All-Camp Sport & Follies," Kadie said, turning to Tania. "As your hosts, we offer you first choice in our first event. Will you shoot first or second?"

Tania considered for a moment, and said, "Second."

The judge in the black, veiled hat cleared her throat.

"Then we are underway. First archer, come forward."

Vivian stepped up first, and Kadie could tell right away that she was still rattled from earlier. She kept looking back over her shoulder, as though Tania still had a bow trained on her head. Perhaps loaded this time. Vivian's first arrow barely hit the target at all, and the second was no better.

Before she took her third shot, Kadie raised her hand and called for a time-out.

"She can't do that," one of Tania's minions protested.

After conferring for a moment, the judge in the purple suitcoat stepped forward.

"Sixty-second time-out granted to Camp So-and-So. No further time-outs to be granted during this event."

Kadie leaned in and whispered in Vivian's ear, "Inhale when you draw back. Exhale when you let go. It works, I promise."

And it did. Over the next four shots, Vivian's arrows found their way back to the target, and she shared the advice with Kimber when she handed off the bow. However, Kimber was even more nervous than Vivian, so it did her little good. Her mind was muddled when she pulled back her bow, and her hand shook. Her first arrow went wild and clattered off the windshield of one of the Inge F. Yancey town cars. Her fingers slipped, her release points were off, and her next two arrows flew in a slow, wobbly trajectory like drunken bumblebees and fell short of the target. By the end, she'd improved somewhat, and the first Inge F. Yancey camper's shooting was only fair, but Tania would have to fail tremendously for them to have any chance at all of winning.

Tania stepped up to the target and removed her sunglasses, surveying them all with a look that said she wondered why she'd even bothered to show up. She drew her bow and fired six arrows in quick succession so they formed a perfect circle around the inner target ring, then shot a seventh exactly in the center. That accomplished, she dropped her bow on the dewy grass, slipped her sunglasses back on, and got into the backseat of one of the town cars. A driver, unseen behind the tinted windows, put the car in gear and drove up the winding dirt road toward the art barn, where the next event in the All-Camp Sport & Follies would take place.

The judges and the rest of the Inge F. Yancey campers followed suit, and one by one the town cars departed, leaving the girls from Cabin 1 standing in the meadow alone. The sun was barely up, and they were already behind.

"Who's supposed to clean all this stuff up?" Dora asked.

Kadie handed Dora a quiver and started pulling arrows out of the targets.

"Who do you think?"

Inge F. Yancey: 1
Camp So-and-So: 0

They left Dora to lug the archery supplies back to the equipment shed while they hiked back up the hill to meet the rest of the Inge F. Yancey campers at the art barn. The art barn had been constructed many years before by someone who had despised art and wanted to ensure that campers spent as few happy hours there as possible. It was made entirely of poured concrete and allowed no natural light save what could enter through a poorly fitted garage door on the front. While the Inge F. Yancey campers loitered in fashionable, bored poses around the perimeter, Kadie wrestled with the door until it slid up, releasing the old, wet, and rotten odors that had been pent up inside for an entire year.

Tania held her wrist up to her nose and said, "We can't possibly work in there."

Cressida glared at Tania with such rage that her left eyelid twitched. Kadie sympathized. It was infuriating enough to be beaten by the Inge F. Yancey campers without their contempt and sneering piled on top.

"If you think it's so awful, why don't *you* host the All-Camp Sport & Follies?" Cressida asked.

"Because I don't want you and your friends putting your grubby fingers on all my nice things," Tania said, peering over the tops of her sunglasses. "Besides, you'd probably steal anything that wasn't nailed down."

The candelabra of judges took their places atop a fallen log that was upwind from the art barn. The judge who wore the sleeveless, floral-print dress and could have been forty or a hundred and two cleared her throat and said in a warning tone, "Now, ladies . . ."

Cressida and Tania took a step back from one another and stood at attention with the other campers.

"Artists, step forward," said the judge in the veiled hat. "The next event in the All-Camp Sport & Follies is about to begin."

A pair of witchy-looking twin girls from Inge F. Yancey peeled themselves off the rock where they'd been sheltering from the sun. Both wore their long brown hair parted over their ears like a pair of lute-playing princesses at a Renaissance Faire.

From Camp So-and-So, Kadie and Cressida stepped forward. Kadie had taken metal shop at school and Cressida said she could draw a little bit, making them Cabin 1's most accomplished artists. Vivian and Kimber hung back, but Dora returned from putting archery targets away in the equipment shed in time to give them a small but enthusiastic round of applause.

The judge in the purple suitcoat produced a fistful of matchsticks, broken into different lengths.

"We'll draw straws to determine the artistic medium for this event."

"What's a medium?" Kimber asked, as Kadie and one of the witchy-looking girls drew and compared their straws. Kadie's was shorter by two inches.

The witchy-looking girl pressed her lips together smugly and said, "We choose textiles."

"Very well," said the judge in the purple suitcoat. "You have one hour to create a textile-based craft. The team that makes the best craft wins the event for their camp. Your time starts now."

Kadie and Cressida dashed inside the art barn and tripped and stumbled through the dark to the rack of supplies. They rummaged through shelves of crusty paint brushes and water-logged crepe paper and dried-out pots of rubber cement, looking for any supplies that could possibly be applied to fabric.

What had her cabin done last year? Kadie struggled to remember last year's camp craft event, but couldn't. It wasn't that the memory was fuzzy or dim. It wasn't there at all.

"What's wrong with you?" Cressida asked, giving her arm a tug, and Kadie realized that she'd frozen in the center of the art barn, staring at the shelves of art supplies.

"Tie-dyed t-shirts," Kadie said, forcing herself to snap back into the moment. She pointed at a stack of plain white t-shirts on one of the shelves that didn't look too water-stained.

"Let's do it," Cressida said, and together they filled a basket with shirts, stencils, Rit powder dye, and rubber bands. An hour wasn't much time, but they could certainly manage some tie dye, a classic camp craft if ever there was one. Cressida mixed the buckets of dye while Kadie started twisting rubber bands around the fabric to make swirls and stripes and rosettes. Nearly half their time had passed before either of them realized that the witchy girls from Inge F. Yancey had not followed them into the art barn.

"I guess they meant it when they said they couldn't possibly work in here," Cressida said.

"But they don't have any supplies or anything. It's weird. I'm going to see what they're up to," said Kadie, removing her dye-stained gloves and walking toward the light.

A moment later she was back, grimly picking the rubber bands out of her designs and shaking the wrinkles out of her shirts.

"What are they making out there?" Cressida asked.

"They're knitting," said Kadie.

"Is it better than ours?"

"I don't want to talk about it."

At the end of the hour, they had three good-enough t-shirts to show for their effort. One was a rainbow spiral, one was blue and red starbursts, and one was lilac and teal stripes with a row of skulls stenciled in white across the front. They brought the still-damp shirts outside and laid them out on the concrete steps in front of the art barn. It was only then that Cressida looked up and saw what the Inge F. Yancey campers had done for their camp craft.

They hadn't needed supplies from the art barn. They'd brought their own.

Each girl grabbed two corners, and together, they unfurled an ivory sleeping bag that looked so soft it might been knitted out of clouds.

"It's qiviut," said one of the witchy girls. "We thought about using cashmere . . ."

The other one finished her sentence. ". . . But that seemed *common.*"

"Besides, qiviut is much more functional. Eight times warmer than wool, you know. Eight times more expensive, too."

Tania touched her cheek in mock astonishment. "I *did not* know that. Fascinating."

Even though she'd gotten a sneak preview, Kadie was still gobsmacked by what she saw. How had they knitted an entire sleeping bag in an hour? She'd tried knitting once, and it took her an entire week just to make a potholder. Kadie forced herself to stop admiring the impossibly even and tiny stitches.

"And now, let's see what Cabin 1 has for us."

Chin held high, Cressida picked up the t-shirt with the skulls, still damp and wrinkled, and held it up to her chest.

"We decided to go with 100 percent cotton," she told the judges with a defiant gleam in her eye. "Polyester blends just seemed so . . . common."

Inge F. Yancey: 2
Camp So-and-So: 0

It was barely nine a.m. when they finished cleaning up the dye, but the art barn was already sweltering. Mosquitos swarmed around their heads as they trudged along the dirt road toward the north shore of Lake So-and-So, where the rowing event was about to begin. Kadie was in a foul temper, still upset about the t-shirts. They should have pushed themselves harder, been more creative. Of course they were never going to win with something stupid like a tie-dyed t-shirt.

Winning wasn't just about getting to stay at the Inge F. Yancey camp, where she was sure the art barn was well-ventilated and the cabin mattresses were free from vermin. How could you look at their smug faces and not want to beat them at something? Cressida could make wisecracks about polyester blends, but to Kadie there was nothing funny about it.

Fueled by clench-fisted rage, Kadie had pulled ahead of the judges and the rest of the girls in Cabin 1, who lagged fifty yards back, shuffling their feet in the dead leaves and dreading whatever the next event held. Kadie was sure that even though the Inge F. Yancey campers had driven up ahead of them in their town cars, they'd be fanning themselves in the shade while the girls from Cabin 1 hauled the canoes out of the equipment shed and lowered them into the water.

When she rounded the corner in the road, though, that wasn't what she saw. Kadie resisted the urge to call out and ask the Inge F. Yancey campers what they were doing and, instead, ducked behind a tree to watch. Their town cars were parked in a line next to the equipment shed. The Inge F. Yancey campers had already changed into their rowing gear. They had gotten two canoes out of the equipment shed and laid them out on the dock. They were all gathered around one of these canoes in a way that made Kadie suspicious. She looked around, but there was no sign of the judges' car. Perhaps the three timeless, shapeless, ageless oddballs had fallen back, opting to walk instead.

Kadie waited behind the tree until her cabinmates caught up, and their little group walked down the dirt road toward the equipment shed together. The moment the Inge F. Yancey campers spotted them, they fell away from the boat and scattered, striking poses of impatience and indolence. Tania waved to them from the boat dock.

"You look tired," she called out. "We can save this until tomorrow if you want to. You know, postpone your inevitable defeat."

The other girls looked ready to take her up on the offer, but Kadie shook her head as they approached.

"We're ready," she said. "We just want to switch boats."

Cressida tugged on Kadie's arm and muttered through clenched teeth, "Are you crazy? Take the extra day."

Kadie turned her back to the Inge F. Yancey campers and pulled the girls from Cabin 1 into a huddle.

In a whisper so quiet she was really only mouthing the words, Kadie said, "We've been sabotaged."

Kadie whispered a few more instructions to her cabin-mates, then Vivian and Kimber peeled away from the group and into the equipment shed. A few minutes later, they emerged toting a new boat over their heads.

Looking as though she had just been pickled, Tania sneered, "You can't do that. It's against the rules."

"No, it isn't," said Kadie.

"Judges!" Tania shrieked. "We need a ruling."

In no hurry, the trio of judges shuffled onto the dock, clutching one another's arms for stability.

"What seems to be the trouble?" asked the judge in the floral-print dress, smoothing her skirt and freshening her lipstick.

Tania glared at the judge. "They can't just *change boats*. Tell them they can't do that."

"Let's see," the judge said, pointedly tucking the tube of lipstick back inside her purse before turning to confer with the other judges.

After a moment's discussion, the judge in the veiled hat cleared her throat and said, "The young lady is quite within her rights. There is nothing in the All-Camp Sport & Follies rules that would prevent the campers from getting a new boat."

Kadie gave the Inge F. Yancey campers a triumphant smile.

"Besides, there's something wrong with this one," she said, pushing the sabotaged boat off the dock and into the water with a hard shove. The moment it splashed into the lake, pieces of the hull began to dissolve in the water like an Alka-Seltzer tablet.

Tania took Ron by the arm and made a simpering pouty face at him. "Well, a girl's gotta try, doesn't she?"

"Yeah," Kadie said, looking over her shoulder to the other end of the boat dock, where her cabinmates were wrestling their new boat and oars toward the water. "Yeah, she does."

The race wasn't even close.

Fueled by determination, vengeance, and righteous indignation, Cabin 1 won by more than five lengths.

Inge F. Yancey: 2
Camp So-and-So: 1

A NOTE FROM
THE NARRATOR

Before we continue, a word about the camp.

Of course, Camp So-and-So is not its proper name. There is something a little more formal inscribed on the letterhead.

It is not a secret; it is not hidden.

It is just that every time it is read or heard or spoken aloud, it goes up like a scrap of flash paper set alight, and all that remains is the memory of a place called Camp So-and-So.

Of course, it was not the intent of the first Inge F. Yancey that Camp So-and-So should have become a summer camp at all.

When he bought the land sight unseen, he had envisioned a lavish lakeside retreat where his friends and cronies could hobnob with Jazz Age luminaries. However, the stock market crashed before construction could begin, and, disappointed, Inge F. Yancey found himself preparing to sell off the land. He needed as much ready cash as possible to conceal from his family the extent of their financial ruin.

Inge F. Yancey acquired so much real estate that all his land deals tended to blur together, but there were things about this plot of land, which was nestled on a hard-to-reach hilltop on the outskirts of an obscure Appalachian town, that stood out to him as unique. He remembered that the land agent had been seedily eccentric with his purple pinstripe suit and hair that hung over his eyes. They'd drunk elderberry wine in Inge F. Yancey's office as they finalized the details of the contract, and Inge F. Yancey remembered how excited he'd been about the prospect of opening his resort. He could almost see F. Scott and Zelda Fitzgerald clinking glasses by the lakeside.

Now, in retrospect, he realized he'd been giddy, which was unlike him. He was never giddy over a simple business deal and certainly not over a couple of freeloading inebriates like the Fitzgeralds. Why had he bought that land in the first place? he wondered. It was not practical, it made no business sense, he loathed the company of artists and writers, and so he bought a train ticket to the obscure Appalachian town to make the arrangements for selling the land.

Ordinarily, his chauffeur would have driven him, but Inge F. Yancey had fired the man, ostensibly for tardiness, the previous week. He'd been only five minutes late and claimed it was because his baby was ill, but Inge F. Yancey had no money to pay a driver and was looking for any excuse. He told his wife he'd been unable to find a suitable replacement, and that he'd enjoy the train ride for old time's sake. He disliked lying about all these things, but found, paradoxically, that they were the kinds of lies that allowed him to face himself in the mirror.

Upon arriving in the Appalachian town, Inge F. Yancey hired a local man named Oscar to drive him up the hillside. When the truck would carry them no farther, they parked it in the middle of the dirt road and continued on foot. At first, Inge F. Yancey found the land to be utterly disappointing. The forests were infested with gnats and mosquitos. The the trees were gnarled, knotty, scrubby little things.

Not only was it wholly unsuitable for a glamorous luxury resort, but it wouldn't even be good for lumber.

Still, when he and Oscar crested a hilltop and emerged in a clearing that looked out over a pristine lake and a rolling green meadow, Inge F. Yancey had to admit that the view was lovely. But he had not come to this place to be charmed by views. He had expected to make a quick study of it, to determine how fast he could unload it and for how much, and to hope that it would be enough to finance his eldest son's schooling abroad, his middle son's summer at equestrian camp, his daughter's debut into society, and the trip to Paris his wife had already paid for with money the Yanceys did not have.

He had not expected to fall asleep there on top of the hill overlooking the lake, the meadow, the forest-covered hillsides.

And when he woke, he had not expected to meet Tania.

What she offered him seemed impossible, and yet Inge F. Yancey found himself inclined to believe she could deliver on her promise to reverse his fortunes. And what she asked in return was so modest.

It was lonely here, she'd said, and she and her people had lived here so long with only each other for company. Perhaps Inge F. Yancey could arrange for some small entertainment?

The more he thought about it, the more perfect it sounded. What if, instead of having to sell the land for extra cash, word got out that he was developing it to start a luxury summer camp? A camp that would be open to the children of his friends and colleagues, and since there was so much land, he'd build a camp for the deserving poor, too. It would cement his reputation as a philanthropist, a magnanimous and generous tycoon, who, even at the height of international financial crisis, could muster the resources to give and give and give.

Within a few months, and with the help of Tania and her people, of course, Inge F. Yancey had made several shrewd and prescient business deals, cash flowed into his coffers, and construction was underway on what would become the Inge F. Yancey Young Executives Leadership Camp and Camp So-and-So. Thanks to Tania, there was now plenty of money again for his houses, for his sons and daughters, for their sons and daughters, for trips to Paris and trousseaus and parties.

And in the thirty years that Inge F. Yancey would oversee Camp So-and-So, before turning over control of the family interests to his eldest son and expiring in his bed, it never once troubled him that he'd gotten so much for so little, or that he did not entirely understand what Tania was getting out of the arrangement.

KITCHEN REQUISITION

To: Victoria Aviles, Director, Yancey Corp. Foods

From: Theda Green, Head Cook, Camp So-and-So

Bread, white
Bread, wheat
Milk, lowfat 1%
Butter pats
Beef, ground
Ketchup
Mustard
Tomatoes
Lettuce, iceberg
Cereal
- Raisin bran
- Crisped rice
- Shredded wheat

Carrots
Graham crackers
Chocolate bars
Eggs

DENIED

TO: Inge F. Yancey IV, CEO, Yancey Corp.

FROM: Octavia Henry, Director, Camp So-and-So

Dear Mr. Yancey,

Things have gotten rather desperate at Camp So-and-So. Due to the outrageous negligence of your assistant, Mr. Langley, the camp is without an operating budget, the bank seems never to have heard of us, and I can't even afford to stock medical supplies, much less hire a counselor.

Now, Mr. Langley may think I can run this camp with no money, but I assure you, the girls will at least need to eat! I've attached the Kitchen Requisition form, submitted May 28 by Head Cook Theda Green, which was returned from your offices on June 5 stamped "Denied."

I have seen the list of names and the signed waivers, and as far as I know, twenty-five girls are set to arrive in less than a week. However, without your immediate intervention, Mr. Yancey, I cannot in good conscience open Camp So-and-So to campers.

It may be too late to remedy the situation; the whole thing may be too far gone. If nothing else, I at least wanted to let you know how Mr. Langley has acted on behalf of your family's interests—perhaps you should be looking for a new assistant!

Please let me know if help is coming, if I should even open the camp. If not, I have no choice but to resign as Director of Camp So-and-So.

Sincerely,
Octavia Henry

TO: Octavia Henry, Director, Camp So-and-So

FROM: Inge F. Yancey IV, CEO, Yancey Corp.

Ms. Henry,

Prepare the camp to the best of your ability, and open it to campers on the appointed date. When this has happened, and only after this has happened, I will accept your resignation.

IFY4

CABIN 2

KILLER IN THE WOODS

*[SCENE: WALLIS, CORINNE, SHEA, HENNIE, and
BECCA discover their counselor's body hanging from the rafters
of Cabin 2 and realize that ABIGAIL, a dangerously
insane former camper, is likely to blame.]*

That first night at camp, the girls from Cabin 1 slept soundly in their beds, but for Wallis, Corinne, Shea, Hennie, and Becca, the hours between dusk and dawn would hold no rest.

The crime scene inside their cabin had been carefully staged, from the bloody letters splashed on the ceiling to the flashlights taped to the corner posts, spotlighting poor Megan, dangling by her ankles with X's drawn over her eyes with black marker.

It had the desired effect.

At first, the girls from Cabin 2 stood paralyzed with fear, unable to do anything but sob and scream. Then a terrible thought crossed Wallis's mind.

"What if Abigail's still here?" she whispered. "What if she's watching us?"

With a yelp of fear, Corinne ripped a flashlight down from the corner of the cabin ceiling, Shea ripped down another, and they all ran for their lives.

A Note from the Narrator: They went to the other cabins for help, but the girls from Cabin 1 were still recovering from their run-in at the beach with Tania and her force field. Cabin 3 had set off on a quest to fulfill a prophecy. Cabin 4 was in the woods gazing at their soul mates for the first time, and where Cabin 5 had been, there was now only an impenetrable wall of brambles. The counselors were nowhere to be found, either by coincidence or design (though whose design, I wouldn't dare to venture at this point).

It was Corinne's idea to go back to the mess hall, where the camp director's office and private quarters were housed on the second floor. However, what they found there was no better. The phone lines were dead. At first, they suspected that this was Abigail's doing, but the real reason was actually a matter of housekeeping.

The camp director's office and quarters were empty and looked as though they'd been abandoned in a hurry. The computer hard drive was gone, but the monitor remained. A wall safe hung open, emptied out. On the desk, Wallis found a stack of unpaid phone and utility bills dating back six months. No wonder they'd been eating gray hot dogs for dinner. There was no power, no phone service, no computer, no gas.

"The director must have left right after the Welcome Campers dinner," said Hennie.

Corinne groaned. "Which means she probably took her car. But there has to be some other kind of vehicle around here, a bus or a truck or something."

"THERE'S AN EQUIPMENT SHED AT THE NORTH END OF THE LAKE. THERE MIGHT BE A TRUCK THERE," Shea said.

They all shushed her at once. Not even the prospect of being stalked by a murderous lunatic had encouraged Shea to lower her voice.

"I'M TRYING," Shea said. "I DON'T SEE WHY IT MATTERS, THOUGH. WE'RE PRETTY EASY TO SPOT WITH THESE FLASHLIGHTS ANYWAYS."

"Shea's right," Corinne said, swallowing hard. "We should turn off the flashlights."

Of all of them, Wallis observed that Becca's shift into survival mode was the most tenuous. Since fleeing the horrors of Cabin 2, she'd done little but whimper and sob and whisper under her breath, "I want to go home. I want to go home." When Corinne introduced the prospect of turning off their flashlights, she began to hyperventilate.

The only thing holding her together was Shea. She'd held Becca's hand and dragged her along with the rest of the group as they'd run from cabin to cabin, and then to the camp director's quarters above the mess hall, all the way bellowing reassurances that had no basis in reality but, nonetheless, helped a little bit. Now, she pulled Becca into a hug, saying, "IT'S OKAY. I PROMISE IT'S ALL GOING TO BE OKAY," until Becca's breathing slowed again, and her sobs subsided to a less distracting level.

Still, it was clear that the notion of trekking nearly a mile in the dark to an isolated shed, with or without flashlights, appealed to no one. For a moment, they stood there, staring at each other and trying to think of a better plan, until finally, Wallis mustered the courage to speak.

"What about Oscar?" she asked. "He'd know."

"The creep on the lawn mower?" Corinne asked. "Sorry, but that doesn't sound any better to me."

"YEAH, FOR ALL WE KNOW, HE'S ABIGAIL'S ACCOMPLICE OR SOMETHING. HE DIDN'T SEEM SCARED OF HER OR ANYTHING."

"Well, isn't that a good thing?" asked Wallis. "An adult who is actually here and not scared of Abigail?"

"But what if he's not here?" Hennie asked.

She had a point. It was likely that most camp staff—if there were any—did not actually live on the campgrounds. Still, Wallis thought, Oscar had been mowing long after the Welcome Campers dinner had ended, and he didn't exactly seem like the sort of person who went home to a loving family at the end of each day. Maybe he had some kind of arrangement with the camp director to maintain the grounds and keep an eye on the place during the off-season in exchange for room and board.

He'd stay in a cellar or a broom closet, Wallis thought. Some place small and out of the way. Some place like the small storage shed right behind the mess hall. Yes, that seemed about right.

"If he's here, I know where he'd be staying," Wallis said, feeling suddenly sure of herself. "It's not far either."

"FOR ALL WE KNOW, HE MADE UP THAT STORY ABOUT ABIGAIL," Shea said, then added with a gasp, "WHAT IF HE'S THE ONE WHO KILLED MEGAN?"

"He wouldn't have had time. We went straight back to the cabin after we talked to him," Wallis said.

"He could have done it beforehand," Hennie offered, and the other girls in Cabin 2 were startled by the sound of her voice. She'd been so quiet, even in the midst of discovering Megan's body, they'd almost forgotten she was there.

Wallis shook her head at Hennie's suggestion. "Megan put up all those decorations after dinner, so the cabin must have been fine then."

Corinne cradled her forehead in her hands and massaged her temples for a moment before looking up, a plan of action glinting in her eye.

"All in favor of going to the equipment shed to see if there's a truck, raise your hands," she said, raising her own hand. A second later, so did Shea.

She nodded, thoughtfully. "And those in favor of finding Oscar, raise your hand."

Wallis and Hennie raised their hands, then turned their eyes to Becca, who stood there quaking, her eyes closed and her arms crossed.

"What do you want to do, Becca?" Corinne asked.

"I want to go home," Becca said, clutching at her arms and twisting from side to side.

"You're the deciding vote, so you have to make up your mind and tell us," Corinne said, her voice gentle, but with a hint of impatience at the edges.

"I want to go home."

Wallis took Becca by the shoulders and gave her a shake.

"Becca, if you don't make up your mind, Hennie and I are going to go look for Oscar, and Corinne and Shea are going to go to the equipment shed, and we will leave you here by yourself."

Becca's eyes flew open, and she began to cry. Corinne hissed at Wallis to shut up, and Shea decided to take a gentler approach. "BECCA, WE NEED YOU TO BE BRAVE NOW. WHAT DO YOU WANT TO DO?"

"Becca," Wallis whispered, "the equipment shed is really far away. Oscar's shed is only a few yards from here."

It was not the nicest thing she had ever done, manipulating poor Becca like that, but Wallis had a feeling she was right about Oscar. Maybe Corinne thought he was creepy, but Wallis trusted him. What's more, she knew that if there was anyone at camp who could help them, it was him.

Becca considered her answer, and said at last, "Oscar's shed."

Corinne shot Wallis a dirty look and issued the group's next instructions: "Lead the way, Wallis. But if Oscar's not there, or if anything about his place seems even the slightest bit off, we run straight to the equipment shed. Agreed?"

They all nodded and went down the stairs from the camp director's quarters to the deserted mess hall. The sticky varnished tabletops gleamed eerily in the moonlight. Megan had made the girls from Cabin 2 clean up after themselves, but some of the tables were still strewn with crumbs, half-eaten hot dog buns, and greasy paper plates. Wallis led them through the kitchen, past the racks stacked high with canned pudding and green beans. Corinne picked up a paring knife that had been left on the butcher block. Following her lead, Shea took a meat tenderizing mallet and put it in her back pocket. Hennie took a ladle for herself and handed a whisk to Becca. Clutching her flashlight like a weapon, Wallis led them out the back door and into the yard behind the mess hall.

A few yards away stood a wooden shed that looked ramshackle, but homey. Yellow checked curtains hung in the windows, and a pair of work boots sat on a reed mat by the door. Wallis breathed a sigh of relief that she'd been right, and now hoped that Oscar would be able to help them. She crossed the yard and knocked quietly at the shed door. From inside, a familiar voice called, "Who's there?"

"It's us," Wallis whispered. "From Cabin 2. We need your help."

The door flew open, and Oscar filled up its frame, still wearing his coveralls. He ushered them inside, scanning the woods around the mess hall for movement before closing the door behind them.

"So she's struck again?" Oscar asked. He sounded like he'd been expecting it.

The girls nodded as they peered around Oscar's shed. It was nicer than they'd expected, and bigger, too. Around the utility sink and garden tools, he'd made room for a cot, an oval-shaped rag rug on the floor, a nightstand with a candle and a transistor radio on it, a small table set with a single plate, fork, and coffee cup, and a straight-backed wooden chair.

"We need to go for help," Corinne said. "Is there a car or something around here?"

"There's a truck up at the equipment shed, but it hasn't been driven in a while. Some rats got at the hoses and chewed them up pretty good."

"Can you fix it?" Wallis asked.

"Well, sure, I can fix it. It'd be easier to wait until morning when there's light, though."

"I don't think this can wait until morning," Corinne said.

"WE'LL HELP," Shea said. "WE'LL HOLD THE FLASHLIGHTS AND STAND GUARD."

Oscar gnawed thoughtfully on his lip, then said, "Well, let's get a move on."

They took the dirt road from the mess hall to the equipment shed, running past the art barn and the campfire pavilion. Oscar knew every inch, every pebble of Camp So-and-So, so they ran without flashlights to guide their way, following instead the soft footfalls and panting breaths before them.

When Wallis felt a hand close around her shoulder, she stifled a scream, then realized that it belonged to Corinne. Without slowing her pace, Corinne leaned forward and whispered, "It was a good idea going to get Oscar."

"Thanks," Wallis whispered back, surprised to find that even in the midst of all of this, Corinne's approval still meant rather a lot to her.

Corinne gave Wallis's shoulder a squeeze, and then she ran to the front of the pack with Shea and Oscar. Wallis allowed herself a moment to beam, then turned her focus back toward keeping up with the other girls, all of whom seemed to be in much better shape than she was. Hennie was gawky, but her strides were long, and even though Becca was being pulled along every step of the way by Shea, she wasn't winded. Wallis was small and inclined toward stoutness. She knew that if she stopped running, she was as good as dead, but even so, it was tempting to take a break.

If this works, you'll be riding in the truck back into town by sunrise, she reminded herself.

But then, just as Wallis had known that they needed Oscar's help and where to find him, she knew something else. Wallis knew that this wasn't going to work.

This happened to her sometimes, knowing what was going to happen next. Not because she was psychic, or at least she didn't think so. It felt different than that.

A Note from the Narrator: I believe I already made it clear that there are no psychic girls at Camp So-and-So this year.

Wallis always knew who the murderer was on crime shows, and when she went to the movies, she always figured out what the big twist was ages before everyone else. It happened in real life, too. The moment she unwrapped the talking cat toy her parents gave her for her seventh birthday, she'd known that she was never going to play with it again after that day, that wanting it had been the best thing about it.

It wasn't always as boring or depressing as it sounded. Sometimes it was reassuring. When Wallis had butted heads with her English teacher, Miss Kriss, last September, she'd known that they'd learn to appreciate each other by the end of the school year, and that's exactly how things had turned out.

Still, it was nice to be surprised every now and again. That was why she read the Isis Archimedes books. It had been a year since she finished reading the fifth one in the series, and still, she didn't have the slightest idea what the author, Eurydice Horne, was going to do next. This was mostly because Isis

Archimedes was murdered in the last scene, and try as she might, Wallis couldn't see a way out of it.

But this wasn't like that.

As they ran toward the equipment shed and the truck that Oscar could fix, the truck that would get them to safety, Wallis knew that he couldn't, that it wouldn't.

There was nothing she could do about it. If she warned the others, they'd think she was crazy, especially since it had been her idea in the first place. All she could do was brace herself for failure and be ready to act before Abigail could strike again.

When they reached the shed, Oscar took a ring of keys out of his pocket, felt out their shapes in the dark until he found the right one, and unlocked the padlocked door. Once they were safely inside, Corinne turned on her flashlight, and Shea followed suit.

The truck was there, just like Oscar had said it would be. None of them had ever been so happy to see a 1989 Toyota 4Runner in all their lives. It turned out that Corinne was halfway handy, so she and Oscar worked to replace the tattered hoses while Wallis and Hennie shone Corinne's flashlight under the hood. Meanwhile, Shea stood guard, shining her flashlight into the corners of the shed and along the walls, keeping an eye on the still-shaky Becca, and looking for any signs of Abigail. The shed was cluttered and packed full of canoes and life jackets, harnesses, spools of net, and half-rotted lifeguard chairs. Plenty of things for a person to hide behind.

Suddenly, Shea caught something in the beam of her flashlight and let out a shriek that made Corinne drop her wrench on the ground. When they turned around to see what had happened, Shea's face was deathly pale, and she was pointing her flashlight toward an archery target stained with blood.

"Don't think about being afraid," said Corinne, who seemed almost incapable of becoming rattled. "Think of it like a row of hurdles we have to jump over. We fix the truck. We drive into town. We get the police. We call our parents. Then everything goes back to normal. We can all be sitting in the police station drinking hot chocolate in less than an hour."

Corinne's speech seemed to have a calming effect on everyone, even Wallis.

Why not hope? Wallis thought. She hoped that the plan would work. She hoped the feeling in her gut was wrong.

"Okay, I think that just about does it," said Oscar, helping Corinne to her feet and slamming the hood shut. "Let's see if she'll start."

Corinne stood with the other girls as Oscar climbed behind the wheel and put the key in the ignition. The truck sputtered and choked, but then Oscar nudged the gas pedal, and the engine turned over. He let out a whoop and stuck his arm out the window, motioning to the girls from Cabin 2.

"Climb in!" he said, and put his foot on the clutch, shifting the truck into first gear.

The explosion killed him instantly.

It ripped through the dashboard and shattered the windshield, and then the cab burst into flames. Thick white smoke poured from under the hood as the girls screamed.

To Wallis, the whole thing seemed to happen in slow motion. *What happened? What went wrong?* she wondered. She hadn't seen anything under the hood while Corinne and Oscar were working. Clearly, they hadn't seen it either. Whatever the device was, it must have been well-hidden, not that this mattered now.

Small fires began to ignite around the shed as flaming debris rained down. The fires spread and joined up with each other, and Wallis realized that if they didn't hurry, they'd be surrounded.

It was Corinne who found the stack of buckets by the door and began thrusting them into the arms of her cabinmates.

"Go to the lake. Get water," Corinne instructed.

A small boat dock separated the equipment shed from Lake So-and-So. Wallis and Hennie took the buckets from her and ran toward the lake.

Shea had been knocked to the ground by the explosion. Blood streamed down her face and arms. Her eyes were half-open and unfocused, and she couldn't stand on her own. While Wallis and Hennie ran to the end of the dock to fill their buckets, Corinne got behind Shea, hoisted her up under her arms, and dragged her outside. Once she'd moved her out of harm's way, Corinne went back for Becca, who was still cowering near the flames, her eyes blank with shock.

By this time Wallis and Hennie had returned with the buckets of water. Corinne pointed them toward the small fires threatening the shed, while she went back to the truck. Even if Oscar hadn't been beyond help, there was no way she could have reached him. The entire cab was engulfed in flames and smoke.

Once the girls had gotten the smaller fires under control, Corinne motioned them toward the truck. They formed a line, and the three of them passed bucket after bucket to the front, where Corinne stood and tossed the water onto the flames.

Finally, after five dozen buckets, the blaze was out. Their faces were smeared with ash and sweat, their throats raw from smoke inhalation, their arms aching. But they were better off than Oscar.

"Check on Shea and Becca," Corinne barked at the other girls, her voice ragged.

They found the two girls propped up against the boat dock railing. Blood oozed down Shea's face from a deep cut on her forehead, and yet, she was still more lucid than Becca, who clung to her arm, quaking.

Hennie dropped to her knees, ripped a strip of fabric from the bottom of her t-shirt and pressed it to Shea's head while Corinne headed back to the shed.

"Help me," she said, motioning Wallis to follow her, and in a horrifying, sickening second, Wallis realized what it was that Corinne needed her help to do.

The two of them climbed inside the sodden cab of the truck and pulled Oscar's body out. A piece of metal had speared him through the eye in the explosion. He probably didn't even have time to wonder what hit him. Corinne took his hands and Wallis took his feet, and in that way, they carried him out of the equipment shed and laid him down on the dock.

"Should we bury him?" Wallis asked.

Corinne shook her head. "No. We're still going into town to get the police. They'll want to see the . . . body."

Corinne choked over the last word and buried her face in her hands.

"We should cover him, though," Wallis said. "He said there were rats."

"We should have covered Megan, too," Corinne said, her voice heavy with guilt. "We should have at least cut her down."

Wallis didn't know what to say. She pulled a tarp off of a pile of firewood stacked outside the shed and handed Corinne a corner of it, and the two of them pulled the tarp over Oscar's body and weighted it down with stones from the shore of the lake.

All of this was her fault. She was the one who'd made them bring Oscar into this, and now he was dead. Worse, she'd known something bad was about to happen, and she hadn't kept him from starting the truck. Of course, it wouldn't have made sense to any of them if she'd tried to explain: *No, we shouldn't take the truck. We should try to escape from camp by walking twenty miles or so in the dead of night to the nearest town. Why? Because I just have a feeling.* She would have sounded crazy, they wouldn't have listened to her, and the same thing would have happened, but Wallis still wished she'd tried to stop them when she had the chance.

"How did she do it?" Corinne wondered aloud as they worked.

"Abigail?"

"I looked under the hood. Oscar and I both looked, and there wasn't anything there."

"You couldn't have known," Wallis said, patting Corinne on the shoulder. It wasn't a gesture she was used to making; however, if she was doing it wrong, Corinne didn't seem to notice.

"What should we do next?" Corinne asked.

The truck was done for, that much was clear. They discussed waiting until morning or trying to go on foot immediately, but neither idea sat well with them. Had Kadie Aguilar been in their cabin, she would have told them about the existence of the Inge F. Yancey Young Executives Leadership Camp, and they might have chosen to row across the lake for help. However, all five were new to Camp So-and-So, and on that moonless night, they saw only acres of dark, wooded nothingness on the far side of the lake.

They rejoined the other girls. After bandaging Shea's head wound, Hennie had inspected her for any other injuries and, finding none, helped her to her feet. Shea was still dizzy, dazed, and probably mildly concussed, but they all knew how much worse it could have been.

"Can you walk?" Corinne asked.

"I THINK SO," Shea said, and then suddenly Wallis came up with a plan so Shea wouldn't have to.

"We can take the horses," she said. "The stables are just through the woods behind our cabin."

"What about her?" Corinne nodded grimly at Becca, who was still crouched on the ground, arms wound tight around her knees, rocking, rocking, rocking.

"Get up," Wallis said, stretching out a hand to her, but Becca ignored it.

"SWEETIE?" Shea asked, touching Becca's shoulder. Becca flinched, but the sound of Shea's voice made her lift her eyes and transform back into a person who could be reasoned with.

"WE NEED TO MOVE," Shea said. "DO YOU UNDERSTAND?"

"Don't leave me here," Becca whispered.

"NOBODY'S LEAVING ANYBODY, BUT YOU HAVE TO GET UP," Shea said. Wallis wondered how she was standing at all, much less counseling the shell-shocked Becca.

"OKAY?"

Shea met Becca's eyes and refused to let her look away until Becca nodded and whispered a small "Okay."

"OKAY," Shea said, helping Becca to her feet. It was too much exertion for her, though. She swayed briefly, and the other girls in Cabin 2 lunged forward to catch her. But she waved them away and caught the boat dock railing to steady herself.

"LET'S GET THOSE HORSES AND GET OUT OF THIS PLACE."

It was a plan they could all agree on.

INTERMISSION

From the spot in the treetops where the two stagehands sat, they could see the girls from Cabin 2 fleeing toward the stables. In the other direction, shadowy figures raked the smoldering remains of the equipment shed. Soon enough the two stagehands would be down there with the rest, tidying up, clearing the set, making it look like the whole thing had never happened.

But it would be at least a few more minutes before they were missed. Might as well sit in the treetops and enjoy the night while they could.

One stagehand turned to the other and asked, "That wasn't supposed to happen, was it?"

"It wasn't in the script," the other replied, adding, "Poor Oscar."

"Yeah, poor Oscar," the first stagehand agreed. "He had a good run, though."

"Did he?"

They sat without speaking—a moment of silence for the fallen groundskeeper.

At last, the first stagehand spoke again. "If they're not following the script, that means . . ."

"Better hold on to our hats."

The first stagehand frowned and shook his head.

"Better hope we end up on the right side of things."

CABIN 3

THE HERO'S QUEST

[SCENE: On a path in a wood that holds a cave that holds a beast]

As dusk fell on that first night, they set out from the stables on foot into a forest so thick that it seemed to swallow them up. They traveled in single file, speaking only when absolutely necessary—which, when they came to a fork in the path, it was.

First you must slay the beast inside its lair
And then set free the one imprisoned there.

The girl with beads in her hair shrugged the backpack from her shoulders and unzipped the side pocket. Inside was a copy of the prophecy they'd found written in the rafters of their cabin and a map of Camp So-and-So she'd sketched from the disk of lumber outside the mess hall. At the time, it had seemed like good planning, but now she worried that a map carved into a piece of wood might not divulge every twist and fork in the vast forests of Camp So-and-So. She didn't even know what she was looking for. It wasn't like there was a spot on the map labeled BEAST'S LAIR.

This was not her only worry, though.

As long as they kept moving, it was easy not to think too much about what they were doing out in the woods. Or at least it was easy not to feel silly about it.

We're just having fun, thought the girl with beads in her hair. *There's no way this is really happening.*

But deep in a secret corner of her heart burned a hope that it was real.

The girl with beads in her hair had spent years staring down the barrel of *real*, an endless barrage of SAT practice tests; community service hours; tedious, venal boys; and girls who turned into simpering invertebrates in their presence.

Real had nothing to do with anything she'd spent the past decade and a half of her life caring about. Nobody was going to pay her to daydream, and it wasn't like she could write a college admissions essay about the difference between a merrow and a selkie, or why Perseus was cooler than Hercules.

The girl with beads in her hair knew you could want and hope and wish all you wanted, and it wouldn't make a difference, but when she saw the prophecy written on the ceiling of Cabin 3, something in her heart had opened up and whispered, *Please.*

"There's supposed to be a cave down the trail to the left," she said, and the rest of the girls from Cabin 3 fell in behind her. "Maybe that's the beast's lair."

It was nearly dark when they found the cave, set twenty yards back from the trail at the edge of a clearing. The earth around it was dusty and pounded hard, and a ridge of craggy boulders rose up on either side.

"What do we do next?" asked the girl with the upturned nose. "Should we just go in?"

"It looks dangerous," said the sticklike goth girl.

"It probably is," said the girl in the orange hoodie.

"Maybe we should come back in the morning," said the girl with thousands of freckles.

"We're already here," said the girl with beads in her hair, turning on a flashlight.

The five of them huddled up, whispering over their plan and how they would approach the cave and who would keep a lookout. The girl with beads in her hair stuck her hand into the center of the circle and one by one, four more hands settled on top of it.

"On the count of three," she said.

"Let's do it," said the girl with thousands of freckles.

They counted, they mustered their courage, and they broke out of the huddle to find a tiny young woman in cargo shorts and athletic sandals sitting on a boulder by the cave with her knees gathered up to her chest, squinting at them in the dusk.

"What are you doing out here by yourselves?" she asked. "Where's your counselor?"

The girl in the orange hoodie rested a hand on the hatchet she kept hooked to her belt loop and stared back at her.

"Do we know you?"

"My name's Robin," she said, sounding annoyed. "I work here. Counselor-in-training, remember? I checked you into your cabin three hours ago, not that any of you noticed me then."

The young woman gave them a pointed look as she slid down from the rock and dusted off her backside. The girl in the orange hoodie let go of the hatchet, and her hand fell to her side.

"Where did you get those hatchets? You're not supposed to have weapons here." Robin's brow furrowed.

A Note from the Narrator: It was curious. She'd checked all their bags for contraband a few hours before and hadn't noticed any of these hatchets and Swiss army knives then. Of all the cabins, this bunch of straight arrows seemed the least likely to break the rules.

"It's not a weapon," said the girl in the orange hoodie. "I mean, not unless there's an emergency it's not."

"It's camp," added the girl with thousands of freckles. "Who comes to camp without a hatchet or a Swiss army knife?"

The other girls nodded in agreement, and Robin sighed.

"Where's your counselor?" Robin asked again. "Aren't you supposed to be playing Capture the Flag or making friendship bracelets or something?"

The sticklike goth girl unhunched her shoulders and rose to her full and considerable height.

"We're on a quest," she said.

Robin came over to them and walked up and down the line they'd fallen into, and after inspecting them all, she stifled a burst of laughter behind her hand before regarding them with an apologetic smile.

"Don't take this the wrong way, but aren't you girls a little old for that?"

The girl with beads in her hair felt her cheeks burn as she realized how they must have looked to the counselor-in-training. Of course the poem they'd found written on their cabin ceiling wasn't a call to adventure. Of course there was no beast, no lair, no quest, no magic. It was probably a joke. There were probably a bunch of people hiding in the bushes pointing and laughing their heads off, and filming the whole thing so they could put it on YouTube.

They were freaks who believed in monsters and talking animals. They were idiots who found a goofy poem and actually thought it was real. They were losers who should have grown out of things like this by now.

None of them looked up. They stood there, hands dangling uselessly by their sides, ears burning with shame.

That was when the beast sprang from the mouth of the cave and pounced on top of the sticklike goth girl.

It had the body of a spider and the head of a snake, and it hissed as it picked up the sticklike goth girl with its hairy front legs and began to wind her up in a sickly green web.

The girl in the orange hoodie unhooked her hatchet from her belt and raised it, letting out a battle cry that rang through the night air and sounded braver than she felt. Heartened by her boldness, the rest of Cabin 3 exchanged glances and nods, and charged the beast.

None of the girls saw which way Robin went when she fled. One minute she was there, taunting them for believing in the quest, and the next she was gone, but there was no time to pursue the counselor-in-training. They had to save their friend.

They jumped on top of the beast and began hacking at its legs with their hatchets and Swiss army knives. The beast yowled and dropped the sticklike goth girl, who rolled toward the cave, still bound up in webs. It reared up and shook the girls from its back, flinging them to the ground. Before the girl with the upturned nose could regain her footing, the beast shot her with a mass of sticky web that pinned her to a sheer rock wall next to the cave entrance.

Though two of their number were now immobilized, the three remaining girls continued to fight the beast. The girl with thousands of freckles struck a devastating blow to the underside of the beast's reptilian neck, which unleashed a geyser of black, oily blood, while the others managed to remove two of its legs. The beast swung its remaining limbs wildly about, reeling from pain and rage. One hit the girl in the orange hoodie in the gut and sent her flying into the mouth of the cave, where she landed with a sickening thud. The girl with thousands of freckles raised her knife high and brought it down in a killing blow, but before she struck, the beast curved its snake head around and sank its teeth into her calf. The girl with thousands of freckles screamed and fell back, clutching at her leg and writhing in pain.

Only the girl with beads in her hair was left to finish the fight. She wielded her hatchet and gritted her teeth, inching away from the cave while the beast hissed and struck at the ground before her. Wounded though it was, it was still more than a match for her.

The girl with beads in her hair despaired. Behind the beast, her friends lay wounded or trapped. She wanted to hold her ground, but found herself retreating step by step across the pony trail as the beast snapped at her. She took another step back and bumped into a fallen log at the side of the trail. She lost her balance and fell backwards over the log, landing on her shoulder with a grunt before rolling onto her back.

As she went down, the beast rose up on its hind legs and drew back its head to strike. The girl with beads in her hair braced herself, but held her eyes open and lifted her blade in the hopes of landing one more blow before the beast sank its fangs into her and ended it all.

But just when it should have happened, it didn't.

A pack of wild girls, their faces streaked with ash and blood and tears, tore down the trail on horseback. One had pigtails and wore overall shorts. One had a blood-soaked strip of cloth wrapped around her head, curly red hair sticking out from under it. One of them whimpered over and over again, "I want to go home. I want to go home." There were five of them in all, and they rode in such a fervor that not even the sight of the beast looming before them on the path slowed their pace. In fact, they seemed not to see it at all. They charged straight down the middle of the path, trampling the beast. Its back snapped beneath the hooves of their steeds; its legs gave out and splayed across the path.

They never even slowed their pace as they laid waste to the beast, and before the girl with beads in her hair could begin to make sense of what she'd seen, the girls from Cabin 2 were gone.

The beast lay on the trail, twitching and hissing. The girl with beads in her hair struggled to her feet, raised her hatchet, and lopped off its head.

Then she collapsed onto the dry, packed earth feeling like she might like to curl up on the trail next to the carcass and rest, just for a few minutes. Just to catch her breath. Just to wipe the tears from her eyes. The girl with beads in her hair had never killed anything before.

It was a cry from the girl with thousands of freckles that lifted her off the ground and sent her running back toward the cave. Gray-faced and shivering, the girl with thousands of freckles had rolled up the leg of her jeans to reveal an angry red wound where the beast's fangs had punctured her skin. The girl with beads in her hair knelt down next to her, trying to hide the worry in her eyes. There was nothing in their first aid kits for a bite like that, nothing they could do for the girl with thousands of freckles, except hope that the venom would not travel too quickly through her veins.

But the girl with thousands of freckles didn't care about that, not then. She tried to shout out, but her words were too slurred from the venom. Finally, and with great effort, she raised her arm and pointed toward the mouth of the cave.

When the girl with beads in her hair turned around, she saw the girl in the orange hoodie emerging from the cave, dragging behind her a large wooden cask that had been water-logged and sun-baked so many times it had turned almost to driftwood.

"Come give me a hand," she called out, unaware that few of her cabinmates were in any shape to do so. "I think I found what we're supposed to be looking for! *And then set free the one imprisoned there!*"

She pointed her headlamp toward the cask and began to inspect the latch that bolted its lid shut.

A Note from the Narrator: The cask was not sitting out in the open. It would not have been easy to find. When the beast had hurled the girl in the orange hoodie into the cave, she'd landed in the first chamber, then tumbled down an almost hidden gravel slope, coming to rest at the bottom of a small crevice. A person exploring the cave on foot, searching from chamber to chamber, would have missed it entirely. Fortunately, the crevice was not deep and its walls not terribly steep, and the girl in the orange hoodie fumbled in the darkness until she found a good foothold. But first she had found the cask. Immediately, she'd known that it didn't belong there, and when she'd heaved it loose from the debris, she found it was light enough to drag up the slope by herself. Opening it, however, was proving to be more difficult.

Wounded bodies surrounded the cave. The sticklike goth girl lay near the mouth of the cave, still wrapped like a spindle in sticky green webs. Ten feet up, the girl with the upturned nose was pinned to a boulder, sawing at the beast's webs with her Swiss army knife. The girl with thousands of freckles convulsed in the dirt while the girl with beads in her hair fished through the first aid kit for anything that might provide the slightest bit of relief.

And yet, all the girl in the orange hoodie could see was the cask and the problem of opening it. It had fixated her, and that should have been her first indication that whatever was inside was not going to be the end of their quest, but a complication to it.

The girl in the orange hoodie lifted her hatchet, preparing to break open the cask.

Only the girl with thousands of freckles understood what was about to happen. Through shivering lips, she whispered, "No," but it was too quiet and too late to make a difference.

The girl in the orange hoodie swung her hatchet like a baseball bat, striking the latch and knocking loose a hundred years of rust.

The hinges groaned. Then the lid fell open. Then a cyclone of feathers and dust rose up from the cask and enveloped the girl in the orange hoodie.

At that moment, the girl with the upturned nose cut herself free from the webs that strapped her to the sheer rock face of the cave, and she dropped to the ground. As she fell, she cracked her leg on a jagged rock and landed with a bloodcurdling howl.

With all of her friends now in distress, the girl with beads in her hair froze, unsure where to intervene first, or whether she'd only make everything worse.

"Close the lid," whispered the girl with thousands of freckles.

Of course.

The girl with beads in her hair leaped to her feet and circled around to the other side of the cave. The cyclone whistled around her, its winds shaking the trees and whipping beaded strands of hair against her cheeks like BB pellets. She could see nothing of the girl in the orange hoodie now, nor any of the other girls. She couldn't get close enough to reach out and close the lid. Even if the winds hadn't been holding her back, there was no way to do it without stepping into the center of that black, swirling vortex made up of who-knows-what.

The girl with beads in her hair bent down and picked up a large stone, then threw it as hard as she could at the lid of the cask. It was a tough shot in the dark, but she heard a thump followed by a creak as the lid fell shut. At once, the cloud of feathers and dust stopped spinning and drifted gently to the ground, and standing there in the center of it was the girl in the orange hoodie.

It was only the wind that had been holding her upright. As soon as it died and the feathers fell away, she toppled to the ground.

Renata, thought the girl with beads in her hair, for that was her friend's name.

The girl with beads in her hair ran to her and knelt by her side. She stroked her hair and shouted her name over and over again. She slapped Renata's cheeks and begged her to answer, but though the girl's eyes were open, all the life had gone out of them.

This can't be happening, thought the girl with beads in her hair as tears filled her eyes. She should have known. If she was willing to believe in beasts and lairs and things held prisoner in caves, she should have known that this was just as possible.

The girl with beads in her hair cursed herself for ever wishing that the quest was real, then buried her face in her hands and sobbed. She did not notice the unusually clumsy raven that hopped from the lid of the cask onto the ground, until it stumbled over to her and pecked her on the knee.

"Stop crying," the raven said in a voice the girl with beads in her hair recognized at once. "It's me. I'm okay."

"Renata?"

Wiping the tears from her eyes, the girl with beads in her hair scooped the raven up and folded it into her arms.

INTERMISSION

In a remote, undesirable corner of Camp So-and-So, there was a clapboard tool shed that was unremarkable in every way except for the sheet of parchment tacked to the door that read:

THE STAGE MANAGER'S CREED
Dealing with Actors, Crew, Producers, Directors, and Other Difficult Sorts

1. Be where you are supposed to be. Do not make me have to send someone to look for you.

2. Do not mistake your place in the cast for your place in the production. All of you can be replaced. I cannot be replaced because no one else wants to be the stage manager.

3. Things that do not belong backstage: your sass, backtalk, significant other, or diva attitude.

4. You will attempt to usurp, disrespect, and undermine my authority. You do so at your peril. You will try to make me cry. Stage managers never cry.

5. The stage manager cares not for glory and status. The stage manager strives for higher things. Without the stage manager, nothing works. Without the stage manager, there is only chaos.

A pair of stagehands stood before the door, reading the sign absentmindedly as they waited to be let in, even though they had read it many times before and it had long ago stopped being intimidating, funny, or even pathetic to them. It was just Robin. That was how she was, that was what she kept tacked to her door. Maybe it made her feel better. In any case, all the stagehands knew it was better to stay on Robin's good side, to do what she said without asking too many questions, to tell her about little problems before they became big problems.

"What is it?" Robin asked as she opened the door, searching the faces of the stagehands for hints that anything was amiss.

"We're checking in," said one of the stagehands.

"Like you asked us to," said the other, sounding a bit snottier than Robin liked, but she decided to let it slide. There was too much to do. She didn't have time to make them *like* her, too.

She motioned for them to step inside the tool shed, though they would have preferred not to. It was a dim, claustrophobic place, and every available inch of wall was papered with maps, drawings, diagrams, and lists like the basement lair of a psychopath obsessed with set design instead of serial murder. A heavy oak desk took up most of the room, leaving little space for Robin, much less for the two stagehands, but they crowded in around it. As Robin settled in with her clipboard and pen, the stagehands studied the shelf that hung over the desk. It was littered with a sad menagerie of clay and papier-mâché figurines made and abandoned by several decades' worth of former campers. There was a mermaid, a gryphon, a leprechaun, and what looked to be a werewolf, as well as an assortment of monsters and swamp creatures. Two of the models sat in the middle of Robin's desk, and if the stagehands hadn't known better, it would have looked as though they'd interrupted her in the middle of playing with them. One was shaped to resemble some kind of half-serpent, half-arachnid creature, and the other was a black horse with glowing red eyes.

The first stagehand pulled a notepad out of its pocket and read from its notes.

"Cabin 1 is on board for the All-Camp Sport & Follies. As you know, Cabin 2 went to the equipment shed for the truck . . ."

"Which failed to start," added the second stagehand.

A Note from the Narrator: This was, of course, an incredibly loose interpretation of the truth, but being truthful with Robin did not seem to be a very high priority for the stagehands that summer.

"Now they've got the horses," said the first stagehand in an effort to distract Robin from any further inquiry about the truck and the equipment shed.

"Excellent," said Robin, picking up the spider-snake model from her desk. "And Cabin 3? How are they doing with the beast?"

"They dispatched it. With a little help from Cabin 2, as it happens."

Robin frowned at the model, then crumpled it in her fist, just as the second stagehand added, "They opened one of the casks in the cave, and whatever was inside it turned one of the girls into a raven."

Robin pursed her lips. Her eyes shifted to the left, considering the angles. Over the years a number of things had been locked up in the cave—so many that Robin had almost lost track of them. As to which the girls in Cabin 3 freed in their effort to fulfill the "prophecy," almost any would have made for an interesting story. Some would have been grateful to be freed, while others had been sealed up in casks and crates and bottles for such a long time, they were liable to have worked up some dangerous, vengeful grudges.

And then there was the thing in the deepest recesses of the cave. When Robin had written the prophecy, she hadn't worried about the girls finding it. The cave was too dark, too frightening, and no one had ever ventured in that far before. Of course, Robin considered, if they'd stumbled into *that* particular chamber of the cave, there was no denying things would've become interesting.

"Anything else?"

The stagehands exchanged glances before casting their eyes toward the ground. Neither of them wanted to share the next bit of news with Robin.

"Don't tell me Tania's already got her claws in one of them," Robin said, practically baring her teeth as she spoke.

"Cabin 4," said the first stagehand, daring to lift its eyes. "It was the one called Addison."

"The girl picked up a button," the other stagehand explained. "Right after it fell off the boy's shirt."

Robin made a fist and pounded it on her desk. "That is exactly what I warned you about, exactly the thing I told you to keep from happening."

"It wasn't like one of us could dash out and snatch it off the ground," the second stagehand said with an insouciant shrug.

Robin rolled her eyes.

"An epic failure of imagination," she said. "A puff of wind could have blown in a leaf to cover it up. You could have changed the color so it blended in with the dirt. And we have squirrels at this camp, don't we? Last time I checked, there were squirrels, and it wouldn't have been the hardest thing in the world to nudge one of them out into the clearing to pick up a stupid button and run off with it."

The longer she spoke, the louder and angrier her voice grew. The stagehands inched backwards toward the door.

"And that's just thinking off the top of my head," she said. "Now go to the equipment shed and get that battery out of the truck. I'm going to find Pam and see if it's not too late to get this mess straightened out."

CABIN 4
SOUL MATES

[SCENE: ADDISON, ANNIKA, ALIX, AMBER, and VERITY prepare to sneak out and return to the woods in search of their soul mates.]

The girls from Cabins 2 and 3 would spend their first night at Camp So-and-So on the run and fighting for their lives. Cabin 4, however, would spend it plotting one of the most venerable and ageless camp traditions: sneaking out after dark.

From her bunk, Verity saw four pairs of eyes glittering in the dark, peering out from sleeping bags that concealed the fact that the girls from Cabin 4 were sleeping in their clothes and shoes, ready to spring out of bed the very instant they knew that Pam was asleep. Wind rippled through the tarps that hung from the cabin eaves in place of walls. They didn't keep out bugs or forest creatures. They didn't even keep out the moonlight.

As darkness fell, Pam had ushered them to the latrine with

flashlights since the power seemed to be out. It happened all the time, Pam said. Something to do with old circuitry at the camp. Oscar, the groundskeeper, would have it taken care of by morning.

A Note from the Narrator: Except, of course, he wouldn't.

Verity hoped that the moonlight would be bright enough to guide them through the woods, that the magnetic current they'd followed that afternoon would lead them back to the cabin again.

If only Pam would fall asleep. She was older than the other counselors Verity had seen at Camp So-and-So and had grown suspicious with age. She slept like a cat, and even though her eyes were closed, her breathing never turned slow and heavy. It was only when Amber started to snore lightly that it seemed to dawn on the others that they would have to act soon if there was to be any hope of making their journey that night.

Addison crawled out of bed first and stumbled up the path to the latrine, shaking Amber's shoulder on her way out the door. After a discreet minute or two, Amber followed her. Then Alix. Then Annika.

And finally Verity. When she joined them, the four girls were all huddled together, shivering in their thin t-shirts and miniskirts. Verity felt underdressed—though warm—in her sweatshirt and jeans. If the others looked chilly, Addison looked positively miserable. Her teeth chattered as she clutched at her gooseflesh-covered arms, but she seemed to be sweating, too, Verity noticed. The honey-blonde curls near her forehead were damp with it.

"Are you okay?" Verity whispered.

Addison didn't answer.

Verity knew they shouldn't be doing this. Something about it wasn't right. Not one thing about it was right, and they all had to have known it, yet Verity couldn't quite bring herself to mention it.

And then Addison reached into her pocket and pulled out a button. It looked ordinary—round and white with four holes—but as she held it in the palm of her hand, a change came over her.

Verity saw the whole thing happen.

Addison had looked ready to collapse, but then instantaneously, the sweat evaporated from her skin, and the curl returned to her hair, and the pits faded from beneath her eyes, and she smiled.

What did I just see? Verity wondered, before deciding that she must have been mistaken, that what happened to Addison was just a trick of the starlight.

That was when she heard Amber ask, "What are we going to do when we get there?"

"We talk to them," Annika said, looking at her friend as though this was the most obvious thing in the world.

Verity's face drained of color. She didn't know if she was ready to talk to the girl with the radiant smile, or if she was ready to have the others *see* her talk to the girl with the radiant smile. For a moment, she thought about going back to bed, and then it dawned on her.

She was about to go on a secret mission by moonlight, led by a supernatural force toward a mysterious destination, and if she balked at a chance like that, she might as well toss her Isis

Archimedes books into the trash. She might as well go back to her bunk and stay there for the rest of the week.

"Then let's go," Verity said with resolve she didn't know she had.

They crept down the path from the latrine, whispering and giggling a little more than Verity would have liked. None of the other cabins stirred, but Verity still cringed at the amount of noise they made. They cut behind their cabin and onto the path they'd found earlier that day. Except this time, they didn't find the magnetic current waiting to lead them to their soul mates.

What they found was a very angry Pam.

"What on earth are you doing out at this hour?" she asked. She stood in the center of the path, blocking it, her arms folded across her chest. "And what in God's name are you wearing? Get back to the cabin right now. Tomorrow morning, you're all on kitchen duty."

The morning after their thwarted plot, Pam was chilly with them. She said nothing about the previous night, though judging by the dark circles under her eyes and the way she stifled one yawn after another, they knew she hadn't gone back to sleep. After they'd showered and dressed and made up their bunks, they walked to the eerily dark and deserted mess hall and through the swinging metal doors to the kitchen. There should have been a kitchen crew scraping trays and scrubbing pots, but the kitchen was as quiet as the rest of the mess hall. The stainless-steel countertops, the dishes and pans in the drying rack, the sink, the floors were all bone dry. No faucets dripped. No film of steam and dish soap hung in the air. Not so much as a piece of toast was laid out. If this was any cause for alarm, though, Pam gave no sign of it.

Annika peered over Verity's shoulder and groaned. "What are we supposed to eat? I'm starving."

Verity's own belly rumbled. They'd had nothing to eat since the s'mores Pam had made the night before. She and Annika moved from the refrigerator to the cupboards, where they found a canister of powdered eggs and some instant coffee. They brought these to the others, who were examining the scanty contents of the wire baker's rack.

"Good find, girls," said Pam. "We'll just mix these up with a little water and have ourselves a good, hot breakfast. Addison, put some water on to boil, why don't you?"

Addison was looking unwell again this morning, sweaty and shivering, but she did as she was told, hefting the giant copper kettle from the stovetop and filling it to the brim. Meanwhile, Pam measured out the powdered eggs into a mixing bowl and stirred in a cup of water.

"Amber, find me a frying pan," she said, testing the ropy texture of the reconstituted eggs. "Verity and Annika, you look for some cutlery and plates. And some coffee mugs while you're at it."

Kettles and skillets and cutlery were easy to come by. Food in the kitchen was scarcer, and meager as the available stores were, Verity could tell they had been picked over. Canned pie filling and green beans. A sack of rice. Half a cardboard flat of snack-sized raisin boxes.

"The stove isn't working," Addison said, fiddling with the knobs. Pam put down her whisk and went over to help.

"The pilot's probably out," she said. "Let me take a look. Annika, see if you can find me some kitchen matches."

Verity wondered what the other girls in the other cabins had been doing for food. In fact, she wondered if anyone else was still here. Maybe they'd missed some kind of announcement while they'd been in the woods, and camp had been called off. Verity imagined a caravan of annoyed parents snaking up the long, unnecessarily winding road to collect the daughters they'd deposited there only a day before. The thought of the others being rescued, driving away, stopping for cheeseburgers and fries on the way home made Verity feel as though someone had poured concrete into her heart.

Don't be an idiot, she thought. *If your parents actually came for you and you weren't there, they'd look for you. At the very least, they'd wait for you.*

Pam propped up the top of the stove like she was looking beneath the hood of a car. "Yep, just like I thought."

Annika handed the matches to Pam, who struck one and held it to the pilot. Nothing happened.

But if the other girls are gone, and their parents didn't pick them up, where are they? Verity wondered.

"Huh, that's strange," said Pam. Undaunted, she went outside to test the gas line. The moment she was out of earshot, the girls erupted in a flurry of scheming. Addison and Annika thought they should sneak away to the cabin later that afternoon. Alix and Amber thought they should go now while Pam was checking the gas line.

If Verity thought about it for more than a few seconds, it was obvious that something was very wrong at this camp. They should have been going for help, or at least asking a few hard questions about why the entire camp was abandoned and the power and gas were shut off. Instead, they were trying to make instant coffee and planning to sneak into the woods to meet a cabinful of boys and one beautiful girl who were almost certainly dangerous, imaginary, or both.

The problem was, it was hard to think about it for more than a few seconds. Verity was aware of this, and yet, paying attention seemed to take so much more effort than ignoring it. Besides, they had Pam, a sensible adult charged with the responsibility of returning them safely to their parents. If they were really in any danger, Pam would have known it, wouldn't she?

So when Pam came back, clapping the dust from her hands, and announced that the gas was indeed off, Verity helped her set up the propane camp stove.

"I'm going in to town," Pam said, after they'd finished eating and cleaning the breakfast dishes. "We need more food and propane and a few other things. Who wants to come?"

The town lay at the foot of the long, unnecessarily winding road, and Verity and her family had passed through it on their way to Camp So-and So. There was a drugstore there and a hot-dog stand and mini-golf and air conditioning and no mosquitos and a change of scenery, and yet, no one volunteered to go.

"Come on," Pam said. "I'll buy you ice cream."

"But we just got here," Addison said.

Pam looked over her shoulder, then to the corners of the room, then peeked her head out the kitchen doors into the dining hall, and finally, went out back and checked the woodpile and the shed. When she was certain they were alone (but wrongly so), she returned to the kitchen and said, "I just want you girls to have a nice time at camp. Canoeing, sleeping out under the stars, s'mores, stuff like that."

"We are having a nice time," Alix said.

"I'm glad to hear that," Pam said. "Are you sure you don't want to go to town?"

"We're sure," said Amber.

"This might be your only chance to go."

"We don't mind," Annika said.

"What I'm saying is—" Pam leaned in and lowered her voice. "This might be the only chance you get. Do you know what I mean?"

There was a pleading tone in her voice that made Verity suspect she was offering more than just a trip to town. Maybe that's what had happened to the girls from the other cabins. They'd sensed the wrongness of it all and fled the first chance they got. But they didn't have such strong, compelling, unsupervised reasons to stay at Camp So-and-So as did the girls from Cabin 4.

"It'll be fun," Pam insisted.

"No, thanks," Verity said. "I think we'd rather stay here."

Pam shook her head and left them to the breakfast dishes and straightening up, and by the time they'd finished, they heard the sound of wheels coming down the dirt road. They cut through the dining hall and went out onto the front porch to see Pam sitting behind the wheel of a 1989 Toyota 4Runner, windows rolled down, engine sputtering.

"Last chance," she said, beckoning them toward the truck. "Plenty of room for everyone in the back."

For half a second, Verity considered taking Pam up on her offer. All she had to do was get in the truck and things would be normal again.

But then she thought about Isis Archimedes. She thought about saying good-bye to the beautiful girl before they'd even met, and Verity found she couldn't.

Pam waited a moment, and when no one hopped into the back of the truck, she lifted her hand and gave them a cheerless wave.

"Well, bye then," she said. "Be careful. Don't wander off. Watch out for each other. Take care of each other."

It seemed like an overly serious thing to say, considering she was only going to be gone for a couple of hours, but they promised Pam that they would, waved good-bye to her, and watched the truck until it disappeared around a bend.

A Note from the Narrator: At this point, Pam leaves our story. What happens to her is not important, unless you are Pam. If you were, you might be interested to know that you were driving a truck that had recently been rigged to explode and hastily patched up by a crew of stagehands with a very long list of other things to attend to. You would be interested to know about the trail of brake fluid leaking from the Toyota 4Runner's undercarriage. You would drive more carefully, especially down a long, unnecessarily winding road.

Back at the cabin, while Amber gave Annika a manicure, Alix went through the clothes in Verity's suitcase, tossing everything to one side except for a too-tight black tank top that Verity had only packed because she didn't care if it got ruined in a cave or torn while rock climbing.

"This might work," Alix said, burrowing through her own wardrobe until she came up with a pair of drapey pants made out of a soft, silky fabric.

"Cute," Amber said, looking up from Annika's nails.

Verity dressed in the clothes Alix had chosen for her, feeling silly about it until she saw the girls' approving nods. She took the rubber band out of her hair and ran her fingers through it. As the ends of her hair brushed her bare shoulders, she felt a shiver pass up and down her arms. She felt confident. She felt excited. She felt cute.

Until she looked at Addison, who had been resting on her cot while the rest of them primped, and was looking worse than ever. She was soaked in sweat and burning with fever, and her eyes seemed to have sunken in her face.

At least, at first.

Addison reached into the pocket of her shorts, took out the white button again, and squeezed it in the palm of her hand. Again, the change was immediate. The sweat evaporated from her skin, and the curl returned to her hair, and the pits faded from beneath her eyes, and she smiled.

"Are you okay?" Verity asked.

"Of course I am," Addison said.

Her eyes were glassy and her cheeks looked unnaturally flushed.

"Maybe we should go another time," Verity said, "when you feel better."

Addison leapt up from her cot, listed slightly, then sat back down.

"I'm just dehydrated or something," she said.

"I'll get you some water," Verity said. "Maybe some aspirin, too, if I can find it."

She had pulled back the tarp that covered the doorway when Annika got up and said, to Verity's surprise, "I'll go with you."

The longer Verity spent with her cabinmates, the more she began to notice the little differences between them. Amber was the silliest. Alix was the sweetest. Back in the real world, Verity was fairly sure that Addison was the leader of their group, whether they acknowledged it or not. But Annika was quieter than the others, more serious and more thoughtful. They walked toward the mess hall without talking, and Verity wondered what Annika made of the strange things happening at Camp So-and-So. Still, when Annika finally spoke, her line of questioning caught Verity by surprise.

"What's your soul mate like, Verity? You never said."

Verity started to panic. Was Annika really asking or did she already know the truth? They'd all been so besotted with their own soul mates that Verity had not heard anyone compare notes. Now, Verity wondered about Annika's soul mate, the shirtless boy with the slicked-back pompadour, doing pull-ups on a poplar branch. Was that what Annika saw when she looked at him?

"Um, really cute," Verity stammered. "You know. You were there."

Annika nodded gravely. "The one reading a book in the hammock, right?"

Verity nodded back.

Annika looked away, embarrassed, and said, "Promise you won't take this the wrong way."

"I won't."

"Is your soul mate a girl?"

"Oh," Verity said, then fell silent.

"It's okay if she is," Annika said.

"I know it is."

"I'm not saying anything about you."

"I know you aren't."

"So, is she a girl?"

Verity felt as though she'd been lifted out of her own body, and now she was looking down, watching this conversation like it was happening to someone else. It made the next thing she said easier and more difficult at the same time.

"Yeah," said Verity. "My soul mate's a girl."

Her cheeks felt hot and her hands were shaking and she felt a slight buzzing between her ears, but she had done it. She had told someone that she liked a girl. And while neither of them said much of anything as they fished through drawers in the nurse's station, and while Annika seemed too embarrassed to even look at her, it hardly mattered. She had confessed the truth and lived.

Verity felt brave now, and bold enough to go wandering through the woods armed only with a flashlight to see the beautiful girl. She felt like she was worthy of seeing her now.

She wished she felt better about the situation with Addison, though. They found nothing useful in the nurse's station—in fact, the whole place looked like it had been ransacked. They did scrounge some bottles of water from the mess hall, and Verity hoped that hydration and rest would be enough to fix whatever was wrong with her cabinmate.

The other girls seemed to share her worries. One moment, Addison would be writhing and shivering in her sleeping bag.

Then, just when they were worried enough to call the whole thing off, she would hop up and run outside, her eyes sparkling, puzzled as to why they hadn't already set off.

"Hey, wasn't there another cabin here?" she asked, during one of her lucid moments, pointing to the high hedge of brambles that twisted and climbed forty feet in the air.

Verity did a double take. Had there been? She had a vague recollection of speaking to some unfriendly girls the day before, but surely they belonged to one of the three other cabins surrounding the fire pit. Not that she'd seen any of the occupants of those cabins this morning either. Once again, a little voice in Verity's head spoke up to remind her that something was wrong, and only bound to get more wrong if she continued on this course, and once again, she ignored it.

"Are you sure you're feeling well enough to go?" Verity asked. Addison rolled her eyes and kicked her legs up in a handstand to prove how healthy she was.

"I'm fine," she said. "So, let's go already."

Verity didn't quite believe her—none of them did—and yet, she seemed so sure.

"What if Pam comes back while we're gone?" Verity asked.

None of them answered, because though they wouldn't have admitted it to each other, or even to themselves, none of them really ever expected that she would.

CABIN 5

SURVIVAL

[SCENE: A cabin encircled by brambles]

Water.

Food.

Shelter.

Bathroom.

Escape.

After the forty-foot-high wall of brambles erupted from the ground and encircled their cabin, these were their immediate needs. Once the initial panic had settled, these were the things they worked at securing.

The girls from Cabin 5 realized they would have to work quickly if they were going to survive. As darkness fell, they laid out all the tarps and ponchos they'd brought with them to catch the inadequate but life-sustaining amount of dew that would fall through the top of the enclosure overnight.

They rose early the next morning and drank sparingly of

the water they'd collected. Then they fell to the ground and licked the dew right off the blades of grass that grew around the cabin. The water from the tarps that they did not drink right away, they saved in water bottles for later.

Their food supply was perhaps an even greater concern than water. There had been no time for care packages to arrive, and very few of the girls had smuggled any food into camp. They'd piled what little they had by the fire pit and rationed it out to themselves in small quantities throughout the first full day. Half a cracker at dawn. One Twizzler in the mid-morning. A square of chocolate at dusk.

In an isolated area away from the fire pit and the cabin, they dug a latrine and strung up bedsheets around it for privacy. It wasn't a permanent solution. Within a few days, the smell would start to become unbearable, but then again, within a few days, their food supply would be gone, and dehydration would have begun to catch up with them. If any of this went on longer than a few days, a smelly latrine would be the least of their worries.

They slept through the hottest part of the day, rising again around five so they could take advantage of the remaining daylight to plot their escape.

One pine tree grew inside the perimeter of the wall, so close, in fact, that several of its branches had been sheared off when the brambles sprang from the ground. The girls took turns climbing the tree as high as they dared, then leaping onto the wall in an attempt to go over the top. It was a dangerous job. Only one girl managed to get a grip on the brambles at all, and she wished she hadn't because the thorns sank into her arms and legs and tore at her skin, and within a few seconds she was plummeting toward the ground, where her cabinmates waited with a sleeping bag stretched out tight to catch her.

Soon, they gave up trying to go over the top and began to dig under. Unfortunately, their digging implements were less than ideal. They had only one flimsy fire shovel meant for poking at hot coals and campfire ash, not for burrowing through hard-packed earth. They loosened the dirt with anything they could find, then scooped it out with the shovel. They only had some sharp sticks and a few shingles they'd pried off the roof, so it was slow going. And yet, they dug tirelessly, shoveling scoop after scoop, shingle after shingle of dirt away.

The girls also devoted a small amount of time to a third, more experimental strategy: the hope that if they could not go over the wall or under it, perhaps they could go through. These were not ordinary brambles—that much was clear—but perhaps there was some item packed in their duffel bags that would bring them down. They tried rubbing alcohol, sunscreen, and contact lens solution. One bold girl rubbed two fleece blankets together until she'd worked up a heady electrical charge, and ran straight into it. Sadly, the only effect was that, in addition to giving herself a tremendous shock, she sustained dozens of scratches and cuts, many of them quite deep and close to important veins and arteries.

Sometimes they talked, but it was always purposeful. They rarely smiled and never laughed. Everything they did was functional.

They looked as though at any time they might snap, crack, and pop straight out of their skins, like if this went on much longer, all of them might rub blankets together and throw themselves into the brambles at once.

Dear Cressida,

If you get this letter, then you know why that should be impossible.

I need your help. I don't know how you're supposed to do that. I don't even know if these letters are getting through to you.

I suppose there's a chance you haven't even noticed anything is different, but I like to think you know me better than that. And if you hadn't noticed, I'm telling you now. Whatever they sent back in my place, IT'S NOT ME.

They're holding me prisoner here. If you can figure out a way to get here and rescue me, that would be awesome. If you can't, well, at least somebody knows where I really am, and I guess that makes me feel better, too.

    Love,

    ع

P.S. You were right about the Isis Archimedes books. Have read the first one three times now. That is partly because it is excellent, and partly because it is the only book I have. If you decide you're up for a rescue mission, don't even think about coming to Camp So-and-So without the rest of them.

CABIN 1

THE ALL-CAMP SPORT & FOLLIES

[SCENE: Shortly before the equestrian event of the All-Camp Sport & Follies, the Camp So-and-So stables are deserted, except for CRESSIDA.]

If Cressida was going to be forced to participate in the All-Camp Sport & Follies, at least everything so far had gone the way she hoped it would. They'd played the game the way the Inge F. Yancey campers wanted them to—the way they *expected* them to—and now, their guard was down. Even the fact that they'd won the rowing event had turned out to be a stroke of luck that would make it that much easier to carry out her plan.

She'd scoured every inch of Camp So-and-So searching for her friend, and now, to continue her mission, she needed to get to the other side of the lake, to the belly of the beast, to the Inge F. Yancey Young Executives Leadership Camp itself. Tania had made it clear that she didn't want the Camp So-and-So girls anywhere near their camp, but what if they didn't have a choice? What if for some reason, Cressida schemed, the horsemanship event could not take place at Camp So-and-So?

While her cabinmates sat at the campfire pavilion triumphantly eating their lunch of apples and peanut butter crackers after the rowing victory, Cressida claimed to have a stomachache and sneaked away in the direction of the stables.

Her plan was to let the horses out of their stalls and turn them loose in the woods before the Inge F. Yancey campers arrived for the equestrian event; however, when Cressida reached the stables, she found that someone had beaten her to it.

A Note from the Narrator: The horses having been taken, of course, the night before by the girls from Cabin 2.

She circled the stables looking for some trace of them. Maybe they were grazing in a pasture or penned up in a nearby corral? Had they gotten loose? Cressida crouched in the dirt, looking for hoofprints.

Then she heard footsteps coming up behind her, so quiet and stealthy that she only noticed when they were practically on top of her. Cressida didn't have time to stand up, but looked over her shoulder to see Kadie looming over her.

Kadie didn't speak at first. She inspected the pasture, the corral, the stalls, and only when she saw they were all empty did she glare down at Cressida and ask, "What did you do with the horses?"

"Nothing."

"Then why are you here?"

"Why are you following me?" Cressida got to her feet and pointed an accusing finger at Kadie.

"I'm following you because I don't trust you," Kadie said, pushing Cressida's outstretched hand away. "You're always sneaking around. Snooping. Lurking. I've seen you."

"I don't know what you're talking about," Cressida said, taking a step back. She knew Kadie was suspicious of her, but was startled by her intensity.

"Then where did you go this morning before everyone else woke up? Why was the equipment shed already unlocked when I got there? And why are you out here by the stables when you said you were sick to your stomach?"

With each question, Kadie advanced on Cressida, backing her into a fence. When she could retreat no farther, Cressida stood her ground. She didn't want a fight. She didn't have time for a fight. Tania and the rest of the Inge F. Yancey campers would be there any minute, and they needed a cover story.

"What if I'm looking for them?" she asked in her paper-shredder voice. "Care to help, or are you just going to stand around and blame me for losing the All-Camp Sport & Follies?"

Kadie started to argue, but thought better of it and followed Cressida around the back of the stables instead. Losing the All-Camp Sport & Follies was not at the forefront of her concerns at that moment. She had much larger ones.

She thought back to the day before, when Tania had levitated Dora three feet off the ground. She thought about the witchy girls who had knitted a sleeping bag in an hour and wondered what the Inge F. Yancey campers had done to her cabin's canoe to make it disintegrate in water. If Cressida was a spy (and Kadie was beginning to suspect that she was—she knew far too much about Camp So-and-So for a first-year camper), she might not just be out to sabotage Cabin 1's chances. She might actually be dangerous.

The two girls followed the pony trail into the woods to the spot where it forked before turning back. The equestrian event was due to begin, the Inge F. Yancey campers would be there any minute, and there was still no sign of the horses.

Just as they emerged from the woods, Vivian and Kimber arrived. They'd stopped by the cabin to freshen up—Vivian's black hair was teased into a glam-looking bouffant and Kimber was wearing false eyelashes. Both wore their high black boots over their painted-on jeans, equestrian-style. Kadie and Cressida looked at their own mosquito-bitten legs and ratty sweatshirts and, for a moment, felt slightly homely next to their glamorous cabinmates.

"Where are the horses?" Vivian asked.

Just as Kadie was about to open her mouth and lay the blame on Cressida, they heard a thundering of hooves, and five lathered, wild-eyed horses galloped out of the woods.

Some frothed at the mouth; others snorted and stamped their hooves in the dirt as they paced frantically in front of the stables. Kadie gave Cressida an accusing stare, but there was more pressing work at hand.

"We have to take care of them," Kadie told her. "Go find Dora. She said she knows something about horses."

A Note from the Narrator: This was rather an overstatement, Dora's knowledge of horses being limited to a handful of riding lessons and trail rides she'd done in the fifth grade. However, it was enough to qualify her as Cabin 1's designated rider for the equestrian event and resident horse expert.

Cressida set off down the trail from the stables without arguing. Meanwhile, Kadie began filling buckets from the pump and pouring them into the horses' troughs. She didn't know enough about horses to know what attention they required now, but she could tell just by looking at them that water was a priority. They drank as fast as she poured, and by the time Cressida returned with Dora in tow, Kadie's arms ached from operating the pump and filling the troughs.

Dora came running as soon as she saw the horses. "You poor things!" she cried. "Let's get those saddles off you."

Saddles, thought Kadie. *Of course.*

Dora showed the others how to loosen the horses' girths and remove the saddles and blankets. Once they had managed that, they searched the stables for sponges and towels, and wiped the lather, dirt, and sweat from the horses' coats and mouths. Cressida tried to help, despite her allergies, but her horse rolled its eyes and flicked its tail in warning whenever she approached. Kadie's horse was an aged mare that had spent many summers dealing with inexperienced riders and was inclined to give them the benefit of the doubt; however, Kadie was so tentative and jumpy that the horse began to neigh impatiently as she brushed it. Finally, Vivian and Kimber helped them walk the horses back to their stalls, where they plied them with oats and hay and pieces of carrot.

No sooner had they finished tending to the horses when a pack of the Inge F. Yancey campers strode into the stables. Judging from their pinched facial expressions, they considered the facilities to be beyond primitive and beneath contempt.

"Good afternoon, ladies," Ron said, flashing his reptile smile. "Are you ready to ride?"

It was Dora, of all people, who came forward to speak.

"Nobody's riding these horses today. Just look at them!" she said, stepping protectively between Ron and the stalls.

A slow smile spread across Tania's face. "Then you're saying you can't compete. Is that right?"

"No," Kadie said, looking Tania square in the eye. "What we're saying is that these horses are currently unavailable. We can postpone this portion of the competition until they're rested."

Suddenly, Cressida was standing by Kadie's side, chiming in.

"Or we can go across the lake and use the horses at your camp," she said, adding snottily, "You do have horses, right?"

"Of course we have horses," Tania snapped.

The Inge F. Yancey campers whispered among themselves for a few minutes before Ron emerged from the pack, smiling as though he'd already beaten them.

"We propose this," he said. "We will compete today. We will compete using our horses. But we'll compete on our course, not here. Either you agree to those conditions, or you forfeit. 'Kay?"

It was exactly what Cressida had been hoping for, but she knew Kadie still didn't trust her. It wouldn't help her chances to look too eager about it.

"It's your call," Cressida whispered to Kadie. "What do you want to do?"

Kadie's guard was up. What was Cressida playing at? she wondered. If she was a spy or a saboteur from the Inge F. Yancey camp, why was she letting Kadie make the decision here? Then again, if Cressida was a spy, she would know that Kadie would never forfeit. She would be counting on that. And having already established her horse aversion, Cressida would know that she would not be the one to ride.

But then again, if they forfeited now, they would have lost and it would be over. Kadie ran scenarios in her mind, trying to think of an angle Cressida had overlooked.

While she was thinking, though, Dora spoke up.

"We'll do it," she said.

Cressida tried her best to conceal her excitement while slow smiles spread over Vivian and Kimber's faces. Even if they didn't win the All-Camp Sport & Follies, at least they were going to get a better look at the canopied terraces and shining glass edifices of the Inge F. Yancey Young Executives Leadership Camp. Kadie's expression was harder to read, and maybe she alone was considering that this might not be the safest decision.

The girls from Cabin 1 followed the Inge F. Yancey campers back to the main road where their private cars were waiting. There was much eye rolling and complaining as it was determined that several of the Yancey campers would have to share cars in order to accommodate the girls from Camp So-and-So. At last, two agreed to double up, and the Cabin 1 girls squeezed themselves into the extra car, four in the backseat and Kadie up front, quaking with nerves and anticipation. She'd seen the Inge F. Yancey Young Executives Leadership Camp from across the lake and had actually set foot on its boat dock earlier, but beyond that, it was a mystery to her.

Their driver regarded them with indifferent, hooded eyes and stubbed out a cigar on the dirt path before getting into the driver's seat. Unlike the Inge F. Yancey campers' drivers, he did not hold the doors open for them. They traveled down the long, unnecessarily winding road until they came to a turnoff that none of them had spotted before and that almost certainly had not been there when their parents dropped them off at camp. The driver, who had thus far been silent, stopped the car and handed them each a small black sack.

"I'll have to ask that you place these over your heads as we enter the facility," he said, and cracked his knuckles in a way that suggested there would be repercussions if they resisted.

While the experience was humiliating and more than a little bit frightening, the fabric was a brushed Egyptian cotton, a very high thread count and extremely gentle on the skin, the girls had to admit.

After ten minutes of driving, the car came to a stop. They heard the driver roll down his window and punch a series of buttons on a keypad, each one emitting a different tone. Then they heard the mechanical whir that must have been the gates opening because the car began to move again.

"You may remove the sacks," the man said.

When they did, they saw that they were approaching the stables, which had been built to resemble a petite Tudor lodge with a slate roof and a cobblestone walkway leading up to sturdy double oak doors. The entire thing was surrounded by an English rose garden that was at its peak blossoming. As they got out of the car, Kadie and Cressida tried to keep their bedazzlement in check. Neither of them had expected anything so grand.

Inside, a snide-looking groom led them down a corridor with walls tiled in mosaic that depicted scenes of the historical legacy of horsemanship over the course of ten centuries. Their sneakers squeaked on the granite floors. The horses' stalls were varnished teak, intricately carved with leaves and angels.

The horses themselves were sleek, muscled creatures from storied lineages. They were not summer camp nags meant for nothing grander than a trot down a forest trail. They had been bred to be champions. Cedar shavings, heather, and hay lined the floors, creating an intoxicating aroma that was not the slightest bit horsey.

A Note from the Narrator: All the horses at the Inge F. Yancey Young Executives Leadership Camp were shampooed daily, and sprigs of lavender were braided into their manes afterward.

The snide groom guided them outside, where a lush pasture unfolded for acres over gently rolling hills, a sparkling little stream bubbling through it. Ron and Tania stood waiting to greet them, their minions crowded around them. Off to the side, the three judges murmured amongst themselves, largely ignoring the rest of the proceedings.

"Welcome," Tania said with all the warmth of the alpine tundra. "We're so glad to have you here."

"If you'll come this way, we'll show you the course," Ron said, motioning toward a hedge-lined footpath. "Of course, we favor a slightly more *refined* style of riding here, though I'm sure you'll have no trouble adapting to it."

They wound through a labyrinth of hedges, marveling at the delicate beds of tea roses and lavender that had been planted on the sides. Finally, they emerged from the maze onto what looked like an oversized miniature-golf course. Stone walls, high hedges, water hazards, and white lattice fences were arranged in a large oval formation. There was no trail or track, just freshly manicured grass.

Tania beamed, "We're very proud of our steeplechase course here at Inge F. Yancey. It's been certified by the American Cup."

"Don't brag, Tania," Ron said, patting her arm. "But it *is* a fine course. I'm sure you'll enjoy it."

"What's a steeplechase?" Vivian whispered to Dora.

"I'm not sure," Dora whispered back. "I think we're supposed to race the horses through the obstacles, maybe?"

A smug look on his face, Ron said, "If you're not familiar with steeplechase, now would be the time to let us know. This is not for beginners."

None of the girls said a word but looked to Kadie for direction, and Cressida wondered whether Kadie was willing to let one of their cabinmates actually attempt the steeplechase rather than admit none of them knew how to do it.

"I'll be riding for us, of course," Tania said. "Have you selected your rider?"

Kadie suddenly imagined one of them tumbling from the saddle and being trampled beneath a horse's hooves. What if a horse got hurt because of their bad riding? Kadie may have disliked the Inge F. Yancey campers, but she had nothing against their horses. Maybe they should just go back to camp and spend the rest of the week sunning themselves on Mosquito Beach and being bored out of their minds.

Assuming, of course, that they had a choice. Assuming that they would be permitted to leave.

"It's me," said Dora. "I'm riding for us."

Before Kadie could do or say anything to stop her, the groom had already led Dora away to the stables to pick out a horse.

"Do you think she'll be all right?" Cressida asked.

"I hope so," Kadie said.

Ten minutes later, Dora emerged from the stables dressed in silks, breeches, riding boots, and, thankfully, a helmet, leading a dark bay filly by the reins.

"Her name's Helena," Dora said, while the horse nickered into her ear.

A Note from the Narrator: Helena was accustomed to being whipped, goaded, tugged at, and scrubbed within an inch of her life, and found Dora's gentleness and her soft, encouraging voice to be a happy change of pace. Dora wouldn't even take the riding crop or spurs from the groom. Within minutes, the horse was quite devoted to her and resolved to help her in any way possible.

"Are you sure about this?" Kadie asked. "Please don't do this on my account. I don't care if we forfeit. I just don't want you to get hurt over some stupid contest."

"Don't worry," Dora said.

To Helena, she whispered, "You do exactly as much as you can, Helena. If there's an obstacle you don't want to do, *you just go around it*, okay?"

The horse whinnied, as though she understood.

A Note from the Narrator: In fact, she did.

"As our guests, of course you'll do the honors and go first," Ron said.

Dora climbed into Helena's saddle and rode her to the starting line, whispering to her and stroking her mane the whole way, and in return, Helena whinnied adoringly. Noticing that the next event was about to get underway, the three judges elbowed one another and shuffled over to the steeplechase course, leaning on the fence to watch.

"Whenever you're ready," Tania said, tightening the straps of her helmet under her chin. "Once around the course."

"Okay," Dora said, then lightly pressed her heels against Helena's sides, and they were off.

The horse cleared the first obstacle, a low stone wall, landing as gently as possible so that Dora would not be jolted out of the saddle. At the second obstacle, however, the horse slowed, eyeing the high white gate uneasily. Dora said something to her, patting her on the side of the neck, and Helena trotted around it. The Inge F. Yancey campers hooted in triumph, but Dora and Helena paid them no mind. The next obstacle, a hedge with a pool of water beyond it, Helena sailed over effortlessly, and kept her momentum for the next wall as well. Another high, white gate came next, and as before, the horse wanted nothing to do with it. Dora guided her around it, whispering encouragements into the horse's ear. Near the end, they built up speed and vaulted across a terrifyingly high hedge and over a pool of water, clearing it by over a yard before crossing the finish line and circling back to where they'd started. Dora cheered from the saddle and hugged the horse around the neck.

From the sidelines, the three judges clapped politely and made notes on their score sheets. The other girls mobbed Dora, praising her bravery and Helena's skill. Both the girl and the horse seemed surprised by the attention, but enjoyed it nonetheless.

Tania mounted her horse, a chestnut mare, and clapped sarcastically in their direction.

"Nicely done," she said. "Of course, you'll be penalized for the gates you failed to clear, but I'm sure you knew that."

She dug her spurs hard into the mare's flank and gave it a swat with her riding crop. As they trotted toward the starting line, it almost seemed as if Tania's horse looked back at Dora and Helena with longing in its mournful eyes, not that such a thing was possible.

A Note from the Narrator: Of course it is.

Suddenly, a panicked look crossed Dora's face and she dropped to the ground on all fours, scouring the blades of grass with her fingertips. She did not cut a distinguished figure, crawling around in front of everyone like an animal. Some of the Inge F. Yancey campers just stared openly as she did this. Others pointed and howled with laughter.

"Are you okay?" Vivian asked, looking back at the Inge F. Yancey campers with embarrassment at her cabinmate's erratic behavior. "What's wrong with you?"

"Has anybody seen a pocket watch?" Dora asked, crawling toward the starting line, running her hands over every inch of ground she crossed.

"You're not allowed to have a watch here," Kadie hissed at her. "It's against the rules."

"It was my grandfather's," Dora said, sounding more agitated by the second. "I always carry it with me. It must have fallen out of my pocket on one of the jumps."

"Get her out of the way," Ron said, shoving two of his

minions onto the course. They each took one of Dora's elbows and hoisted her to her feet, dragging her away from the starting gate before she could be trampled by Tania.

Oblivious to the small drama unfolding on the sidelines, Tania let out a primordial shriek and bore down on the chestnut mare once again with her riding crop. They thundered toward the stone wall, the horse's eyes wide and rolling. Kadie was horrified. She wasn't a horse person, or even particularly an animal lover, but even she knew this was a loathsome way to treat so noble a beast.

Tania and the mare cleared the first wall, and then jumped the high, white gate that had given Helena problems. As she rode past, Tania turned to bare her teeth at the girls from Cabin 1 in a vicious grin, then rained fresh blows and insults on her horse as they approached the next obstacle.

She's awful, thought Kadie. *She's cruel. She's vain. She's bloodthirsty. She cheats. She doesn't deserve to win.*

The horse leaped over the hedge and was sailing over the pool of water when a curious thing happened. Tania's arm froze in the middle of the beating she was delivering, and she sat up ramrod straight in the saddle. The riding crop fell from her hand, her feet slipped out of the stirrups, and when the horse landed on the far side of the pool, the impact jolted Tania loose from the saddle and sent her flying backwards into the pool of water.

The horse twitched, bucked, neighed loudly, then took off in the opposite direction of the next gate. The water seemed to bring Tania back to herself, and she sat there with dripping hair, spewing curses after the chestnut mare as it bounded toward the hilly pastures.

"Does that mean we win?" Kimber asked.

With great effort, Tania lurched out of the water and around the hedge. She doubled over like she was going to be sick, but instead, she reached down into the grass with a gloved hand, brought up something that glittered silver in the sunlight, and chucked it onto the sidelines like it weighed thirty pounds, not a few ounces.

"What, may I ask, is *that* doing in the middle of the steeplechase course?"

Her breathing was labored and her arms hung limp at her sides, yet every fiber of her being quaked with rage.

No one said a word.

"No foreign objects on the steeplechase course," she said, grabbing onto a fencepost for support. "The horse spooked. I could have been killed!"

Odd, Kadie thought. It was her fellow Inge F. Yaney campers Tania seemed to be yelling at, not the Cabin 1 girls. And it wasn't the horse that had spooked. It was Tania who had frozen, and now there seemed to be something the matter with her. Kadie turned to find Cressida, to see what she made of all of this.

Only, Cressida wasn't there.

She wasn't with the others, who were feeding Helena apples and oats. She wasn't with the Inge F. Yancey campers, who were fussing over Tania. It was as if she'd simply disappeared.

Or taken advantage of the distraction to ditch them.

There was only one way she could have gone. Kadie ran down the hedge-lined path they'd taken to the steeplechase course, calling Cressida's name. She reached the stables and had started to open the door to cut back through, when she noticed a cobblestone path that led in another direction, toward a tulip-covered knoll with a working windmill perched on top. Scrambling up the path as fast as her spindly, chicken legs would carry her was Cressida. Kadie watched as she waded through the tulips toward the windmill, opened a door at its base, and went inside.

Kadie raced after her. Athletic and sure-footed, she arrived at the windmill in less than a minute, but paused outside to collect her thoughts. Kadie knew she could physically overpower Cressida if it came to that. But what if she wasn't alone in the windmill? What if she was meeting someone? Kadie grabbed a shovel that was resting on the ground next to the windmill, slung it over her shoulder, and slowly opened the door.

Inside, it took Kadie's eyes a moment to adjust to the light. Across the room, she spied a crude set of stairs leading toward a loft area. Brandishing the shovel, she crossed the room and began to climb them. When her head popped up into the loft, she heard a small squeak of surprise. Kadie didn't even think. She hoisted the shovel up and made an awkward swing, reeling backwards as she felt it make contact with something soft but solid. There was a grunt, a thud, and then some quiet wheezing. Kadie bounded up the last stair into the loft to see Cressida on the floor, clutching her left calf with one hand and shielding her face with the other.

Kadie raised the shovel over her head, ready to strike again. "Why did you run away? You have five seconds to tell me what you're doing here or else."

"You idiot," Cressida wheezed, still struggling to catch her breath. "Can't you just mind your own business? Or did they put you up to this, too?"

Kadie lowered the shovel and knelt down beside Cressida. "What are you talking about? Who do you mean, *they*?"

Cressida caught Kadie by the arm and squeezed it so hard her bones groaned.

"Don't play dumb," Cressida said. "I know you're one of them. An Inge F. Yancey stooge."

Of course, nothing could have been further from the truth. Kadie's lip curled at the very suggestion.

"*You're* the spy!" Kadie said, struggling against Cressida's grip. "All your disappearing and sneaking around."

"Why do you act like you know so much about this place?" Cressida asked, giving Kadie's arm another tight squeeze.

"Camp So-and-So is *my* camp. It was last year; it is now."

"No, it wasn't," Cressida said, digging her fingernails into Kadie's skin. "You weren't *at* camp last summer. I know for a fact you weren't."

Cressida was rarely wrong about things, and she wasn't wrong about this.

Kadie let out a gasp and sat down hard. The shovel clattered to the floor.

She held out her hands and studied them, first the backs, then the palms. She looked down at her legs stretched out in front of her. Everything looked the same, but Kadie knew that it wasn't.

I wasn't at camp last summer, she thought. *I was never here before in my life.*

CABIN 2

KILLER IN THE WOODS

*[SCENE: After their plot to fix the truck and escape Abigail
ends in tragedy, WALLIS, CORINNE, SHEA, BECCA,
and HENNIE flee on horseback into the forest.]*

For Cabin 2, it was still the middle of the night, that never-ending, dark, terrifying first night at camp. They had not slept; they were still on the run from Abigail. Wallis was afraid and battered, and she had seen terrible things. Her lungs were raw from breathing in smoke and ash, but the moment she swung into the saddle and rode onto the forest path, the shortest way back to the road and safety, her heart flooded with boldness. The horses changed everything. They were speed, they were armor, they were a way out. And even though these horses were more accustomed to plodding trail rides, they sensed the urgency of this journey. With the girls clinging to their manes, they galloped down the path as though the hosts of hell were behind them.

The horses knew every inch of the trail. They were not fooled by the way the moonlight created snares where none existed and hid others. They saw every root, every stone. But they had never seen anything like the creature that stood outside the cave. It had the body of a spider and the head of a snake, and it loomed over a girl with beads in her hair who lay stunned by the side of the path.

They were upon it in an instant. There was no time to stop or slow down. The creature was big—it should have stopped them like a stone wall, but instead, they thundered over it, crushing its head beneath the hooves of their steeds.

A Note from the Narrator: It was pure fear that kept the girls from tugging at the reins, turning around, and fleeing back in the direction from which they'd come when they saw the beast in the middle of the trail. They could not go back. They would not go back. When a terror-stricken girl believes she is fleeing a psychotic murderer, perhaps the girl will dispatch the monster in front of her without fully noticing because it is standing between her and her escape route.

No sooner had it happened than the horses panicked—they reared up and bolted off the path. Wallis just barely managed to hang on as she and her horse crashed through the brambles, and tree branches whipped her across the face.

Just ahead of her, Wallis saw the figure of one of her cabinmates slump to the side and tumble off her horse. In the darkness, she could only make out her silhouette, but the tightly coiled mass of curls was a giveaway. Shea. Wallis tried to stop, but her horse was wild with fear and would not be stopped, would not be directed, would not double back. It dawned on

Wallis that this was not going to be the story of how they escaped either.

The horses weren't going to bring them out of the forest, not unless they were willing to leave Shea behind.

Still, knowing that and willingly throwing herself from the back of a horse were two different things. As her horse galloped past the spot where Shea had fallen, Wallis found she was frozen in the saddle. It was only when she saw Corinne grasp an overhanging tree branch and lift herself from her horse's back, and when she saw Hennie let go of the reins and fall backwards, that Wallis realized she and Becca were in danger of losing the others if she didn't act quickly.

First, she caught up to the catatonic Becca, who was clinging to the saddle and saying over and over again, "I want to go home, I want to go home, I want to go home," and gave her a firm push, breathing a sigh of relief when Becca tucked and rolled clear of the horse's hooves.

Now it was her turn. Wallis tried to tuck and roll like Becca had, but landed flat on her back and had the wind knocked out of her. Wincing, she pulled herself upright just in time to see the horses disappear into the darkness. Then she crawled over to the pile of rotten leaves that had broken Shea's fall. The others had already gathered there and were surveying the damage.

Shea could ill afford another injury. After being hit in the head by that piece of shrapnel during the truck explosion, she had lost a fair amount of blood. The mile-long run to the stables hadn't done her any favors either, though she'd kept up with them fairly well. However, she'd barely spoken since the explosion, and when she did, her voice was a fraction of its usual volume.

Now Shea lay very still. At first, Wallis thought that she had passed out from fear, exhaustion, or loss of blood, but when they rolled her over, she saw that this was not the case.

Abigail had struck again.

Or at least she'd tried to. There was a gash on Shea's cheek and fresh blood in her hair at the temples, but her hands had gotten the worst of it. They were cut to ribbons, and blood streamed down her wrists and arms.

What happened? Wallis wondered, looking around the soft, fecund mulch of the forest floor. There was nothing sharper than a stick around here.

Then she looked up and saw the barbed wire that had been strung between the trees. Her insides twisted as it dawned on her that Shea had avoided a grisly outcome by the narrowest of margins. Whether it was luck or instinct or remarkably good night vision, Shea had raised her hands to protect her face just as her horse passed beneath the barbed-wire snare. She'd been knocked off the horse, but that was a small price to pay for an intact jugular vein.

"We have to stop the bleeding," Hennie said, the first of them to recover from the shock. "Give me some light."

"What about Abigail?" Becca whimpered.

"I don't care," Hennie said. "I have to help Shea."

Wallis drew a flashlight from the pocket of her overall shorts and switched it on, glancing nervously into the woods for signs of movement. Under Hennie's guidance, the others applied pressure to Shea's wounds until the bleeding slowed, then bandaged her hands with strips torn from the sleeves of their t-shirts.

"Her head's bleeding again," Hennie said, mopping Shea's temple with a bandanna.

"Well, then bandage it," Corinne said, a little snappishly.

"With what?"

The bandana was already soaked through. Corinne sucked in a breath and gave Hennie an apologetic look.

"I'm doing the best I can," Hennie said.

After what seemed like hours, they'd managed to stop the worst of the bleeding, and though Shea looked like a crime scene, she had somehow remained conscious.

Of course, by that time, the horses were long gone. Now the girls were stranded in the middle of the woods with no choice but to walk to safety. They'd lost Megan and Oscar. They'd lost the trail. They'd lost the horses.

It was still their first night at camp. They should have been in their cabin, curling up in their sleeping bags right now. Instead, they were on the run from a killer with a flair for booby traps. They were lost. And they still barely knew each other.

"Be careful," Corinne warned them, pointing out more strands of barbed wire strung overhead like macabre Christmas lights. "More of Abigail's traps."

"How do you know it's Abigail?" Hennie asked.

"Who else would it be?"

"Well, if she wants to kill us, why doesn't she just come out here and do it?" Shea asked, weakly. Becca clung to her side, still shaking and muttering under her breath that she wanted to go home.

"Because," Wallis said, "she's only a little bit older than us. Remember what Oscar said? She was a camper here. She's probably not very big or strong, so she's trying to pick us off one by one. She's hunting us."

Shea examined her hands and tested the bandages to make sure they were secure. "But we're not the ones who abandoned her in that cave and drove her insane."

"I don't think that matters much to Abigail."

They continued to walk in the wrong direction, meandering first toward the stables, then making a dogleg turn south just when a straight course would have led them back on the trail. It was slow going. Hennie half-dragged, half-carried Shea, while Becca clung to Shea's arm. Corinne and Wallis led the way, scanning their flashlights over the ground as they walked.

In this way they managed to avoid a spring-loaded bear trap, a tripwire, and a deep pit with sticks filed to sharp points lining the bottom.

These were small victories by themselves, but did little to distract them from the larger goal of getting to safety. And as far as they could tell, they were no closer to that. During the hour before dawn they decided to rest and sat down in a clearing.

Seated between Shea and Hennie, Wallis sneaked glimpses of the other girls. They were all covered in blood—their own, or someone else's—and leaves and twigs clung to their hair. No one had eaten, no one had slept. Their clothes were torn and reeking of smoke, and yet, Abigail had not quite broken them yet.

Despite her head wound and her ruined hands, Shea seemed unperturbed. Her eyes were clear and determined as she stared straight out into the forest, half-daring any evil thing to go ahead and just *try* to attack her again. Shea was a fighter, Wallis decided. The same went for Corinne. Even lost in the middle of the woods, in the middle of the night, with a psycho killer after them, she was like a firefighter or a reporter in a war zone. She never panicked. She *refused* to panic. And while Hennie seemed as daffy and off-kilter as ever, that strange smile still plastered on her face, without her quick thinking and first aid skills, Wallis was afraid to think what might have happened to Shea.

Becca was the only one Wallis remained unsure about. Ever since they had found Megan's body, Becca had been a quivering, useless mess. Wallis understood. Wallis sympathized. But there was no denying that Becca slowed them down, even more than Shea did.

As soon as the thought entered her head, she felt guilty for it and gave Becca a squeeze on the arm. "Hey, are you doing okay?"

Becca did not reply. *Uh oh*, thought Wallis.

"Hey, Becca?"

She put her arm around Becca's shoulder and gave her a shake. Becca's neck swayed from side to side, but the expression on her face didn't budge.

"Corinne, can you come here? I think something's the matter with Becca."

The other girls gathered around Becca. Shea waved a hand in front of her eyes. Corinne took her pulse. Hennie watched all of it thoughtfully, then said, "You know, it's possible that she's fallen under Abigail's thrall."

"Are you insane?" Corinne asked, and she put her arm around Becca's shoulder.

"It happens sometimes on TV shows. One of the potential victims becomes inexplicably drawn to the killer. The killer is aware of this and grooms the victim to become his or her assistant. It's like Stockholm syndrome, only worse. Soon, the assistant begins actively helping the killer, finding victims and offering them up to the killer or even taking part in the murder itself."

"And you think that's what happened to Becca?" Shea asked. It was hard to tell whether she was dazed from blood loss, or if she was actually considering Hennie's suggestion.

"I think you watch too much TV," Corinne said.

Hennie shrugged. "Maybe we should tie her up, just to be safe."

At this, Becca's face crumpled and her eyes squeezed shut and her mouth contorted and she began to sob, wild, hysterical sobs so loud they might have summoned every murderer within a ten-mile radius.

"See? She's trying to draw Abigail to us," Hennie said, so taken with her own theory that she hardly seemed to care if this was indeed what was happening.

Becca opened her mouth and gasped through her tears, "No . . . I'm . . . not. I . . . just . . . I just . . . I'm homesick!"

Having said this, she dissolved into fresh and inconsolable tears.

Corinne and Shea descended upon her with hugs. They patted her back and smoothed her hair and whispered that it was okay. Becca tried to catch her breath, but it only gave her the hiccups, which, for some reason, made her cry all over again. Eventually, even Hennie relented and put her arms around Becca. Wallis told herself she didn't join in because someone needed to keep an eye on the woods, but in truth, Wallis had a horror of hugging or being hugged by people she didn't know very well.

"I just wanted people to like me and to make friends," Becca sobbed.

"We do like you, Becca," they cooed to her. "We are your friends."

"I want my mom! I want to go home!" Becca wailed.

Wallis scowled. *If we weren't lost in the woods together and being hunted by an insane murderer, they'd probably all be making fun of her right now.*

Eventually, Becca got it all out of her system. Her shoulders stopped heaving. She dried her eyes on her sleeves, caught her breath, and discovered that she had almost completely forgotten about Abigail. It was amazing what a good cry could do. It was so amazing, in fact, that she recommended it to the other girls, and as Wallis kept watch, one by one, the others took turns weeping loudly and bitterly for home, for their counselor Megan, for Oscar, for the things they'd seen, and for the inexorably horrible week they were all having. While it happened, Wallis sat away from the others, stony-faced, and then her heart filled with shame and self-pity because she realized that they'd all comforted Becca and she hadn't, and now the four of them sat together weeping and hugging, and she was left on the outside.

In the end, she cried about that.

When it was over, dawn was just beginning to break through the treetops, and they all felt remarkably strong, clear-headed, and ready to begin their journey anew.

Through the pale gray light, Shea thought she spied the trail. Cheered and determined, they set off in the direction she pointed, discussing their new plan.

Wallis had been right, they agreed. Abigail was weak and alone. There were five of them. Together they could take her. They would still go for help, but if they met up with Abigail on the way, they promised each other that they would not run. They would stand their ground and fight her.

"If I see Abigail, I'm going to punch her right in the face," Becca said, with more fire than they'd ever heard from her.

"I'LL SLAP HER WITH A PIECE OF BARBED WIRE," Shea said, back in full voice.

"I'll kick her in the teeth," Hennie said, once again all smiles.

They were all laughing when the net they'd just stepped into scooped them up, lifting them ten feet above the forest floor, where they swayed, a tangle of arms and legs.

Only Wallis remained below. Panicked, she screamed. Her eyes darted through the trees for any sign of motion, and then, not sure if she'd seen anything or not, she screamed some more.

"HELP US!" Shea said.

"Stop screaming, Wallis, and cut us down," Corinne shouted from inside the net.

Wallis looked up at the girls in the net. Her head jerked toward the sound of crackling leaves in one direction, then the sound of a twig snapping in another. The tree branches groaned overhead. They were surrounded—Wallis could feel it. The forest seemed to be closing in around her. In the distance, she could have sworn she heard footsteps approaching the clearing.

This time, though, Wallis couldn't see what was going to happen next. Not until the moment it happened. Not until the moment she did it.

The girls' pleading and curses died in her ears as she turned and ran into the forest.

CABIN 3

THE HERO'S QUEST

[SCENE: At the mouth of a cave and next to the carcass of a recently deceased beast, THE GIRL WITH THOUSANDS OF FRECKLES clings to life, and THE GIRL WITH BEADS IN HER HAIR clings to a raven.]

"Let go of me," said the raven whose name was Renata. "I can't breathe."

The girl with beads in her hair loosened her grip on the bird, who hopped to the ground and over to the spot where her body lay, the orange hoodie spattered with mud from the cave as well as with the beast's dark, murky blood. The body was still, the eyes open to reveal lifeless, black pools.

"I didn't set anyone free, did I?" Renata asked, her voice tremulous as she stared at the body that only a few minutes ago had been her.

The girl with beads in her hair shook her head.

"The beast?"

"Dead," said the girl with beads in her hair.

"And the others?"

The girl with beads in her hair felt her face crumple as she looked up from the ground and surveyed the scene. If there was a silver lining to having your friend turned into a raven by the contents of a supernatural cask, it was that it did distract you from your other problems.

"It's bad," she said at last, the only words she could squeeze out without crying.

She shone her flashlight over to the spot where the stick-like goth girl still lay motionless on the ground, bound up in the beast's webs. They could only hope she hadn't been bitten, too. Then she ran the light along the craggy rock wall until she found the girl with the upturned nose, her leg twisted underneath her at an unnatural angle. She'd stopped screaming and gone frighteningly silent.

And then there was the girl with thousands of freckles, who looked weaker and paler with each minute that the beast's venom coursed through her veins.

The girl with beads in her hair swallowed down the lump in her throat and balled her fists at her sides. She was the only one who could help them now, so she had to—even though she didn't know where to begin, even though it felt like every brave and capable thing about her had been sapped away by the last hour.

"Go to her." The girl with beads in her hair pointed Renata toward the girl with thousands of freckles. "Keep her talking. Keep her awake. See if you can think of anything we can do for her."

"What happened?" Renata asked, testing out her wings

before trusting them to carry her over to the spot where her cabinmate lay.

"That thing bit her," the girl with beads in her hair called out after her.

As Renata went to the girl with thousands of freckles, the girl with beads in her hair went to the sticklike goth girl and examined the thick webs that wound around her whole body like a skein of yarn. She had to cut her free before the girl suffocated, but the hatchet was no good for a job like that. Fortunately, the girl with beads in her hair saw a Swiss army knife on the ground nearby. One of the girls must have dropped it during their battle with the beast. She picked it up, wiped the gore from the blade as best as she could, and sliced the webs free from the sticklike goth girl's face. She could feel her breath—shallow—and her pulse—faint—and thus encouraged, the girl with beads in her hair continued to hack away at the webs until the sticklike goth girl was free. After a minute or two, her eyes fluttered open and the girl with beads in her hair helped her sit up.

"Can you stand?" she asked.

"I think so," said the sticklike goth girl. She was still wearing her backpack. The beast had struck so quickly, she hadn't had a chance to shuck it off. Now, she slid the straps off of her shoulders, brushed away the strands of sticky web, and unzipped the backpack's front pouch, producing a flashlight.

With help from the girl with beads in her hair, she rose, and together, they went to the girl with the upturned nose. She was propped up against a rock, sweat beaded on her forehead. The girl with beads in her hair noticed that the girl's lips had a bluish tinge.

"It's broken," said the girl with the upturned nose, shuddering as she pointed to her leg.

"How can you tell?" asked the sticklike goth girl.

"Because the bone's supposed to be on the inside."

The sticklike goth girl focused the beam of the flashlight on the leg, and when she saw what the girl was talking about, she ran off and was sick behind a boulder.

As gently as she could, the girl with beads in her hair helped the girl to lie down and then straightened the leg out in front of her. The girl with the upturned nose bit down on a belt to keep from screaming or biting off her tongue.

She was brave, but the girl with beads in her hair watched her shoulders quake and convulse, and she knew being brave wasn't enough. Her pulse fluttered like a hummingbird's; her breath was shallow. She turned a pale gray. The girl with the upturned nose was going into shock.

How did you treat shock? She tried to remember, but the only thing she could think of from her first-aid training was that you were supposed to get the person to a doctor. A fat lot of help that was now.

Keep them warm, she thought. *You're supposed to keep them warm.*

She ran over to the spot where Renata's human body had fallen and unzipped the orange hoodie. It wasn't like Renata needed it now. Still, as the girl with beads in her hair pulled Renata's arms out of the sleeves, she noticed that the body didn't seem to be dead like she'd originally feared. It was still warm and breathing, but that was all. The limbs were limp, the eyes still gaping open—no sign of life in them. No pupils, either. No whites. No irises. Nothing but solid black. It made the girl with beads in her hair shudder to look in them for very long.

She took the orange hoodie and ran back to the spot where the girl with the upturned nose rested. The sticklike goth girl had recovered from her queasy spell and now sat by the girl's side, clutching her hand.

"Can you stay with her?" asked the girl with beads in her hair, tucking the orange hoodie around the girl's chest and shoulders.

The sticklike goth girl nodded.

"I'll be right back," said the girl with beads in her hair. "Try to make her as comfortable as possible."

Then she got up and ran across the clearing again. A compound fracture was deadly serious, but it was the girl with thousands of freckles whose wound needed the most tending.

The raven was perched on a boulder near the girl's head, whispering soothing words in her ear. Her head slumped to one side, but as the girl with beads in her hair approached, she lifted it and said with as much strength as she could muster, "Can you carry me?"

The girl with beads in her hair felt her heart sink. She doubted she could carry even one of the girls out of the forest to safety, not even if the sticklike goth girl helped. Not without doing more harm than good.

"Not all the way. Just across the clearing," said the girl with thousands of freckles. She nodded toward the girl with the upturned nose. "That way she won't be alone."

When I go for help, thought the girl with beads in her hair, then looked over toward the sticklike goth girl. *When we go for help.* After what they'd seen, going anywhere alone in these woods was out of the question.

She slid one arm under the knees of the girl with thousands of freckles, the other behind her back, and hoisted the girl up in her arms. She carried her past the mouth of the cave to the other side of the rocky embankment and set her down next to the girl with the upturned nose, who was clutching her broken leg. Renata followed along behind them. She seemed to have gotten the hang of her wings already, gliding back to earth without even a stumble.

It was the witching hour by the time they'd done all of this. The injured rested, but they'd all resigned themselves to the fact that none of them would be sleeping that night.

"What do we do now?" asked the sticklike goth girl, once all five of them were together again.

"There's a nurse's station above the mess hall," said the girl with beads in her hair. "We should go see if they have a snakebite kit and a stretcher."

The sticklike goth girl nodded gravely.

"A phone, too," she said. "We have to get them out of here or . . ."

"I'll go, too," Renata said, interrupting that morbid thought with one of her own. "If something goes wrong, I can fly back here and let you know. No matter what happens, I'll come back. I promise. We won't leave you here."

"I know you won't," said the girl with thousands of freckles. She turned to the girl with beads in her hair and held out her hand. "But leave one of the hatchets."

The girl with beads in her hair handed it over, hoping her friend wouldn't have to use it.

"We'll come back for you," she said.

The girl with thousands of freckles managed a pained smile.

"You'd better."

And then they were three, setting off down the path toward safety and help.

Or were they? The girl with beads in her hair thought about the girls on horseback. Were they still out here, and what had they been running from? If the girls from Cabin 3 had met a beast in the middle of a well-maintained pony trail, maybe the rest of Camp So-and-So was no safer.

According to the map, if they continued on the pony trail, it would spit them out of the woods near the meadow and not far from the mess hall and the nurse's station. However, when they were half a mile past the cave, the trail became overgrown and gnarled with roots. They picked their way along, mindful of snakes and other perils with each step. At first, Renata flew ahead of them acting as a lookout, but eventually, they realized they felt safer traveling close together.

"Are you all right?" the girl with beads in her hair asked the raven. She felt strange asking, but it seemed like someone ought to. On the one hand, Renata was the same as she'd ever been, so wholly herself that you could almost forget she had turned into a raven.

And then on the other hand, she'd turned into a raven.

"I'm okay," Renata said after thinking about it for a minute. "Better than okay, actually. I just think about what happened to the other girls, and I guess I feel like I got off lucky."

"Broken legs heal," said the girl with beads in her hair, frowning. "What if this isn't like that?"

"That's the thing," Renata said, stretching her wings. "I don't mind that much."

Before the girl with beads in her hair had a chance to consider what she might have meant, they came upon a pile of foliage that seemed not to belong in the middle of the trail. When they cleared away the brush, they uncovered a pit ten feet deep and a yard across.

It was unsettling to find a thing like that without knowing who had dug it and for what purpose. It was hard not to take a thing like that personally. They dragged the branches and leaves that had been used to conceal the pit away from the trail so that it was perfectly visible to anyone who might come that way. At least the girls on horseback seemed to have avoided it, though the girl with beads in her hair couldn't help but wonder how.

Between the cave and the road, they sniffed out other lures and traps and tripwires strung across the path. They were primitive, but abundant, and suggested a hunter whose appetite for prey was limitless. They walked (or flew) with their weapons (or talons) drawn, their eyes searching the trees for any sign of movement, scanning the ground for any lurking holes.

Another thought nagged at the girl with beads in her hair. "Where did Robin go?" she asked.

They compared notes and agreed that none of them had seen the counselor-in-training after the beast first attacked.

"It was like she just vanished," said the sticklike goth girl.

Renata cocked her head to the side. "Abandoned us, is more like it."

They hiked mile after mile until finally, small patches of sunshine began to shine through the thinning trees, and they permitted themselves a quiet cheer. There was little cause for celebration, though, as they walked into the meadow. They might have made it through the night and out of the woods, but none of them had slept or eaten a proper meal, and none of them knew if it was too late to save the girl with thousands of freckles from the venom in her veins.

And so, as they walked through the meadow back toward the place where they'd started, it was with heavy hearts and troubled minds. When they'd first found the prophecy, they'd only seen the glory in it, thought the girl with beads in her hair.

But know the path you walk is thick with traps
All custom-made to hasten your collapse.

They'd ignored its more menacing parts, and so far, all of those things had been accurate. There had been a beast. There had been traps. If they'd known the quest was going to turn out like this, would they ever have agreed to go?

What they found in the mess hall turned the doubts of the girl with beads in her hair to something far more urgent. The nurse's station had been ransacked, the cabinets emptied of everything except for two rolls of gauze and a tube of baby aspirin. The phones were dead, the power was out, and the kitchen was barely stocked. The oddest thing of all was that they did not see a single soul there, neither campers nor staff. The trip was not wholly fruitless, as they found and took a wheelbarrow from behind the mess hall before starting back toward the forest. They were returning without medicine (unless you counted the gauze and baby aspirin), without help, without anything but a dirt-crusted wheelbarrow to transport two gravely wounded girls from the forest.

The darkest possibilities of this escaped none of them.

So troubled were their thoughts as they walked that they almost failed to see the enormous black horse that appeared on the road before them. It was unsaddled and wore around its neck a small, glowing crystal vial on a cord. As soon as it spotted them, the horse whinnied and stamped its hooves. It shook its head so the crystal vial swung from side to side, and they could not help but notice it. Once the horse was sure it had gotten their attention, it raced across the meadow.

The girls and the raven exchanged glances.

"Is it just me, or do you think we're supposed to follow that horse?" asked the sticklike goth girl.

They abandoned the wheelbarrow by the side of the road and took off after the horse, following its crashing path through the meadow until it ended abruptly at Lake So-and-So. The horse stood on the gravelly shore as though it had been waiting to greet them there. It strode up to the girl with beads in her hair until it was close enough to nudge her shoulder with its nose. The girl with beads in her hair smiled, and it nudged her again. Then it dropped its majestic head low so the vial dangled loosely from its neck.

"Should I take it?" asked the girl with beads in her hair.

The horse knelt on one foreleg and nudged the girl with beads in her hair again, snuffling into her hand.

The same thought occurred to all of them: that perhaps the contents of the vial were an antidote to the venom now coursing through their friend's body. It seemed possible. The way things had gone so far, it seemed almost likely.

Of course, it seemed equally likely that the whole thing was a trap, though the girl with beads in her hair couldn't see how. If the vial didn't contain an antidote, what could it possibly do? Poison their friend *more*? And as closely as she scanned the shoreline, the girl with beads in her hair could see no tripwires, snares, or triggers. There wasn't so much as a shrub where an assailant could hide and wait to strike. If it was a trap, the girl with beads in her hair decided, she would have to risk it. For her friend's sake. And because they were otherwise out of choices. She gave a little bow in return, then put her hands around the horse's neck to slip the vial over its head.

What happened next happened in an instant.

The horse lifted its head and with enormous strength, shook its great neck and slung the girl with beads in her hair onto its back. She struggled to get off, but she was stuck—her hands were so tangled in the horse's mane, she might as well have been tied to the creature's back. When the horse reared up, Renata and the sticklike goth girl saw that its eyes had turned red as hot coals. They screamed as it galloped out into the lake, diving beneath the surface, the girl with beads in her hair still clinging to its back.

Renata flew back and forth along the shoreline, hoping that the horse and her friend would resurface. The sticklike goth girl, though, did not wait. She unlaced her boots and plunged into the lake after them. As she disappeared beneath the surface, Renata stopped hoping and began to count. Thirty seconds passed. A minute. A minute and a half passed, but there was still no sign of the sticklike goth girl. Renata trembled, and she thought about having to return to the cave to tell her friends that there was no help coming, that everyone else was dead.

Before she could begin to think about what she would do

if the worst happened, she heard a splash from the center of the lake, and a plume of water arched through the air, bearing a tangle of arms, legs, hooves, and hair. It cannonballed back toward the water, then shot up again twenty yards closer to shore. This time, in the foam, Renata could see the horse with its flared nostrils and wild, red eyes. The sticklike goth girl sat astride the beast, one hand clutching its mane, the other wrapped around the waist of the girl with beads in her hair. Again, they plunged into the water, disappearing for such a long time that the riot of bubbles rising to the surface slowed to a weak protest.

Then all three of them hurtled to the surface again, this time galloping up onto the shore. The sticklike goth girl's hair was dripping and knotted with water weeds. Yet she sat triumphant upon the back of the horse, which had stopped trying to twist away from her grasp and now lowered its head and whinnied meekly.

The sticklike goth girl leapt down and pulled the girl with beads in her hair from the horse's back, stretching her out on the rocky strip of beach. She listened for breath, and finding none, pinched the girl's nose closed and began to perform mouth-to-mouth resuscitation. After a tense minute, the girl with beads in her hair coughed, tilted her head to the side, and choked up a stream of water.

Then the sticklike goth girl got to her feet and glared at the animal.

"You could have killed us," she said.

"Then you should feel lucky that I didn't," said the horse.

None of them was terribly shocked that the horse spoke. It was the animal's candor that surprised them.

The sticklike goth girl wrung out a hank of her hair, and began to pick out the water weeds. "What kind of horse are you anyway?"

The horse reared up, kicking its forelegs inches from the sticklike goth girl's head. She gasped and stumbled backwards, landing hard in the stony sand.

"Idiot girl," it said, towering over her. "Do you really take me for a common horse?"

She scrambled to sit up and raised her arms over her face to shield it. "I beg your pardon," she said, then added, "What are you really, then?"

The horse—for that is exactly what it resembled, and excepting its remarkable underwater feats and murderous tendencies, that is what any person who saw it standing on the shore would take it for—seemed placated by the girl's apology, and put its forelegs down.

"I am the last of the proud and ancient race of kelpie. For five hundred years I have lured wretched humans onto my back and dragged them to the depths of this lake, and in all that time, not one has ever survived." The kelpie hung its head until its muzzle touched the ground. "Today is a sad and shameful day for the kelpie. Bested by a human. Worse, by an idiot girl who cannot even tell me from a horse."

Caught up in its mournful soliloquy, the kelpie did not notice the looks the girls from Cabin 3 exchanged.

At last, Renata spoke. "Forgive us, noble kelpie. Our ignorance blinded us to your true nature. We did not see you for what you were, for we did not know to look."

"Now that your majesty is revealed to us, O impressive beast, I curse mine own eyes for failing to see it from the first," the sticklike goth girl chimed in. "Your coat gleams like onyx polished by the sun's own rays."

"Your eyes could burn a thousand villages," said the girl with beads in her hair, coughing up another stream of lake water from her lungs as she sat up.

"And how great your wisdom that you chose to spare us so that we might complete our quest and save this land from ruin, chaos, and darkness," said the sticklike goth girl.

The kelpie snorted with disdain, but it also stopped visibly sulking.

"Tell me, girls, what has brought you to my shores? What is it that you seek?"

They described the quest they'd set out on, and the beast in the cave, and the prophecy, and the one they were supposed to free, and what had become of their other friends. With every syllable, the kelpie grew more agitated and began to pace on the rocks. When they finished, it gave a long, low whinny.

"I fear any advice I can give will be unequal to the task before you. When first you beheld me, all you saw was a horse. All I see before me now is a pack of fools. Have you even the slightest idea who sent you out on this quest? No, you do not. You found a message written on your ceiling, and that was all the encouragement you required. Has it not occurred to you that your entire quest might be in service to some dark and wicked cause?"

Cabin 3 murmured amongst themselves, admitting that they had no assurance the message in their cabin was sent by someone or something that wished them well.

"But what about the beast?" asked the girl with beads in her hair. "It was definitely evil. It nearly killed us all."

"I also nearly killed you all. Do you think me evil?" asked the kelpie.

The simple answer to this was "yes," but none of the girls dared say that to the kelpie. Besides, it was more complicated than that. Five hundred years of self-admitted human drowning aside, the kelpie was as good as its word. Since the sticklike goth girl had bested it, the creature had not so much as nipped at them. In fact, it seemed inclined to help them. What remained to be seen was whether or not the kelpie's advice could be believed.

The girl with beads in her hair thought about the lines from the prophecy:

Beware! The Knave who only speaks in lies!

Beware! The Knight who plots out your demise!

"It depends," said the girl with beads in her hair. "Are you telling us the truth?"

The kelpie's eyes danced. "Are you a fan of puzzles?"

The girl with beads in her hair nodded.

"Do you know how to play Knights and Knaves?"

"I've heard of it," said the girl with beads in her hair. It was an old riddle about a shipwrecked sailor who finds himself on an island of knights who can only tell the truth and knaves who can only lie. In the riddle, the sailor comes upon two paths, one that leads to certain death, the other to safety, and each one is guarded by a man.

"Then I propose a game. You may ask me three questions, and if you are able to guess correctly whether I am the knight or the knave, I will give you the vial around my neck."

"And if we don't?" asked the sticklike goth girl.

The kelpie gave her a filthy look. "Then I will take you for another ride on my back."

The girl with beads in her hair tried to remember the trick to this logic puzzle. There was some question you could ask that would reveal which man was the knave and which was the knight. "Will whatever is in the vial around your neck save our friend?" blurted the sticklike goth girl.

The kelpie polished off the lake weeds that the sticklike goth girl had pulled from her hair and began to graze on the spindly bulrushes at the water's edge. Only after it had cleared a section the size of a beach towel did it answer the girl's question.

"In truth, child, the vial is as likely to contain a curse as a cure. But if you like, I could tell you where Robin fled after she gave it to me, or the name of the soul who delivered that prophecy to your cabin."

That didn't help, thought the girl with beads in her hair. In fact, their first question to the kelpie had only confused the matter more. Now there were options to consider that they hadn't even known existed. Proof that the counselor-in-training was involved in all of this. Information about who sent them on the quest in the first place.

But only if the kelpie actually knew those things.

Knights can only tell the truth. Knaves can only lie.

The girl with beads in her hair combed through the recesses of her brain, trying to think of the question she could ask the kelpie that would reveal it as a truth-teller or a liar. A simple question would be best. Something direct, something the kelpie could only answer with yes or no.

"If I knew what was in that vial, would I give it to my friend?" Now it was Renata who spoke up to ask the kelpie a question. The girl with beads in her hair let out a quiet groan. Once again, it was the wrong question.

"No, you would not," said the kelpie.

The kelpie could still be the knight: the vial could be filled with rat poison or hydrochloric acid, and its answer could be the truth. Renata and the sticklike goth girl exchanged nervous glances and looked to the girl with beads in her hair. She was their last chance.

There was one way through this that the girl with beads in her hair could see, and that was to ask a question she already knew the answer to. She laughed bitterly to herself as she thought about the prophecy, the beast, who'd sent them on this quest, why her friend had been turned into a raven.

She didn't have any answers. There was nothing she knew that would help her now.

Except for one thing.

The girl with beads in her hair lowered her eyes modestly. "I know a little bit about kelpies," she said.

"Oh, do you?" asked the kelpie, giving a little chuckle.

"I know you usually take the form of a horse. You tend to crop up in the Scottish stories." The girl with beads in her hair had read every book of fairy tales, folklore, and mythology in the library at least twice. She closed her eyes and thought about those books now, how the pages were yellow and water-stained and so brittle they threatened to disintegrate in her fingers when she turned them.

"Luring people onto your back, then drowning them? That part always happens, but you've been known to mix things up. Sometimes you devour the people you've drowned, and let their entrails drift back to shore. Sometimes you're a demon. In some of the stories, a bold fool will try to capture you and harness your powers, and you lay curses on their heads."

At first, the kelpie looked proud as the girl with beads in her hair listed off these stories, but then annoyance flickered across its face.

"What are you driving at, girl?"

That was when the girl with beads in her hair knew the question she was about to ask was the right one. "Since when do you go around asking riddles?"

The kelpie looked away and, after a long moment, muttered, "Since always. Kelpies are great lovers of puzzles."

The girl with beads in her hair tried to keep a neutral face as she thought about all the lies and half-truths that the kelpie had told them: that they should feel lucky it hadn't killed them; that their quest might be in service to an evil cause; that the vial around its neck would not save their friend's life.

"You're the knave," said the girl with beads in her hair.

The implications of the prophecy dawned on the others as well.

"You said you'd give us the vial if we guessed correctly," said the sticklike goth girl.

The kelpie tossed back its head and laughed.

"Oh," said the sticklike goth girl. "That part was a lie, too."

Still laughing, the kelpie turned and started to walk back into the lake. "Of course, you're welcome to take it from me, if any of you fancies another ride on my back."

"Give us the vial," said Renata, perched on the sticklike goth girl's shoulder.

"I owe you nothing," said the kelpie.

The two girls and one raven from Cabin 3 exchanged a wordless glance. Their friend's life was at stake. They'd tamed the kelpie, then answered its riddles. They'd beaten it fair and square. The idea that it owed them nothing at this point was the biggest lie it had told yet.

At once, all three of them were swarming around the kelpie.

"If there's one thing we know, it's how these stories work," said the girl with beads in her hair, standing between the kelpie and the lake with her arms outstretched. "And if you're the knave, and everything you say is a lie, and you say you owe us nothing . . ."

"Drop it on the ground, or I will peck your eyes out," said Renata.

"No funny stuff," added the sticklike goth girl, linking arms with the girl with beads in her hair.

"You owe us," said the girl with beads in her hair.

The kelpie rolled its eyes, but lowered its head so the cord slipped off of its neck and the vial fell into the sand with a plop. When it had done this, the kelpie waded into the water up to its haunches before it turned around and said, "This is why I always drown the humans I meet. So I don't have to talk to them."

With that, the kelpie snorted out a laugh, then lowered its head beneath the lake's surface and disappeared.

The girl with beads in her hair picked up the vial and inspected it. She had no idea what it was, but she hoped it would save her friend's life.

"Let's go," she said to the others, starting back across the meadow toward the pony trail in the woods that would lead them back to their friends. From a distance, she could see the wheelbarrow by the side of the road where they'd left it.

The two fell in line behind her, Renata fluttering overhead, but when they reached the road, the sticklike goth girl's face was troubled.

"All of us?" she asked.

"Where else would we go?" asked the girl with beads in her hair.

"What about the quest?"

The girl with beads in her hair stared incredulously at her cabinmate. "Who cares about the quest now?" she asked. Even if the antidote worked, they'd still have to wheel the girl with the upturned nose, with the broken leg, down the long, unnecessarily winding road until they reached help, civilization, or cell phone reception, whichever came first.

"I don't think we really have a choice about it," said the sticklike goth girl.

The girl with beads in her hair looked to Renata for help. The raven landed on a fence post, pecked a grub from the rotting wood, and nodded. "She's right."

"That's insane," said the girl with beads in her hair.

Renata took flight from her perch on the fence post, landing at the feet of the girl with beads in her hair.

"You can turn back if you want to. You can quit, you can leave, you can do whatever you want to do. But look at me," Renata said, spreading her wings and looking down at her feathered body. "I can't."

"Maybe there was a moment when we could have turned back, but it's long past now," said the sticklike goth girl.

Renata cawed and recited the prophecy they'd found in their cabin. "*Beware! For you will lose before it's done! First five, then four, then three, then two, then one.*"

The sticklike goth girl reached out her hand and took the vial from the girl with beads in her hair.

"This is where I go," she said.

"That's ridiculous," said the girl with beads in her hair. "We'll go back to the cave together and see if the antidote even works. We'll go to the hospital, and then after that, we can come back here and continue the quest."

The sticklike goth girl had tears in her eyes as she put her arms around the girl with beads in her hair.

"I don't think so," she said, hugging her good-bye.

Suddenly, a strange gust of wind blew down from the north. They turned toward it just in time to hear a sound like a wave crashing and to see a column of fire erupt from the treetops just past the mess hall.

"Our cabins," said Renata.

"We have to go help," said the girl with beads in her hair.

But when she turned around, only Renata was there, flapping her wings to steady herself against the foul-smelling wind.

The wheelbarrow, the antidote, and the sticklike goth girl were gone, and the girl with beads in her hair knew she could run toward the cave or the fire, but she couldn't do both.

INTERMISSION

At the end of a hallway in a wing of the Inge F. Yancey Young Executives Leadership Camp that was forbidden to most, Robin stood in front of a dressing room door. She didn't have time for the usual niceties that generally accompanied a visit like this one.

Typically, she would knock and be told to go away. She would apologize and attempt to justify the necessity of her interruption. She would grovel and beg until she was admitted to the room, where she would find Tania sitting at her vanity, arranging her hair. She would be in an ill temper and, before Robin could get a word in edgewise, would subject her to a long treatise about how she suffered and toiled and was surrounded by idiots. Following her humiliation in the All-Camp Sport & Follies, Robin knew she could expect this to go on even longer than usual.

So she did not knock. Instead, she cupped her hand to the door and shouted, "Tania, Cabin 5 is on fire."

From inside, there was a long pause, followed by the sound of a glass being smashed.

"Let them burn."

"But two of the campers from Cabin 3 are heading toward the fire."

"If they're that idiotic, they *deserve* to burn."

It was worse than Robin had feared. She should have done a better job checking the girls for contraband, but honestly, Dora was the last one she would have suspected of smuggling in that steel pocket watch. If she hadn't been spread quite so thin, it might have occurred to her to cancel the feast honoring Cabin 1 in the wake of their second victory in the All-Camp Sport & Follies. Robin knew how much Tania hated a fair fight, and feared that in her boss's current mood, the girls from Cabin 1 might not be altogether safe at the feast.

Not that it would come as any great shock to her, the way things were going so far this summer. Ordinarily, her productions ran like well-oiled Rube Goldberg machines, like gorgeous little jewel boxes with all the surprises on the inside. This year, though, things kept getting away from her. Damage she should have been able to curb raged unabated. Maybe she was slipping. In any case, it couldn't hurt to remind Tania of the rules.

"Tania, these girls are under your protection," she said.

From behind the door, Robin heard Tania let out a snort.

"Tell it to Inge F. Yancey IV. It's his name on the letterhead, not mine," she said.

CABIN 4

SOUL MATES

[SCENE: Out from under the watchful eye of Pam, VERITY, ADDISON, ANNIKA, ALIX, and AMBER venture into the woods in search of their soul mates.]

Together, they crept around to the back of the cabin where the trail started, and just as it had before, the mysterious force tugged at them and drew them into the dense woods.

While Amber and Alix carried on an effervescent flurry of conversation as they walked, and Annika listened graciously, chiming in every now and again, Verity noticed that Addison wasn't paying the slightest bit of attention to any of them. She'd pulled ahead of the group, but even from a distance, Verity could see that something was wrong. Once again, she looked awful, like she'd had the flu for a week. Rivulets of sweat ran down her face and neck, and her eyes looked sunken and dark.

"Are you okay?" Verity asked, trotting ahead to catch up with her.

"Fine," Addison muttered.

She took something out of the back pocket of her shorts, and in a flash, her eyes brightened, her cheeks flushed, and the sweat dried from her brow.

"Okay, what was that?" Verity asked.

Addison feigned wide-eyed ignorance. "What was what?"

"You know what. I saw you do the same thing last night outside the latrine. You've been doing it all afternoon in the cabin. One minute you look like you're going to die, the next minute you pull something out of your pocket and you're fine. So tell me, what's going on?"

"Nothing's going on."

Ordinarily, Verity wouldn't have pushed the matter, not with someone she barely knew, especially not with someone who radiated popularity like Addison did. But Verity worried that if she didn't speak up now, something truly terrible might happen.

Magic was a curious thing, and Verity was sure that it was at least partly responsible for what had been happening to them. She didn't like admitting it to herself because it sounded crazy, but Pam was gone, the camp was deserted, something was wrong with Addison, and they were currently following an invisible current through the woods to find their soul mates, who had no business being there. There was no other explanation Verity could think of that made sense.

Of course, if that was the truth, what were they supposed to do about it? In Isis Archimedes, magic was always a thing that had to be acknowledged. It wasn't a thing to be played with or controlled, and it certainly wasn't a thing to be ignored. The best you could hope for was to understand it, and pray it didn't lay waste to you.

She took Addison by the arm.

"What do you have in your hand?" she asked.

Addison yelped like she'd been burned and wrenched free from Verity's grasp. As she did, Verity saw a button pop out of her hand, land on the path, and bounce into the underbrush. At once, Addison fell to her knees and began combing through the brush without regard for any poisonous spiders, snakes, or thorns she might find there.

"No, no, no, no, no, no, no," she said, tossing handfuls of dead leaves over her shoulders. "Where is it? Where did it go?"

Verity dropped down next to her on the path.

"I'll help you look," she said, reaching into the brush.

Addison slapped her hand away and shouted, "No!"

"I'm sorry," Verity said, clutching her stinging knuckles. "I didn't mean to make you drop it."

Addison sat down on the path, suddenly looking exhausted. She leaned back on her elbows, then actually lay down flat on her back right there in the dirt.

"It's not that," Addison said, her voice scarcely a whisper. "If you see it, don't pick it up. Don't even touch it."

It was then that Verity realized Annika, Alix, and Amber should have caught up with them by now. She looked back the way they'd come, but the path was perfectly empty. She called out to them, but the woods were perfectly silent. It was as if the other three girls had been lifted right off the path.

A Note from the Narrator: It is perhaps more accurate to say they had been diverted by the stagehands.

This was bad. This was very bad. Verity closed her eyes and allowed herself a pointless moment of wishing that they'd all gone to town in the truck with Pam, but that being off the table, she set about the business of getting Addison upright. Verity pulled her up to a sitting position, then dragged her to her feet.

"Come on," Verity said. "We're going back. We're going to find them."

The woods were different now. The invisible, magnetic current that had ushered them along was gone, and without it, the path seemed less distinct. Verity looked ahead and saw a mossy boulder she felt sure they'd already passed. She looked back the way they had come and saw nothing she recognized. It was as though someone had swept in while she and Addison were distracted by their search for the button and moved all the identifying landmarks around.

Even the path itself had changed. It was treacherous in a way it hadn't been before, paved with slippery stones and gnarled roots at every step. And on top of everything else, now it was dark.

Verity and Addison linked elbows and shuffled their feet along the path like elderly widows on an icy sidewalk. Careful though they were, after a few minutes, Addison tripped on a rock and fell to the ground, clutching her scraped shin.

"Are you all right?" Verity asked.

"I think so," Addison said. "Can we just sit and rest for a second?"

She seemed smaller now, frail and fragile. Verity felt slightly guilty for wishing that it was capable, matter-of-fact Annika she was out here with. Or even Alix or Amber, whose exuberance and giggly good cheer would have at least

202

distracted her. Being with Addison only served to remind her how dangerous and foolhardy this whole adventure was, and that if anything went wrong, she would be on her own and far from anyone who could help her.

Addison seemed to sense Verity's disappointment because she held out her hand and said, "Help me up. I'm ready," even though Verity saw her wince as she stood.

"We can rest a little bit longer if you need to," Verity said.

"No, let's keep going."

They trudged forward, slower now, and whispering as they went.

"The button fell off my soul mate's shirt when we were in the woods yesterday. Ever since I picked it up, this has been happening to me," Addison confessed.

She was sweating again now, and Verity had to stop every few minutes so Addison could rest.

"Who do you think they are?" Verity asked.

"Our soul mates?"

"Do you think they're real?"

"It feels real," Addison said with a shiver.

"It feels real to me, too."

Verity realized that they could have been anywhere now, and if they didn't find a way back to their cabin soon, they'd be lost in the woods after dark. She watched Addison, who was leaning against a downed, moss-covered tree, her arms clutched tightly to her chest. Suddenly, though, she loosened her grip and looked up, and her eyes fixed on something across the clearing.

"It's glowing," Addison whispered. "Can't you see it? It's so beautiful."

"What are you talking about?"

"Their whole cabin is glowing."

Even before Verity's hand came to rest on Addison's forehead, she could feel the heat radiating from it.

"Come on, let's go back," Verity said. "You're burning up."

Addison jerked away from her. "I've never felt better."

Verity squinted but still couldn't see the cabin. Yet Addison staggered to her feet and limped into the clearing.

"Addison, wait!" she called after her, but Addison acted like she hadn't heard. Without thinking, Verity got up and ran after her. Even with her injured leg, Addison navigated the rough and uneven terrain easily, while Verity lost her balance more than once.

"There you are," Addison said, when Verity finally caught up. "Now do you see it?"

Verity looked where Addison pointed and gasped. The cabin wasn't there, and then, it was—just as Addison had said. A soft, golden light emanated from its walls, and when Verity saw it, it was like walking up the driveway to her house after the last day of school before Christmas break, or like the smell of coffee and the tinkle of bells that greeted her when she walked through the door of her favorite bookshop back home.

Verity gulped down deep breaths until the lump in her throat disappeared and the tight feeling in her chest subsided. Then the boy appeared in the door.

It was the same boy they'd seen the day before, the one who had gathered the firewood. He had sun-bleached hair that was probably brown in the wintertime and eyes that were two different colors—one blue, one hazel. Or at least that's what he looked like to Verity. Whatever it was that Addison saw must have been to her liking, though. Her upturned face was bathed in light from the cabin, and she was smiling.

"Hi," she said. "I'm Addison."

"My name's Tad," the boy said.

What kind of stupid name is Tad? Verity thought, her face twisting into a scowl that she instantly regretted.

Because then, there she was.

She appeared in the doorway next to Tad and squinted out at them.

"Who are you talking to?" she asked. Her voice was a silky alto, rounded at the edges, and Verity loved it at once.

"Two of the girls from the other camp," Tad said. "Addison and . . ."

"Verity," she squeaked, her eyes flitting nervously from Addison to Tad to the girl. Verity was too embarrassed to make eye contact with her, but unable to stop looking at her either.

The girl laughed. "You mean you can see us?"

"Uh huh," Verity said, the syllables barely squeezed out before her throat closed up altogether.

The girl smiled. "Do you know how long it's been since anyone saw me? Other than these jackasses, I mean."

Still unable to form words, Verity shook her head, an idiotic grin pasted across her face.

"You don't talk much, do you?" she said. "That would be just my luck. I haven't seen anyone new in a year, and when I do, she doesn't talk."

Just then, out of the corner of her eye, Verity noticed Addison.

One year, Verity had sung in the middle school chorus, and their director had insisted on rehearsing for an entire morning to prepare for the annual holiday concert. After two hours of being packed on the risers like lunch meat in a warm deli case, the girl next to Verity had gone gray in the face and passed out cold, taking Verity down with her. Verity had split her lip open and couldn't sing with her stitches, so she had missed the concert and had spent three months in tri-weekly choral practice for nothing. Even after all this time, the memory rankled.

On the bright side, at least now she recognized the telltale signs. So when Addison's knees buckled underneath her, Verity tore her gaze away from the beautiful girl's face in time, and caught Addison under the arms.

"Help me," she said, struggling under Addison's dead weight.

Tad ran down the cabin steps and helped Verity lay Addison down. He peeled off his camp sweatshirt, folded it neatly, and tucked it underneath Addison's head.

"She's burning up," he said, smoothing back the damp strands of hair that stuck to Addison's forehead. Had she been conscious, Addison would have perished from delight.

"We should get her back to the cabin," Verity said.

"No, we need to take her inside now," Tad said. "Erin, she's been marked. I have no idea how she walked all the way here like this."

Erin. Her name was Erin.

The girl knelt by Addison's side and gasped when she touched Addison's face. Verity did, too. The fever had spiked, and now Addison seemed to be approaching temperatures that only existed on thermometers for meat, not humans.

"Can you help her?" Verity asked.

"We can," Erin said, "but—"

"Erin," Tad said, his voice filled with worry and warning.

"She should know," Erin said.

"We have to take her inside," Tad said. "She's been marked. She's one of us now."

"What do you mean 'one of you'?" Verity asked, clutching Addison protectively to her chest. "What do you mean 'marked'?"

"We used to be campers here," the girl said. "Now we're Tania's prisoners."

Tad gave her a look that made Erin correct herself with a sigh.

"Guests, I mean. Guests who can never leave."

Addison's skin was so hot to the touch now that Verity could no longer hold onto her.

Tad knelt by Addison's side and felt her wrist for a pulse. "Erin, we don't have time for this now. We have to get her inside. It's getting worse."

The beautiful girl met Verity's eyes, waiting for instructions, but all Verity could say was, "Prisoners?"

Tad nodded impatiently. "What do you want us to do?"

"What happens if I won't let you take her?"

Tad didn't hesitate. "She'll waste away and die, probably in the next few minutes."

Verity would never have believed him if she hadn't seen Erin nod, seconding his implausible, impossible words.

"And if you do take her—is she going to be okay?" she asked feebly, her chin wobbling.

"We'll take care of her," Tad said.

It was no choice at all, though Verity acknowledged that she was taking a good deal on faith. Tad picked Addison up in his firewood-hauling arms and carried her inside the glowing cabin. Verity looked after them, but beyond the cabin walls everything disappeared in a golden haze.

"You did the right thing," Erin said, putting her arm around Verity's shoulder.

"What happens now? When will she get better? Should I wait for her?" Her voice shook when she spoke.

"Verity."

The sound of her own name on the girl's lips was like a soothing balm.

Then she spoke again.

"She's gone."

CABIN 5

SURVIVAL

*[SCENE: Inside the flaming ring of brambles, the girls of
Cabin 5 fight for their lives.]*

The brambles resisted their efforts to climb over them or dig
under them, or to tunnel through them, but in the end, they
could not resist fire.

One girl, a birdwatching enthusiast, took out the binoculars she'd smuggled into camp. Surely it was a mistake, she'd
thought, that binoculars were included on the contraband list,
and she'd felt no compunction about hiding them inside her
sleeping bag. Now, she was glad she'd done so. She disassem-
bled the binoculars and polished the lenses, then bit her lip and
focused a ray of sunshine through them.

As she watched a puff of smoke rise up from the thorns,
she thought that this was how Archimedes must have felt as
his burning glasses reflected the sun's rays and incinerated the
Roman fleet as they approached Syracuse.

But what she felt a moment later, as the entire wall went up in a sheet of flames, as the smoke engulfed them, as the blistering heat closed in around them and the sky was blotted out, I could not say.

A NOTE FROM THE NARRATOR

It is difficult not to marvel at the advances in changeling technology in recent years. The brutalities you tend to read about in fairy stories—infants switched in their cribs for hobgoblins and that sort of thing—have been happily relegated to the past. So primitive. It is hard to believe that anyone ever got away with it, that anyone ever fell for it. And really, it was only ever possible with infants who were still in that most unformed and blob-like of stages.

Today, what is done is much different. When a creature like Tania takes a liking to a human, she might decide to keep that human for herself. One basic principle from the old days does remain, however. You have to send something back. Otherwise, there would be an outcry.

Unlike the old days, it's now possible to work with humans of any age. Tania can send back the same girl who'd gone to Camp So-and-So—or most of her, anyway.

The girl would look the same, sound the same. She'd mostly even be the same. It is possible to slice out a representative strata of personality, disposition, likes, and dislikes so that you ended up with two almost identical people.

And if you didn't get the proportions completely right (and you never did), well, people changed. Concerned families were liable to chalk it up to hormones, the influence of new experiences and new friends, and the like.

The best thing was, when someone Tania had adopted angered her or began to bore her, it was easy enough to dispatch him or her because there was a perfectly adequate copy back in the human world. Tania had been at it for decades now, and she had never been caught. No one ever noticed.

My knowledge of this secret procedure might lead you to believe that I am complicit in the creation of these changelings, or that I somehow condone it, but nothing could be further from the truth.

I come by this information honestly.

My hands are clean.

All that I know, I know firsthand.

CABIN 1

THE ALL-CAMP SPORT & FOLLIES

*[SCENE: Inside a windmill at the Inge F. Yancey Young Executives
Leadership Camp, KADIE has walloped CRESSIDA with a shovel,
and CRESSIDA has revealed to KADIE a shocking truth.]*

"Of course I was at camp last summer," Kadie said. "I remember it."

But even as she spoke the words, she knew they were both true and not true. The faces of last year's cabinmates, the prime rib at the Welcome Campers dinner, the counselor who taught them show tunes and how to modulate their vibrato—all of it turned to smoke. It was like a spell had been broken, and Kadie knew that none of those memories was real.

"If I wasn't here, then how do I remember it?" she asked, a tremor in her voice. "And how do you know I wasn't?"

Cressida, who had by this time recovered from being hit in the leg with a shovel, pulled herself up and knelt beside Kadie.

"This place isn't what it seems," she said.

It occurred to Kadie that Cressida was perhaps responsible for this, that her cabinmate was both a spy and a witch.

Inching away from Cressida, she said, "I don't know who you are or what you're up to, but stop messing with me. This isn't funny."

"I'm not trying to be funny," Cressida said. The sunlight that shone through the narrow windows of the windmill lit up her frizzy hair from behind so that she resembled a dandelion on fire.

"I know you weren't here last year because my best friend was. I was supposed to come, too, but at the last minute I broke my arm and Erin had to go by herself. She felt bad that I couldn't be there with her, so she promised to write me letters and tell me *everything* that happened. And she did. She told me about all the people in her cabin and the food and the counselors. She told me about the Inge F. Yancey Young Executives Leadership Camp and the stupid All-Camp Sport & Follies. She was right there in the thick of all of this, and you know what? She never mentioned you once."

A Note from the Narrator: As it tended to lead to panic and misunderstandings, letter-writing was discouraged at Camp So-and-So. However, since to ban it outright would have attracted suspicion, the camp directors simply allowed no time for it, provided no paper or stamps, and when asked, feigned ignorance about when or where mail was picked up. Cressida's friend, Erin, was inordinately persistent to have managed to get not just one letter out, but several.

"When camp was over and Erin came back, though, she was a completely different person. She wore different clothes, listened to different music, and hung out with different people, and the weird thing was, nobody else seemed to notice it at all."

Kadie twisted her lips into a skeptical little bow. "People *change*, Cressida. Especially over the summer."

"I *know* people change, Kadie. But this was different."

Kadie folded her arms across her chest and glared down at Cressida. "Because she used to be your super-special best friend, and then all of a sudden she wasn't? *That's* what this is all about?"

Cressida reached into the pocket of her shorts and pulled out an envelope that had grown almost silken from being unfolded and refolded so many times. The handwriting on the outside was looping and threadlike, with letters that looked as though they should have vines growing off of them.

"No, because she wrote me this."

Kadie took the letter from Cressida's hand and read it, whispering the words aloud.

"*If you get this letter, then you know why that should be impossible,*" she muttered, then a moment later, "*Whatever they sent back in my place, it's not me. They're holding me prisoner here.*"

When she had finished, she folded the letter up and handed it back to Cressida.

"What's it supposed to mean?" she asked, still unsure whether Cressida was playing some sort of game with her.

"Don't you get it?" Cressida asked. "She wrote it to me *a month after she got home from camp.*"

Nothing about the way Cressida looked at Kadie suggested she was anything but ferociously serious.

"What makes you think she's here?"

"Because Erin said, 'They're holding me prisoner.' They. And because I already looked for her everywhere at our camp. And because there's something strange about this place. And because I don't think Tania's really a camper and I don't think the Inge F. Yancey Young Executives Leadership Camp is really a camp. Do you?"

Kadie took all of this in, chewing nervously at her lip.

"If you're right," she said slowly, "then what would happen if Tania's horse threw her off its back into the mud, and we beat them in steeplechase? Would that be bad?"

Even on her worst day, Kadie was the faster runner, but upon hearing the outcome of the steeplechase event, Cressida shoved Kadie aside and bolted down the stairs. By the time Kadie regained her balance and stumbled down the ladder, Cressida was out of the windmill and halfway down the tulip-lined path. Kadie called after her, and Cressida's head whipped around. She raised a finger to her lips.

"What's wrong with you?" she hissed. "Do you want them to know we're coming?"

"You think they haven't already noticed we're gone?" Kadie replied.

"Too late," Cressida said, a smile pinned to her lips. "Act like nothing's wrong."

Kadie looked up to see Tania, Ron, and some of the other Inge F. Yancey campers gathered in a semi-circle at the trail-head, arms folded tightly across their chests. With as innocent and carefree a smile as she could muster, Kadie waved.

Tania tapped her foot impatiently as they approached. "You're not supposed to go wandering off by yourselves," she said.

"The grounds here are just so lovely," Kadie gushed. "We couldn't help exploring a little bit."

Ron gave them an easy smile that showed off his immaculate dental work but never quite reached his eyes.

"Well, you're holding up the luncheon we've prepared for you. To celebrate your victory in the steeplechase, I suppose. I mean," he added with a chuckle, "it was supposed to be the luncheon we prepared to celebrate *our* victory, but that's the fun of the All-Camp Sport & Follies, isn't it?"

Tania clapped her hands, and in almost perfect unison, the others turned on their heels. They followed her back the way they'd come, past the stables, and through a gap in the hedgerow. There lay a stone-cobbled terrace, tastefully appointed with long, low tables made from redwood slabs and wicker chairs.

Tania indicated the table at the center of the terrace and invited them to sit. It was the largest and most lavish, laid with silver-rimmed china, ivory linen napkins folded in the shape of swans, and an arrangement of foxtails and calla lilies in the center. Tania snapped her fingers, and at once, five Inge F. Yancey Young Executive Leaders stepped up to pull out their chairs, snap their napkins out of the swan fold, and smooth them across the girls' laps.

Once Tania had left them and taken a seat at the next table with Ron and a few of her preferred followers, a squadron of blandly attractive servers clad in identical black trousers and oxford shirts appeared, each holding a silver pitcher, each with a crisp tea towel folded over his arm. They began to fill water goblets, starting with the girls from Cabin 1 before moving on to the other tables. No sooner had they finished when another wave of servers swooped in, and a basket of rolls, a tureen of gazpacho, and a tray of petit fours were laid before them. Kadie's mouth watered as she started to reach for a roll. It seemed like ages since the last time they'd eaten a proper meal.

"Please," Tania insisted, "don't wait for us. Enjoy your lunch."

Vivian and Kimber had the petit fours nearly to their lips when Cressida stood up, lifted her water goblet, and cleared her throat.

"If I may have your attention," she said, casting a pointed look in Vivian and Kimber's direction until they took the hint and put the petit fours back on their plates, "I'd like to thank our gracious hosts for this splendid lunch and their hospitality. They are the very model of sportsmanship, and it is an honor to compete against them in the All-Camp Sport & Follies."

Something was wrong, Kadie thought. Cressida didn't sound at all like herself. She sounded pleasant and proper and sincere. For a moment, Kadie's suspicion that Cressida was some kind of double agent reared its head. But as it did, she felt a tap on the back of her hand, and looked down to see that Cressida was trying to pass her a note underneath the table. Kadie took it, and opened it underneath the table. It read:

Don't eat anything. Don't take anything from them. That's how they get you.

"And so, let us raise our glasses high in honor of our hosts, and in honor of the Inge F. Yancey Young Executives Leadership Camp," Cressida said, with a smile that brightened her pinched and homely features considerably. "Hear, hear!"

The other girls recovered from their surprise in time to raise their glasses and murmured, "Hear, hear."

Under the table, Kadie tapped Kimber's leg and tried to press the note into her hand, but Kimber was more interested in food. She and Vivian were about to pick up their petit fours, but no sooner had their fingers grazed the plate when Cressida tipped the tureen of gazpacho over so it drenched the sweets, the rolls, the table, and the fronts of Vivian and Kimber's shirts. They squealed and frantically blotted at the stains.

"Oh no!" Cressida wailed, and began trying to help them clean up. When an irritated Kimber recoiled from her touch and brushed her off, Kadie saw Cressida whisper something in her ear.

At the next table, Tania raised a single finger and Vivian and Kimber were flanked by two of her minions, each bearing a look of grave concern that was entirely disproportionate to the scale of the crisis.

"I do apologize about this," said one.

"Come with us," said the other. "We'll launder these things for you and get you some fresh clothes to wear in the meantime."

"It won't take but a minute," said the first minion, offering his arm to Vivian, which, after a moment, she took.

"Right this way," said the second.

Cressida stood up, a desperate look on her face.

"You don't have to go. You look fine. You shouldn't miss lunch."

Vivian and Kimber stared daggers at Cressida.

"Don't tell us what to do," Kimber said.

"You've done enough," Vivian agreed.

"I am so, so sorry," Cressida said to Kimber.

"Whatever," Kimber said, and allowed Tania's minion to help her to her feet.

As Vivian and Kimber disappeared through the hedgerow, Kadie gazed longingly at the overturned tureen. Oddly, though their servers cleaned up the mess, they did not offer to bring another.

Looking to Kadie and Cressida with her wide, docile eyes, Dora started to reach for a relatively unsoggy roll in the bread basket and asked, "Can I eat now?"

Kadie and Cressida exchanged glances that were filled with equal parts pity and contempt. Dora may have been a natural at steeplechase, but she still couldn't have made a decision for herself if her life depended on it.

A Note from the Narrator: Of course, if either of them had asked, Dora would have explained that she was asking if it was all right to eat because she suspected that it wasn't. It was very clear to her that something was wrong with the whole camp, and that Kadie and Cressida had a far better idea what it was than she did. Dora didn't think of herself as a follower so much as a noticer. Watching the things that other people did and said was far more interesting than thinking about what she thought. She knew what she thought.

So, while Vivian and Kimber knew no more about Dora than they had on the first day of camp, Dora knew that the two girls had stopped having much in common with one another months ago. She also knew that Kimber was just beginning to realize how bored she was with her own boredom, but that Vivian wasn't. Dora knew that Kadie sometimes pretended to know things she really didn't, and she knew that Cressida had tipped over the gazpacho on purpose.

Knowing all these things, Dora felt absolutely no shame in asking if it was all right to eat.

Kadie shook her head almost imperceptibly, and Dora put the soggy roll down. Kadie didn't understand everything Cressida had said back at the windmill about her friend Erin, who'd come back from camp the same but different, or the letter she'd sent a month later claiming to be held prisoner here. Yet somehow, she felt in her bones that Cressida was right about the food. The question now was, why?

Kadie looked at their hosts. It was not the first time that she'd wondered if they might be dangerous, but now she found herself wondering if they might be something other than human as well. They were all terribly tall and thin, not identical exactly, but they shared a bone structure that announced itself loudly in the girls' cheeks and the boys' jawlines. All of them had the same dewy, burnished complexion, not a freckle or a pimple to be seen. They didn't walk so much as they glided—almost floated, really—with an impossible grace and fluidity, and was it her imagination, or did they shimmer just a little bit? She hadn't seen any of them after nightfall, but wouldn't have been surprised to learn that they glowed in the dark.

She thought back to the first day of camp, when Tania strolled right through the force field that had blown Dora off her feet. At the time, she thought it was some sort of invisible security fence, the kind that people use on their dogs. But if she and her cabinmates were the dogs in that scenario, what did that make Ron and Tania?

The force field, their perfect faces, and the way that none of the staff seemed to be any older than the campers—in fact, if you looked closely, none of them seemed to be any age at all. It reminded Kadie of television shows where people in their twenties were cast as high school students, and while they were youthful, occasionally someone would smile or raise an eyebrow in a way that broke the spell.

At that moment, Vivian and Kimber came through the hedgerow dressed in silk robes with hems that brushed along on the grass and made it look as though they were floating toward the table. The heavy eyeliner and false eyelashes were gone, and in each of their hands was a tall glass filled with ice and something pink and fizzy, and—judging by the enthusiastically large sips they drew through their straws—intoxicating. Their cheeks were flushed, their smiles merry. The other girls had seen Vivian smirk once or twice, but now she let loose a pretty laugh that trilled up like a set of wind chimes. They had never even seen Kimber's teeth, as she had a tendency to look at the ground and mumble when she spoke, but now she threw her mouth open wide and grinned with gleeful enthusiasm.

When they reached the table, they glided past it without giving Kadie, Cressida, and Dora so much as a glance. They were being waved over by a trio of Inge F. Yancey campers. Whatever they were, each camper was deeply tanned with straight white teeth, and each had eyes more smoldering and dreamy than the last.

"What happened to them?" Kadie asked.

Cressida groaned. "I told them not to eat or drink anything. But they didn't listen. "

At the next table, Kimber giggled and clapped as two campers competing for her attention began to arm wrestle.

"Is there anything we can do for them now?" Dora asked.

"I'm not sure," Cressida said.

Kadie balled a corner of the tablecloth in her fist and squeezed it until her knuckles turned white. "If you'd told us sooner that this was dangerous, we could have stopped them."

Cressida narrowed her eyes. "I didn't know they were going to bring us here. Anyway, when was I supposed to tell you? On the ride over? Because when someone stuffs you in the backseat of a car and puts a bag over your head, that's usually a pretty good sign not to go around accepting food and drinks from them."

"At the beginning," Kadie shot back. "You should have told us everything at the beginning."

"Like you would have believed me then."

"Um, guys," Dora said, tapping insistently at the tabletop. She nodded to her right.

From her table, Tania was staring at them intently. "Is everything all right?" she asked.

"Fine, thank you," Dora said with a smile that seemed, despite everything, sincere.

At this, Tania stood up and clapped her hands. A fleet of servers descended upon the tables, clearing away plates and whisking away crumbs. After they had gone back to the kitchens, Tania clapped her hands again, and all her minions went quiet and stared up at her expectantly.

"And now it is my turn to say a few words about our guests today. They have proven to be worthy competitors, and it is, as ever, an honor to face them in the All-Camp Sport & Follies."

Though her words were gracious enough, like Kadie's had been, she spoke them in a sneering monotone that made it clear exactly how little she meant them. But with her next words, a cruel smile spread across her face even though her voice retained its even, honeyed timbre.

"The final portion of the Follies will be held here, tonight. You will have the rest of the afternoon to prepare your song and dance number. Our staff will show you the theater and the props and costumes available to you."

Just like that, their escorts appeared, arms outstretched to help them up from their chairs. Kadie, Cressida, and Dora stood, but declined to take an elbow.

"The performance will start promptly at dusk. As our guests, you may choose whether you perform first or second. As I'm sure you know, if you win the song and dance competition, you will secure a victory for Camp So-and-So in the All-Camp Sport & Follies, but if you lose, the victory will be ours. Best of luck to you."

Vivian and Kimber made no motion to join them. They sat with the Inge F. Yancey campers, giggling and sipping their beverages.

"Come on," Kadie called to them. "We have to rehearse."

Tania smirked, but Kadie caught a glimpse of her teeth, and could have sworn they'd been filed to points.

"I think you'll find your friends have renounced their former allegiances," Tania said. "You'll have to go on without them."

One Inge F. Yancey camper draped his arm around Vivian's shoulder, and Kimber leaned her head onto the shoulder of another. In their silken robes, their faces scrubbed clean until they glowed, they hardly looked like themselves. Every so often, the air around them would pulse, and Kadie could have sworn that a mirror image of each girl fluttered alongside her, pale and translucent. Then, just as quickly as the second figures had appeared, they vanished.

Then with a sickening flip of her stomach, Kadie knew. She knew the thing that had lingered at the edge of her thoughts since she and Cressida left the windmill, the thing that she'd known all along but had refused to take seriously. This wasn't about Vivian and Kimber throwing them over for the cool kids the first chance they got. It wasn't about sneaking drinks and boys with dreamy eyes and pillow lips. It wasn't about loyalty, it wasn't about winning, and it certainly wasn't about the All-Camp Sport & Follies.

It was about Cressida's friend, Erin.

It was about how she'd gone away to camp last year and something else had come back in her place.

It was about whatever forces had tampered with Kadie's memory, filling her head with a summerful of things that had never happened.

It was about magic.

She turned to Dora and whispered, "We have to get out of here."

Dora said, "I know."

A NOTE FROM THE NARRATOR

I feel I should explain a little more about how I came to have this information, how I came to have this job as narrator in the first place.

It began twelve years ago when I was brought here. I believe it was meant to be a special treat for that summer's guest of honor. I do not think they intended to keep me around such a long time, especially not when I'd failed to do what they'd brought me here to do in the first place. Tania always was a bit careless about reuniting the souls she'd split in half, though.

I was here, and there were stories to tell, and even if they stopped letting me make them up after what happened twelve years ago, they couldn't stop me from narrating them. Robin does all the inventing of stories now, but the thing she's never understood, even after all these years, is how stories tend to take on a life of their own.

That was what happened to me.

I want you to understand how simple my intentions were, how completely they went off the rails. And if you can think of aany way I might've prevented it, I'd appreciate it if you kept it to yourself.

TWELVE YEARS AGO . . .

No one could remember who had announced the treehouse-building contest or the prize trophy that would go to the winner, but all of the campers were wholly committed to the idea.

A Note from the Narrator: It was me, of course, but moving on . . .

Somewhere around the second day of camp, they began to ignore their counselors' pleas to join them on nature hikes or boat rides across Lake So-and-So, and instead devoted all of their time to the task of building, stopping only to sleep and take their meals.

In Cabin 1, the unofficial leader was a lantern-jawed youth named Beau Krest. Beau Krest was big for his age and good with his hands. He knew how to operate a circular saw without killing anyone, and had helped his father build a deck the previous summer. At his right hand was Inge F. Yancey IV, though no one called him that. He was known to his cabinmates as

Iffy, which suited him, for he was not a boy of great certainty. His shaggy hair was neither blond nor brown. He was neither short nor tall, neither nice nor not nice. And even with his famous name, he might have been ignored by his cabinmates had he not shared his architectural plans for the treehouse with Beau.

Beau knew a good design when he saw it, knew how to build what Iffy described, and in giving his stamp of approval, rescued poor, overlooked Iffy from obscurity. Soon the other boys sought his counsel as they constructed the treehouse, courting his favor, and in no time, it had gone to Iffy's head.

His father had insisted on sending him to Camp So-and-So, not the much posher Inge F. Yancey Young Executives Leadership Camp on the other side of the lake. He said this would build character. He told his son that it would do him good to work and play alongside young people who did not have all the advantages he'd had.

What Iffy quickly came to believe, though, was that he was superior to them all. He began to view himself as the brains of the operation, Beau as nothing more than manual labor. He began to contradict Beau's orders in front of the others and talk down to him.

Beau was confused and a little annoyed at the sudden change. He spoke to Iffy in private, said there'd be no hard feelings if he'd lay off the power trips. But Iffy believed that support for him within the cabin exceeded that for Beau. He believed himself surrounded by loyal friends. What's more, he believed that Beau's interpretation of his plan for the treehouse was pedestrian, that his genius vision was being hampered by Beau's workmanlike execution.

Among his cabinmates, he found a willing accomplice who would follow his plans as he had written them, without compromise or question. Another agreed to spy on Beau and his followers, to sabotage their tools, loosen their nails and screws, steal their timber. The gradual shift in power soon left Beau the odd man out. At first, he spoke up, but as his words were neither heeded nor appreciated, he began to spend his days playing guitar back at the cabin or swimming in Lake So-and-So.

Construction continued under Iffy's watch, and soon, a remarkable treehouse rose from the branches of the old oak they'd selected. A spiral staircase wound around the trunk, leading to a grand entryway. The design from there was a series of individual pods connected by rope bridges. There was one for each boy, a solitary place for the hatching of plans, as well as a small common area, for the rare occasions when they might want each other's company. Some of the pods balanced in the crooks of branches, while others were suspended by cords from sturdy boughs like oversized Christmas ornaments. It was striking and odd and imaginative, and it was the proudest accomplishment of Iffy's thus far short and uneventful life.

The other Camp So-and-So cabins had produced treehouses that looked like the products of a first-grader's imagination. Platforms, rope ladders. Iffy was embarrassed for them. Their competitors at the Inge F. Yancey Young Executives Leadership Camp had produced work that was little better, and Iffy felt superior to them as well, and realized that it was no coincidence, no fluke that it was his name on the camp and not any of theirs.

Therefore, it was with grave horror that Iffy discovered on the eve of judging that Beau had been correct all along. Iffy had just settled into the pod he'd designed for himself—it was the largest and the nicest, with both the best view and the most privacy—when he heard a creaking sound, then a snap. His pod separated from the branch that had supported it and fell four feet before catching between two sturdy boughs. Iffy scrambled out of the pod just in time to see it roll off the end of the branch and crash to the ground, where it splintered to bits.

It was then that he saw his treehouse as it must have looked to Beau, as it would certainly look to the judges the next day. As it truly was, not as it existed in his imagination. The structures were precarious, the construction was not square, the bridges that connected the pods sagged. Nothing beyond the staircase and grand entrance, both of which had been constructed by Beau, was any good at all.

Spite and bile filled his heart. He was furious, but it was the night before judging, and it was too late to do anything about it. He had been wrong, and now his cabin was going to lose the trophy, and Iffy would have to go home and explain to his father why the scion of Yancey Corp. had come in dead last not only against his wealthy peers, but also against a camp full of plumbers' sons and bus drivers' daughters. His father would be disappointed and disgusted, and then he would go back to ignoring Iffy. Again.

It was more than he could stand. And so, under the cover of night, Iffy sneaked to the equipment shed; stole some rags, kerosene, and archery gear; and shot flaming arrows into the oak tree. Then he fled back to his cabin and, on the morning of the final judging, joined his cabinmates in looking shattered and dumbstruck at the sight of their masterpiece in ashes.

"It must have been Beau," said the boy Iffy had placed in charge of espionage and sabotage.

The others murmured in agreement that Beau had been jealous and disgruntled and hostile to their cause. Iffy did nothing to dissuade them of the notion—not even when Beau appeared in the clearing, his eyes fixed not on the smoldering remains of the oak tree but on the splintered pod that had fallen out of the tree, and correctly surmised what Iffy had done.

His eyes met Iffy's and he shook his head, saying, "I told you it wouldn't work."

Iffy was startled at being found out so easily, then worried about what Beau might do with the information.

He turned to his friends, narrowed his eyes, and said, "Get him."

The boys descended upon Beau, beating him savagely with their fists and feet. Never much of a fighter, Iffy hung back, watching with a sick smile on his face as the carnage unfolded. Beau might have been killed had the judges not shown up then and the boys come back to their senses and stepped back in horror to see what they had done. As it was, Beau was hospitalized for the rest of the summer with a damaged spleen, a broken jaw, and a skull fracture. By the time he could talk again, he had decided it was best not to speak up about Iffy Yancey and what he had done.

Though he'd spurred the others to action, Iffy had kept his own hands clean in the melee, and so it was he who made his case to the judges that because of the act of sabotage, the integrity of the whole contest was soiled and it would be unfair to award a trophy to anyone. And because his name was on the camp and because the parents were beginning to arrive, and questions were being asked about what had happened to Beau, and charges were being pressed, the judges agreed.

A Note from the Narrator: No one was very happy with how my story turned out, and no one would listen when I tried to explain how little I'd had to do with any of it. My understanding of Robin's role, of Tania's, of the stagehands', was rudimentary then compared to now, but they'd played no role in the sabotage, the fire, the beating, the tragic ending to my harmless little treehouse story.

Everything that had happened that summer, Inge F. Yancey IV brought about on his own.

CABIN 2

KILLER IN THE WOODS

[SCENE: When her cabinmates were swept up in Abigail's net, WALLIS panicked, fled, and now finds herself quite alone in the forest.]

Wallis ran through the woods in a mindless panic. She crashed through branches and the low, thorny scrub until her arms and legs were latticed with cuts, not caring whether the next clearing in the forest contained a SWAT team, another trap, or Abigail herself.

Had the adrenaline that coursed through her body and fueled her flight existed in unlimited quantities, nothing could have contained her. But, as adrenaline always does, it ran out. One moment, she was racing through the forest; the next, she was crumpled in a heap, her legs useless, her muscles the consistency of pulled taffy.

As Wallis gulped air into her raw, singed lungs, the terrible thing she had done began to dawn on her. She curled her legs up to her chest and rolled onto her side with an ear pressed to the ground. She could hear the chewing, rustling, skittering sounds of insects and snakes going about their morning business. At first, it was creepy, but after a few minutes, Wallis began to find it soothing.

Maybe I can just stay here forever, she thought, closing her eyes. *I'll never have to face them again, and no one else will have to know what I did. Because I'll be here, alone, until I die, which will probably be soon.*

The worst part was, Wallis knew she didn't deserve to be the one who lived. Her cabinmates had needed her, and she'd abandoned them. She'd panicked, and while it was only a momentary lapse, it was still the worst thing she had ever done.

Abigail would come for her, would find her separated from the others, and then she'd shoot her full of arrows, or string her up by the heels and cut out her eyes, or blow her to bits.

She swallowed hard and forced herself to sit up. If death was coming, she wanted to see it coming. She wanted to meet it with honor, not with her face buried in a pile of leaves.

You know, if it's honor you're so concerned about, you could always go back for them, you unbelievable moron.

How long had it been since she ran away? The sun was up now, but it had certainly been less than an hour. Sitting there in the dirt, she realized it was a little premature to resign herself to death—or her cabinmates, for that matter. They'd managed to stay alive in the woods for an entire night. There was no justifying what she'd done, but the only way out of the whole mess, if there was a way out, was to get up off the ground.

As Wallis pulled herself to her feet and started to run back toward the clearing, two sets of visions ran through her mind. In the first, the girls from Cabin 2 greeted her with contempt, despising her because of the unforgivable thing she'd done. In the second, no one greeted her at all because they were all dead.

Wallis blinked her eyes shut and forced herself to stop thinking about it. Instead, her mind went where it always went when it needed to escape—to the last scene of the fifth book in the Isis Archimedes series, the scene where Isis Archimedes is unambiguously, unquestionably murdered by her archenemy, S'ulla, two books before the series was supposed to end.

Once again, she let her mind drift down avenues she'd already explored, looking for something she'd missed the first time around. Necromancy didn't work in Isis's world, nor could she have shifted away at the last minute. The room was bound, and her magic didn't work there. If she really had been killed, maybe she could fight her way out of the realm of the dead in the sixth book . . . but somehow, that didn't feel right to Wallis either. If Eurydice Horne ever wrote the sixth book, Wallis hoped she wouldn't go in that direction.

The mental exercises ended the way they did back at home: Isis Archimedes was dead, and Wallis couldn't see a way that she wasn't.

These reflections kept her mind occupied until she'd run back through the woods and returned to the clearing to find . . . nothing at all. The net hung from a stout hickory branch, empty.

At first, Wallis thought that Abigail must have captured her cabinmates. Her legs turned to water under her and she sat down hard. But quickly enough, she realized that didn't make sense. If Abigail had come for them, there would have been some sign—arrows, hints of a struggle, blood.

The light in the forest was soft and gray now, and Wallis got on her hands and knees and crawled into a thicket near the tree where the net was strung up. She followed the tangle of cords and pulleys until she found a great wooden spool and crank wound with lengths of rope. Wallis reached into her pocket for her Swiss army knife and cut down the ropes so that the trap could not be reset. The remnants of the net fell into the clearing.

When Wallis bent down to inspect them, she saw that the girls from Cabin 2 had cut themselves free. Of course, that didn't mean they were okay, she told herself. It was an awfully long way to fall, and while—encouragingly—there was not a pile of bodies beneath the net, it was possible that at least one of them had been injured when they jumped to the ground. If that had happened, Abigail would have a much easier job tracking them through the woods. Unless, Wallis thought grimly, the rest of Cabin 2 was like her and not above leaving behind a fallen cabinmate.

Wallis circled the clearing until she found a spot in the brush where the twigs bowed out and a few had been peeled back to reveal the soft green wood beneath the bark. Beyond them, she saw the unmistakable beginnings of a footpath. They must have gone this way.

There was an unusual number of ravens in the woods. At first, Wallis noticed one every few paces. After half an hour of walking, she began to notice them on every tree. A shower of pine needles fell to the ground in front of her as a well-fed raven came in to roost. Wallis looked up and saw that it held something in its beak.

"Hey," Wallis shouted up at the bird.

It cawed in reply, and when it did, the thing in its mouth fluttered to the ground. Wallis picked it up, and her heart sank when she saw the blood-soaked strip of bandage.

It didn't mean anything, she told herself. It might have gotten snagged on a branch. It might have been from three summers ago. It didn't have to be Shea's, and even if it was, it didn't mean the worst.

The woods were thick with ravens now. Wallis was afraid to look at them, not wanting to know what other things they carried in their beaks. At some point, she realized, she had lost the girls' trail and was now mostly following the sounds of these scavenger birds.

The woods thinned, and up ahead, Wallis could see light shining through the tree trunks. She paused, half afraid to see what lay beyond them, then pulled aside the brambles and stepped into the clearing.

I've been here before, she thought. It had been dark and she'd been on horseback at the time, running for her life, but Wallis recognized the cave and the pony trail. They'd seen a hideous creature there, and before they could slow their horses down, they'd trampled it flat.

Now, every rock, every ledge, every craggy spot around the cave entrance was covered with perching ravens. The noise they made was awful, and the smell was worse, though, to be fair, the ravens were not to blame for that. Wallis crossed the pony trail—looking both ways first—and approached the mouth of the cave. Lying before it were the picked-over remains of what might have once been some sort of reptile or insect creature, but was now just a bloody, smelly mess of scales and legs. Thankfully, nothing human seemed to be mixed in with it.

"Hello?" she called out. "Is anyone here?"

There was no answer, but as Wallis explored the area, it was clear that several people had been here, and not long ago. There were footprints everywhere, and at the base of the craggy rock wall, the dust was soaked with blood. Leading away from the cave, the carcass, and the blood was a single tire track, too thick to belong on a bicycle.

What had happened here, Wallis wondered, and where was everyone now?

From a long way off in the distance, she heard a series of clipped, staccato caws. A raven sitting on a rock in front of the cave laid down the scrap of intestines it was eating and cocked its head to the side with great interest. One by one, the rest of them followed suit, and soon, every raven on the path, by the mouth of the cave, and on the craggy rocks had gone completely still and silent.

"What's wrong?" Wallis asked, forgetting for a moment that the ravens couldn't answer her.

The big raven that had been eating intestines flew up to the highest rock, tossed back its head, and burst forth with an oration that held all the other ravens at attention. Wallis could have sworn it was giving them orders—and they seemed to be listening.

When the raven finished cawing, there was a rustle of wings and a cacophony of raven chatter, and then, as one, they rose from the rock face of the cave like the sail of a pirate ship riding up the mast. They flew up past the treetops and disappeared from view. Wallis couldn't even tell which direction they'd flown, and she wondered whether something had frightened them away, whether she was in danger if she stayed here.

Wallis sat down on a rock near the mouth of the cave. The woods felt empty now, and she felt more alone than ever.

It was fitting that she'd end up here, Wallis thought. After all, this was the place. The place where the other campers had left Abigail in Oscar's story. The place where she had gone crazy after being left.

If the story was true, it was probably a significant place for Abigail. Maybe she lived there now or brought her victims there. If Wallis wanted to find her friends, the cave seemed like a good place to look for them, though the thought of going inside by herself made her heart race. What if she lost her way? What if she were driven mad, just as Abigail had been?

Of course, had you not abandoned your friends like a twitchy little coward, you wouldn't even be here, Wallis thought.

At that moment, Wallis realized that she'd called the other girls in Cabin 2 her friends, and meant it.

In the next moment, she felt herself tap into the veins of the story—of *their* story—the way she sometimes did. The way she'd known that Oscar wasn't going to save them, that the horses weren't going to bring them out of the forest; the same way she'd known those things, Wallis suddenly knew that Abigail was not going to kill her.

She recognized the story she and the rest of Cabin 2 were supposed to be part of, the story of the killer in the woods. There were hundreds of low-budget popcorn stories like that, and they all played out the same way: girls scream; girls run;

girls get separated; girls get picked off one by one. Maybe it was an arrow through the neck or a hatchet between the eyes. Maybe one girl survives. Maybe not. There were variations, but that was the basic gist of it.

Once upon a time, a girl was abandoned in a cave, and when she came back, something about her was broken. So she murdered a camper, then she murdered a counselor, then she blew up a truck, and she laid barbed-wire traps and nets in the woods.

Some of the things that had happened to them fit right into that story, but what had happened here last night, when she and the girls from Cabin 2 rode their horses down this trail and mowed down a gigantic spider-snake—*that* didn't belong.

Wallis might have thought she'd made the whole thing up. It had all happened so fast that in her panic and hysteria, she'd barely had time to think about it. But the evidence lay before her, with scales and fangs and hairy legs and beady eyes, and Wallis knew that a beast like that had no business being in a story about a psychotic slasher chasing girls through the woods.

There was another force driving this story—Wallis was sure of it. It wasn't Abigail; it wasn't the question of whether the five of them would escape from her clutches. It was bigger than that.

The cave beckoned to her, promising answers, and Wallis, who could never resist a story she didn't know the ending to, took a step inside. She trusted herself, and she trusted where this story was taking her. Maybe she was going to meet her death in this place, but it wasn't going to be at the hands of Abigail.

Was there even an Abigail? They'd never seen her. For all Wallis knew, maybe there had never been any such person.

Before she could change her mind, she took another step.

She inched through the cave's winding passageways, using her flashlight to navigate, although it was hardly necessary. The high vaulted chambers of the cave were made of limestone so white, they seemed to glow in the dark.

Deeper in the cave, there came a sound. It was a sound like chains dragging on rock. It was the sound of something that knew Wallis was there. It was the sound of something that wanted her to know it knew. She froze, turned off her flashlight, and clutching it like a weapon, scanned the chambers for any flicker of motion.

The sound of the chains grew louder with each corner she turned. Wallis passed through one chamber, then another, and finally one more, until she came to a wooden door, soggy with rot. Behind it, the chains went silent.

Wallis kicked the door open and held her flashlight aloft.

It was not a large room, but every inch of every wall was covered in thousands of mirrors, each one no bigger than a deck of playing cards. Wallis saw a bench in the center of the room that had been taken over by mosses and molds and bat guano. The other thing she saw in the room, chained to the bench, clad in rags, undernourished, not very fresh-smelling, and babbling all these things to herself like a crazy person, dear friends, was the face she'd seen on the back inside flap of every Isis Archimedes book, the face she'd looked at when she thought about the books she'd someday write that would have her own picture printed on the back.

A Note from the Narrator: I'd never much cared for that picture. Much too moody and self-important, the way I'm staring off into the distance, like the photographer just happened to catch me in the middle of a critical thought. It was the kind of photograph that, at a certain point in my life, I thought an author was supposed to have.

"I know you," Wallis said. I saw the doubt on her face as she tried to reconcile what she knew to be possible with what she saw before her. She saw me, she knew me, and yet, she couldn't quite bring herself to say it aloud.

"Where are my friends?" she asked instead.

"Not far from here," I said. "They're safe."

Wallis looked at me, and I cannot say that I liked the sensation one bit. I was accustomed to being listened to. I was accustomed to the certain amount of authority that comes with my station, one of the few perks of the job. It had been a long time since I had been subjected to the scrutiny of anyone, and I can't say I liked being on the other side of things.

What did I look like to her?

When I'm spinning a tale, I always imagine myself looking like one of those fireside storytellers with bits of day-old stew in my beard and a walking stick that conceals a sword and a glass eye that I pop out of its socket from time to time, just to unsettle folks and fascinate small children. I like to imagine that if you saw me the way I see myself, you wouldn't be a whit surprised to hear that I could fly short distances or conjure and speak to the dead.

But, of course, in saying all this, I'm only postponing the inevitable.

"You're Eurydice Horne," Wallis said, gripping the wall as she studied my face, the chains that bound me to the stone bench in the middle of the cave.

"It's been a long time since anyone called me that."

I watched my words sink in and take hold, and for a moment, Wallis looked as though she might cry, overwhelmed by the terror, the whiplash of the last few days—a long, reeling path through the wilds of Camp So-and-So that ended with me.

"Why are you here?" whispered Wallis.

I mustered my dignity, drew myself to sit upright, and fixed the girl with my one-eyed storyteller stare.

"Because I am the Narrator. I am here to tell the story of what happens to all of you."

CABIN 3

THE HERO'S QUEST

[SCENE: From the meadow, THE GIRL WITH BEADS IN HER HAIR and RENATA see a column of fire rise up into the sky above their cabins.]

The flames roared and crackled and hissed like a living thing, and though they were at least a half a mile away, it sounded like it was right on top of them.

A Note from the Narrator: Cabin 1 was, at this moment, safely across the lake, preparing for the equestrian event of the All-Camp Sport & Follies. Wallis was at the cave, the whereabouts of the rest of her cabinmates unknown. The girls from Cabin 4 had just been separated from one another during their search for the soul mates, and you don't need me to tell you where Cabin 5 was.

The sky above their cabins was on fire. The girl with beads in her hair and Renata exchanged a glance, and without discussing the matter any further than that, they began to travel as fast as their legs and wings would carry them toward the cabins. They went up the long, unnecessarily winding road until they reached the mess hall, then took the path that forked left into the woods, already thick with smoke.

When they emerged into the clearing where the semicircle of doorless, wall-less cabins stood, they saw a column of fire at least three stories high burning hot and thick. The fire raged loudly, but even so, both of them could hear the screams coming from the other side, where Cabin 5 stood.

The girl with beads in her hair grabbed an overturned ash pail by the fire circle and ran to the latrine to fill it up with water from the sink. Then she ran back down the hill and heaved the water into the flames, before racing back to do it all again.

As the girl with beads in her hair worked, Renata scanned the clearing for any signs of life, frustrated that she could not do more. All of the other cabins seemed to be deserted, and even the animals had fled at the first whiff of smoke. Then she caught a flash of movement in the branches of a fir tree and looked up to see another raven perched in the branches.

Long ago in some elementary school science class, Renata remembered learning that ravens were scavenger birds—that, like vultures, they congregated around things that were dead or dying. Years after that in English class, she learned they were widely considered to be an ill omen.

That wasn't how being a raven made Renata feel, though. She'd tried to explain it to the girl with beads in her hair back in the woods, but it hadn't come out right. The truth was, Renata felt better about being a raven than she'd ever felt about being a girl. Renata knew she was not a great beauty—her hair was lank, her face round and cratered with acne. That wasn't what bothered her, though. There was nothing wrong with her face, nothing wrong with her body, but Renata had never been able to shake the feeling that she was in the wrong one.

And now she wasn't.

Since the change had happened, a tiny, glowing hope had kindled in her brain: that it would last, that she would get to stay like this.

But when she saw the raven in the tree, another idea took hold of her. She flew up to the branch where the bird was perched, and hovering before it, flapping her wings frantically, she said, "I'm Renata."

The raven on the fir branch cocked its head and considered her for a moment. Then it opened its beak and croaked, "Renata."

Renata looked down at the ground where the girl with beads in her hair continued to battle the fire, pouring bucket after bucket of water on the flames. It was brave, but hopeless. Alone, it was all she could do to keep the small blazes contained, and she wouldn't be able to do even that much longer.

Renata told the raven her plan.

"Renata," it croaked again, then spread its wings and left the fir branch swaying in its wake.

A terrible amount of time passed, during which terrible things happened.

The wind picked up and the flames rose, raining down a shower of sparks. As the girl with beads in her hair tried to smother a small fire with her ash pail, a puff of wind goaded it up her leg, and her jeans ignited. She panicked for a moment and started to run, but only made it a few steps before she came to her senses and dropped to the ground, rolling to extinguish the flames with her own body.

Renata began to wonder if the raven had even understood her message, much less passed it along.

Worst of all, she could no longer hear the girls from Cabin 5 screaming.

When Renata looked down, she saw that for every small fire the girl with beads in her hair had beaten out, two more had sprung up. Was this where their quest had led them? she wondered. To be swallowed up by a forest fire, to stand by while five girls burned to death, knowing there was nothing they could do about it? They didn't have a phone to call for help. They didn't have so much as a garden hose.

Hope was lost, and then Renata heard something in the distance. It sounded like one wet sheet after another being snapped smooth and flung over a clothesline. It grew louder and drew nearer.

Within moments, every inch of the sky was filled with thousands and thousands of ravens.

Her message had gotten through.

Now, if only it would work, Renata thought as she flew up to join them.

As she did, the first platoon of ravens flew over the pillar of flame and hovered there, the flames almost licking at each bird's talons. There, it was joined by another. And another. And another. And another. Then the sky above Cabin 5 was so thick with them that they blocked out the sun. Aside from the flapping of their wings, they didn't make a sound. Not a caw, a squawk, a bark, or a chirp.

Once the first group was in position, Renata's voice rang out, "Now!"

All at once, the ravens opened their mouths and streams of water fell from their beaks into the fire. This accomplished, they flew straight up into the air while another platoon of birds took their place.

Wave after wave of ravens flew in, a hundred birds in each platoon, letting loose a cascade of water onto the flames. Each wave flew in a circuit over the treetops, the mess hall, the meadow, until they dipped down over the lake and skimmed up as much water as their gullets could hold, water to pour over the fire and extinguish the flames.

From where the girl with beads in her hair stood, it seemed like too little. How could a few mouthfuls of water put out a four-story tower of fire? And yet, somehow it did, beak by beak by beak. Under Renata's command, thick gray smoke began to rise from sections of the wall, and eventually, the flames died down. As the smoke began to clear, the only sign that a wall of thorns had once stood there was the circle of ash that surrounded the blackened eaves of Cabin 5 and some rather curious artifacts: half-melted tarps mounted on sticks, shingles bent into shovels, a rope made out of bra straps. It was odd what burned and what didn't.

Of the campers, there was no sign at all.

A few of the ravens were overwhelmed by the smoky air and fell out of the sky like downed fighter jets. The girl with beads in her hair did her best to dodge them as she ran toward the cabin, looking for some indication that there were survivors.

"Hello?" she called through the cabin doorway, hesitant to run inside. The structure looked as though it might crumble to ash at any moment. There was no answer, so the girl with beads in her hair went carefully up the concrete steps and stuck her head inside the door, but it was impossible to see through the haze.

"Hello?" she called again, more frantic this time. She stood there for a full minute, but the only sounds she heard were the pops and hisses of the last remaining embers and the caws of ravens, retreating in search of cleaner air.

The girl with beads in her hair ran down the steps and circled around the back of the cabin. She got down on her hands and knees and peered underneath. *They were here*, she thought. *They hid under here. They had to have hidden under here because there was nowhere else, and because if they weren't here, that means they're—* Before she could finish the thought, the girl with beads in her hair crawled underneath the cabin. The air was dank and earthy, the ground littered with decades' worth of camper debris and rotting things. It was also full of holes, dens, and burrows for whatever creatures lived under there. The girl with beads in her hair ran her fingers over every inch, not caring whether she was scratched, cut, or bitten so long as she brushed up against a hand, a sneaker, a leg.

She crawled from corner to corner and back again twice before giving up, before lowering her head so that her braids fell forward like a curtain around her face and her arms began to shake beneath her.

There was nothing left of the girls from Cabin 5.

Inch by inch, the girl with beads in her hair forced herself to crawl out from under the cabin, and rose weakly to her feet. The moment she looked up, she gasped and stumbled backwards, scraping the backs of her singed legs against the remains of Cabin 5.

Standing there before her, her face gray with smoke and ash, was Robin, the counselor-in-training. Robin, the closest thing to an authority figure they'd seen since arriving at camp. Robin, who'd taunted them, then abandoned them to be slaughtered by the beast. Robin, who might have had something to do with their entire predicament, if what the kelpie had said had even a shred of truth to it.

The girl with beads in her hair tried to collect herself, but the moment she opened her mouth to speak, the words stuck in her throat.

"They're all dead," she said at last, tears beginning to stream down her cheeks.

If Robin was rattled by this news, she did not show it. Instead, she unclipped a walkie-talkie from the waistband of her shorts and held it to her lips.

"Cabin 5 clean-up crew, I need you here yesterday," she barked, over an eruption of static. "All hands. This is a code red situation here."

A soot-covered Renata glided down to earth and perched next to the girl with beads in her hair. Like her friend, she had been scanning the clearing for signs of life, and likewise had found none.

"What happened?" Renata asked Robin, who was clipping the walkie-talkie back on her belt.

"Something that wasn't supposed to," Robin said, not batting an eye at the talking raven.

Renata surveyed the remains of Cabin 5, the circle of char and ashes that surrounded it. Then she looked at the girl with beads in her hair, at her crumpled face, and at the tears in her eyes.

"So they're—"

Renata could not finish the question.

"It looks that way," Robin said. She sighed heavily, then turned and began to walk away.

The girl with beads in her hair exploded.

"What is *wrong* with you?" she asked, running after Robin. "Don't you care? This isn't just something that needs to be cleaned up. People are *dead*!"

Robin got on her walkie-talkie again.

"Cabin 5 crew, report immediately. Anyone not reporting in the next thirty seconds will be *severely* punished."

Ignoring glares from the girl with beads in her hair, Robin began to walk around the perimeter of Cabin 5, casting her eyes back and forth over the ruined earth. At one point, she bent down and picked up a pair of binoculars that had been warped almost beyond recognition by the heat. With a primal shriek, she whipped them over her head by the strap and flung them into the forest.

Thirty seconds passed. Then a minute. Whoever Robin had tried to summon on the walkie-talkie was not coming, never mind the consequences.

Renata flapped her wings and caught up with the girl with beads in her hair, who was still stalking after Robin, waiting for answers.

"What are we supposed to do now?" Renata asked, landing on the ground in front of the girl with beads in her hair.

The girl with beads in her hair stopped in her tracks and stared down at her friend. Looking like she'd been struck between the eyes, she slumped to her knees.

"I don't know," she whispered.

If there was anyone left at Camp So-and-So who could answer that question, it was Robin, but why would they believe anything she told them?

When she called after Robin, her throat felt raw from smoke and tight with anger.

"You left us," she said. "Back at the cave. You just left us there with the beast. If we hadn't killed it, would you be calling for help to clean up what was left of *us*?"

Robin stopped walking but didn't turn around.

"That wouldn't have happened," she said wearily. "I wouldn't have let that happen."

The girl with beads in her hair sprang up on her toes, and in an instant, she had caught up with Robin. She tackled her from behind and pushed her to the ground, pinning a knee in the small of her back and twisting one of the counselor-in-training's arms behind her back.

"I don't believe you," she grunted, giving Robin's arm a sharp tug so the counselor-in-training hissed in pain.

This was where the quest had been leading them. It must have been. They were in evil times where darkness threatened day, and Robin seemed to be the cause. There had probably been more "accidents" like this one all over camp. The girl with beads in her hair thought about her friends, about the girls who'd ridden through the forest on horseback the night before. Where were they now? Were they still alive, or had Robin picked them off one by one?

Renata had followed her and now hovered at the girl's shoulder as she dug her knee into Robin's back.

"What are you doing?" she asked, horror filling her raven eyes.

"*In evil times when darkness threatens day,*" said the girl with beads in her hair through gritted teeth, "*one soul among you must hold it at bay.* I'm the soul. She is the darkness."

"Please," Robin pleaded. "The prophecy, it's not what you think."

"How would you know?" asked the girl with beads in her hair.

"Because I wrote it. *First you must slay the beast inside its lair,*" Robin said, gasping for breath. "*And then set free the one imprisoned there.*"

The girl with beads in her hair eased some of her weight off Robin's back.

"I'm the one who left the so-called prophecy in your cabin and sent you off on your so-called quest," she said, coughing into the dirt. "I didn't know you'd all take it so seriously."

The girl with beads in her hair felt her head spin.

The doubt she'd harbored from the beginning was true, but it was all so much worse than she'd feared. The monsters and the talking animals and the magic were all real, but none of that mattered. The quest wasn't real. It was a hoax, a thing made up by their counselor-in-training. And while they'd been sucked into it, terrible things had happened all around them. People had died, and they'd been too busy—risking their lives on a quest that didn't matter—to save them.

And Robin was so nonchalant about the whole thing. She appeared to feel remorse about what had happened, but it was the way you'd feel about the death of a gerbil or a houseplant you were fond of. Maybe Robin hadn't wanted it to happen, but she also wasn't appropriately, humanly upset about it.

Of course she isn't, thought the girl with beads in her hair, suddenly realizing the truth. *Robin isn't human.*

While the girl with beads in her hair processed that, Renata, who saw things in a different way, had arrived at a conclusion that was completely different, but no less correct.

She landed on the ground and perched next to Robin's head, giving the girl with beads in her hair a pointed look until she took her knee off of Robin's back.

"What are we supposed to do?" she asked the counselor-in-training.

Robin sat up and dusted off the front of her shirt. "After you killed the beast, which, by the way, I knew you would, you were supposed to go inside the cave. After all, the prophecy did say you were supposed to 'set free the one imprisoned *there.*'"

Renata spread her wings and turned around, showing off her plumage as if Robin might have missed it earlier. "Was *this* supposed to happen?"

Robin considered this for a moment.

"You were supposed to free some*one*, not some*thing*. Of all the casks you could've brought out, you picked *that* one. Then again, the cave is full of all kinds of things. Trust me. There are worse things than turning into a raven."

Trust me.

Renata did. She had suspected, but now she was convinced.

"You're the knight," she said, fixing her black eyes on the counselor-in-training.

"Beware! The Knave who only speaks in lies. Beware! The Knight who plots out your demise," Robin said with a nod. "I think it went a little something like that."

The girl with beads in her hair wasn't sure what to feel now, but her mind honed in on one point.

"You can only tell us the truth," she said.

Robin nodded.

"Why did you send us on the quest in the first place?" asked the girl with beads in her hair, puzzled. If it had all been for her own amusement, Robin certainly didn't seem to be enjoying herself very much.

"I didn't mean for it to happen," Robin said. "Not like this, anyway."

"But you did mean for it to happen in some way," Renata said. "Why?"

"Because I'm the stage manager," Robin said, almost like she was trying to remind herself of the fact.

"Stage manager of what?" asked the girl with beads in her hair. "This isn't a play."

"But it is," Robin said, walking up the steps to Cabin 5. "We put it on every year."

"And we're the . . . *actors?*" Renata asked.

Robin nodded, then paused at the threshold to Cabin 5.

"It works best with humans," she said. "They can be managed, but they never do exactly what you expect them to. Keeps the stories fresh."

Robin disappeared inside the cabin, unconcerned about the stability of the load-bearing beams. The girl with beads in her hair was dumbfounded, then furious. Their actions had all been choreographed from the beginning, all for the amusement of some backward, forest-dwelling creatures with nothing better to do.

"Haven't you heard of television? Or books?" she called after Robin.

A moment later, Robin reappeared in the doorway, brushing soot from her shorts.

"Is it always like this?" Renata asked.

Robin frowned. "What do you mean?"

"You know what I mean."

Robin pursed her lips and seemed, for a moment, unwilling to answer. At last she relented.

"No," she said. "Nobody dies during my productions. At least nobody ever has before. I believe I have some kind of sabotage on my hands. Or mutiny."

Not for the first time during this conversation, the girl with beads in her hair stifled the urge to scream. The way Robin was going on about it, you'd think *she* was the one who was suffering.

"I'm going to get to the bottom of this," Robin said. She walked down the steps and went back to circling the area around the cabin. "I know you don't like me very much right now. I know you blame me, but you have to believe me. I never intended for any of you to get hurt. Not Megan or Pam or Oscar or anyone . . ."

Robin looked around at the clearing where the five cabins stood, and she considered what she knew about the current whereabouts and well-being of each cabin.

A Note from the Narrator: Which, to her knowledge, was as follows: Cabin 1 was in Tania's clutches at the Inge F. Yancey Young

Executives Leadership Camp. Cabin 2 was on the run from Abigail, or rather, from the crew of stagehands who manufactured her traps, none of whom seemed to be following their notes anymore. She hadn't heard from Cabin 4 in hours, and Cabin 5 was presumed dead.

As the girl with beads in her hair watched Robin, she realized that she felt more committed to the quest than ever. To Robin, this was just about cleaning up a mess and sorting out her mutinous crew, but in truth, the girl with beads in her hair realized that what was at stake was nothing less than all of their lives. Everything Robin had written in the prophecy had come true, even the parts she couldn't possibly have controlled. Robin hadn't known what she was writing, hadn't taken it all that seriously, but it didn't matter. The prophecy had taken on a life of its own, and it was *real*. Five of them were lost, but the rest were still out there, and if the girl with beads in her hair didn't try to save them, who would?

"We're coming with you," said the girl with beads in her hair.

Robin may have been telling the truth, but she couldn't be trusted to act in their best interests. The girl with beads in her hair and Renata would keep an eye on her. Together, they would make this right. They would save the rest of the girls at Camp So-and-So and face whatever darkness lay ahead because, deep down, the girl with beads in her hair knew there was more at the root of this than a few rebellious stagehands.

She didn't think Robin would argue with her, and she didn't. After all, who else did she have to help her clean up this mess?

But once again, Renata saw things in a different way, and arrived at a different conclusion that was no less correct. She cleared her throat.

"I'm not coming with you," she said. Her voice trembled as she spoke.

"Why? Where will you go?" asked the girl with beads in her hair, even though she already knew the answer.

"I promised the others I'd come back, no matter what," Renata said.

Doubt tugged at the girl with beads in her hair, and she began to wonder if she was making the right decision. Renata's way made sense. Maybe they should stick together, especially now that they knew what was happening, and exactly how bad things could get.

The girl with beads in her hair was about to change her mind, about to tell Renata that she was going back to the cave with her, but Renata kept talking.

"The prophecy said we were supposed to go into the cave and free someone. It's the part of the quest we missed, and it's my fault. I have to go back and fix it so you can finish. If I don't, I have a feeling that nothing is going to turn out the way it's supposed to."

It was what the prophecy said would happen, thought the girl with beads in her hair. *First five, then four, then three, then two, then one.*

It was what always happened in stories like this. The hero started off surrounded by friends who helped out, who stepped up and were heroic at different moments along the way, but in the end, when things were darkest and most uncertain, the hero always ended up alone.

In evil times when darkness threatens day,
One soul among you must hold it at bay.

It had flashed across her mind when she tackled Robin and pinned her to the ground. *I'm the soul. She's the darkness.* Now, the girl with beads in her hair realized what that meant.

She was supposed to be the hero of this story.

Immediately, she knew she didn't want it. Renata would make a better hero. She'd been cursed into the body of a bird, and she turned around and commanded a raven army to put out a terrifying inferno. She was braver and smarter, and the girl with beads in her hair didn't want to finish this quest without her.

She felt like she might cry again, but instead she held out her hand to Renata and said, *"There is a world above and a world below and a world between, and in all of them, always, you are my friend."*

It was the next-to-last line of the third book in the Isis Archimedes series, the one everybody liked best. After infiltrating S'ulla's armies as a soldier and spy, Isis Archimedes is captured and thrown in prison. There, she meets Melchior, who tells her the truth about her parentage and reveals that she comes from a long line of realm-walkers. Melchior doesn't know the magics himself, not properly, but he teaches Isis a bastard form, more dangerous and unstable than he lets on. Together, they harness the magics to open a portal and break out of prison; however, the portal ruptures, and the book ends when Melchior throws himself into it, sealing himself inside and saving two worlds in the process.

Renata croaked down the sob in her throat and gave Isis's reply, the last line of the book: *"And nothing, not even the walls between worlds, can keep us apart for long."*

"Good luck," said the girl with beads in her hair.

"You too."

With that, Renata spread her wings and rose up through the treetops. The girl with beads in her hair kept her eyes on the sky until Renata vanished into the smoke.

The girl with beads in her hair stumbled across the clearing, tripping over piles of smoldering rubble, her vision blurred with tears. A few yards away, she saw that Robin had dropped to her knees and was sifting through the dirt with her fingers.

Before the girl with beads in her hair had a chance to wonder why, she realized that the ground beneath her feet was suddenly, inexplicably gone.

CABIN 4

SOUL MATES

*[SCENE: VERITY stands outside a possibly enchanted cabin with
her soul mate, ERIN, who is as lovely in person as she is from afar.
They are alone, and at last they are talking.]*

Once Tad had carried Addison through the glowing door,
Verity was left alone with the beautiful girl. At first, she
found this almost as alarming as the events that had just
unfolded.

It had all happened so fast. One moment, Addison was
running toward the cabin, her face bathed in light. The next,
Tad and Erin were telling her that Addison had been marked
by someone named Tania, whatever that meant, and that she
was going to die unless Verity let them take her.

It hadn't been hard to believe this might happen. Nobody
else seemed to have noticed it, but Verity had watched Addison's steady decline. And then there was the terrifying turn
for the worse she'd taken in front of the soul mates' cabin, her

face completely drained of color, her skin so hot Verity could hardly bear to touch it.

"Where is he taking her?" Verity asked. She started to go up the stairs, but Erin positioned herself in front of the cabin door.

"You can't go in there," Erin said, putting a hand on each of Verity's shoulders. Verity's skin tingled at the girl's touch, and the feeling spread down her arms and up the back of her neck.

"But—"

"I promise, your friend isn't going to die," Erin said. "But Tad's taking her somewhere you can't go. Please trust me."

It was crazy, but the solid feel of Erin's hands on her shoulders, the way she looked Verity right in the eye when she spoke, the even calm of her voice made Verity believe her.

"I trust you," she said, hoping for Addison's sake that she wouldn't regret it.

"Do you need to sit down?" Erin asked. "You look like you're about to be sick."

Great, thought Verity. *She thinks I look sick.*

"Where's everybody else?" Verity asked, forcing herself to look less unwell.

"What do you mean, 'everybody else'?"

Erin stepped out of the cabin doorway and took a seat on the steps, leaving enough room for Verity.

"Before, when we were all watching you, there were five of you," Verity said, almost immediately wishing she could take it back. *Why, yes, that's what I saw earlier when my friends and I were creepily spying on you.*

However, that wasn't the part of Verity's revelation that Erin latched on to.

"When you were *all* watching us? How many of *you* are there?"

"There are five of us, too," Verity confessed. "Addison and I got separated from the rest of them in the woods."

"Then shouldn't the others have found you by now?"

It was a valid point. There was no good reason why they should have gotten separated in the woods in the first place, and even if there were, there was no explanation for why they had not immediately found one another. Annika, Alix, and Amber had followed the trail to the soul mates' cabin once, had even been pulled to it, and certainly should have found their way here by now. What if something had happened to them?

Verity decided to take Erin up on her offer to sit down. She was feeling light-headed, a condition that was not improved when Erin's leg brushed against hers as she sat down next to her on the cabin step.

"Where did they go?" Verity asked.

"Robin's crew probably diverted them off the path," Erin said, then added, "Oh, wait. I forgot, you have no idea what that means."

"The counselor-in-training?"

"Counselor-in-training. Stage manager. She gives herself a lot of different titles," Erin said, a disgusted tone in her voice. "Mostly, though, she's Tania's flunky."

"I don't know who that is either," Verity said, though it was only partly true. She'd heard Erin and Tad say that name before. Whoever Tania was, Verity was beginning to realize she was behind what had happened to Addison, to all of them.

Erin gestured toward the woods, then back to the cabin, then up to the sky.

"All of this is hers," Erin said. "It's her show. We're just here to do her bidding, to keep her and her people entertained."

As she said this, a strong gust of wind rattled the tree branches, and dust blew up and circled their ankles. Verity could have sworn she smelled smoke.

A different girl might have taken this as a cue to seek shelter or run back into the woods to look for her friends, but Verity stayed where she was on the cabin steps. This was partly because in the woods she'd be alone, and here she wasn't, and partly because of the way that Erin's leg brushed against hers every so often in a way that might have been accidental or not.

"How did you get here?" asked Verity, who felt like she had frogs in her stomach and jackrabbits in her knees each time their legs touched.

"The same thing that happened to everybody else. They caught me."

"Like, with a net?"

When Erin didn't answer right away, Verity cringed. Nearly everything she said sounded idiotic in her own ears. Erin was smart, and she said what was on her mind; Verity could tell that about her immediately. She felt sure that at any moment, Erin was going to decide she was tired of talking to Verity and follow Tad and Addison inside the cabin. Verity braced herself, but it didn't happen. Erin stayed where she was.

"It doesn't really matter what they use," Erin said. "They might offer you a drink or a pretty necklace or an extra blanket. It doesn't matter to them if you don't know what you're agreeing to. If you reach out and take it, you're marked. You're their prisoner."

"What did you take?"

"Stamps," Erin said. "I really needed to send a letter. I'd promised my best friend I would—she was supposed to be here with me, but she broke her arm and couldn't come. Anyhow, one day my stamps went missing, and then the next day, I found a sheet of stamps on my pillow. I thought that whoever took them was squaring things up, so I peeled one off the sheet, stuck it on my letter, and mailed it to my friend. When I think about it now, I don't even think I said anything important in it. The names of people in my cabin. Where they were from. What they were like. What we did all day. Boring stories about a bunch of people she didn't know. And that's why I'm here now."

"Addison took a button," Verity said, unsure whether this was betraying a confidence. "It fell off of Tad's shirt."

Erin wrinkled her nose. "That's weird. Why would she want a button?"

The cabin wasn't any bigger than theirs. It seemed strange to Verity that they hadn't heard a sound coming from inside since Tad had carried Addison in her arms through the door. Verity looked over her shoulder, but beyond the door frame, it was completely dark.

"Erin, what's happening to her now?" Verity asked, with a sharp intake of breath.

Erin went quiet, staring intently at the tops of her shoes. After a long silence, she said, "You're the first person I've told this to."

Erin trailed off and was silent another long minute.

"And you seem really cool, and I'm worried that . . . I don't know if you'll believe me. I don't know what you'll think when I tell you."

The chorus of frogs rose up in Verity's throat, and though she was afraid to open her mouth, the pressure was such that she knew keeping it closed would not remain an option much longer.

"Youseemreallycooltoo," she said, before squeezing her eyes closed, afraid to see the look on Erin's face.

Verity felt the back of Erin's hand brush against her leg as she wrapped her hands around her knees. Slowly, Verity opened her eyes, and she saw that Erin had leaned forward and was resting one of her perfect cheekbones on her perfect knees. Verity leaned forward and wrapped her hands around her own knees. Their fingers touched.

Her voice more confident now, Verity said, "You can tell me."

"This camp is one big set. Tania, Ron, Robin, and all of their minions. Some of them pretend to be campers or counselors. Some of them just sit back and watch.

"Before camp starts, they find out all about us, and then, they set the stage and plop us down in the middle of whatever little stories they've made up. They wind us up, sit back, and watch to see where we go."

"Are they watching us now?" Verity asked, twisting to look up into the tree line, which was perfectly still. The sun was low on the horizon—there were still a few hours of daylight, but the sun would be setting soon.

"Someone's always watching," Erin said. "Somewhere."

From the very first time she'd seen her, Verity had known that Erin and the soul mates weren't ordinary campers, and yet, she always found herself thinking about her that way, pushing the uncomfortable truths to the side so she could think of Erin as a girl she liked. But Erin knew things, things she couldn't have picked up in a couple of days at Camp So-and-So.

"How long have you been here?" Verity asked, then wished she hadn't. Erin's dark eyes filled up with tears. She blinked them back, but one slid down her cheek and dripped onto her knee.

"That's the part I'm not sure how to explain," she said. "It happened last summer. Apparently, it happens all the time. They find a camper they like and decide to keep him or her around. It's the same thing that just happened to your friend, Addison. It's what happened to Tad and all the other guys, too. Of course, they can't just steal us. People would notice. Our parents would notice. So instead, they carve out a little piece of you and send the rest of you on your way. You're not the same person you were, but then again, you're not *not* yourself either."

"Like a copy of yourself?"

"More like a reflection," Erin replied. "I guess there's another version of me out there right now, living in my house, going to my school, but I don't know what she's doing or if she feels like I do."

Verity wondered how you carved out a piece of another person, whether you used a knife or a melon baller or a magic wand.

"Does it hurt?" she asked.

"Not exactly," Erin said. "I just feel kind of hollowed out. Empty. I'm not myself, and you'd think that after a year, I'd be used to it, but I'm not. I never forget that I used to be someone else, that that's who I really am, and, Verity, that person is *gone*."

It took a minute for Erin's words to sink in, but once they did, they nearly took Verity's breath away. Erin was alive, she was unharmed, she wasn't in pain or in danger, and yet, it was clear that a terrible thing had happened to her. It wasn't just that Erin was trapped here, separated from her friends, from her family. She was separated from herself, too. Verity thought about the conversations she had inside her brain multiple times each day, the check-ins and assessments and commentary and pep talks between herself and herself. She thought about what it would mean if someone took that away from her.

"You must be so lonely," Verity said at last.

The moment she said it, Erin began to sob.

"All the time," she said through her tears.

Verity felt terrible. She hadn't meant to make Erin cry, and didn't know how to make her stop. She reached out and put one arm around Erin's shoulders and gave it a tentative squeeze. Erin buried her head in the crook of Verity's neck and wept. Verity didn't say anything, just sat there with both her arms now wrapped around Erin until her crying subsided. At last, Erin peeled herself off of Verity's shoulder, pulling up the collar of her t-shirt to wipe her face. When she was done, the fabric was blotched with tears.

"I'm so embarrassed," she said, looking away.

"Don't be," Verity said.

"Thank you for believing me," Erin said. "Thank you for understanding."

She took Verity's hand and laced their fingers together.

A moment earlier, Verity had been too caught up in the immediacy of the crying girl to think of her as The Girl She Liked. Now, it was all she could think about. A shiver passed through her fingers and up her arm.

"Are you cold?" Erin asked.

"I'm fine," Verity said. In truth, she was better than fine. She was sitting on a step, hip to hip with a beautiful girl, so captivated by the luxurious feeling of Erin's thumb stroking the back of her hand that she couldn't imagine it ever ending.

"What stories are they doing this year?" Erin asked, shaking Verity out of her reverie.

At first Verity was confused, but then she remembered what Erin had said about every camper being plopped down into the middle of Tania's stories.

"I have no idea," Verity said. "I've hardly even seen the other girls."

"No boys this year?" Erin asked, raising an eyebrow. "I guess that makes sense. They did stock up on quite a few of them last summer. Maybe they're evening the numbers."

"I hope not," Verity said with a shudder. The idea of more campers being stolen away was terrible to consider even though she didn't know them.

"Last summer, they stranded a cabin of campers in the high ropes course. They cut down all the ladders and left them there."

Verity gasped. "How did they get down?"

"Actually, it wasn't that big a deal. Everyone in the cabin just slept up there for a couple of days, then when they got bored, they picked apart one of the rope obstacles and just climbed down. Tania must have been pissed because she expected everyone to freak out, and instead, everyone had fun.

"Some of the other cabins didn't have it so easy, though. One got really unpleasant superpowers, and I think another spent the whole week on a quest to find buried treasure at the bottom of Lake So-and-So."

"What about your cabin?"

Erin rolled her eyes. "Verity, count yourself very lucky that you have never had anything to do with the All-Camp Sport & Follies."

Verity laughed and pretended to shudder. "I don't know what it is, but it sounds horrible."

"It was!" Erin said. "We rode horses and made crafts and shot bows and arrows and went canoeing and did these little skits. And there were all these stuck-up rich kids we were competing against. They were extremely fixated on kicking our asses, and I remember they all had matching Gucci flip-flops."

As Erin listed off the activities, her eyes squeezed shut and she began to giggle like these were the most hilarious things anyone on the face of the planet had ever done.

"It all sounds so normal and . . . campy," Verity said.

Erin let out a fresh peal of laughter.

"I know! And look at me now!"

Verity didn't reply, and the smile vanished from Erin's face.

"I guess it's not actually that funny," she said.

"No, not really."

Erin took a deep breath and went back to stroking Verity's hand with her thumb. She hadn't let go of it, not even when she was giggling so hard Verity thought she was going to fall off the step. She held it so casually it might have been an accident, like when their legs brushed together. And though the hand-holding was consuming a sizable chunk of Verity's concentration, she didn't dare say anything to call attention to it.

"Earth to Verity," Erin said, waving her hand in front of Verity's face.

"Sorry. Did you say something?"

"I said, you never told me what story your cabin is in. Are you going to jailbreak us or something like that?"

Tell her the truth, Verity thought, but when she opened her mouth to speak, nothing came out.

"Are you going to tell me, or are you going to stare off into space like a hypnotized trout?" Erin asked, making a goofy face at her.

Tell her the truth. We're already holding hands. How badly could it go?

"We're the love story. Something led us to your cabin, and when we saw you and the guys, all of us thought the same thing at once. That you were our—" Verity cringed at the last word, then spat it out as fast as she could. "Soul mates."

Erin's lip curled and she drew her hand away from Verity's.

"Soul mates?" she mumbled into her knees, turning the word over in disbelief.

Verity's stomach lurched. Erin sounded so quiet, so calm, but there was also something in her voice that sounded like it was about to snap.

"That's not fair," Erin said at last. "They can't do that to people. They can't just mess around with the way we feel. What did they think would happen? Did they think we'd just go along with it?"

Quite suddenly, Verity found that she was too upset to breathe and certainly too upset to reply. Erin wasn't finished talking, though.

"Don't tell me you actually think I'm your soul mate," she said, her voice dripping with scorn. "You don't know me. I don't know you. How could we be anything to each other?"

Verity felt like her heart had been smashed. She believed

everything that Erin had told her—how could she not?—and yet, *this* was the point she couldn't force herself to accept. She had no trouble believing that whoever ran this freak show of a summer camp could scoop out part of a girl's soul, or manufacture a cabin in the woods that had no business being there, with a magnetic path that would draw her right to it.

But Verity couldn't bring herself to believe that they could make her feel something she didn't really feel.

"I never expected you to like me back," Verity said, her voice shaking. "I never expected anything at all."

"Well, good."

Erin was sitting up now, her arms folded across her chest, her face stony and unreadable. Except, Verity found she could read it anyway, like a language she'd picked up in childhood and forgotten she knew.

"But you do," Verity said.

It wasn't arrogant or pushy the way she said it. It wasn't maneuvering; it wasn't manipulative. Verity was merely reading aloud what had been unmistakably written there in the language of Erin's face.

"Excuse me?" Erin asked.

Verity closed her eyes and took a deep breath. When she opened them, she turned to face Erin and looked her in the eyes.

"You do like me a little bit," she said, then braced herself for the next part. "And I like you. I know it doesn't make sense. I don't even know if you like girls, so this might all be really presumptuous on my part, but the first time I saw you, I felt something."

"They made you feel it."

"Maybe," Verity said, "but I believe it anyway."

"Why would you?"

"Because I don't think they can tell me what to feel," Verity said.

"I'm not your soul mate."

That word again. They'd all been throwing it around since the first time they'd seen Erin and the boys, and now she could see why Erin rankled at it.

It was a word that took away all your choices. It was a word that meant there was no one else in the world to find, no one else to look for because it had all been decided and the matter was settled and you never even got to have an opinion about it.

If that's what a soul mate was, then it was bullshit. So much had been taken away from Erin already, and Verity had no desire to be one more thing she hadn't gotten to choose.

Still, there was one thing she needed to know.

"When you saw me standing in front of your cabin, what went through your head? What did it feel like?"

Despite herself, a smile spread across Erin's face as she thought back to the moment that had taken place not two hours ago, but somehow felt like it was from another age.

"I felt like I'd been found," Erin said. "For a moment, I felt like I wasn't alone."

Verity was so happy to see her smile, she wanted to jump up from the cabin steps and do a pirouette and throw her hands up in the air and sing, but she didn't want to scare Erin off either.

"I know what you mean," she said.

"I felt hope," Erin continued, "and I knew it was stupid to pin so much hope on someone I'd never met, but I felt it anyway."

"Hope for what?" Verity asked.

"That I'd be happy again."

It was the most beautiful thing that anyone had ever said to Verity, and she felt her eyes well up with tears at Erin's words.

Wiping them away, she asked, "Can it just mean that?"

Erin's eyes dropped to her knees, but she reached over and placed one of her hands on top of Verity's, interlacing their fingers.

"*There's a danger in thinking another person can make you happy. Which has never stopped anyone from doing it,*" Erin said. "That's a line from this book I like. There's a character named Nikolai. He's a healer who falls in love with the main character, Isis Archimedes, and she falls for him, too. Only, he has to stay in the village and heal people, and she has to go out on this quest to fulfill her destiny. Anyhow, that's what he says to her before she leaves, when they both know it won't work out."

Verity knew the scene she was talking about. And unlike Erin, who'd obviously not read the next four books, she knew that wasn't the last Isis saw of Nikolai, not by a long shot. But even so, that line had always meant something different to her.

"I always thought Nikolai was saying, you shouldn't go around expecting other people to make you happy, but that doesn't mean they won't."

"It makes more sense the other way," Erin said.

"I know it does."

"But I like your way better."

Then she leaned over and touched Verity's chin and kissed her.

At first, Verity panicked, fearing that she'd kiss too prudishly or sloppily, or that their teeth would clack up against each other, or that she'd lose her balance and fall off the steps, or that this was all some sort of joke that Erin was playing on her, and that in another moment, a crowd of people would leap out of the bushes, including her mother, the paparazzi, and Lionel Hernandez, who'd given her her first kiss at a dance in the seventh grade and told everyone she was terrible at it. And all of them would point and say, "We knew it! We knew it all along!"

But more than anything, more than she was scared, Verity wanted to keep feeling this girl's lips against her own. And their teeth did not clack together, and it was neither too prudish nor too sloppy, and no one lost her balance. Verity reached out and put her arms around Erin's waist and Erin put her arms around Verity's shoulders, and Verity breathed in the smell of wood shavings that clung to Erin's hair.

The air around them was full of electricity and a warm golden light, and when Verity opened her eyes—just for a second, just to convince herself it was really happening—she saw hundreds of golden sparks drifting around their faces like fireflies.

Then she heard a gasp from the edge of the clearing. Then another. Then a nervous giggle.

Because Verity's eyes were already open, she saw the peaceful expression on Erin's face curdle before she pushed Verity away.

Erin parted her lips to speak, and the golden light that had enveloped their faces darted inside her mouth, and then it was gone. All the firefly sparks buzzing around their heads froze and dropped out of the air like stones.

"What happened?" Erin asked. "What did you do to me?"

Erin leapt up from the concrete step and staggered backwards, in such a hurry to get away from her that she tripped on the top step and nearly toppled inside the cabin.

"Did you know they were there? Is this some kind of joke to you?" Erin asked, her face contorted with rage.

Before Verity could reply, Erin pointed at her and said, "Don't. Just don't."

She fled inside the cabin. Verity heard the fall of her footsteps, and then nothing. The darkness swallowed her up.

At the edge of the clearing stood Verity's cabinmates, too stunned to say a thing.

CABIN 5

SURVIVAL

[SCENE: Twelve feet beneath the smoldering remains of Cabin 5]

They could not squeeze through the thorns or cut them down or go over them, and when the hedge went up in flames, they found themselves surrounded, trapped behind a wall of fire with no way out.

They could not go under the wall of thorns either, but they had tried, and in the end, that was what saved them.

One of the girls had the idea to jump into the tunnel they'd been trying to dig under the wall. It wasn't a proper tunnel yet. It was only a hole, not more than six feet deep. However, when the girl from Cabin 5 jumped down it, the ground at the bottom crumbled under her weight. Her right foot punched through and dangled beneath her into an unseen nothing. She dug her fingers into the dirt, hoping to catch hold of a root, but the earth gave way and she fell through it, discovering that the bottom of their hole was the ceiling of someone else's tunnel. Fortunately, it was not a large one, only about eight feet in diameter, and the girl did not have far to fall. She even landed on her feet.

One of her cabinmates saw her fall down the hole and ran over to pull her out. However, when the cabinmate looked down the hole, her friend was nowhere to be seen, and when she called out her name (which was Haley, though I hardly expect you to care about that at this stage in the game), Haley called back to her to get the others and jump.

It was a tunnel for the stagehands, used for cutting from one side of Camp So-and-So to the other quickly and without being seen. It was big enough to accommodate a loaded dolly, a wheelbarrow, or, in a pinch, a very agreeable horse. At that moment, though, the girls from Cabin 5 did not care about its purpose or its terminus.

They followed it under the mess hall, alongside the long, unnecessarily winding road, deep into the woods, beneath the pony trail, until it joined up with the limestone-walled network of passageways in my cave.

They followed it.

CABIN 1

THE ALL-CAMP SPORT & FOLLIES

[SCENE: Their numbers depleted, KADIE, CRESSIDA, and DORA prepare their song-and-dance number for the final contest in the All-Camp Sport & Follies.]

Kadie refused to let herself be awed by the theater. It was impressive, she admitted, but it was also ridiculous. They were miles away from anything like a real city, and yet the walls were draped in brocade, the seats upholstered in gold velvet. Heavy brass chandeliers hung from the vaulted ceiling, and the stage had been recently sanded and finished. Who were they trying to impress out here in the middle of nowhere?

The costume and props department was equally opulent and stocked with every sort of wig, frock, and set piece imaginable. There were flapper dresses, top hats, hoop skirts, gold lamé jumpsuits, fringed hippie vests, straw boaters, gowns with puffed sleeves, pantaloons, silk smoking jackets, feather boas, and sequined hot pants. The makeup table was laid with spirit gum and latex, baby powder, false eyelashes, and dozens of pots of eye shadow, rouge, pancake concealer, and gloss, all of it brand new.

"Do you do theater at your school?" Cressida asked the other two girls.

"Assistant director," Kadie said.

"Props," said Dora.

"Stage crew," Cressida said. "And lights."

"I was going to guess costumes."

Cressida sniffed at this suggestion. "And publicity, too, for all the good that will do us. We've got a whole crew, but no cast."

Kadie turned to Dora with a hopeful grin. "I don't suppose you're secretly good at singing, too?"

Dora belted out a few bars of the national anthem before Kadie held up her hand, cringing in dismay.

"What about you?" said Cressida.

Kadie shook her head vehemently. "The only thing I've ever done is backup and harmonies. And I can't dance at all."

"Is there anything you're actually good at? I mean, besides telling other people what to do?" Cressida asked, her pointed chin jutting out. "You're afraid of horses, you're bad at crafts, you can't sing. Why did you ever care about winning the All-Camp Sport & Follies in the first place?"

Kadie briefly considered slapping Cressida, but instead blew out a long, cool yoga breath.

"I guess a bunch of magical beings filled my head with lies, then stuck me in a cabin with you," she said, then stalked out of the room.

Dora watched her go, then gave Cressida an accusing stare.

"What?" Cressida said, daring her to say another word about it.

"I'm going out to check on her," Dora said. "She's been through a lot."

"I've been through a lot, too!" Cressida called after her, but Dora was already gone.

Cressida sat down at one of the vanity tables and buried her head in her arms. She felt especially small and ugly at the moment, and knew that her reflection would only make those feelings worse. Not only was she small and ugly, but she was failing at what she'd set out to do.

If she had it to do over again, she would have slipped away from the group the first night of camp and gone off in search of Erin on her own. But no, she'd hesitated. She'd doubted herself, and now not only was she small and ugly and failing, but she'd dragged all the other girls into this mess with her.

My name is Kadie Aguilar. I live in Pittsburgh, Pennsylvania, with my mom. I have friends. I go to school and do Model UN and debate and theater. That is my real life. That is real.

Except what if it wasn't?

After her spat with Cressida, Kadie had gone back out to the stage wanting very badly to be alone, to have a few minutes of quiet, a few minutes to think about what she now knew had happened to her.

What they had done to her.

Up until a few hours ago, Kadie had believed herself to be a Camp So-and-So veteran. She remembered friends, counselors, and experiences from last summer, but apparently, none of that had happened. None of those people had even existed. They'd gotten inside her head, tampered with the contents, and now, and as far as Kadie could tell, they'd done it so that she would convince her cabinmates to get on board with the All-Camp Sport & Follies. If Tania, or whoever was running the show, wanted a competition that badly, why not just make it mandatory? Better yet, why not make every cabin do it?

And then Kadie thought about the other cabins and felt a sinking in her gut as she wondered what had happened to them. What kinds of manufactured drama were they being forced to act out? Or was something even worse happening to them?

Kadie sat down in the center of the stage under the comfortingly hot lights, closed her eyes, and tried to concentrate. It was difficult to tell where the false memories ended and the real ones began, so one by one, she began to prod at them, looking for places where the stitches showed.

She thought back to the first day of camp, her mother's harried expression as she'd chewed antacids and unloaded Kadie's bags from the trunk. She thought about the ridiculous argument they'd had on the drive up about whose job it should be to scoop out the litter box.

You had the cat before I was even born, so I don't see why I should be responsible for its upkeep now.

But you love him, Kadie. He sleeps at the foot of your bed like a dog.

Where Jasper sleeps is irrelevant, Mom.

She thought about the snotty way she purposely used words like "upkeep" and "irrelevant" when she had ridiculous arguments with her mother like they were a trump card, like she deserved to win because she threw around words like that and her mother didn't. When she conjured up her mother's face, the way it had looked when she'd sighed and said, "Maybe you should just do it because I'm your mom and I asked you to," Kadie felt tears prick at her eyes.

That memory was real. She felt sure of it.

She rubbed at her eyes, annoyed with herself for crying at a time like this. Tears wouldn't help her, and they wouldn't make this right. Neither would getting angry, although what she wanted most in the world after a good sob in the middle of the stage was to smash the floodlights, slash the curtains, and punch Tania in the face.

She thought about the people she'd met at Model UN, some of whom she had little doubt would grow up to become the kind of people who would wield real power and inflict great harm on the world at large because they would always act like the whole thing was a game. Crying didn't help you against people like that, and neither did getting angry. In fact, they loved it because it confirmed what they already thought: that they were strong and you were weak.

Kadie crossed her legs in front of her and rested her hands on her knees. She tried to clear her head, to blow out her anger and frustration one breath at a time.

This is who I am, she thought.

They can play games with my head. They can think I'm dumb and weak, and that they're better than me, and I'll still come up with a way to beat them.

Because that is who I am.

Kadie opened her eyes to see Dora sitting in the front

row of the theater, watching her like she was a grenade with a pulled pin.

"Dora, could you get Cressida out here?" she asked.

If only Kadie hadn't followed her to the windmill, Cressida thought. If only they'd all just left her alone.

Do you really believe it would have been that easy?

Of course, she still didn't know where Erin was. The Inge F. Yancey camp was so big, its boundaries so far-reaching, Cressida didn't even know where to begin looking. And now they'd lost Vivian and Kimber, and whatever Tania and her minions had done to Erin, Cressida felt sure they had something similar in mind for her cabinmates.

For the first time since she'd arrived at Camp So-and-So, Cressida gave herself over entirely to despair. She wondered how long she could sit there, arms tented over her head, forehead resting on the cool marble vanity table, before someone came to find her. She hoped no one ever would. She hoped they'd put on the show without her and leave her for Tania and the others. It was no less than she deserved.

Then she heard Dora clear her throat.

"Kadie and I have an idea," she said.

Cressida looked into the mirror and saw Dora standing behind her in the dressing room doorway, wearing a strange expression on her face.

"You guys can do whatever you want," she said. "I don't care."

Cressida put her head back down on the vanity table. A moment later Dora cleared her throat again, and Cressida looked up to see that the girl was now standing by her side.

Dora took Cressida by the elbow and hoisted her up from the velvet-upholstered chair.

"We can't do it without you."

Of all the things Cressida had come here to do and had not done, finishing the All-Camp Sport & Follies was at the very bottom of the list. That Kadie and Dora were still making plans after everything that had happened made Cressida a little sad for them. It was like they wanted this to be a normal summer camp so much that they were willing to overlook all evidence to the contrary. Kadie, especially, should have known better. Cressida was a little disappointed in her—and just when she'd been starting to like her.

"I told you," Cressida said. "I don't care."

Dora sighed, but did not let go of Cressida's elbow.

"They took her memories and put something else in their place, Cressida," she said.

Cressida wrenched her arm out of Dora's.

"They took a whole *person* away from me," Cressida cried.

Dora nodded thoughtfully. "Then you should at least hear what Kadie has to say. After that, you can tell her to her face how much you don't care."

Grudgingly, Cressida allowed herself to be led from the dressing room.

In the center of the stage, Kadie sat in the lotus pose with her eyes closed and a calmness in her face that Cressida envied.

"I hear you have an amazing idea," she shouted from the wings, but not even her buzz-saw voice could break Kadie's concentration.

When she was good and ready, Kadie opened her eyes and stretched her legs out in front of her.

"Every year Camp So-and-So loses the All-Camp Sport & Follies, but every year the games go on exactly the same. Do you know why?"

"No," Cressida admitted. This bit of camp lore still seemed a bit strange to her. It seemed like maybe after a few decades of guaranteed wins, Tania would have lost interest in carrying on this particular tradition.

"Two reasons," Kadie said, massaging the back of her neck. "They think we're entertaining, and they think we're idiots."

Dora stretched out a hand to Kadie and helped her to her feet.

"Our idea is to give them what they want," Dora told Cressida. "What they expect from us."

Cressida studied Kadie's face, certain she had misunderstood. Altered memories and all, the All-Camp Sport & Follies were no joking matter to Kadie.

"I thought you wanted to win," Cressida said.

"This isn't about winning," Kadie said. "It's about ending the All-Camp Sport & Follies. For good."

"How do we do that?"

"First, we have to lose."

A NOTE FROM THE NARRATOR

When Inge F. Yancey III invited me here twelve years ago, it sounded too good to be true, and it was.

He offered me more money than I'd ever seen in one place, simply to spend a single week at Camp So-and-So, to spin one little story in the hopes that it would make his gloomy son smile.

"You'll be a choreographer, camp director, and storyteller all in one. If you can dream it, Tania and her people can make it happen."

It sounded like no camp I'd ever heard of, but I didn't care. I'd just killed off Isis Archimedes, had no idea how I was going to finish writing the series, had no idea if I even wanted to. Mr. Yancey's offer sounded like just the escape from my own life I'd been hoping for.

"He has trouble with other people his age, doesn't make friends easily, but he's a good boy. He likes to design buildings. Maybe you can do something with that."

You already know what a disaster that turned out to be. An innocent boy nearly had his spleen beaten into jam, and I almost alerted the outside world to the existence of this strange camp. That was what came of my efforts to bring a smile to the sour lips of Inge F. Yancey IV.

After that, his father decided he'd had his fill of storytellers, and Tania decided it was too dangerous to send me back to the real world intact. No telling what someone like me might write down—and besides, she'd thought of another use for me.

There is a Eurydice Horne back in the real world, and then there is me, and if there's a reason why we never finished the Isis Archimedes books, I suppose it's because we couldn't do it without each other.

The other version of me, the one who lives in a farmhouse and raises chickens, doesn't quite have the imagination or guts to finish them. And me? I'm too scattered and wild to finish anything. No discipline, no craft.

Together, maybe we could have written them. Together, maybe we could have found a way to stop Tania, to shut down the whole camp, but by myself, I wasn't up to the challenge.

Sometimes I would forget about my chains, about the fact that I was a prisoner, about the part of me that was missing, all because I was too caught up in the story.

I was sucked in. I was so worried about missing something that almost without noticing, I missed twelve years of my life.

I could only relate the wonderful, terrible, gobsmacking things that I saw from my cave. I never could see an ending to any of it— could not stop it, could not even be bothered to try to save myself—not until these girls came along.

Not until they freed me. Not until they showed me the way out.

Humans really are such amazing creatures.

We never do what you expect us to.

CABIN 2

KILLER IN THE WOODS

[SCENE: In a chamber of the cave, covered with bat guano and thousands of tiny mirrors, WALLIS and the NARRATOR, EURYDICE HORNE, consider their situation and its implications.]

Wallis was bewildered. She was overwhelmed. She was standing in a cave with Eurydice Horne, who'd just informed her that Abigail wasn't real, and confirmed the awful truth that Wallis had abandoned her friends in the woods because she'd been afraid of something that didn't exist.

"Have a seat," Eurydice Horne said, patting the spot next to her on the bench. "You look a little frail."

Wallis pushed the chains aside and did as the author suggested. While Wallis recovered her nerves, Eurydice Horne explained how the stagehands rigged the booby traps, how the scenes were viewed—either as live theater or in edited broadcasts, complete with narration—by a forestful of creatures who delighted in watching humans flail and struggle and cower in terror.

"Then my friends are still in danger," Wallis said, imagining a platoon of blood thirsty stagehands setting traps in the forest. "Even though there is no Abigail."

"Yes," said Eurydice Horne.

"Tell me where I can find them," she said.

Facing her friends would be terrible. She'd have to throw herself on their mercy, apologize for being a coward and leaving them in danger. And when she was done doing that, she'd get to break the news that Abigail wasn't even real, and that Megan and Oscar had died, and Shea had been hit with shrapnel and had her hands slashed to ribbons by barbed wire booby traps, and they'd all been frightened out of their senses for someone else's entertainment. Going to them with a story like that—would they even believe her?

Wallis turned her attention to the mirrors that covered every inch of the chamber walls and ceiling. On some of them, there were only swaths of trees or grass or water with no other movement, but on others, Wallis could see human-looking figures dashing around the frame so quickly their figures blurred. Each time they flashed across the screen, something changed—the mossy side of a rock now faced south, one fork of a trail was covered over by rotting leaves—until the scene was unrecognizable from what it had been.

"Are those the stagehands?" she asked.

Eurydice Horne raised her eyebrows and nodded. "Didn't take you long to find that, did it?"

Wallis let her eyes skim over more of the mirrors. In some of them, Wallis could see her fellow campers. She saw two girls sitting on a concrete block step, their knees bumping together in a way that might have been accidental or not. On another screen, she saw two girls sitting on the stage inside a theater, sketching plans in a notebook. Wallis's eyes darted to the opposite wall, to a mirror where a third girl with thin blonde hair like dandelion fluff sat at a vanity, her face buried in her arms.

"How did you know where to look?" Eurydice Horne asked.

Even if Wallis had known that Kadie, Dora, and Cressida were all in the same cabin, the mirrors they'd appeared on were nowhere near one another. And yet, Wallis had located both as though a string connected them.

Wallis shrugged. "I just did. Why?"

"It took months of practice before I was that quick at it," said Eurydice Horne. "And I was stuck here. I didn't have anything else to do."

Before she could elaborate, Wallis pointed to a mirror wedged in a corner near the cave floor where she could see half of Corinne's unsmiling face.

"There they are!" she said.

One by one, four girls crossed the frame. They were all whole and alive and, as far as Wallis could tell, unharmed.

"I have to get them," Wallis said. "I have to bring them back here where it's safe."

"And how are you going to convince them to come?"

"I have no idea," Wallis admitted before starting for the chamber door. Before she passed through it, she turned around and said, "Don't worry, though. I'll come back. I won't leave you here."

"I'll be watching," Eurydice Horne said.

Wallis made her way back to the mouth of the cave and onto the pony trail. It was easy to find the girls from Cabin 2, but then, it was easy to find anything if you had a picture showing you the way, and easy to see booby traps and snares when you weren't hysterical with fear. As it happened, the rest of Cabin 2 had wandered lost in the woods after cutting themselves out of the net, but had eventually stumbled upon the pony trail less than half a mile from the mouth of the cave.

They had stumbled upon other things, too, but more about that in a moment.

Up ahead, Wallis could hear twigs and leaves crackling under her cabinmates' feet. Gulping down her fear, Wallis cleared her throat and called out to them.

"Hey!" she said. "It's Wallis. I'm here. Is anybody there?"

The crackling of leaves went still. A moment later, Corinne stalked around the bend in the path looking as though she might box Wallis's ears. Wallis had heard that expression in old books, but had never before seen anyone who looked as though they might actually do it.

"You left us up there to die," Corinne said, now just a dozen paces away from Wallis and closing, her face livid.

Becca and Hennie came around the bend in the path next, calling after Corinne.

"Stay away from her!" Becca cried.

"She's trying to lure you to Abigail," Hennie warned.

Thankfully, Shea came around the bend next. As soon as she laid eyes on Wallis, she trotted past Becca and Hennie and stepped in front of Corinne. She threw her arms around Wallis's shoulders and swallowed her up in a hug.

"SWEETIE, I'M SO GLAD YOU'RE ALL RIGHT!"
she said. Her throaty twang that sounded like honey and clover and being outdoors had returned to its full volume.

Wallis had never been so glad to hear anything in her life.

"I'm so sorry," she said, tears rolling down her cheeks.

When she pulled away to dry them with her sleeve, she
noticed there was something different about Shea.

"Where'd you get those bandages?" she asked.

Gone were the scraps of t-shirt sleeves they'd used to
staunch Shea's bleeding the previous night, and in their place
were fresh strips of gauze, expertly applied. She looked better,
too, and Wallis noticed that she and the other girls were all
carrying bottles of water. Hennie had a package of granola
bars sticking out of her shorts pocket.

"Where'd you get all that stuff?" Wallis asked.

It was then that another party of girls rounded the bend in
the trail. One was tall and spindly with dark bangs that covered her eyes. She was pushing a wheelbarrow that held a girl
with a prominent upturned nose and the limp body of a girl
wearing an orange hoodie. Behind them walked a girl with a
fearsome puncture wound on her leg and more freckles than
Wallis had ever seen on a person. The girl with thousands of
freckles carried a raven on her shoulder.

Shea pointed down the trail to these new girls. "FROM
THEM. THEY'RE FROM CABIN 3, AND WAIT UNTIL
YOU HEAR WHAT HAPPENED TO THEM."

There were only four of them, Wallis noticed. Was the
fifth girl in Cabin 3 dead? Was she still out there?

The trail was getting crowded now, and though Hennie
and Becca still hung back, suspicious of Wallis, and Corinne

didn't even bother hiding her resentment, the girls from Cabin 3 were eager to regale her with stories of their quest. At first, Wallis was skeptical that anything they'd faced could be worse than Abigail, but when she heard about the spider-snake monster and the murderous horse that had tried to drown them in the lake, she was forced to admit that, far-fetched as those terrors sounded, at least they were real.

The girl with thousands of freckles had the fang marks in her leg to prove it, though the contents of the kelpie's vial had stopped the venom from killing her. The girl in the orange hoodie had been magically transported into the body of a raven, leaving her human body an empty shell. Wallis's own troubles seemed almost mundane compared with that.

The raven's name was Renata, and she caught Wallis up on what she'd already told the others. She told her about the quest, about the fate of Cabin 5, and about what she'd learned from Robin—how they were all actors in the middle of some woodland theatrical production.

So they knew about it too, Wallis thought, but before she could chime in to compare notes, Renata began to talk about some kind of prophecy.

All the girls from Cabin 3 could recite it by heart, and did. Even knowing what they knew, all four of the girls seemed to take it very seriously, which Wallis thought was odd. Most of it sounded like nonsense to her, except for one part that made her ears prick up:

First you must find the beast inside its lair
And then set free the one imprisoned there.

If the girls from Cabin 3 had already dispatched the beast, Wallis had a theory about the next line.

"I think I know who you're supposed to set free," she said.

"You do?" asked the girl with thousands of freckles.

"Eurydice Horne, author of the Isis Archimedes series, is chained to a bench in the cave. The same people who are putting on this 'play' are holding her prisoner there. She's the narrator," Wallis said, then added, when she saw the wary looks the girls were exchanging, "If you want, I can show you."

The girls from Cabin 3 muttered amongst themselves, but it was Corinne who spoke up first.

"Why would we follow you anywhere?" she asked. "Are you going to abandon us in the cave, too?"

Wallis shoved her hands into the pockets of her overall shorts and looked at the tops of her shoes. It was clear that the girls from Cabin 3 were torn. Wallis could tell how badly they wanted to see what was inside the cave, but knew they also didn't want to risk alienating their new allies by appearing to take Wallis's side.

Finally, the sticklike goth girl could bear it no longer.

"I'm going," she said, bold at first, but careful to avoid eye contact with Corinne.

"I'm going, too," said the girl with thousands of freckles, who'd thought her quest was over once before and wasn't about to let the chance slip away again.

"I THINK WE SHOULD ALL STICK TOGETHER," Shea said.

At last, Corinne relented.

"Fine, then I'm coming, too," she said.

As they made their way back to the cave, Wallis broke the hard truth about Abigail to them. After hearing everything that happened to Cabin 3, it was easier than it might have been to tell them. Still, she could tell it was little consolation for them to learn that the danger had been real even if Abigail wasn't. Fleeing into the night with a psycho killer on your heels was one thing. It was as familiar as apple pie and televised football. But finding out you'd been pursued through the woods, driven half-mad with fear by a crew of stagehands? It was hard to know what to do with that.

While the information sank in, Wallis quickened her pace and fell in step with Corinne, who was leading the way. She knew an apology was unlikely to make a difference, and yet, she needed to do it anyway.

"I'm sorry I ran," she said.

Corinne pressed her lips together tightly and said nothing.

"You kept them all alive, Corinne," she added, admiring the girl for her cool head, her sheer nerve. "I wanted to say thank you."

"For what?" Corinne said, looking her in the eye at last.

"For being braver than I was," Wallis said. "I know I messed up, and I hope that someday I can make it up to you."

"We're on the same side. You don't need to make anything up to me," Corinne said unexpectedly. "Whoever did this to us, though, I'd like to even the score with them."

Wallis felt the twisting guilt in her chest loosen its hold. If the rift between her and Corinne was not fully mended, it was at least patched.

When they reached the cave, Wallis took the lead. Wheelbarrow and all, the nine of them wound through passageways into the heart of the cave and, finally, into the chamber that held the thousands of mirrors and, of course, Eurydice Horne.

The sticklike goth girl pushed the wheelbarrow, and the girl with thousands of freckles held the raven on her shoulder. They rushed toward Eurydice Horne with their hatchets drawn, causing the author to shriek and hold her hands up to her face.

"Don't worry," said the sticklike goth girl. "We're here to free you."

Eurydice Horne did not seem to appreciate their efforts, however. She would not uncover her face. She would not look at them. She had been almost entirely alone for the past twelve years, this cave the only home she'd known, and suddenly, it was full of overwhelming girls, very loud, very insistent on changing things.

"Wait," said the girl with the upturned nose, whose seat in the wheelbarrow gave her a better vantage point. "You don't need the hatchets."

The girl with the upturned nose reached out and pulled the chains off of Eurydice Horne. Every movement was agony for her with her torn flesh and broken leg, but she gritted her teeth and did it anyway. Link by link, the chain tumbled to the floor. Eurydice Horne's hands dropped from her face as the girls from Cabin 3 stared at her, puzzled.

"These chains aren't attached to anything," said the girl with thousands of freckles.

A Note from the Narrator: If I wanted to drape my body in chains and hide in a cave for twelve years, that was my business, wasn't it? But before I could open my mouth to explain, five more girls burst into my chamber.

Each one of their faces was streaked with sweat and ash. Their hair was singed; their clothes reeked of smoke.

Wallis stepped forward, stuck out her hand to one of the girls, and shook it.

"Cabin 5, I presume?" she asked.

The singed-haired girl looked a little taken aback, but nodded.

"You're not dead!" cheered Renata, who'd last seen Cabin 5 a smoldering ruin.

"How did you know it was us?" asked one of the girls, wiping soot from her face with a bandanna.

Wallis pointed to a mirror on which she saw an empty tunnel about eight feet in diameter.

"I saw you coming through there a few minutes ago," she said.

"But how did you know where they came from? And how did you know they were going to end up here?" Corinne asked.

Wallis looked to Eurydice Horne for help as she fumbled with her explanation, but the author said nothing.

"It's something about the way the mirrors are connected," Wallis explained. "It's like they talk to each other, and if you look at them closely enough, they tell you where to look next."

"What else do you see?" Corinne asked, looking up at the part of the ceiling that Wallis was studying. Like the rest of them, Corinne only saw her reflection.

Wallis pointed to one mirror, and told them about the All-Camp Sport & Follies and the Inge F. Yancey Young Executives Leadership Camp. She pointed to another and told them about the imprisoned soul mates. She told them how the remains of Cabin 5 still smoldered and smoked and that no one had come to clean up despite Robin's threats.

A Note from the Narrator: Some of the girls looked angry as they listened, some looked like they might cry, and a few looked as though they might like to take a swing at me.

But not Wallis.

I think that Wallis understood my position better than anyone. Wallis knew that even if you were a victim, a prisoner, or a sacrifice, you could still make terrible mistakes. You could fail to act. You could fail to do enough.

But that is where the similarities between us ended.

"This room would make a great battle station," Wallis said, studying the tangle of mirrors and stories. "I can see where they are, where they're going, which parts are undefended."

"We can set traps of our own," said the sticklike goth girl.

"And make sure the others are safe," Renata added.

"We can make them pay for what they did to us," Corinne said, setting her jaw.

"And when that's done, we make for the theater," Wallis said. "All the other cabins are starting to head that way. I can see it on the mirrors. We join forces, and together, we finish this."

"We'll need walkie-talkies," said the sticklike goth girl, frowning. "Otherwise, I'm not sure how it can work."

Wallis went quiet for a minute as she considered this.

"Can you find us a couple of those stagehands, Wallis?" Renata asked as she flew around the chamber, scanning the screens. "Preferably some who don't look so spry."

Wallis grasped the implications, and a slow smile spread across her face. She pointed to a screen that showed two stagehands napping in the rocks near the mouth of the cave.

"Corinne, would you like to do the honors?" she asked.

A Note from the Narrator: Wallis would have made a spectacular narrator, I am sure, but as I have pointed out, Wallis and I are different. She gathered together all these stray girls and led their charge, and I stayed behind to narrate and buy them some time.

That's what I told them, anyway, and it's half true. The other half is that I couldn't quite give up that old need of mine to see what happened next—to see everything that happened next. It's not a nice need. It's not a healthy one. It's the kind of need that keeps you trapped in a cave for twelve years.

When I first found I could pick out the stories on the screens, I was intoxicated by it, and I still am. But Wallis could look even deeper. She could see right away what I had not yet learned.

That this was a story that needed to be ended forever.

CABIN 3
THE HERO'S QUEST

[SCENE: After parting ways with the rest of her cabin, THE GIRL WITH BEADS IN HER HAIR casts her lot with ROBIN in the hopes of finishing their quest. However, while crossing the clearing, she feels the ground begin to give way beneath her.]

One of her legs plunged into the earth, and the other skidded after it into the hole. She reached out frantically, digging her fingertips into the crumbling dirt. Below, she could feel her legs dangling into nothing. She kicked out to the side, looking for a foothold, but could find nothing solid. Her arms wouldn't hold her for much longer.

"Help!" she called out to Robin, wondering how the two of them could have missed a hole of this size in the middle of the clearing. It *had* been covered over by a cluster of blackened brambles, but still, the girl with beads in her hair felt as though she ought to have noticed.

Robin came running over, her face flooded with relief.

"Of course!" she said. She reached out to the girl with beads in her hair and took hold of her arms. Instead of pulling her to safety, though, she said, "Meet you at the bottom," and let go.

It wasn't a long drop, and the shock barely had time to register before the girl with beads in her hair landed with a thump and a grunt.

"Get out of the way," came Robin's voice from the top of the hole. "I'm coming down."

The girl with beads in her hair pulled a flashlight from her backpack and turned it on. She wasn't standing in the bottom of a hole at all. The hole she'd fallen into seemed to have punched through the ceiling of an enormous tunnel. She scooted off to the side just in time to see Robin fall through the hole and land on the dirt floor of the tunnel, graceful and sure-footed as a deer.

"Are you okay?" Robin asked. The girl with beads in her hair glowered at her, understandably cross after having been dropped into a pit without warning. She shone her flashlight in one direction down the passageway, then in the other. It continued farther than her beam in both directions, and aside from her and Robin, it was deserted.

"Is this where Cabin 5 ended up?" she asked.

"They must have dug the hole, then jumped in once they hit the tunnel," Robin said. "I thought it was strange that there weren't any bones up top."

"Are we going after them?"

"Why would we?" Robin asked. "They're fine. What do they need with us?"

The girl with beads in her hair shone her flashlight down the passageways again, then up the sides. The tunnel was perfectly round, like it had been made by a machine, but the girl could see no beams, joists, or supports keeping the earth above from crashing down on their heads.

"Then where are we going?"

"Across the lake," Robin said. "Corporate headquarters, if you will."

The girl with beads in her hair wondered what her role in this was to be. Was she just fooling herself into thinking that tagging along on this errand would somehow help the others?

One soul among you must hold it at bay, she thought, repeating it to herself a few more times as she followed along behind Robin.

"What did you mean when you said you had a mutiny on your hands?'" asked the girl with beads in her hair, thinking back to what Robin had said at Cabin 5.

With each step, Robin seemed to quicken her pace, and she sounded almost winded when she answered.

"Ordinarily, if something like what happened at Cabin 5 happened, a whole crew of my stagehands would have been there on the double. The fire would have been out before it started. Even more, it never should have happened in the first place. Those girls didn't have binoculars when I searched their bags on the first day."

"Is there a chance you just missed them?" asked the girl with beads in her hair.

Robin looked over her shoulder and gave her an icy look.

"No. There is not a chance I 'just missed' them," she said. "And I didn't 'just miss' the pocket watch that the girl from Cabin 1 smuggled in either, and I definitely didn't 'just miss' the explosives wired to the gas tank of the truck."

The girl with beads in her hair had no idea what she was talking about, but the way Robin talked about things like it had all just been some sort of glitch made her blood boil.

"It's still wrong," said the girl with beads in her hair. "Even though you didn't kill anyone."

"No one important anyway," Robin muttered, but the girl with beads in her hair did not hear her.

"Don't you see that you can't just do this to people?" she asked.

Robin stopped, looking genuinely puzzled.

"Why not?"

"Because we're not puppets. We're not toys."

Robin's face was impassive and unmoved. The girl with beads in her hair sighed as she realized that this line of reasoning was getting her nowhere.

"Because someday, we might try to fight back," said the girl with beads in her hair, trying again.

Robin shrugged. "You'd lose."

The girl with beads in her hair shook her head.

"I don't think so," she said. "Not if you don't know where all of us are. Not if your plans can be undone by a pocket watch or a pair of binoculars. Not if your underlings won't even pick up their walkie-talkies when you call."

Robin gasped.

"You're right," she said, and without further explanation, she broke into a sprint down the tunnel.

The girl with beads in her hair raced after her.

"Right about what?" she asked, panting.

"Now I know what she's up to," Robin said, grinning triumphantly. "Divide and conquer. She's never liked me. This is

307

her chance to put someone else in charge. She'll use everything that went wrong this summer as an excuse to have me replaced."

The girl with beads in her hair didn't understand a word Robin had said, other than that there seemed to be someone else involved, someone Robin reported to, and as they continued along the tunnel (they were underneath Lake So-and-So by then, only ten minutes on foot from the Inge F. Yancey Young Executives Leadership Camp), she worried whether she'd made the right choice in following the counselor-in-training. It seemed less and less likely that she'd be able to do anything to protect the other campers from Camp So-and-So from where she stood.

The whole time they ran, Robin muttered things under her breath about someone named Tania. How Tania was a diva, Tania was selfish. How Tania was irresponsible enough as it was, but that all of this marked a new low.

The girl with beads in her hair wondered: would it be worse if Robin were leading her somewhere actually dangerous, or if it turned out she was just tagging along to watch someone have a fight with her boss?

As if she could read her thoughts, Robin interrupted her own monologue and turned to face the girl with beads in her hair.

"There's something I need you to do," she said. "When we get to where we're going, Cabin 1 is going to be there. They ended up with one of the more normal stories. No beasts, walls of fire, or anything like that. They might not be prepared for what happens."

"What's going to happen?" asked the girl with beads in her hair.

"I just need you to stay with them, keep them from doing anything stupid," Robin said. "The winner of the All-Camp Sport & Follies is being announced tonight. Almost everyone will be there, and the last thing I need is one of the campers panicking."

As the girl with beads in her hair wondered what the All-Camp Sport & Follies was, they came to a ladder, which they climbed, and a trap door, which they opened. Robin went up first, then thrust out a hand to help the girl with beads in her hair clamber out into a small round room. Robin opened another door, and the girl with beads in her hair discovered that the room they had been inside was a windmill that she was certain was not located on the grounds of Camp So-and-So. She was on Robin's turf now, and even if she'd wanted to turn back, she doubted the doors that opened to Robin would open to her.

The girl with beads in her hair wondered where the rest of the girls in her cabin were right now, if they were safe, if they were together. She hadn't been afraid when the kelpie dragged her beneath the waters of Lake So-and-So—it had happened too fast and she'd been fighting too hard—but she was afraid now.

What kept her moving forward was the reason she'd chosen to come with Robin in the first place. She wanted answers, she wanted the truth, and whether it was a mistake or not, she wanted to see her quest through to the end.

But first, she wanted to find the girls from Cabin 1.

CABIN 4

SOUL MATES

[SCENE: Outside the soul mates' cabin, VERITY stands between her cabinmates, who have just witnessed what Verity thought was a private kiss, and ERIN, who has just stormed inside.]

Her cabinmates wore a thousand questions on their faces, but Verity was too angry to answer any of them. They'd spied on her! They'd spied on her, and now Erin was gone. All Verity could think about was going after her, apologizing for her stupid cabinmates, explaining how she hadn't known they were in the bushes. She hoped Erin would listen to her.

She hoped that was why Erin had run away—not because she wished she had never kissed Verity at all.

"We're sorry, Verity," Alix said, inching toward the steps, her hand outstretched like Verity was a feral cat who might dash off. "We were just surprised, is all."

"We just got here, I swear," Amber added. "We didn't mean to barge in on you."

"Please, don't be mad," Annika said.

Verity wanted to believe them. She did believe them, but the thought of losing Erin without even getting a chance to explain was unbearable.

"I—" Verity stammered, unable to find the words for what she was feeling, for what she wanted to say. "I have to go," she said, scrambling to her feet and following Erin through the cabin door.

Inside, it looked nothing like their cabin. It was bigger, for starters. Verity couldn't even see the back of it from this first room. Skateboards, guitar cases, and comic books lay on the floor, along with half a dozen pairs of shoes.

It was only when Verity was through the first room that she realized that she had seen *Addison* standing with the rest of the girls from Cabin 4 at the edge of the clearing just seconds before.

It couldn't have been her imagination, but it couldn't have been possible either. How could Addison be in two places at once?

She froze in the hallway, realizing that everything Erin had told her was true. Addison had been split in two, just like the soul mates, and now half of her was outside the cabin and half was somewhere else. She'd never doubted Erin's word, but it was a different matter to see it for herself. She thought about turning back just to make sure, but then she heard Erin's footsteps ahead of her and followed them.

She ran through the living room, which was furnished with lumpy couches and wagon-wheel tables. A half-finished game of Life was laid out on one of them. There was a dining room, a boys' dormitory, and two bathrooms. Finally, Verity reached the last room. She peeked around the door frame and saw that Erin had thrown herself belly-first on one of the beds and buried her face in a pillow. Not wanting to seem like a sneak, Verity called attention to her presence by rapping on the door frame with her knuckles.

Without looking up, Erin said, "You shouldn't be here. I mean, you *really* shouldn't be here."

"I don't care," Verity said. "Are you okay?"

Erin didn't answer right away, which Verity understood. Given the circumstances, it was a complicated question.

While she waited, she studied the handful of artifacts Erin had pinned to her wall. There were a few comic book covers with ripped edges, a pretty red maple leaf, and a single photograph of Erin and another girl with wispy, blonde hair that stuck out around her head like dandelion fluff. They'd both painted their fingertips with an array of monster faces and had been wiggling them at the camera when the shot was taken.

Verity felt a pang of jealousy, which she knew was stupid.

Don't assume things, she told herself. *Besides, you're here because you're worried about her. She doesn't owe you any explanations.*

Finally, Erin rolled over on her side, and Verity saw that her eyes were puffy.

"You can come in if you want to," she said.

Verity came in and took a seat on the rag rug next to Erin's bed.

"I feel different," Erin said at last.

Verity understood, or at least she thought she did. Talking to Erin, holding hands with Erin, kissing Erin—it made her feel confident and right, and even though the kiss had ended like it did, the feelings stuck around. Verity's heart was light, her mind easy. Even her skin felt good.

"I feel different, too," Verity said.

Erin shook her head. "I wasn't talking about that."

"Oh," said Verity, feeling dumb and also a little bit hurt. Erin's tone was brusque in a way it hadn't been out on the cinder-block step.

"What I mean is," Erin explained, "I feel like myself again. The way I used to be."

Verity remembered what Erin had said before about feeling like a part of her had been hollowed out, about feeling lonely all the time.

"Isn't that a good thing?" she asked.

Erin nibbled her bottom lip as she turned over the thing she was trying to say.

"Have you ever hated a food, then one day, you eat some by mistake and realize you like it? Like olives—one day you hate olives, the next, you'd eat them on everything. And it's weird, because it's not like you set out to like olives and trained and built up a tolerance to them. You just changed without knowing you'd done it."

Verity wondered what Erin was trying to tell her. Was it that she'd changed her mind? That kissing her had been a mistake? Something seemed different about her, but only in the smallest ways. Only in ways you'd only notice in someone you'd known for years.

Some of the sweetness and joy had gone out of her face, replaced by something more no-nonsense and serious. She still talked like someone who said what was on her mind, but she seemed more patient, less likely to wander off in search of someone better to talk to.

Verity shouldn't have noticed these things, but she noticed them anyway.

"Back home, my best friend was always trying to get me to read those Isis Archimedes books, and I never wanted to. Then I came here, and I swear, I must have read the first book seven times. I loved it, I memorized whole paragraphs of it, and now, I feel the way I used to. Like, reading that book no longer seems like something I want to do with my time."

"You don't want to read Isis Archimedes anymore?" Verity asked. She had no opinion about olives, but was stricken to hear Erin dismiss the Isis Archimedes books so casually. More than anything, though, she was confused. "Are you talking about what happened back on the steps? With us? Or are you talking about something else?"

"I'm talking about *everything*," Erin said, sitting up and swinging her legs over the side of the bed. "Don't you get it, Verity? This is *me*. The whole me. The put-back-together-again me."

In the hallway, they heard a stampede of feet, and then Addison, Annika, Alix, and Amber were standing in the doorway.

"Where's everyone else?" Amber asked, looking a little disappointed to find only Verity's soul mate inside the cabin.

"Never mind that," Annika said. "Where's Addison? The real one."

The changeling really did look exactly like Addison. She had the same springy, blonde curls, the same wine-colored birthmark on her neck, the same ropey volleyball player's body. However, when Annika, Amber, and Alix had stumbled upon this version of Addison in the woods without Verity, her explanations had proven entirely unsatisfactory.

They had been best friends with Addison since the fourth grade. They knew she ate her string cheese by biting right into it rather than peeling it apart, and that she had a lucky bra that had been washed so many times it was practically gray. They could tell the difference between when she said she was okay and wasn't and when she said she was okay and was. They even knew that she always checked the underside of a toilet seat before sitting down on it because she was afraid there'd be a spider.

The moment Addison joined them in the clearing and opened her mouth to explain what had happened, they knew she was a different person.

Annika and Alix explained what had happened when they'd been lost in the woods and how they'd found the soul mates' cabin. Then Erin explained about the camp and how the soul mates—and now, their friend—had been split apart, one half to be sent back to the real world, and one to remain at camp forever, or until Tania tired of them and dispatched them.

"We should go get her," Alix said.

"You can't just go pick her up," Erin said. "They'd stop you. It's too dangerous."

"I don't care," Alix said.

"And even if we did find Addison, there'd still be two of her," Annika added, looking discouraged. "And neither one of them would actually be *her*."

While they argued about what to do, Amber listened and pored over the pictures on the wall over Erin's bed. It wasn't that she was a snoop exactly. Amber had a puppyish curiosity about her, and a habit of going through other people's jewelry boxes and glove compartments and peeking in open windows when she went for walks, not because she was looking for anything in particular, but just because she wanted to see what was there.

"I've seen her before," she said, pointing to the girl with dandelion-fluff hair and monsters painted on her fingertips. "She's here at camp."

Erin jumped up from the bed so roughly, the springs rattled. She ripped the picture off the wall and shoved it in Amber's direction.

"This girl? *This year?* Are you sure? Are you positive?"

Amber pushed the picture away and wrinkled her nose.

"Yeah. I saw her getting into a black town car with a bunch of other people over by the stables this morning."

"Why didn't you say anything?" Verity asked, getting caught up in Erin's fervor.

"It didn't seem like a big deal."

"Shhh, I'm trying to think," Erin said, pacing from one side of the rag rug to the other.

"I heard them say something about going across the lake to use the horses at the other camp," Amber added.

Erin stopped pacing and gripped the sides of her head.

"Oh no no no no no," she muttered, then met Amber's eyes. "Are you absolutely sure that's what you heard?"

"Of course I'm sure."

Without offering any kind of explanation, Erin dashed out of the bedroom and into the hall.

Addison, Annika, Alix, Amber, and Verity followed after her. They saw her unlatch a door, open it, and disappear down a dark set of basement stairs. They followed her there, too, and when Erin saw that she was not going to be able to outrun them, she said, "I told you. You can't go there. It's too dangerous."

"But that's where Addison is," Annika said.

"That's where everyone is," Erin said. "It's the All-Camp Sport & Follies. I'm supposed to be there, too."

Annika was perplexed, never having heard of the All-Camp Sport & Follies until that moment; however, Amber honed in on the crucial bit of information at once.

"*Everyone* is there?" she asked.

She exchanged glances with her friends, and without speaking a word, knew they were all in agreement. "I'm not leaving here without getting to meet my soul mate," Amber said.

"Or without Addison," Annika added.

That settled it. There was no argument Erin could offer that would sway them, and so she led the way from the dormitories into the secret network of tunnels that connected the grounds of Camp So-and-So with the Inge F. Yancey Young Executives Leadership Camp. When they came out on the other side, they followed a trail from the windmill to the English rose garden and, at last, into the theater.

Every few paces, Erin would shush them or tell them to walk more quietly, or would halt their entire procession in its tracks because she thought she saw a flash out of the corner of her eye. However, they came to the theater doors without being stopped, without even seeing another soul. Before going in, Erin gathered them together for a briefing.

"The lights will be turned down and the show will be going on, so we should be able to sneak in without attracting any attention. Once we're inside the theater, we find the door to the light booth along the back wall. We go up to the light booth, take whoever is working up there by surprise, and knock them over the head with something. Then we should have a good view of the audience and we'll be able to find Addison and the rest of them."

"What do we do after that?" Verity asked.

"I haven't the slightest idea."

Since no one else had a better plan, they followed Erin into the deserted theater lobby. They paused, momentarily dazzled by the ornate chandeliers and wood paneling. But soon, they came back to their senses and the task at hand, and they stole across the room on tiptoe until they came to the door, which Erin opened just a crack.

Inside, they could hear singing.

CABIN 5

SURVIVAL

[SCENE: In the NARRATOR's cave, WALLIS directs the girls from Cabins 2, 3, and 5 to their battle stations.]

They drew up a map of Camp So-and-So, dividing it into a grid.

"First, we clean up. We gather intel. We plan. And then we attack," Wallis said.

Wallis sent the girls from Cabins 2 and 3 out to disarm traps and gather supplies, marking the sectors where these things could be found with the information she gathered from studying my screens.

She also set out to learn as much as she could about Cabins 1 and 4, who were already on the other side of Lake So-and-So. Neither Shea nor the girl with the upturned nose was in any shape to go out in the field, but both wanted to be helpful, so Wallis found a few particularly useful screens and told them to soak up as much as they could. The girl with the upturned nose sat with her fractured leg propped up in front of her, filling Wallis in on the final event of the All-Camp Sport & Follies, which was about to begin. Meanwhile, Shea not only located all of Cabin 4's soul mates—she was also able to figure out that Addison liked the lumberjack, Annika liked the bodybuilder, Alix liked the skateboarder, Amber liked the guitar player, and Verity liked the girl who read Isis Archimedes books (or used to read them).

However, it was the girls from Cabin 5 who landed the most interesting missions.

First, Wallis sent them to the basement of the mess hall, where they found rope, a cinder block, and a grappling hook just where Wallis said those things would be. They loaded everything into the wheelbarrow, then set off down the long, unnecessarily winding road until they came to a blind curve in the road, a spot where the guardrail had nearly rusted away. There, hanging by its rear wheels on the precipice, was the 1989 Toyota 4Runner. Pam, the counselor from Cabin 4, was slumped over, unconscious, in the driver's seat.

It was a delicate operation. First, they braced the wheels with the cinder block. Then, they created a human chain, leaning out over the guardrail to open the door of the truck and hook the rope to Pam's belt loop. There was no other way to reach her, and none of them was strong enough to heave her out of the truck with only one arm.

It would take all of them. They would have to be strong, and they would have to be quick. They would have to pull the counselor from the seat of the truck and lift her out of harm's way before the shifting weight sent the truck careening over the edge.

Wallis might have sent another cabin on this mission. The girls from Cabin 5 had been lacerated by thorns, scorched by flames, choked by ashes. Of all the cabins, they were the most exhausted, the most worn down, and yet, Wallis knew the grit that had helped them escape made them exactly the right girls for this job.

They took their positions behind the guardrail, they dug their sneakers into the dirt, they counted to three, and in one swift motion, they pulled.

ACT 6

Where everything happens in a slightly different order

CABIN 1

THE ALL-CAMP SPORT & FOLLIES

[SCENE: *As the curtain goes up on the final contest in the*
All-Camp Sport & Follies, KADIE, CRESSIDA, and
DORA hatch a daring plan.]

Backstage, Dora and Cressida had put the finishing touches
on their props and their harmonies. On the other side of the
stage, they could just make out the soft shuffling of feet and
hushed whispers of their competitors.

The lights went down, and Kadie took center stage alongside Tania and Ron in front of the closed velvet curtain. Every
seat in the theater was filled, a sea of perfect, cruel faces staring
up at them. Halfway back, Kadie saw Vivian whisper something to Kimber, and the two of them snickered behind their
hands. However, when the spotlight fell on Tania, everyone in
the room fell silent and applauded their leader dutifully.

"Thank you, thank you," she said with a demure bow.
"Welcome to the song-and-dance portion of the All-Camp

Sport & Follies. And welcome to our judges, though they need no introduction."

The audience applauded again as the Inge F. Yancey Young Executives Leadership Camp Board of Directors shuffled onto the stage: the woman in the veiled hat and gloves who seemed to be transported from another time, the woman in the floral-print dress whose age was impossible to tell, and the lumpen creature in the purple suitcoat, his, her, or its face hidden beneath a thicket of black hair. After they were introduced, the three judges filed into the front-row seats that had been reserved for them.

Tania's smile turned venomous as she shifted her gaze from the judges to Kadie.

"As winners of the steeplechase, you'll have the opportunity to choose whether you'll perform first or second."

"We'll go second," Kadie said.

"Very good," Tania said in a way that suggested she was prepared to defeat them soundly either way.

"Then without further ado, let the Follies begin!"

Kadie and Tania shook hands and exited to opposite sides of the stage as the curtains opened.

The sets had been transformed into something marvelous, a canopy of artificial trees and twinkling lights against a backdrop painted to look like the forest at night. A group of Inge F. Yancey campers stood in a ring around a maypole, each one of them holding a long silk ribbon. From the orchestra pit, a flutter of woodwind notes rose, and they began to dance. Their skirts and hair flowed behind them as they glided around the maypole, tying their ribbons into a pastel braid.

Then they dropped the ends of their ribbons all at once

and completed a series of perfectly executed grand jetés before floating offstage. The maypole was lifted out on wires, and the lights dimmed so it looked like the stage was bathed in moonlight.

Three more performers danced onstage to a lively fiddle tune. One wore a donkey mask over his head, while the other two wore wreaths of flowers in their hair. Then a fourth camper came out wearing a sandwich board that had been carved out of Styrofoam and painted gray to resemble a stone wall. The audience all laughed and applauded wildly, these apparently being familiar and much-loved characters from some fairy story or another. After they had frolicked and kissed and chased one another around the stage for a few minutes, they bowed.

The curtain fell, and the audience erupted in applause so raucous that after a few minutes, the curtain was lifted once again and the cast stepped forward and took another bow. The audience came to its feet, and no less than ten bouquets of flowers flew up onto the stage. The cast bowed again, then left, then were called back for yet another bow before they finally exited the stage for good and the curtains closed.

Two days ago, Kadie would have been seething with frustration and rage, but as she stepped into the spotlight, all she could do was hope.

"Good evening, ladies and gentlemen," she said with a smile that she hoped looked more natural than it felt. "We are Cabin 1 from Camp So-and-So, and we are here tonight to dazzle you with our feats of daring, to woo you with song, and to move you to tears with our camp spirit. Without further ado, I give you—Dora!"

When the curtains reopened, the backdrop painted to look like the forest at night was gone. The trees, the twinkling lights, even the musicians in the pit orchestra had vanished in a matter of seconds. Dora stood in the center of the bare stage, beaming like a goon.

They had the whole costume room at their disposal, and unable to decide between frocks, Dora had chosen all of them. She twirled across the stage in a flurry of feathers and sequins and rainbow-striped tights and launched into a series of cartwheels before lunging into a split she was unable to get out of for some moments. At least she did manage to keep from braining herself on her last tumbling pass.

Next, Kadie juggled a set of clubs which she dropped only twice, and Cressida surprised them all with a competent tap dance number.

Then all three of them stepped to the center of the stage, pulling with them an artificial campfire they'd made using cellophane and gold foil and a battery-operated fan.

Dora stepped forward and sang:

On top of spaghetti all covered in cheese
I lost my poor meatball when somebody sneezed.

Then Cressida joined in:

Little Bunny Foo Foo hopping through the forest,
scooping up the field mice and bopping them on the head.

And finally Kadie's song blended in with the rest, her voice a clear, unadorned alto:

Make new friends, but keep the old.
One is silver and the other's gold.

The audience, which had ranged from politely scornful to actively hostile throughout their performances, went completely silent as the girls from Cabin 1 sang in a round. Alone, none of their voices was anything special and none of the songs was anything they hadn't heard a hundred times, but together, they somehow blended into a magical thing.

This number had been Kadie's idea. It was camp, after all. Camp was supposed to be hot dogs and sleeping bags and horseback rides and singing little-kid songs at the top of your lungs. It was not about steeplechase and gazpacho. It was not qiviut sleeping bags and bad dinner theater.

They linked arms and sang in unison:

Make new friends, but keep the old.

One is silver and the other's gold.

That was when one of the lobby doors at the rear of the theater opened and light poured in. Kadie, Cressida, and Dora paused and looked up to see who had passed through them.

Neither Kadie nor Dora recognized the group of girls, but Cressida squinted, sure that her eyes were mistaken, that it was a trick of the light.

They were only through the first third of their plan, and the look on Kadie's face said that she was about to move into the next phase. Cressida stopped singing for a moment, caught Kadie's eye, and mouthed the word, "Wait."

If Kadie had been nervous before, now her heart raced. The heat from the stage lights made her dizzy, and she willed herself to stay on her feet.

From the back of the theater, a girl's voice rang out, filling the entire room. She called Cressida's name.

And Cressida knew that whatever their plan had been, they were going to have to improvise now.

CABIN 4

SOUL MATES

[SCENE: Six girls interrupt Cabin 1's performance in the All-Camp Sport & Follies: ERIN, VERITY, ANNIKA, ALIX, AMBER, and one of the two ADDISONs.]

Erin opened the theater doors quietly and just a crack, but the moment she passed through them and looked down the aisle to the front of the theater and saw who was standing there, she forgot all about being stealthy.

She ran down the center aisle, screaming at the top of her lungs, "CRESSIDA!"

A murmur rose up all through the theater. Heads turned and the audience got up from their seats to get a better look at what was happening. No one was sure if it was part of the act.

Erin vaulted onto the stage and tackled Cressida in a hug that nearly knocked them both off their feet.

"Are you trying to kill me?" Cressida rasped, but tears streamed down her cheeks as she spoke, and a smile that no one at Camp So-and-So had ever seen lit up her face.

"You magnificent bastard! You got my letter," Erin said, eyes wide in disbelief. "You came for me. You believed me."

"Of course I believed you, idiot face," Cressida said. Her voice shook as she threw her arms around Erin again and bear-hugged her. "You're my best friend."

The entire audience had fallen silent and hung on every word the two girls exchanged. Meanwhile, the rest of Cabin 4 threaded through the aisles, looking for their soul mates. It didn't take them long. Alix recognized the skateboarder from across the room and made a beeline for him. Amber waved to the soul mate with the guitar, and Annika introduced herself to the one with the pompadour and well-defined biceps.

It was just Verity and Addison now—one of the Addisons. Across the room, Verity could see the other one laughing with Tad, her soul mate with the firewood-carrying arms, but mostly, Verity's eyes were glued to the stage, where Erin was hugging a girl with translucent skin and hair like dandelion fluff, tears streaming down both of their faces. It was the girl from the photograph in Erin's room. Verity wished Erin were holding her like that, and tried to brush away an ugly prickle of jealousy.

Before Verity's brain could stir up any more trouble, though, Erin found her in the crowd and motioned for her to come up onstage. Guiltily, Verity made her way down the aisle and climbed up the stairs, joining the two girls.

Erin beamed and said, "Verity, this is my best friend, Cressida. Cressida, this is Verity."

They shook hands and smiled, then Erin gave Verity a strange look.

"Can I talk to you for a second?" she asked, taking Verity by the hand and pulling her to the side of the stage. "Are you okay?"

It took Verity a while to answer. After all, it was a complicated question, given the circumstances.

At last, she said, "You do seem different."

"I'm me again," Erin said. "I was trying to explain it before when your friends showed up. You brought me back, Verity. When you kissed me."

Of course, that was what Erin had been getting at with all the talk about olives and Isis Archimedes, and Verity saw that now, but she was still skeptical.

"How do you know it was the kiss that did it?"

Erin gave her a scornful look. "Oh, does golden light usually pour into your mouth when *you* kiss someone?"

"I don't know," Verity said truthfully. "I've never kissed anyone like that before."

"Me neither," Erin said, taking her hand.

Two by two, the rest of Cabin 4 joined them onstage, hand in hand with their soul mates, each one of them brimming with happiness and talking like they'd known one another their whole lives.

"I almost hate to tell them," Erin said.

"I feel badly for them," Verity said. "They don't know what's going to happen."

Erin touched Verity's face gently with her fingertips and kissed her on the cheek.

"Nobody does," she whispered in Verity's ear. "Nobody ever does."

Then Alix kissed the skateboarder.

Amber kissed the guitar player.

Annika kissed the boy with the pompadour.

Addison kissed Tad.

Out in the audience, Verity saw the second Addison flicker, then fade, then disappear altogether.

"Do you want to kiss me again?" Verity asked. "I mean, even though . . ."

Erin laughed. "Of course I want to kiss you again. It's not like I changed *that* much."

A helix of sparks encircled each pair of faces, and light flowed from the stage, bathing the upturned faces in the audience. Not everyone was enchanted—not Tania, certainly—but more than a few found themselves swept up in the passion. The creatures in the audience might have been vicious, they might have been cruel, but they knew a good story when they saw it.

Verity stood on her tiptoes and cupped Erin's face in her hands, and they kissed. It was different this time. This time, there was no shower of sparks, no ray of light emanating from their faces. They weren't outside on a warm summer evening at sunset, crickets chirping as the breeze licked at their hair and tickled them behind the knees. They weren't alone.

And they weren't the same people they had been.

None of this was bad, but none of it was the same either.

As the other soul mates kissed the girls from Cabin 4, one by one each one of them felt himself wake up and, upon waking, discovered he felt like himself—his true and whole self—for the first time in a very long time.

Verity felt Erin's fingers in her hair. She touched her neck. Somewhere, Verity was sure she heard singing.

CABIN 1

THE ALL-CAMP SPORT & FOLLIES

*[SCENE: While everyone is distracted by romance, Cabin 1
resumes their plan with CRESSIDA taking center stage.]*

Cressida was surprised to see her best friend kissing the girl
from Cabin 4 onstage, but only a bit. Erin had come out to her
last summer, right before she left for Camp So-and-So, right
before Cressida had broken her arm—the very night, in fact,
that Cressida had broken her arm.

At the time, Cressida had done her best to be supportive.
She could tell how terrified Erin was to tell her, never mind
that they were best friends and had always told each other
everything.

"How long have you known?" Cressida had asked as the
two of them sat on top of the monkey bars at the playground
behind the elementary school, their preferred venue for serious talks.

"Awhile," Erin said, dropping down through the bars to

hang by her knees. "Deep down, probably a long time. I knew *something* was different. I just didn't know exactly what it was. It's harder to figure out than you'd think it would be. Which is not fair, by the way."

"I'm happy for you," Cressida had said.

"Why?" Erin asked. "It's not like I won something."

They both laughed at this as they got down from the bars and got on their bikes.

"I'm happy because you know," Cressida said. "And because you told me."

"I hope this doesn't make things awkward between us," Erin said, her voice sounding strangely formal and nervous.

"Don't be stupid," Cressida said, pedaling out of the grass and into the teachers' parking lot. "Why would it?"

"Because that's what scares me the most," Erin said. "That you're going to get all weird around me."

"I promise I won't get weird," Cressida said.

That was when she'd hit a patch of loose gravel with her front tire and gone spilling onto the ground, cracking her elbow on the pavement. Erin had ridden home as fast as she could and gotten her dad to pick Cressida up and take her to the emergency room. That was the last time they'd talked about any of it because the next day, Erin left for camp and Cressida stayed on the couch trying not to scratch underneath her cast, and when Erin came home a week later, Cressida wasn't the one who'd gotten weird.

Erin had been distant the rest of the summer, hadn't returned most of Cressida's texts, and the few times they did see each other, Erin had acted like a different person, like Cressida was a casual acquaintance.

The first two months of the school year had been a misery for Cressida without her best friend by her side. And then the letter had come with its postmark from that obscure Appalachian town and the handwriting that she knew so well she could practically forge it, and Cressida's heart had flooded with hope.

And now after a whole year, she was back, she was here, and she was the old Erin. That she was kissing the girl from Cabin 4 was the least astonishing thing about any of it.

There wasn't time to muse further about any of it, and she certainly wasn't about to interrupt Erin so they could compare notes. Cabin 1 had a plan, and now there was more reason than ever to move forward with it. Kadie and Dora had already taken advantage of the chaos and the kissing to creep offstage. That left Cressida to pick up the plan where they'd left off.

She wished she had Kadie's boldness and leadership skills, as they would have come in handy for this part of the plan, but Cressida was determined to do her best. She only wished there were some way to let Erin and the others know what was about to happen.

While the soul mates kissed and the sparks swirled around their faces, Cressida picked up the musical cue and resumed Kadie's song:

Make new friends, but keep the old.
One is silver and the other's gold.

She wished the song were longer so she could buy Kadie and Dora more time, but since it wasn't, she gestured to the audience. They were slow to join in, but soon, the Inge F. Yancey campers and the judges and everybody in the entire theater except Tania was singing along.

Cressida led a sing-off between the left and right sides of the theater, between the front and the back, between the guys and the girls. She made up new verses on the fly and taught them those:

Win or lose, it matters not,
Brave we stood, and hard we fought.
Shoot and knit and ride and row,
All-Camp Sport & Follies, what a show!

She led them in song until finally it could go on no longer. Exhausted, her throat ragged, Cressida threw her arms into the air and called out, "Tonight, we are all friends! We are all friends here!"

She fell to her knees in a deep bow, her forehead nearly touching the stage. At first, the theater was so quiet that Cressida was afraid to look up. Then the clapping started. Cressida lifted her eyes from the floor and was surprised to see more than a few damp eyes in the crowd, not least of them belonging to the judge in the floral-print dress.

"Encore!" someone shouted.

"Bravo!" came another cry from the audience.

Cressida smiled and lifted her arms and bowed again at the waist.

"Bring them out! Bring out the others!"

The spotlight shifted over toward the wings of the stage, ready to light the paths of Cabin 1's other stars.

Cressida hoped they were ready. She hoped they'd be able to convince Vivian and Kimber to let themselves be rescued. She hoped every single Inge F. Yancey Young Executives Leadership camper—or whatever they really were—was sitting right here in this room. She hoped that Kadie had had time to bar the exits. She hoped that if this didn't work, nothing very bad would happen to them.

She hoped with all of her heart, but had to admit, there were a lot of things that could go wrong.

The applause began to fade and turned to grumbling as the rest of Cabin 1 failed to materialize.

Cressida took a deep breath, and when her pulse had steadied itself, she spoke:

"That's not true," she said, then looked down at the spot in the front row where Tania sat grimacing like the wicked queen in a fairy tale. "We are not friends. Not after what you did to us. Not after what you did to Kadie's memory. Not after what you did to Erin.

"So, let us go now. Let *all* of us go, and promise not to do it again."

Tania wrinkled her nose in displeasure.

A Note from the Narrator: This happened every now and again. A few of the campers would figure out what was happening to them. They always got so angry, so self-righteous, but humans were so easily distractible. It had never taken much effort for Tania to nudge their brains back into line. Still, she hated it when they figured things out. They always broke character.

"Or what?" Tania stood up and folded her arms across her chest.

"Or we'll make you sorry."

For a moment, Tania was silent. Her lips quivered, then split apart in an ugly smile, and she burst out laughing.

"You'll make *me* sorry?"

She sat down, clutching the arm of the chair to hold herself upright while she shook with laughter, tears streaming down her cheeks.

They'd agreed to try diplomacy first—it would be less messy for everyone if it worked. Still, Cressida had known that it was a long shot.

"Now!" she called out, lifting her voice to the rafters of the theater.

From the catwalk above the stage, Dora tossed her grandfather's pocket watch out into the audience where it landed in the lap of a still-cackling Tania.

Just crossing the path of the pocket watch on the steeplechase course had been enough to make Tania fall off her horse, and afterward, she'd had to lean on a fencepost to hold herself upright. They'd hoped direct contact would yield more drastic results, and they were not disappointed.

The change came over her at once. All the color drained from her face, and all the youth and beauty as well, leaving her gaunt and haggard, a creature who looked centuries old, not eternally seventeen. With enormous effort, she lifted the pocket watch from her lap and flung it onto the stage. The recovery began the moment the watch left her hand, but it did not happen at once. The rest of the audience sat stunned and motionless as they watched Tania gasp for breath as the color came back into her cheeks. Nobody made the slightest move to help her.

Now was the perfect moment for the next phase of their plan. From her perch on the catwalk, Dora tugged the ropes that she'd spent the afternoon rigging for this very moment. At once, the ceiling of the theater seemed to open up, and a shower of straw and compost and horse dung rained down on the first two rows.

Over the course of the afternoon, Kadie, Cressida, and Dora had spent fifteen minutes planning and rehearsing the number they would perform. The rest of the time they spent wheeling cartload after cartload from the Inge F. Yancey stables and compost piles, hefting them up to the tarps Dora had hidden in the rafters.

And now the fruits of their smelly labor were beginning to pay off.

The Inge F. Yancey campers in the front of the theater leapt from their seats and ran down the aisles, skidding on clods of greenish-brown manure as they fled. When they reached the back, they pulled on the doors to the lobby, only to find them bolted shut.

Cressida breathed a sigh of relief—she'd bought Kadie enough time to lock the doors and trap them all in here.

A loud panic erupted and spread row by row through the theater until everyone there was on their feet, climbing over the backs of chairs, running for the emergency exits, slipping in piles of horse dung.

Clumps of it stuck in Tania's hair and soiled her white sundress. She howled and dragged herself toward the stage. She was still weak, but her fingernails sank into the stage like the claws of a mountain lion, and she hefted herself onto the boards.

Then Cressida's relief curdled as she realized that their plan *had* worked—the problem was, there wasn't enough of it. They'd thrown everything they had at Tania and her minions, and all it had done was make them angry. She hadn't counted on Erin being here, much less the girls from Cabin 4 and their soul mates. So many people were in danger because she, Kadie, and Cressida had hatched this sticky, smelly, underdone plan.

The only thing she could do now was take advantage of the confusion and panic to slip all of the humans out the back. They'd lock the door behind them, row across Lake So-and-So in stolen boats, and when they made land, they'd run down the long, unnecessarily winding road, and they wouldn't stop until they found a proper human adult.

"We left the back door open for ourselves," Cressida whispered to Erin and Verity, pointing backstage. "Take your friends, and I'll catch up with you."

They ran, pulling the other girls from Cabin 4 and their soul mates along behind them, and they disappeared backstage. Cressida turned around just in time to see Tania advancing on her. She dropped to her knees and rolled off the stage as Tania delivered a punch that would have struck her in the face had she been at full strength. Still wobbly on her feet, though, Tania missed and went stumbling across the stage.

Without looking back, Cressida crawled through the orchestra pit to the front corner of the darkened theater, where she found Dora with Vivian and Kimber. The unassuming girl had made her way down from the rafters, crept out into the audience, found the two, and dragged them from their seats. Now, she had each one by the elbow.

"Are they okay?" Cressida asked. Back in the garden, Vivian and Kimber had been starry-eyed and giggling at the attention from Tania's minions, but now they looked as though they'd just woken up from bad dreams.

"I think so," Dora said. "They're a little rattled, but I'm not sure that anything actually *happened* to them."

"Get them out of here," Cressida whispered to her. "We'll meet at the docks."

"What about Kadie?" Dora whispered back.

"I'll find her. I'll make sure she gets out," Cressida said.

"We'll wait for you."

"Don't wait too long," Cressida said. "If we're not out in ten minutes, start rowing across the lake without us."

In the dark, Dora caught her hand and gave it a squeeze.

"We're not going anywhere without you."

Cressida squeezed Dora's hand back. She'd held them together, been quietly brave and resourceful and clever, not at all the spineless sap Cressida had taken her for at first. She found herself wishing she'd been nicer to Dora from the beginning.

The moment she let go, Dora was gone, and Cressida found herself alone in the dim theater packed with screaming, dung-covered minions. They crowded near the doors and shoved at each other, their curses filling the air.

Only the three All-Camp Sport & Follies judges acted as though nothing out of the ordinary had just unfolded. They sat in their seats in the front row, covered in straw and manure, quietly scribbling notes on their scoresheets.

There was no sign of Kadie. Cressida ducked down low and inched her way toward the back of the theater to avoid being noticed. When one of Tania's minions looked in her direction, she dived behind a marble bust in a recess. She began to despair of finding her friend, of escaping the theater, of ever leaving the Inge F. Yancey Young Executives Leadership Camp, and then she heard Kadie's voice in her ear.

"Where are the others?" Kadie asked. She'd huddled behind the marble bust as soon as the chaos broke out and had been waiting there until she could work up enough nerve to make a run for it.

"They got out," Cressida whispered, not knowing whether this was true or not. "I came back to look for you."

Kadie grumbled as they started inching back toward the stage, but Cressida could tell she was glad not to be the only human trapped in this theater with Tania and the rest of them.

They had just reached the stage and scrambled onto it when the locked double doors to the entrance of the theater began to rattle. There came a terrible sound of fingernails scraping against wood, then a clatter on the marble floor, and then the doors flew open, but in the dark, they all heard her before they saw her:

Make new friends, but keep the old.

One is silver and the other's gold.

They craned their necks to see who was doing the singing, squinting against the darkness until they could just make out the shape of a young woman coming down the center aisle. She was hardly more than five feet tall, and she wore cargo shorts and athletic sandals. It was Robin, the counselor-in-training. Cressida realized they hadn't seen her since the first event of the All-Camp Sport & Follies, and wondered where she'd been all that time.

Behind her walked a girl with vagabond eyes and beads in her hair.

What's going on? Cressida thought.

All at once, every Inge F. Yancey camper froze and gaped at the center aisle, aware that they were about to see yet another showdown. They knew who Robin was, even if they looked down their noses at her. She was only the stage manager, after all; they were *actors*. They knew about her long-standing feud with their leader, known it would come to a head someday, but now? The timing was so bad it was almost tacky, not that they expected anything less of Robin.

If Robin was even aware of their presence, she didn't let it show.

She began to sing again.

Make new friends, but keep the rest.

Old friends know just how to hurt you best.

In the dark, her teeth glittered like knives.

CABIN 2

KILLER IN THE WOODS

[SCENE: From her battle station in the NARRATOR's cave,
WALLIS lands upon the truth.]

One question had been nagging at Wallis ever since she sent
the others out on rescue and reconnaissance missions around
Camp So-and-So, and it was this: How did you do battle against
a species of creatures that thought you were . . . amusing?

She and the other campers might as well have been a pod of
trained seals to the true inhabitants of Camp So-and-So. Ador-
able, entertaining, and absolutely nothing to take seriously.

So we turn on them, Wallis had thought at first. *We show*
them our teeth, advance on them as a pack, and teach them that we're
not so cute after all. And maybe they'll decide we're too much trouble.
They'll give up and let us leave.

That was the best-case scenario Wallis could think up,
and it wasn't what she wanted. She didn't want to escape from
Camp So-and-So by the skin of her teeth, or even by wearing

Tania down, and leave everything just as it was for the hapless campers who would show up next summer.

It wasn't enough, and the more Wallis thought about it, the more certain she was that it never *would* be enough. Not if they burned the place to the ground. Not if they tore down every cabin, poisoned the lake, and dynamited the road. Wallis had no doubt it would all be rebuilt within a fortnight.

No, another batch of campers would have to go through the whole thing again. Only, the creatures in charge would be smarter about it next time. They'd find more docile campers and use stronger magics. They'd make sure there was never a revolt like this one again.

Until she'd found Eurydice Horne and the cave, Wallis had never seen this "they," only the shape of the havoc they wreaked. But now she'd seen some of their faces in the screens. They didn't look like particularly wicked faces, and Wallis began to wonder if they only acted this way because they didn't understand the damage they did. Maybe if they knew, they'd stop.

Were they the ones who had located all the campers, researched them, mailed them letters, and offered them scholarships? Something about that didn't feel right to Wallis.

There was something else behind this place, something petty and earthly and spiteful and human.

So when Wallis saw Inge F. Yancey IV appear on the screens a moment later, she understood.

Tania and her minions may have put the girls through these horrible paces and worked these horrible magics on them, but they did it because Inge F. Yancey IV enabled them to do so. Wallis remembered the brochure she'd received in the mail what seemed like a lifetime ago:

Welcome to Camp So-and-So! For over 75 years, the Yancey family has been proud to provide young people with opportunities for physical, mental, and social growth through independently directed study, wilderness activities, and cultural enrichment . . .

Maybe some version of this had been happening since the days of Inge F. Yancey IV's father, when Eurydice had been invited to the camp.

And now, Inge F. Yancey IV was here, and Wallis didn't know why, but she knew that he was not on their side, that he was not there to help them.

He walked through the rose garden and past the stable, stopping outside the theater. Wallis saw him open his suitcoat and reach in, giving something at his side two soft pats before buttoning the coat back up and smoothing the front, straightening the French cuffs on his dress shirt. Wallis did not get a good look, but she saw a quick glint inside the coat, and that was enough to make her pick up the walkie-talkie.

She took a deep breath before pressing the button. She didn't want to have panic in her voice when she spoke to Corinne and the others, who were heading through the tunnel under Lake So-and-So. Wallis found them on the screens. They were just coming out of the windmill.

"Turn around," Wallis said. "Come back to the cave now. Whatever you do, don't go into the theater."

But when they had entered the tunnel, Corinne had turned the walkie-talkie off so no sudden beeps and hisses of static would alert anyone to their presence. So nobody heard Wallis's warning, and all she could do was watch on the screens as they marched toward the theater, into the worst kind of danger.

CABIN 3
THE HERO'S QUEST

[SCENE: ROBIN makes her grand entrance and prepares to confront TANIA. The others having fled to the wings, THE GIRL WITH BEADS IN HER HAIR is the only human left in the theater.]

Robin stood in the center aisle, every eye on her as she sang, every face in the room stunned by her audacity. However, it didn't last.

The moment she had finished singing, Tania cocked her head to the side and regarded Robin with a cool smile.

"Old friends?" Tania asked, tossing her hair over one shoulder. Covered in filth and at less than her full strength, she was still imperious-looking. "I suppose I've never thought of us that way. I suppose I've never thought of us as friends at all."

Even in the dark, the girl with beads in her hair could see that Tania's words had struck their mark. Still, Robin recovered quickly, swallowing and setting her jaw. She sauntered the rest of the way down the aisle, shooting filthy looks at everyone she passed in the audience.

"Maybe not," she said, surveying the filth flooding the aisles and Tania's dung-smeared sundress, "but look what happens when I'm not around."

Tania looked down at her dress, then rolled her eyes. "Oh, I bet you're loving this. Acting like this is your show, like the whole thing would just fall apart without you."

Robin's resolve crumbled a little more. Well aware she'd find no support among the audience, she turned toward the girl with beads in her hair.

For her part, the girl with beads in her hair was surprised to find herself giving Robin a nod of encouragement. It wasn't that she considered Robin an ally exactly, but in this room, without another fellow camper in sight, Robin might have been the best thing she had.

"You're always undermining me," Robin said, vaulting one-handed onto the stage and landing nimbly on her feet. "You've never appreciated what I do. Cleaning up *your* messes, fixing all the damage *you* do."

Tania did not take kindly to criticism on the best of days, and certainly not on a day when she'd been bucked from a horse, showered with manure, and attacked with an item made of dreaded steel. She crossed the stage and snatched Robin by the wrist, gripping it so tightly that Robin winced in pain.

"First the singing, now this," she muttered, then added loudly enough for the whole theater to hear, "You're crew, Robin. Theatrics don't become you."

"Theatrics?" Robin said. Her wrist turned purple, then white, in Tania's grip, and her eyes filled up with tears. "You're lucky you didn't kill half of the campers trying to bring me down a peg or whatever it was you were trying to do."

Every creature in the audience sat perfectly still, perfectly quiet, their eyes fixed on Tania and Robin, waiting to see what would happen next. The girl with beads in her hair would not have been surprised if they'd started munching popcorn.

"First, you try to sabotage *my* camp," Tania hissed, "make *me* look like a fool, and then you have the nerve to whine that I'm undermining *you?*"

As Tania spoke, little flecks of spit hit Robin's cheek and glistened under the stage lights. Her anger was violent, dangerous, but for all that, the girl with beads in her hair saw that it was controlled, too.

"And now you're all by yourself," Tania said with a malicious grin as she squeezed Robin's wrist tighter. "I guess your stagehands aren't as loyal to you as you thought."

The confusion registered on Robin's face even through her pain.

"The truck, the pocket watch, the fire, you think *I* did those things to sabotage *you?*" Robin asked.

Tania seethed. "I know that you did." Tania kept looking out into the audience as she spoke, like she was trying to gauge the reaction her words had on the audience. "This is what happens when you cross me, Robin."

Suddenly Robin screamed as Tania crushed her wrist bones to powder. An ordinary person would have been capsized by the pain, but Robin retaliated.

"I never crossed you!" she snapped.

Then, gripping her walkie-talkie in her free hand, she clobbered Tania in the face. Tania staggered backwards, never letting go of Robin's shattered wrist. Once she'd recovered her balance, she gave Robin's injured arm a sharp tug and dislocated her shoulder from its socket. Robin's head snapped back and she let out a howl of pain that echoed off the rafters.

The girl with beads in her hair hung back as they fought, too afraid to step between these two preternaturally strong creatures, and not entirely sure what she would be intervening *in*. Robin thought Tania was behind the sabotage and had come here to confront her about it, but it was clear that Tania was convinced the opposite was true.

"You can't win," said Tania, sneering in Robin's face. "I'll always be stronger."

Robin refused to surrender. She let the walkie-talkie fall from her good hand, grabbed a hank of Tania's hair, and pulled it as hard as she could. Tania shrieked and let go of Robin's wrist, her hands flying to her scalp. Robin fell backwards, clutching a handful of Tania's golden hair, the other arm dangling limp at her side.

They only nursed their wounds for a second before both were back on their feet, rushing at one another, throwing punches, kicks, and curses. Neither trusted the other, both seemed ready to fight until they'd torn the other to shreds, and the girl with beads in her hair realized that no one in the audience had moved to help either of them.

And then she knew.

It was them. The audience. The stagehands. Tania's minions. *They* were behind this. *They* were the ones who'd tried to kill Cabin 5, and done who knows what else.

And if Tania and Robin were at one another's throats, and

each was accusing the other of orchestrating the chaos, it was playing right into their hands.

"STOP!" shouted the girl with beads in her hair.

She knew that if they'd just quit fighting for a minute, they'd see it, too, and maybe they'd know why it was happening or who was behind it.

But by the time the girl with beads in her hair shouted at them, it was already too late, and when Tania and Robin lowered their fists, it wasn't because of anything she'd said. It wasn't because they were tired of fighting. It wasn't even because of the murmur that rose up from the audience or the way they all began to shift in their seats.

It was because at that moment, Inge F. Yancey IV, famed and reclusive businessman and philanthropist, stepped out onto the stage, drew an old-fashioned pistol from a holster concealed beneath his suitcoat, and fired two shots.

CABIN 4

SOUL MATES

[SCENE: After being reunited with their soul mates, and after their soul mates are reunited with their whole selves, they make a break for freedom.]

Erin's friend Cressida, from Cabin 1, had told them to run, and so they did. Verity and the others fled to the wings, but it was dark and they weren't familiar with the backstage area. Verity could hear shuffling feet and confused whispers. Hands flailed in the dark and grasped onto each other, desperate not to be separated and lost.

After a long moment, Verity heard Erin's voice and reached toward it.

"What's going on?" she asked, as her fingers linked with Erin's. "What are we supposed to do?"

But the voice that answered her wasn't Erin's.

"Follow me," it said. "I'm Dora. From Cabin 1."

"Where are we going?" Erin whispered.

"Out the back," Dora said. "We'll wait for the others to join us, and after that, we're getting out of here."

It sounded like a good plan to Verity. Still holding Erin's hand, she grabbed onto Dora's shoulder and let her lead them through a stage door, then down a dimly lit hallway. Verity looked back over her shoulder and saw that they were all there—all the girls from Cabin 4 (and thankfully, only one Addison now), all their soul mates, and two black-haired girls with retro bouffant hairstyles that Verity had never seen before but whom Dora seemed to know.

"The door's just around the corner," Dora said. "I'll be back with Kadie and Cressida in two minutes."

But when they turned the corner, standing between them and the exit were a dozen men and women dressed in black pants and turtlenecks.

Erin gasped.

"Stagehands," she said. Then clutching Verity's hand, she turned to run.

With lightning-quick reflexes, one of the men stepped forward and caught Erin.

"No," he said. "Nothing like that."

"We're with Mr. Yancey," said one of the women, circling around the girls from Cabin 4 and the soul mates until she was standing at the back of their group. "We're here to help you."

Addison's soul mate, Tad, whirled around to face her, his eyes narrowed.

"Now?" he asked. "About a year ago would have been nice."

"We came as soon as we were alerted to the situation," said the man, who had not yet let go of Erin's arm.

Alix looked back over her shoulder nervously.

"Well, get us out of here then," she said.

By now the rest of the men and women in black turtlenecks had fanned out around them, surrounding them completely. Verity didn't like what she saw in Erin's face, the tension in her jaw, the worry line that creased her forehead.

Their eyes met, and Erin's said, *Run*, and Verity's replied, *Where?*

"First, we'll need the five of you to come with us."

The man who'd been holding on to Erin started to pull her away from Verity. The woman who'd said they worked for Mr. Yancey grabbed Tad. Three more men in black turtlenecks grabbed Alix's skateboarding soul mate, and Amber's guitar player, and Annika's boy with the rockabilly pompadour.

"What's going on?" Erin asked. Her voice had a hard edge, but Verity could hear a quaver just beneath the surface.

The man holding her arm cleared his throat.

"Back in the real world, you and your friends here just disappeared from your beds in the middle of the night. Or at least, that's how it will look to your families if we don't get you back immediately," he said.

Of course, Verity thought. Each one of the soul mates had been split in half, and when they'd kissed, those halves had been reunited here. There would be 911 calls and missing persons reports and panicking parents. And if it just so happened that four boys and one girl who'd gone to Camp So-and-So the previous summer had disappeared on the same night, it would attract attention. People would start asking questions, poking around the camp. If Inge F. Yancey IV knew even half the things that went on here, Verity was sure that scrutiny would be the last thing he wanted.

But if Inge F. Yancey IV knew even half the things that went on here—knew even a quarter of them—what kind of monster would that make him? Verity wondered.

"You don't have to haul them off like criminals," Addison said, shooting murderous looks at each of Inge F. Yancey IV's hired guns. "It's not like *they* did anything wrong."

Tad looked at each of them, like he was nervous that Addison's words might set them off, might result in someone getting hurt.

"We'll go with you," he said, "but let us say good-bye first."

The woman holding on to Tad's arm said, "Make it fast. We're in a bit of a rush, and Mr. Yancey's orders were clear."

Verity turned to Erin, suddenly overwhelmed by a hundred thoughts at once. It wasn't supposed to be like this. They were supposed to have more time. Verity was terrified she'd never see Erin again, that this moment in the hallway, on the run and surrounded by a shady security team, was the last time she'd see her face.

"I don't even know where you live," Verity said.

Erin reached out and touched Verity's face, her fingertips tracing the contours of her cheek.

"Cleveland," she said.

As Verity laid her hand on top of Erin's, she realized she wasn't the only one losing her. And she only had to lose Erin once. Cressida had just gotten her back, and now, she wouldn't even have a chance to say good-bye.

"Cressida," she said.

"Tell her what happened," Erin said. "Tell her I'll see her when she gets home."

Verity looked down the hallway and listened for footsteps.

Dora and the other girls from Cabin 1 should have been coming any minute. Erin could tell Cressida those things herself.

But the hallway stayed empty.

"I'll tell her," Verity said.

"Thank you," Erin said, leaning in to kiss her on the cheek. "For everything."

It sounded so final the way she said it, but before Verity could tell her to wait, or promise that they'd see each other again, she felt a sharp tug, and Erin was pulled away from her and down the hall by the man in the black turtleneck.

The girls from Cabin 4 reacted differently as their soul mates were ripped away from them. Alix burst into tears. Addison tried to chase after Tad and was restrained by two men in black turtlenecks. Amber stood there without saying a word, her face devastated by sadness.

But Annika was the first to look away, the first to size up their captors, the first to ask with suspicion in her voice, "What else did Inge F. Yancey tell you to do?"

They ended up locked in the prop room, with a guard posted at the door.

A few minutes later, on the other side of the theater, Kadie and Cressida and Dora were detained by a separate crew of Mr. Yancey's mercenaries and found themselves tossed into the prop room as well.

CABIN 3

THE HERO'S QUEST

*[SCENE: Onstage, with TANIA, ROBIN, and
INGE F. YANCEY IV]*

The first bullet struck Tania in the arm. The second hit Robin
in the calf. There was no blood, but both fell to the ground,
their skin turning an unnatural shade of gray. Robin rolled
from side to side, clutching her leg, while Tania lay flat on her
back, wailing in agony.

"One more of these would probably be the end of you,"
said Inge F. Yancey IV, as he began to reload the pistol using
powder, a musket ball, and a ramrod. "Let's hope it doesn't
come to that."

It was the same face the girl with beads in her hair had
seen smiling from the glossy Camp So-and-So brochure. He
looked too young to be running one of the biggest compa-
nies in the world—he wasn't even thirty. He had curly brown
hair, and his face was athletic-looking and tanned. He wore an

expensive-looking suit with French cuffs, and black wingtips that had been polished within an inch of their lives. His eyes were cold and carried the suggestion of a threat. They were the eyes of a man who was not accustomed to being denied anything, no matter how inconsequential.

The girl with beads in her hair came forward anyway. She climbed up onto the stage and knelt by Robin's side, examining the gunshot wound in her leg. Robin gasped for breath, too weak to sit up or drag herself to safety. Still, she looked up at the girl with beads in her hair and shook her head, as if to warn her away from whatever course of action she was about to take.

"It was you," said the girl with beads in her hair as she got to her feet and turned to face Inge F. Yancey IV. "All of this happened because of you."

"It's not what it seems, sweetheart."

Being called "sweetheart" by Inge F. Yancey IV like she was a good little girl in pigtails made her skin crawl. She was tired of being jerked back and forth between what was real and what wasn't. Her clothes were singed. She was almost too tired to stand, she'd barely eaten, her body ached, and she was sick of being lied to.

"Then what is it?" she asked, her voice thin and wrung out.

"Business," Inge F. Yancey IV said. "Nothing more. Where are the rest of you?"

"I don't know," said the girl with beads in her hair. "What kind of business?"

"Nothing for you to trouble yourself with, sweetheart. I'd hoped not to involve any of you girls in this in the first place. In fact, you're free to go. All of you. Go find your friends, go back to your cabins and pack your bags, and you'll find cars waiting to take you home to your families. Go now, and I assure you, nothing will bar your way."

With a magnanimous smile, he gestured toward the back of the theater. However, the girl with beads in her hair kept her feet planted where they were.

"What are you going to do then?"

Inge F. Yancey IV gave her a patronizing grin.

"I don't see how that's any of your concern, sweetheart."

"Do you even *know* what's happened here?" asked the girl with beads in her hair, looking around the dung- and garbage-smeared theater.

"I know that it costs me a great deal of money each year to maintain an accredited summer camp for the benefit of a handful of sniveling, selfish, demanding pests."

These seemed like needlessly harsh words to the girl with beads in her hair until she realized they weren't directed at her.

"I should have drowned you in Lake So-and-So when you were fifteen," hissed Tania.

Startled, the girl with beads in her hair turned to see Tania, pale and shaking, but sitting upright. In her right hand she held a wooden hairpin, and pinched between its ends was the musket ball she'd dug out of her own arm.

"You seem to be forgetting what you get out of our arrangement, Inge—as do the lot of you," she said, tossing the pin and ball into the audience in disgust. They parted like tall grass in a breeze where it landed.

"The 'arrangement' you made with my great-grandfather is long overdue for renegotiation."

"Renegotiate?" Tania said, laughing. "I miss your great-grandfather. He was a sensible Yancey. Your grandfather was a bit dim, but still someone I could work with. Now, your father, on the other hand, was a complete turd of a man, and yet, compared to you, he seemed a scholar and a saint."

Inge F. Yancey IV looked out into the audience and gave a slight nod. Immediately, five of Tania's minions, including Ron, rose to their feet and ascended the stage to take their place by Yancey's side.

"You seem to labor under the delusion that any of this is still yours to command," said Inge F. Yancey IV. "Perhaps if you hadn't been such a self-absorbed diva, if your incapacitated colleague here hadn't been such a tyrant, you wouldn't be in this situation right now. Ron, how long did it take me to convince you to join me? Was it over lunch?"

"Over coffee," Ron said with an insufferable smile.

"It's important to listen to your employees, Tania. Recognize what they bring to the organization. Let them know that their contributions are valued. Otherwise, you risk losing their loyalty," Inge F. Yancey lectured. "I believe your associates' talents could be better put to use at Yancey Corp., and they happen to agree with me."

Tania started to speak, but nothing came out. Her mouth just hung open as she stared at Ron and soaked in his betrayal.

"I am here to shut down the camp, neutralize the two of you, and bring all of this untapped, underutilized talent back to New York with me."

Then Inge F. Yancey IV turned toward the girl with beads in her hair.

"And I'm sure it's not difficult to see how this benefits you. All of you. No more Camp So-and-So. No one will ever have to go through anything like this again. This twisted compromise my great-grandfather struck will be a thing of the past."

The girl with beads in her hair had to entertain the notion that this might be the truth, at least for a moment. Shuttering Camp So-and-So would be unequivocally good, even if it was only the side effect of an amoral business tycoon getting his way.

This place had been Tania's kingdom, but for most of its inhabitants, even Tania's most favored minions, it had been a prison as well, the girl with beads in her hair realized. A posh one, but still, a small, primitive corner of the world. Inge F. Yancey IV was offering them more.

But what was he offering them, exactly? she wondered.

He'd described it in an odd way: *This twisted compromise my great-grandfather struck will be a thing of the past.*

Us, thought the girl with beads in her hair. *We're the compromise.*

That was how it worked. She and the other campers who came to this place each year were what whetted the minions' taste for mayhem and what kept them in line. That wasn't to say that what Tania had done was right, but at least she'd acted as the buffer. She'd stood between the two worlds and kept them apart, except for a few unfortunate campers every once in a while. Now, it was all about to be set loose, from the offices of one of the largest corporations in America, and Inge F. Yancey IV was just vain, arrogant, and stupid enough to believe he could control it.

In evil times when darkness threatens day.
One soul among you must hold it at bay.

This was what the prophecy meant. In the end, not even Robin had known this, even though she'd written it.

"I'm sorry I was so harsh before, Inge," Tania said, pulling herself unsteadily to her feet. "But you haven't thought this all the way through. You know what we can do. We can bend reality to our whim, split souls in two, plant the memories of things that never happened, erase the memories of things that did. How long until one of your new recruits turns some of that energy against you? It's not too late, though, Inge. You can still take it back. We can go back to the old arrangement. No hard feelings."

Shakily, Tania extended a hand to him.

"I'd even be willing to revisit a point or two on the old contract if you like."

Inge F. Yancey pressed his lips together. His eyes bored into Tania, radiating resentment and mistrust, but something else, too. Twelve years of it.

"I'm surprised you mentioned that summer I came to camp," he said. "It's never come up between us before. You weren't wrong about my father, though. He was a turd of a man, not least of all for sending me here. His father had done the same thing to him, to make a man of him or some such rot, so off I went, too, to keep up the family tradition."

Tania took a step closer to him and cocked her head to the side, her hand still outstretched.

"I don't remember anything terrible happening to you. You were more or less off limits, if I recall. Your daddy even brought in that big-time author you liked so much."

"So you're saying it was supposed to be special for me?"

"I'm saying it would be very, very sad if you were terminating this long and mutually beneficial partnership, putting innocent people at risk, jeopardizing everything your family name stands for, just because you'd been holding a grudge for twelve years."

As Inge F. Yancey's jaw tightened and the tips of his ears turned red, Tania clapped a hand to her mouth.

"Oh," she said. "That's exactly why you're doing it."

"I always swore I'd shut this place down if I ever had the chance."

Her hand still outstretched, Tania took another step toward Inge F. Yancey.

"I'm sorry, Inge," she said, "sorry we hurt you in any way."

As Tania reached out to touch the sleeve of his coat, the girl with beads in her hair saw Inge F. Yancey's flinch, saw his eyes flicker toward the pistol in his hand and set his intention. Before reason got the better of her, before Robin could reach out and catch her by the heel, the girl with beads in her hair sprang up from the stage and took a running leap toward the two of them.

Inge F. Yancey had flinched away from Tania's touch when the girl stood up, had just drawn the pistol when her feet left the ground. The first shot, which had been meant to strike Tania in the heart, instead grazed the outstretched fingers of the girl with beads in her hair. The second flew wild, as the girl with beads in her hair threw an elbow into Inge F. Yancey's stomach, causing him to misfire. The musket ball burrowed a hole through the velvet curtains before lodging in the wall.

It was an incredibly brave and incredibly risky thing to do. The girl with beads in her hair intervened on behalf of someone who was not even on her side, but she had made her choice.

In evil times when darkness threatens day . . .

It wasn't even a difficult decision. She knew this much, and it was the only thing she needed to know: Inge F. Yancey was holding a gun and Tania wasn't.

She landed and rolled into a crouch, then stood up. When she looked down at her hand, the girl with beads in her hair saw that the musket ball had blown off the tip of her right index finger. It was gruesome, but not terribly serious if she could staunch the bleeding. More serious at that moment was the question of how many shots Inge F. Yancey had left in his pistol, and if any of his minions had come to his aid.

"What have you done?" she heard Robin whisper from the center of the stage.

When she spun around to look at her, the girl with beads in her hair staggered backwards and fell down. Panic flooded her as she struggled to sit up, but her body would not respond, would not do what she wanted it to do. She looked down at her hand again, and saw that her finger was no longer bloody.

It had turned to stone.

Of course, Inge F. Yancey wouldn't have used an ordinary musket ball against Tania and Robin. She should have known it. She should have expected the danger. The stone spread down her hand and started up her arm. Fingers of it began to spread along her throat. The girl with beads in her hair choked out a cry for help, but no one was there to help her.

She thought about the last part of the prophecy, the part she hadn't thought of once, not since the first time she read it.

This quest is not a summer's game.
It is not safe, it is not tame.
Consider this before you pack—
Some of you may not come back.

She was not coming back. She felt it in her heart, and she knew that it was true.

She tried not to cry. She kept her eyes open.

Even if this was how it ended, she didn't want to miss it.

It was her life, after all.

She'd been proud of it.

CABIN 5

SURVIVAL

*[SCENE: The girls from Cabin 5 burst in through the back door
of the theater, with Cabins 2 and 3 following on their heels.]*

They came through the door just as the shots rang out. Even if
Wallis's warning had gotten through, nothing could have prepared them for the sight of the girl with beads in her hair. Even
from a distance, they could see the confusion in her eyes as
her legs gave way beneath her and she tumbled to the ground,
holding her wounded hand aloft. One second it was covered in
blood; the next, it was stone.

"Stop it."

It was only when they heard the powerful baritone voice
that they turned their attention to Inge F. Yancey IV. He stood
on the stage surrounded by a half dozen of the stagehands, all
of them dressed entirely in black. It was to them he turned
after he'd shot the girl from Cabin 3.

The stagehand who stood to his right, a young man

with a shock of wavy black hair and unsettlingly white teeth, shrugged.

"I can't," he said. The rest of the stagehands sent up a murmur of agreement.

Inge F. Yancey IV set the pistol down on the stage and backed away from it, as though that could erase what he'd done. He looked to Tania as the stone spread up the girl's arm.

"Make it stop," he said.

"There isn't anything that can make it stop," Tania said.

The members of the audience who had come for the All-Camp Sport & Follies got up and quietly filed out of the theater. They had come for music and drama, for kissing and fight scenes. They had come to be entertained. But a dying girl? This was the time to slip out discreetly, to hide in the woods for a few days, the way they generally did when something messy happened to one of the humans.

The girls from Cabin 5 waited no longer. They ran down the center aisle of the theater and vaulted onto the stage with purpose. They surrounded the girl with beads in her hair and knelt by her side. One of them picked up her good hand and squeezed it. Another patted her shoulder. The rest spoke soothing words to her as the stone snaked down her side and up her neck. They avoided one another's eyes as they told the girl lies, like "It's not so bad" and "Everything is going to be all right."

They were girls who had battled the elements and stayed alive on sheer nerve.

They were girls who faced fire, burrowed through the earth, and came out in one piece on the other side.

They had rescued a camp counselor from the brink of

death with nothing but a rope and a hook and the strength of their arms.

They had found out the truth, taken a stand, and fought to make things right again.

They did all of those things.

But there was nothing they could do about this.

CABIN 3

THE HERO'S QUEST

*[SCENE: Behind Cabin 5, the girls from Cabin 3 stream
into the theater.]*

There was no blood, but right away, they knew something
was terribly wrong. The sticklike goth girl and the girl with
thousands of freckles burst into the theater and ran toward the
stage, but Renata flew ahead of them both. She flapped her
wings so hard they ached, but when she reached the stage, a
voice called out and stopped her like a tether.

"Renata," it said.

She looked down and saw Robin, the counselor-in-
training, lying on her back on the stage. Her lips were cracked
and there were dark circles beneath her eyes. Her arms and
legs were sticks, all the muscle and fat leached out of them, as
though she'd been suffering from a wasting illness for months
rather than minutes.

"Help me," she called out.

The raven was torn. What she wanted was to be at her friend's side, to give her what comfort she could as she faced death. Renata wanted a chance to say good-bye. Robin could wait at least that long. But then a cry of pain tore loose from Robin's throat, and Renata wondered if maybe she couldn't wait after all.

Renata landed next to her head and asked, "What can I do?"

"Your beak," Robin gasped. "Dig out the bullet. Please."

Robin pointed to her leg and Renata hopped down the length of her body until she spotted the hole that had been left by Inge F. Yancey's musket ball.

"Please get it out," she said.

Renata felt ill at the prospect of performing surgery like this, but she bent her head and placed her beak on the wound. As Robin screamed in agony, Renata closed her eyes and went to the deepest corners of her mind, to the knowledge that had been in the raven before she even got there. She imagined she was pecking a stump for a grub or burrowing at the ground to uncover something shiny. There was a clinking sound as her beak hit the musket ball. She clamped down on it, pulled it out of Robin's leg, and spat it out. The ball rolled off the stage and landed in the orchestra pit.

Robin looked better at once. As she sat up, the color returned to her cheeks and her eyes brightened.

"Thank you," she said.

Renata shrugged, then looked back over her shoulder to the spot where the girl with beads in her hair lay dying.

"Is there anything you can do for her?" Renata asked.

Robin looked down at her knees and let out a long sigh.

"Seven breaths," she said.

Renata felt a surge of hope. "What do you mean, 'seven breaths'?"

"That's how long before her lungs turn to stone."

Renata's heart sank. A throng of campers surrounded the girl with beads in her hair. Some of the girls tried to make her comfortable. Some talked to her, some stood in reverent silence, and some knelt by her side weeping, but all of them knew that she was dying.

On the first breath, Renata saw Inge F. Yancey IV s turn his back as though he'd had nothing to do with this. She felt her entire body go hot with rage, and fought the urge to go peck out his eyes.

On the second breath, she flew across the stage and descended in the middle of the circle that had formed around the girl with beads in her hair. The stone almost covered her face now, and though her eyes were still open, there was fear in them.

On the third breath, Renata thought about how she'd become a raven. They'd done it to her, they'd changed her, and it seemed profoundly wrong and unfair that they couldn't change this.

Or could they?

Before she'd been a raven, she'd been a girl in an orange hoodie. Her imperfect, but perfectly good body, was still back at the cave. Last she'd seen it, it had been comatose, but breathing and alive. Her cabinmates had propped it up in the chamber next to Shea and the girl with the upturned nose.

On the fourth breath, Renata said, "Don't give up. This isn't over. Breathe slowly." From across the stage, Robin shook her head and said, "Her body will be stone in seconds."

On the fifth breath, Renata rose up on her wings and called out to Robin, "Then give her mine!"

On the sixth breath, Robin looked puzzled and asked, "Are you sure?" and Renata said, "Of course I am."

Renata liked being a raven, and if she never changed back, it was a small price to pay for keeping her friend alive. Her spirit soared. There was a way out of this after all, and the girl with beads in her hair would not have to die.

On the seventh breath, Renata drew back her head and screamed at Robin, "Do it!"

As the girl with beads in her hair exhaled the last breath she would ever take, several things happened at once.

Call it a spirit, call it a soul—whatever it was that made Renata herself fled the raven's body. It traveled across Lake So-and-So, over the meadow, through the forest, into the cave, and rejoined the orange-hoodied body that lay in Eurydice Horne's chamber.

The raven dropped out of the air like a stone and landed motionless on the stage.

As it did, whatever it was that made the girl with beads in her hair herself fled into the bird. Her eyes flickered open, and she staggered to her feet, cawing hysterically, one wing dragging behind her on the floor. She wasn't dead, she wasn't made of stone, but still, this wasn't where she was supposed to be. This wasn't right.

She looked down at herself, at the girl she used to be, now a solid block of stone. Her arms were folded across her chest so that she looked like the burial effigy placed atop the tomb of some medieval queen.

The girl she used to be was gone, she told herself, trying

not to hyperventilate, but she was alive. She was here. It wasn't over.

She recognized some of the girls from Cabin 2 and from Cabin 5. The sticklike goth girl and the girl with thousands of freckles were still by her side.

Of Robin, however, there was no sign. She'd abandoned them at the cave when the beast attacked, and now she'd done it again. At least this time, the girl with beads in her hair wasn't surprised.

There was no sign of Renata either, and the girl with beads in her hair forgot about her own considerable troubles to be afraid for her friend. When her soul had entered the raven's body, had it crushed Renata's? Had it pushed it out? Where was she?

"Where's Renata?" The girl with beads in her hair cried out urgently through her raven's beak.

Before anyone could answer her, Inge F. Yancey IV spoke up. While she had been dying, he had been calculating his next move, and now, it seemed, he had arrived at it.

"Are you ready for your first assignment as employees of Yancey Corp.?" he asked the creatures dressed in black that surrounded him onstage.

As one, they nodded.

"Then kill these witnesses."

CABIN 2

KILLER IN THE WOODS

[SCENE: The NARRATOR's cave]

As it all unfolded, Wallis did not speak until the walkie-talkie in her pocket crackled to life. When Corinne's voice came through, it was faint and staticky, but its urgency was not lost. The girls from Cabins 2, 3, and 5 had watched the girl with beads in her hair turn to stone, heard Inge F. Yancey's directive to his minions who were once Tania's.

"How does it end, Wallis?" Corinne asked, her voice as close to panicked and pleading as Wallis had ever heard it. "You have to tell us how it ends."

Wallis's thoughts were tangled as her eyes darted from scene to scene in the mirrors. She needed more time. Time to sift through each of the stories—the All-Camp Sport & Follies, the hero's quest, the soul mates, the tale of wilderness survival, and of course, her own cabin's story.

She felt sure that somewhere in all of this, there would be

something that would enable them to defeat Inge F. Yancey IV. Some nugget from the legend of Abigail or the kelpie's riddle would stop him from carrying out his plan, and would shut down Camp So-and-So for good.

She'd read enough stories in her life to know that this was how they worked.

The only problem was, she didn't know where to start looking. She'd had days of stories, but only minutes to make a decision.

"Cabins 1 and 4 are locked in the prop room," Wallis said. "Get them out of there. And be careful. There are stagehands guarding the doors. You'll need to create a distraction to lure them away."

As Wallis barked her instructions into the walkie-talkie, she knew it wasn't the answer Corinne was looking for, but it needed to be done, and maybe it would buy her time. By the time they'd rescued the others, maybe Wallis would know what they needed to do.

Wallis turned to Eurydice Horne. "Tell me where to look," she said.

Eurydice Horne looked up at the screens sadly and shook her head. "I don't know."

One of the minions picked up the pistol that Inge F. Yancey IV had dropped on the stage. He pointed it at Hennie, who dove over two rows of seats and fled the theater before he could shoot. He turned and aimed at Corinne.

"Help me!" Wallis shrieked at Eurydice Horne in frustration. She couldn't bear to watch, but did so anyway as Corinne ran for the exit, holding the walkie-talkie in one hand and dragging Becca with the other.

"I don't know how to stop it. I'm not a storyteller anymore," said Eurydice Horne. "I'm just the narrator."

"You were never a storyteller," Wallis said, narrowing her eyes as she towered over Eurydice Horne, who had still not moved from her bench. "You were a quitter. If I'd had twelve years to think about it, I could have come up with at least five ways to bring Isis Archimedes back from the dead. I can think of five ways *right now*. Instead, you decided to sit in a cave for almost as long as I've been alive, telling stories to yourself, and the instant one of those stories might be useful and save some lives, you clam up and say you don't know where to look or what to do. So as far as I'm concerned, you're not just a quitter; you're a coward, too."

Wallis was understandably upset. She was worried about the other girls across the lake, worried she'd sent them into grave danger, and now she had no way to get them out of it. She didn't say any of it to be cruel, but still, Shea, who had been quietly listening, touched Wallis's arm and said, "THEY HURT HER, TOO, WALLIS."

Wallis jerked away from Shea and folded her arms across her chest.

"Tell me," said Eurydice Horne after a long silence. "How would you do it? How would you bring Isis Archimedes back from the dead?"

"It doesn't matter!" Wallis cried, looking at Eurydice Horne in disbelief. "We don't have time for that right now."

Wallis stalked from one side of the chamber to the other, looking for answers on the screens, so upset she could no longer follow anything at all.

Eurydice Horne stood up for the first time any of them

had seen. Eurydice Horne herself could not quite remember the last time it had happened. Her back hunched, her legs quaking, she crossed the room and laid her hands on Wallis's shoulders. They looked like the hands of a much older woman, Eurydice Horne noticed, gnarled from years of clutching the seat of her bench in suspense and anticipation, waiting to see what would happen next. Eurydice Horne wondered why she'd cared so much all those years, unless it was to bring her here, to this moment, to this sentence:

"Tell me anyway."

"But—"

"You said you could think of five ways to save Isis Archimedes. What are they?"

Wallis took a deep breath and looked into the author's eyes.

"One: you could reveal that someone had tampered with S'ulla's memories so he believed that he'd killed her even though he hadn't.

"Two: we could find out that S'ulla never existed, that Isis Archimedes was being chased through the woods by nothing but a scary story.

"Three: you could put her soul in the body of a raven.

"Four: you could split her in half, so that even if S'ulla killed her, at least one part of her would still be alive.

"Five: you could have the ground give way beneath her feet in the nick of time.

"There. Those are five ways you could save Isis Archimedes. Are you happy now?"

Shea and Renata and the girl with the upturned nose gaped at Wallis, who felt ashamed and small. Their friends were going to die any minute, and instead of doing something about it, she was having a fight with a traumatized author who had quite possibly not spoken to another human in twelve years.

"I like the fourth one," said the girl with the upturned nose.

Twelve years.

"Me too," said Eurydice Horne.

She'd been here twelve years, thought Wallis. What had happened twelve years ago?

I should have drowned you in Lake So-and-So the summer you were fifteen.

Tania's words stuck in Wallis's head, and she felt the beginnings of an idea begin to glom on to it.

"What happened the summer Inge F. Yancey IV came to camp?" she asked.

Eurydice Horne told the story of the treehouse and the trophy and of what Inge F. Yancey IV had done to Beau Krest, and by the time she was done telling it, Wallis knew what they had to do.

She lifted the walkie-talkie to her lips.

"Did you get them all?" she asked.

There was a long silence, then a crackle of static, then Corinne's voice, weary but strong as ever.

"We're all here."

They'd pushed so hard, faced so much—Wallis hoped they could face just a little bit more.

FIRST 5, THEN 4, THEN 3, THEN 2, THEN 1

From a box seat high up in the theater, Kadie, Cressida, Dora, Vivian, and Kimber pelted the judges with a handful of drywall screws they'd found in the prop room to get their attention. Since Cabin 1's All-Camp Sport & Follies performance—which seemed like an eternity ago now—the three judges had not budged from their seats in the front row, not even when manure and compost rained down on them from the catwalk, not when Tania and Robin turned on each other, not when Inge F. Yancey IV shot them and the girl with beads in her hair. The theater was almost empty now—just the judges, a handful of stagehands keeping watch, and Inge F. Yancey IV.

After he'd issued his orders for the stagehands to kill all the witnesses, it had been pandemonium. The girls had fled, and the stagehands had scattered off in a dozen different directions after them. Some ran into the secret tunnels and hallways that honeycombed the building, while others took to ceilings, storage cupboards, and the light booth.

Inge F. Yancey IV had come down from the stage and sat in a front-row seat. The stone body of the girl with beads in her hair was still there, all alone, but he would not look at it. He dug a fingernail into his seat's varnished armrest and scratched at it, picking off the finish, a sullen look on his face.

Kadie was beginning to lose hope that they would attract the attention of the judges without also alerting Inge F. Yancey IV to their presence, when Robin sat down next to her in the box. Kadie hadn't seen her come in. One minute she wasn't there, then suddenly she was. That was how Robin seemed to make her entrances and exits.

"Just between you and me, the smart money is on running for your lives," she whispered to Kadie. "What are you still doing here?"

Kadie looked down to make sure Inge F. Yancey IV hadn't heard them, but he was still scowling at his armrest and pointedly ignoring the girl he'd killed.

"This isn't over," Kadie said.

"You're waiting around for them to kill you then?"

"No, we're trying to get *their* attention," Dora whispered, discreetly pointing down at the judges in the front row.

Cressida tossed a screw that landed a few inches from the judges' feet, but they didn't stir.

"The judges are neutral," Robin whispered.

"Maybe it's time someone asked them to pick a side," Dora said.

A strange look passed over Robin's face as she reached her hand into the paper bag of drywall screws and plucked one out. She tossed it over the railing and it struck the judge in the black tailored suit and veiled hat on the nose.

"Of the three, I've always liked her the least," Robin muttered.

The judge touched her hand to her face and, at last, looked up. Kadie snaked a hand over the railing and motioned for the judges to come up. The judge with the veiled hat leaned over and whispered something to her colleagues, and then one by one, they rose from their seats and filed out of the theater as silently as they'd entered it. If Inge F. Yancey IV noticed, he did not care.

A moment later, the girls from Cabin 1 and Robin met them in the stairwell leading up to the box seats.

"You have something we need," Kadie said, by way of a greeting.

The girls of Cabin 2 had been on the run from the stagehands since the beginning. They recognized their traps and knew how to avoid them. The sticklike goth girl and the girl with thousands of freckles had already faced far more terrifying creatures. Likewise, the gritty, wily, and battle-scarred girls of Cabin 5 were not afraid to run interference.

With Wallis's help, they lured the stagehands with their kill orders from Inge F. Yancey IV across catwalks, down hallways, through secret tunnels, and far away from what the other cabins were doing.

Wallis told the girls from Cabin 4 where Tania was hiding, and they had no trouble locating the cramped storage cupboard behind a wardrobe in the costumes room. Verity swallowed down her anger as she led Addison, Annika, Alix, and Amber into the cupboard. Tania seemed almost pitiful now that she was cornered, weakened, and alone in the dark, but it didn't change what she'd done to Erin and Addison and the rest of them.

It felt obscene to be standing before this despicable being, asking her to do the very thing she found so despicable. Verity didn't want to work with Tania, didn't want to be her ally, even for a few minutes. But when Wallis explained how the story had to end, she knew it was the only way, and when Wallis said she should be the one to ask, Verity knew she was right.

Because of what Erin had told her, Verity understood better than any of the other girls at Camp So-and-So how Tania split people in half, kept half of them at Camp So-and-So and sent the other half back into the world, both the same and not the same as they'd been before. She understood it better than Cressida, who'd lost her best friend to the process, better than Addison, to whom it had actually happened.

She'd seen the tears on Erin's cheeks when she'd explained how lost and lonely and estranged she felt from herself now that there were two of her. She'd observed the little changes in Erin's personality, in her smile, in the way she kissed, once she'd been made whole again.

Verity explained to Tania that when she did this to Inge F. Yancey IV, the proportions needed to be significantly different.

When she divided his soul in two, one of them needed to be the sullen, awkward, overlooked boy who'd come to Camp So-and-So twelve years ago, the one who knew himself to be a fraud and a disappointment.

And the other one should be the arrogant, venal man he'd grown into, only with none of the childhood resentments and setbacks spurring him on to ruthlessness.

Verity was not sure there was much good in Inge F. Yancey IV, but even so, it seemed possible that he could be made less dangerous, that his wickedness could be diluted if it was divided.

Tania listened thoughtfully as Verity explained the plan, mindful that she was surrounded by five girls, all of whom disliked her intensely and looked as though they'd rather spit in her face than ask for her help.

"It'll never work," Tania said when Verity was done.

Verity understood why she doubted.

Erin had picked up a book of stamps, Addison had taken a button, and Verity knew that Inge F. Yancey IV would never take anything that he knew had come from this place.

"It'll work," Verity said. "Wallis thought of that part, too."

In evil times when darkness threatens day,
One soul among you must hold it at bay.

Inge F. Yancey IV sat in one of the less-soiled theater seats looking ill at ease.

The girl with beads in her hair had known that she would have to face him alone in the end. She just hadn't imagined that it would happen like this.

But know that you will lose before it's done.
First five, then four, then three, then two, then one.

She felt like she was suffocating in the raven's body, like it was squeezing in on her from every side. She wanted to sit beside her stone body—a body she hadn't particularly appreciated or thought much about when it was still hers—and weep for what she'd lost.

But that was not what she was here to do.

She walked awkwardly across the stage until she reached the stone figure and hopped up onto its folded hands. She was still herself, and looking into a face that was brave and strong and had faced even the worst thing with open eyes made her feel less alone when she opened her beak and spoke from the throat she was still getting used to.

"Mr. Yancey?" she said.

"Who are you?" he asked, looking up from the tops of his knees.

"I'm the girl who died," she said. *The girl you killed*, she thought to herself, though she managed to keep her voice neutral.

"Oh," he said. "Not so dead after all, I guess."

The girl with beads in her hair narrowed her eyes. She waited for him to summon his gang of stagehands to finish her off, ready to fly up into the rafters if she had to, but Inge F. Yancey only looked over his shoulder, then the other.

When he saw that they were alone, he asked, "Why did you step in front of that bullet? That was a stupid thing to do."

"Probably," said the girl with beads in her hair.

"There's nothing I can do about it, if that's why you're still here," he said.

"That's not why I'm here," she said. She had no trouble imagining the petulant, sulky child he must have been not so long ago. "I'm here to tell you that you won."

Inge F. Yancey IV chuckled bitterly. "And they sent you to make the concession speech? I don't need you to tell me I've won."

"No one wants to die, Mr. Yancey," the girl with beads in her hair said. "You don't have Tania, and we do. We're prepared to hand her over to you. You call off the stagehands and let us go, we give you Tania, you close the camp, and no one will ever say anything about what happened here."

Inge F. Yancey IV got up from his seat, cracked his knuckles, and approached the stage, looking like he was about to negotiate with a room full of executives instead of a raven.

"People make a lot of promises they can't keep when they're afraid," he said. "It happens in business all the time. What happens six months from now when your friends are safe at home? What kinds of stories will they feel like telling then?"

The girl with beads in her hair held her ground as he drew nearer, and when she answered, there was steel in her voice.

"We keep our mouths shut because nobody would ever believe us," she said. "You get everything you want, and the camp gets shut down, so we get something we want, too. And Tania loses everything."

"What about you? Won't you still be a raven?"

"I said we got something we wanted, not everything we wanted," said the girl, looking longingly at her strong, muscled stone arms, at the strands of beads that hung from the ends of her stone braids, before adding, "But then again, why should we? We didn't win."

At those words, the three judges came onstage wheeling the All-Camp Sport & Follies trophy behind them. The original trophy had been a champion's cup, tall and gold with spindly, ornate handles, but with Robin's assistance, they had drastically altered its appearance.

"What do you say?" asked the girl with beads in her hair. "Do we have a deal?"

Inge F. Yancey IV did not answer. First, he stared. Then, his eyes danced and a pure, childlike smile broke out on his face as he scrambled up from the orchestra pit and raced across the stage to get a better look at the trophy.

It bore a striking resemblance to the design of his treehouse—not the one he and his cabinmates had actually built, but the one that had existed in his mind and occupied a good-sized portion of his daydreaming life for years now. It was all there, from the grand staircase that wound around the trunk to the individual pods connected by rope ladders, seven feet tall and wrought in gold.

The girl with beads in her hair scarcely dared to breathe as she watched him. He circled the trophy, his eyes following the staircase up to the grand entrance hall, and then on each tier that followed, baubles that looked light as soap bubbles but strong as diamonds. He could imagine where the trophy would sit in his office. It was so large, so perfectly rendered, he could almost imagine himself reclining in the pod he'd designed for himself when he was a boy. He knew he would never tire of looking at it.

It was his at last.

He reached up and laid his hand on the trophy, marveling that this thing he'd desired and dreamed about should at last be his.

He can have it, thought the girl with beads in her hair as the spotlight went dark and the doors slammed shut, and from the wings and the ceiling and the trap doors beneath the stage, Inge F. Yancey IV was surrounded.

CABINS
5, 4, 3, 2, AND 1
SURVIVORS, SOUL MATES, HEROES, KILLERS, & WINNERS

[SCENE: The soon-to-be-renamed Inge F. Yancey Young Executives Leadership Camp]

Banishing the stagehands was the first thing Tania did after the camp had been legally disbanded. Some of them she'd sent into the mountains in the north, some to the forests in the east, while some drifted down the long, unnecessarily winding road and into cities. And some of the more mutinous ones did not leave Camp So-and-So at all, not that anyone ever saw them again.

After locating the original contract and charter in the camp director's abandoned office, Tania and the girls sat down with the more pliable of the two Inge F. Yancey IVs and dissolved it.

As for Inge F. Yancey IV, the one they decided to send

back into the world was cruel and ruthless as ever. However, he was too unimaginative to entertain the notion of supernatural help, and too arrogant to have accepted it, even if he believed it was real. He managed his corporate empire without the aid of Tania's stagehands, and none of his philanthropic notions ever involved the endowment of a summer camp.

However, the end of Yancey Corp.'s entanglements with the supernatural would mark the beginning of a long, slow, expensive collapse. Inge F. Yancey IV remained convinced of his own brilliance and blamed the company's failures and missteps on the economy, the president, and other inconveniences he'd surely surmount. His rivals in the business world saw it differently and whispered amongst themselves that Inge F. Yancey IV had lost his edge, his sparkle, that untouchable air he'd had about him.

Now they spied weakness and quietly made plans to capture his empire, one piece at a time.

The Inge F. Yancey that would stay behind at Camp So-and-So was sniveling and spiteful, and seemed capable of holding grudges the way that pearl divers held their breath. However, all he wanted to do was draw and build things, and Tania said that he was welcome to stay here and draw and build to his heart's content. She did not mention that he would not be permitted to leave, but hoped it would be some time before that topic of conversation was broached.

Before any of that happened, though, there were other complications to be sorted out.

When Renata had been evicted from the raven's body,

her spirit had gone hurtling across Lake So-and-So. The next thing she knew, she was staring down at her body—the old one, the human one. She lifted her hand and ran her fingers over her lank hair, the bumps and imperfections of her complexion, her whole ordinary, disappointing body.

This wasn't what she'd wanted. At first, she cursed herself for not making her intentions clearer when she'd called out to Robin and asked her to work the magic that would save her friend's life. The way it had played out in her imagination, the girl with beads in her hair would happily inhabit Renata's human body, and Renata would go on happily inhabiting the raven. It made so much sense at the time, until she realized that the only person who would be made happy by that scenario was herself.

Inge F. Yancey IV had shot her friend in the hand. Her body had turned to stone, and Renata realized that she'd been naïve to think there was a way to salvage happiness from a thing like that.

"Where is she?" Renata asked, tucking her black hair behind her ears and pushing the bangs out of her eyes.

Wallis showed her on the screens, and together with Shea, the girl with the upturned nose, and Eurydice Horne, they watched as the girl with beads in her hair hopped across the stage, still awkward in the raven's body, and convinced Inge F. Yancey IV to take the trophy.

Renata thought about her friend stuck in the raven's body and felt her eyes fill up with tears. Would it have been better if she hadn't done anything? The girl with beads in her hair had never asked for this. Renata had stepped in and made a choice for her, and now, this was the life she was stuck with.

There'd been time. She could have at least asked her what she wanted.

Golden light poured from the trophy as Inge F. Yancey IV wrapped his arms around it, and even though they all knew it was coming, they gasped when, suddenly, there were two of him standing on the stage.

There was something else on Renata's mind, though.

"Does she hate me?" she asked Wallis, her voice quavering.

Wallis had no idea what the girl with beads in her hair felt in that moment. The screens weren't magic like that. Some feelings were so big and scary and complicated that all the storyteller could do was guess at them.

What Wallis *could* see was the pain on Renata's face as she worried about her friend, and so she spoke to that instead.

"You saved her life." Wallis laid a hand on the girl's shoulder. "Whatever she's feeling right now, she doesn't hate you."

They loaded the girl with the upturned nose into the wheelbarrow. With Robin's help, Hennie, Becca, and Corinne had made contact with the outside world, and an ambulance was currently on its way to Camp So-and-So. It would take the girl with the upturned nose to a hospital to have her compound fracture set. Shea's injuries from the explosion and the barbed-wire booby trap were less grievous, but they'd convinced her to go as well. It would have been maddening to survive Camp So-and-So only to be done in by an infected wound. The two were relieved to be going, but also a bit sad that they wouldn't have a chance to say good-bye to the other girls in their cabins.

Renata pushed the wheelbarrow bearing the girl with

the upturned nose toward the chamber door, and Shea followed behind. Wallis was just about to go after them when she stopped and turned back.

"What about you? Aren't you coming?"

Eurydice Horne looked over her shoulder as though Wallis might have been talking to someone else.

"I hadn't planned on it," she said. "Why should anything change?"

"Because *everything's* changed," Wallis said.

She thought about the chains that Eurydice Horne had draped over herself, pretending that someone else had been holding her prisoner in the cave. Even knowing that, they'd all assumed that on some level, Eurydice Horne wanted to leave. Now, Wallis wasn't sure it would be that easy.

"There's nothing for you to narrate now," Renata pointed out.

Eurydice Horne looked offended. "There will be plenty of other things going on after you're gone. There's the kelpie and that interesting family of squirrels that lives under the mess hall. And of course I'll spend a week or two catching up on my rest before any of that begins. What did you think I did the rest of the year anyway?"

The girls exchanged sad looks, then, one by one, extended their hands to Eurydice Horne.

"Come with us," Wallis said.

"Please," added the girl with the upturned nose. "We won't leave you here alone."

"IF YOU DON'T LIKE IT, YOU CAN COME BACK," Shea said.

"Besides," said Renata, "we can't finish our quest unless

you do. *First you must slay the beast inside its lair, and then set free the one imprisoned there.*"

Eurydice Horne trembled. She hadn't been outside in years, and the thought of it filled her with panic, but she reached out and took Wallis's hand.

Say what you will about Eurydice Horne, that she's a quitter, a monster who dragged readers along for five books only to kill off the main character, but she was not the kind of person who would stand between heroes and the end of their quest.

Kind-hearted Shea took her other hand, and together, they led her out of the chamber. Eurydice Horne dug in her heels once, craned her neck around for one last look at the screens, but then Shea squeezed her hand and Wallis gave her a little tug forward. They wound through the cave with its glowing white limestone walls, and a few minutes later, they were standing at its mouth in the clearing where the girls from Cabin 3 had fought the beast.

Eurydice Horne dropped to her knees and marveled at how big everything seemed.

Once they were mostly on the same side of the lake, Robin gathered all of them together in the English rose garden for a meeting.

"I find myself in the strange position of having nothing to be in charge of except you," Robin said. "I find myself in the equally strange position of needing to make amends for what you have suffered.

"For the next five days, the entire grounds are at your disposal. I will arrange for staff—human staff—to be brought in to see to your every need and want. They will cook for you and clean up after you. They will be your lifeguards. They will teach you how to play the dulcimer or make a wallet out of duct tape. For the rest of the week, you may do as you please."

A murmur went up through the crowd.

"How does that even begin to make amends?" asked one girl from Cabin 5, and more than a few others nodded their heads in agreement.

"I'm not sure that it does," Robin said. "But I thought at the very least, you might appreciate a meal, a shower, and a good night's sleep before we discuss anything further. I will stay out of your way. No traps. No tricks."

"Why should we trust you?" asked Kadie.

Robin lowered her head.

"Because I am in your debt. Tania and I both."

Cressida looked around the garden, then peeked through some of the hedges. "Where is Tania anyway?"

Robin made an incredulous face. "Were you hoping to hang out? Get to know each other?"

"I was hoping to replace her kneecaps with sourdough biscuits."

"Which is why I decided it would be for the best if we all kept our distance," Robin said, then gestured across Lake So-and-So. "Besides, the rules of the All-Camp Sport & Follies state that the winner gets to choose which camp they live at. Keeping her over there seems fair, don't you think?"

Had they been less famished and exhausted, they might have dug in their heels at this proposition; however, at that moment, a dazzled-looking pizza delivery driver entered the English rose garden. Robin tipped him and took a dozen pies out of his hands before sending him on his way.

As the meal was of human provenance, they fell upon it like wolves and, besotted with food, allowed themselves to be led from the rose garden to their suites. Each cabin got its own, complete with feather beds, fireplace, hot tub, private balcony, and complimentary robes and slippers. That night, they slept like the dead, and woke in the morning, ravenous all over again.

After a breakfast of pastries, coffee, and juice (also delivered from the outside), they tentatively explored the grounds. They enjoyed eating and sleeping in and lying on their backs in the English rose garden, looking for shapes in the clouds. Kadie and Dora finally got to feel the sugar sands of Most Excellent Beach between their toes.

Robin was as good as her word. There were no tricks and no traps. By lunchtime, they'd decided they did want to stay there for the rest of the week. They harbored no illusions that Robin's invitation balanced the books between them, or even began to make things right. Just because they'd briefly been allies did not make them friends now.

However, she was offering them something that each girl needed very badly, and that was time.

The idea of going home right away, after everything that had happened to them, seemed unthinkable. Of course, they would go when the time came. They would be grateful for their friends and families, even though they'd never be able to explain to those people what had happened to them. At some point, not talking about it would be a relief, but now, what they needed most was to be with people who had seen the same strange things they had seen. They had been soldiers. They needed a chance to exchange their war stories, and Robin could give them that.

As for Tania, the girl with beads in her hair had not lied to Inge F. Yancey IV when she told him that Tania would lose everything. She had no kingdom now. Her only follower was a sniveling former executive. Worst of all for a creature like Tania, she had nothing to do. She set up new quarters for herself across the lake in the camp director's office at Camp So-and-So. She spent a great deal of time pacing and making lists, then balling them up and throwing them across the room. Eventually, she started entertaining herself by cleaning up the wreckage around the campgrounds. She encouraged Inge F. Yancey IV to make himself useful and design some improvements for the area.

It isn't really possible to punish beings like Tania in any way that appeals to a human sense of justice. Unless you're the kind of person who resolves your problems by trying to blow their brains out with enchanted musket balls, the worst you can do is disrupt their comfortable routines, and hope you've done so in a way that coaxes some self-reflection, change, and possibly a little humility out of them.

Her first night in her own private suite, Eurydice Horne could not sleep. The bed was too soft, the blankets too warm, the pillow too plush. Even the carpet by the fireplace seemed like an enormous luxury, but that was finally where she lay down.

The next morning, by popular demand, she took a bath. The water was scented with rose oil, and Eurydice Horne had a vague memory that in her old life, this was supposed to be some sort of treat. With no screens to look at, however, Eurydice Horne found it difficult to relax.

Eventually, she put on a cotton sundress and a pair of sandals and struck out to explore the grounds of the Inge F. Yancey Young Executives Leadership Camp. Her first excursion was to find Verity, whose stolen diary she needed to return.

She found Verity in the rose garden staring at the sky, a book she wasn't reading tented over her chest. She was alone—Addison, Annika, Alix, and Amber had decided to go for a swim.

"Where did you find this?" Verity asked when Eurydice Horne handed the diary over to her.

"Robin had one of the stagehands steal it for me," Eurydice Horne explained, looking not the slightest bit ashamed. "For character-building and backstory in case you turned out to be important. Which you did."

Had Verity been in higher spirits, she might have inquired further. If she'd been less distracted, she would have been mortified—and just the slightest bit thrilled—that her favorite author had read her most private thoughts. Instead she opened the leather-bound diary to a random page, skimming it and sighing.

"What's wrong?" asked Eurydice Horne, taking a seat on the lounge chair next to Verity's.

Verity flung herself over the chair's arm and let her fingertips dangle in the grass.

"I miss her," she said.

All small talk, posturing, and coyness had vanished from conversations around the camp. People walked up to one another all the time and started talking, whether they knew each other or not. They didn't work their way up to deep conversations; they dove right into them. No one worried very much about what anyone else thought of them.

So even though Verity and Eurydice Horne had never actually met before, the author said, "There's more than that, though, isn't there?"

"I'm worried that when I leave camp, Erin won't be my soul mate anymore."

Eurydice Horne nodded. Summer love was one thing, but soul mates were tricky. She'd always advised Tania and Robin against them, not that they ever listened to her.

"What if you're wrong, and she still is?" Eurydice Horne asked. "What if she never was? What if she isn't your soul mate now, but in ten years, she will be? What if there isn't any such thing as a soul mate? What if you get more than one in your lifetime?"

"What are you talking about?"

Eurydice Horne sat up straight in the chair and tried to conjure up that fireside storyteller with bits of stew in her beard and limitless reserves of wisdom. Then she cleared her throat and said:

The morning after she got home from camp, Verity called Erin and they talked on the phone for two hours. They talked again the next week, and the week after that, but each time they spoke, they found they had less to say to each other. They made halfhearted plans to meet at a county fair halfway between their hometowns, but that fell through when Verity came down with a cold, and after that, the calls stopped altogether.

Verity's heart wasn't broken, but it did feel bruised. How could she feel something that powerful, that meant-to-be, and be wrong about it? Why couldn't she just make herself feel the way she'd felt a month ago?

She decided to call Annika to talk about it, and when she did, she found out that Addison and Tad were still together, but Alix and Amber both liked other guys now. As for Annika and the boy with the pompadour, they still talked, but she was pretty sure they were just friends.

"I thought they were our soul mates," Verity said.

"Maybe they were only our soul mates at camp," Annika said. "Anyhow, we're going out tonight. Want to come with us?"

"Are you sure?"

"Kittanning is only twenty minutes from Butler. Come on. It'll cheer you up."

Time passed, and eventually the memory of Erin faded, and Verity discovered that her heart could feel numb, or heavy, but that sometimes it could feel like someone had opened a window and let in the sunshine.

"I want to be in love every day," Amber said one Friday night while the five of them ate chips and ignored a bad movie. "I just don't know how you do that with the same person."

"You just haven't met the right person yet," Addison said, and they all wanted to roll their eyes because she and Tad behaved like such an old married couple, but they didn't because she was their friend.

They all went to the prom together, and when someone called Verity and her date a nasty name, that person would live to rue the day that they said it within earshot of Alix.

They went to each other's graduation parties, and even though they all went away to different colleges, they exchanged gifts at Christmas and went on a spring break road trip together, and slept on each other's couches in their first crappy apartments. And when

Addison announced, to the surprise of exactly no one, that she and Tad were engaged, they decided that for her bachelorette party they would take her camping, for old times' sake.

As they sat around the campfire, Verity lifted her tin mug and proposed a toast.

"To Camp So-and-So," she said, "and soul mates."

Verity was so engaged by the story, and Eurydice Horne in the telling of it, that they didn't notice until it was over that the girls from Cabin 5 had wandered into the rose garden halfway through and were now sitting, rapt, in the lounge chairs around them.

"Do us next!" exclaimed one of the Cabin 5 girls.

Eurydice Horne demurred, but the girls were insistent and flattered her shamelessly, and though she was unused to all the attention, Eurydice Horne found that she rather liked it.

"Just so you know, this isn't fortune telling," she said, then narrowed one eye and stroked her chin as she leaned back in her chair.

Strange as their story had been, the girls from Cabin 5 seemed to enjoy the rest of their week at camp the most. Having been denied any semblance of normal camp activities, they tried to cram as much of it in as possible. They rode horses, made crafts, climbed rocks, and punctuated each activity with meals that would have stymied a hobbit.

But when they returned home, each found herself drawn toward danger, adventure, and a rush of adrenaline in a way she never had before. Most found constructive outlets for this. One would become a paratrooper. Another would find her purpose by becoming a trauma unit surgeon. One climbed mountains and wrote about it for outdoor magazines. One was a singer and toured the world putting on electrifying shows.

The last, however, lived simply in a sleepy little town. Her pleasures were quiet ones—books, films, museums. Her work was fulfilling, but not dangerous or exciting. Each night, though, when she closed her eyes, she dreamed of magical lands, fantastic journeys, grand adventures, never the same dream twice, and she never stopped being astonished by them. She never wrote them down, rarely spoke of them to anyone, and yet in many ways, out of all of them, she was the happiest.

Eurydice Horne walked the grounds drinking in the sights that for years she'd only seen on the screens. She felt the wind on her face, the sun toasting her shoulders. She often sought out the girls' company, but more often than not, she hung back and did not interfere.

When the sticklike goth girl and the girl with thousands of freckles approached her for autographs, she was startled. She'd forgotten that used to be something she did for people. In her old life, she tended to sign things like "In the world above, the world below, and the world between, I remain EURYDICE HORNE."

What she wrote for these girls was rather more personal.

To the sticklike goth girl, she wrote:

There is something I want you to know about quests. When you finish, they leave you with an ache, a longing. Even when you finish, you are never finished. Quests can get into your blood. They can keep you from finding other ways of being happy.

I do not think this will happen to you, though.

With admiration, EURYDICE HORNE

To the girl with thousands of freckles, she wrote a story:

Ten years from now, a young chemist with thousands of freckles will succeed in creating the world's first synthetic universal antivenom. It will be cheap and easily transportable. One dose will fit into a small vial worn around the neck. And it will go on to save the lives of thousands of people around the world.

When asked how she had thought it up, the girl with thousands of freckles will only say that the idea had come to her many years before at summer camp.

Your friend, EURYDICE HORNE

Next, Eurydice Horne made her way over to the pasture. There she watched as Vivian and Kimber sat propped up against the side of the stable, staring at the sky. Cressida was sitting on top of the fence, watching Dora teach Kadie how to ride a horse. Kadie clung fearfully to the saddle while Dora led Helena by the bridle, the steel pocket watch hanging from a belt loop at her side.

At the end of the week, Dora's mother would worry that her daughter was every bit as pliant and eager to please as she had been before, but the rest of Cabin 1 had learned that Dora was made of steelier stuff. She was bold enough to throw her grandfather's pocket watch at a supernatural creature, stubborn enough to recover it from a manure-soaked theater, and patient enough to open it up and fix its broken gears. Dora would be fine.

Eurydice Horne muttered these stories to herself. She suspected that after what had happened to Kadie's memory, the girls from Cabin 1 would not want to hear stories about themselves from the future any more than they wanted to hear made-up stories about the past.

Vivian and Kimber mostly recovered from their time in Tania's clutches, but from that day forth, there would always be something a little bit starry-eyed and vacant about them. Kimber, who Dora had rightly observed was beginning to be bored of her own boredom, developed a terminal case of wanderlust and spent the rest of her life traveling the globe in search of something like what she'd known during her brief time with those strange creatures. Vivian would never think to look for it at all, and it would make her sullen and bitter. But who's to say that isn't exactly what would have happened to them anyway?

Next, Eurydice Horne turned to Kadie, who by this time looked a little less fearful in the saddle and seemed to be almost enjoying herself.

As Kadie continued to sort out the memories that were real from the ones that weren't, she developed a trick that she would carry with her the rest of her life. If she thought about something, and the only things she could remember about it were fluffy and bubbly and gauzily happy, then the memory was too good to be true.

Eurydice Horne whispered the story to herself, focusing on the smile that danced across Kadie's face.

That was how she knew Cressida was her friend, that the two of them would be pissing each other off for years to come.

And speaking of friends, that brought Eurydice Horne to Cressida, the only camper from Cabin 1 she felt it would be unconscionable not to approach. The girl was suffering, and it wasn't fair. She'd fought so hard to find Erin, only to have her ripped away before the two of them could begin to mend things between them.

Eurydice Horne knew how to ease her suffering. She approached the girl, who was sitting away from the others, perched atop a fence.

"It will be fine," she told Cressida, patting her on the back.

Cressida flinched away from her touch and almost fell off the fence.

"What's wrong with you?" she lashed out instinctively, softening only a bit when she turned and realized it was the author who'd approached her. "You scared me, sneaking up on me like that."

"I'm sorry."

"What were you saying? What will be fine?"

"You," said Eurydice Horne. "You and Erin. She's your friend, she never stopped being your friend, and the two of you will go on being friends."

"How do you know?"

Cressida had many good qualities, but Eurydice Horne

allowed that she would not miss the girl's brusque manner and chainsaw-on-sheet-metal voice.

"Because she asked you to save her, and then you did."

Renata found a hidden staircase that led to one of the rooftops and spent the afternoon gazing out over the lake, the mountains, and the forests. After dinner, she returned to watch the birds, and her heart swelled with longing as they skimmed over Lake So-and-So, their forms silhouetted against the sunset.

The next day, she decided it would be better if she didn't go back up to the roof.

If the girls from Cabin 2 had been angry with Wallis for abandoning them in the woods, any lingering resentments vanished the moment she wrote the story that rescued them. Hennie and Becca even admitted they probably would have done the same thing in her shoes.

Unlike some of the other cabins, they decided they'd had quite enough of the outdoors, and resolved not to venture any farther than the pool. Instead they stayed inside, read books, stayed up all night talking, and slept the morning away. It didn't feel right, though, Shea not being with them, and so they asked Robin if they could go into town to the hospital where Shea was being treated and visit her, and much to their surprise, Robin said they could.

One of the human staff Robin had hired for an exorbitant wage at the last minute agreed to drive (Inge F. Yancey IV grudgingly signing off on the expense), and once the engine, brakes, and everything else had been thoroughly inspected, they started to climb into one of the town cars.

It was then that Eurydice Horne found them and handed them an envelope.

"A get-well card for your friend," she said.

At the hospital, gathered around Shea's bed, they opened and read it.

Dear Shea,

When Becca goes away to college and two weeks into the semester feels herself start to go quiet and timid and tearful, she will recognize the feeling, and you will be the one she calls.

When Hennie feels weak and useless, she will remember the time she bandaged your wounds, and she will know that she is strong and useful.

When Corinne goes on her first major assignment, is helicoptered into the middle of a battlefield, interviews the soldiers under fire, files the story, and flies home with the sound of bombs still ringing in her ears, she won't let on she was afraid until she gets home and tells you about it.

You will always take care of them. They know that. But for now, let them take care of you.

Warmest regards,
EURYDICE HORNE

Wallis was not mentioned in the card because just before she could get into the car with the others to go to the hospital, Eurydice Horne took her by the shoulder, pulled her aside, and said, "Would you mind staying here? We need your help."

She asked it like it was a question, like it was a choice, but Wallis knew better.

When she could delay it no longer, Robin returned for a serious chat with another camper. They met in the English rose garden. Three times, the girl with beads in her hair tried to flap her wings and lift herself two feet onto the bench. Eventually, Robin picked her up under the belly and set her down there.

"You don't have to stay a raven," Robin explained. "You may find that a different animal suits you better."

Robin found she could scarcely look the girl with beads in her hair in the eye. While she held to a certain moral code, at least by her standards, Robin had never experienced anything like guilt before. At first, she told herself it was nothing. It wasn't like she had been the one wielding the gun. It wasn't as though she'd asked the girl with beads in her hair to step in front of any bullets. But still, the guilt refused to budge, and because of it, Robin found she couldn't stop trying to fix things, even though things were unfixable.

"Why can't you change me back like you did for Renata?" asked the girl with beads in her hair.

"You died," Robin said. "It's a whole different thing. You don't have a human body to go back to anymore."

Tears slid down the raven's beak and pooled on the flagstone walkway.

"What about my family?" she asked at last.

"I can make them forget you ever existed. Or we can tell them you died," Robin said, scribbling ideas down on her clipboard. Ideas weren't the problem. She had lots. They were just all wrong.

She continued, "You could stay here if you wanted, and help me run the place. We'd do things differently, of course. It might not be a bad life for you."

The girl with beads in her hair shook her raven head.

"That's not what I want," she said.

Robin was troubled and called upon Eurydice Horne and Wallis, and the three of them stayed up to the small hours of the morning devising a solution, and then they summoned the girl with beads in her hair for a meeting.

When she hopped into the office looking as miserable as a raven can be said to look, she was both surprised and not surprised to see that Renata was already there, seated at a round rosewood table with Robin, Eurydice Horne, and Wallis.

"I'm sorry." Tears began to stream down Renata's cheeks as soon as she opened her mouth.

The girl with beads in her hair hopped over to the table, flapped her wings, and made an awkward ascent to the rosewood tabletop, where she met her friend eye to eye.

"You don't have anything to be sorry for," she said. "You saved me."

"It's all my fault," Renata said, and a jagged cry escaped her throat.

The raven whipped her head around and glared at Robin.

"Don't say that," she said, looking back at Renata. "Don't ever say that."

Robin fidgeted in her chair, uneasy in her guilt. "I'm going to try to make this right for you."

This is the closest she would come to an outright apology.

"How?" asked the girl with beads in her hair, pacing across the tabletop and scarring it horribly with her talons. "I'm dead. That won't ever be all right."

"No," said Wallis, inserting herself between them. "It won't be. You'll never have anything like a normal life. You will see people living lives that might have been yours, and be filled with regret for what you have lost. You will probably be lonely. I don't know if you'll be happy."

"That doesn't make me feel any better!" said the girl with beads in her hair.

"Half a minute," Robin said, and turned to Eurydice Horne. "Let the narrator tell it."

As long as she was in her human body, Renata could never really be happy. The girl with beads in her hair could never really be happy as a raven; however, she also could not be happy as Renata. She wanted to be herself, but since that could not be, they settled on this:

During the school year, Renata dutifully went about in her human form, but in the summertime, she and the girl with beads in her hair switched places, and in this way, both of them were a little bit happier, if not entirely so.

The girl with beads in her hair saw no reason to stay at Camp So-and-So. As there was no need to deceive her parents or be parted from them, she returned home and lived her life in the form of a variety of creatures. She was sometimes a housecat and other times a squirrel, and once she was a firefly, just because she wanted to see what it felt like.

Her family still loved her, of course, and tried their best to understand her, but it was difficult. That was the problem with quests. You came back different, if you came back at all.

The girl with beads in her hair never felt at home anywhere she went, and so she began to venture farther and farther away, for longer and longer spans of time, and for all I know, she is out there still, traveling the four corners of the earth in search of her true name.

"How do you feel about that story?" Eurydice Horne asked.

All the way around the table, their faces were inscrutable.

"It's not the only one there is," she said, then added, "but there was something about it that reminded me of you."

After a long while, the girl with beads in her hair looked at Renata. The two girls nodded to one another, and Renata set the raven on her shoulder.

"It doesn't sound very happy," said the girl with beads in her hair. "All that wandering around."

"Most people don't get happy endings," said Eurydice Horne. "Then again, that's because most people don't have very good imaginations when it comes to being happy."

"I do," said the girl with beads in her hair.

"I know you do. And should you ever change your mind, I have no doubt you will write another story that is twice as fine and suits you twice as well."

"I think I like this one for now," she said.

Eurydice Horne leaned forward and kissed the top of her raven head.

"Then take it," she said. "It's yours."

ONE LAST NOTE FROM THE NARRATOR

"What about you?" Wallis asked once everyone else had left and we were alone.

"What about me?"

"Why haven't you asked Tania and Robin to put you back together again? You should do it now, while they're still feeling grateful to us."

I wrinkled my nose, hoping that Wallis would not pursue the subject, though I should have known better.

"You could go home, see your friends," Wallis said, adding hopefully, "You could finish writing the Isis Archimedes books."

She knew at once it was the wrong thing to say to me.

I thought for a long time about how I might reply, explaining that I was a different person now, that it had been years since I'd thought about my old home and friends.

That I wanted Isis Archimedes's story to remain unfinished.

"Wallis . . ." I began, dragging it out as long as possible.

"Spit it out."

"There is a world above and a world beneath and a world between . . ." I said, quoting the third Isis Archimedes to her.

Everybody always loved that part, but Wallis rolled her eyes, and I realized how obvious it must have sounded to her. After all, that was the quote that was printed on birthday cards and inspirational posters. It was what I wrote to every fan who ever asked me for an autograph.

But just because I wrote it to everyone doesn't mean I didn't mean it. I meant it every single time.

"I wrote that because I wanted it to be true," I told her. "That's the only reason I ever wrote anything in the first place."

Wallis looked at me—well, at the half of me that was standing in front of her—and I saw understanding dawn on her face.

"And now it is true."

"Precisely."

I sat down at the rosewood table, took up a sheet of paper and a pen, and wrote a letter of introduction, which I addressed to my farmhouse in New York.

"If I can be your friend in at least two worlds, I think that would make me very happy."

This time, Wallis did not roll her eyes.

"You're saying I should just show up at her house? I mean, your house?"

"You have five good ways to bring Isis Archimedes back from the dead," I said, handing her the letter. "Trust me, she'll be delighted to see you."

Despite my assurances, Wallis never could bring herself to deliver the letter to my farmhouse.

This is probably for the best.

My intentions were good, but I've probably been living at Camp So-and-So a little too long to be trusted entirely. Who knows what might have happened if she'd gone? The other me might have asked her to stay. She might have ended up stuck there, trying to finish someone else's story when she should have been telling her own.

Wallis didn't go, but she kept my letter.

She never told anyone about it, but she kept it near her as a good luck charm when she wrote her first book.

And her second.

And her seventh.

[Exeunt.]

ACKNOWLEDGMENTS

I'd just about given up on this story when a number of magical things puffed air beneath its raven wings, and sent its spirit hurtling across Lake So-and-So and, eventually, into the world.

The first magical thing: Brady Potts bought me a Miranda July novel, inside which he had written, "To the Head Counselor of Camp So-and-So: Stranger books have been published." Brady, you always believed in this story and its strangeness, and you always believe in me and mine. I love you.

The second magical thing: I met Patricia Nelson—it was at a party full of sociologists, so naturally, we found each other and holed up in a corner talking about books. At the time, I had no idea this would be a significant conversation, that like all the best stories, it would become important later, when I least expected it, when I realized that I couldn't imagine it hav-

The third magical thing: Alix Reid, who is magical in and of herself; who dived into this manuscript with the optimism of Kadie, the vision of Wallis, the bravery of the girl with beads in her hair, the heart of Verity, and the sheer grit of the girls in Cabin 5. Alix, I am in awe of you.

An uproarious Camp So-and-So cheer to the friends who have given me encouragement and support when I needed it the most: Glen Creason, Leah DiVincenzo, Joanna Fabicon, Rachel Kitzmann, Stacey Lee, Carolina and Sarah Marvin, Bob Peterson, Christina Rice, Jon Rosenberg, Angela Serranzana, Gwen Sharp, Mark Walker, Marc Weitz, and John Woolf.

A lanyard, a tie-dye t-shirt, and a duct-tape wallet to my family at the Los Angeles Public Library and to my tribe of YA writers both nearby and far-flung, who always turn my gripes into smiles and my roadblocks into inspiration.

A campfire sing-along and unlimited s'mores to John and Karla McCoy, for sending me to Camp Ligonier, where unbeknownst to everyone (including myself) I was socking away the geography, memories, and lessons about what it means to be brave that would become this book. You are the best parents in the world, and I love you.

And finally, to X.J. Kennedy, who wrote the story about the moonflower that made me want to write this one, I whisper into your ear the secret ending of the Isis Archimedes books, the true name of Camp So-and-So, and the words, "Thank you."

ABOUT THE AUTHOR

Mary McCoy was born and raised in western Pennsylvania. She holds degrees from Rhodes College and the University of Wisconsin. She now lives in Los Angeles with her husband and son, and works as a librarian at the Los Angeles Public Library. She is also the author of *Dead To Me*.